John Wilcox was born in Birmingham and was an award-winning journalist for some years before being lured into industry. In the mid-nineties he sold his company in order to devote himself to his first love, writing. His previous Simon Fonthill novels, THE HORNS OF THE BUFFALO, THE ROAD TO KANDAHAR, THE DIAMOND FRONTIER and LAST STAND AT MAJUBA HILL, were highly acclaimed. He has also published two works of non-fiction, PLAYING ON THE GREEN and MASTERS OF BATTLE.

Praise for John Wilcox's Simon Fonthill novels:

'Wilcox writes with an intimate knowledge of the African continent, an encyclopaedic knowledge of the Victorian era when the British Empire was at its peak, and all the dash of a great adventurer' *Nottingham Evening Post*

'The story rattles along at a tremendous pace and once started, it was difficult to put down' *Eastern Daily Press*

'Vivid descriptions of the battle scenes and perceptive analyses of the strategies behind them' *Yorkshire Evening Post*

'A glorious adventure story that beautifully captures a sense of the wild North Western frontier' *Western Daily Press*

'A rollicking account of a turbulent period in Britain's imperial past' *Good Book Guide*

THE
GUNS OF
EL KEBIR

JOHN WILCOX

headline

First published in 2007
by HEADLINE PUBLISHING GROUP

First published in paperback in 2008
by HEADLINE PUBLISHING GROUP

1

Cataloguing in Publication Data is available from the British Library

ISBN 978 0 7553 2721 8

Typeset in Sabon by Avon DataSet Ltd, Bidford on Avon, Warwickshire

Printed and bound in Great Britain
by Mackays of Chatham plc, Chatham, Kent

Headline's policy is to use papers that are natural, renewable and recyclable
products and made from wood grown in sustainable forests. The logging and
manufacturing processes are expected to conform to the environmental
regulations of the country of origin.

HEADLINE PUBLISHING GROUP
An Hachette Livre UK Company
338 Euston Road
London NW1 3BH

www.headline.co.uk
www.hachettelivre.co.uk

For Betty, again.

Acknowledgements

As always, I must offer my thanks to my agent, Jane Conway-Gordon, for her constant help and encouragement, and my editor at Headline, Sherise Hobbs, whose assiduous eye for detail and creative suggestions on plot improved the text greatly. As usual, I would have been lost without the ready assistance offered by the staff and the facilities at the London Library in guiding my journey back in time to the London and Egypt of 1882. The internet can only take a researcher so far on such a journey; a good library is essential in producing contemporary accounts that give a flavour and a feel for the period.

My old friend David Goodenday, a former Justice of the Peace, offered sound advice on the procedure of a magistrates' court, while pointing out that he was not quite old enough to have experienced it at first hand in 1882! At the London Press Office of the Egyptian Embassy, Miss Nashwa Hamid worked hard to help me gain permission to enter the military area that now includes the site of the el Kebir battle, and in Cairo Mr Ahmed Sharaf kindly opened further doors for me. I must also thank Mr Ehab Fahmy, of the Ismailia Press Centre, for escorting me to the battlefield itself. The site has slipped back now, quite unmarked, into the flat gravel of the northern desert and it would have been a frustrating journey without his cheerful company.

My neighbour and good friend, Neil Pattenden, allowed me free run of his library, which included a vital contemporary account of the war, and, as ever, I owe love and gratitude to my wife, Betty, who helped me hugely with the research and, as always, accompanied me on my travels.

For those who would like to read further on the subject of the Arabi 'revolt' and Wolseley's invasion, the following books will be helpful. Some are undoubtedly out of print but the London Library and the British Library should be able to provide them.

The War in Egypt and the Soudan by Thomas Archer, Blackie and Son, London, 1887

Campaigns: Zulu 1879, Egypt 1882, Private Journal of G.C. Dawnay, Ken Trotman Ltd., 1989 (originally published 1887)

War on the Nile by Michael Barthorp, Blandford Press, Dorset, 1989

Cairo by S. Lane-Poole, J.S. Virtue & Co, London, 1892

Lifting the Veil by Anthony Sattin, J.M. Dent, London, 1988

Miss Brocklehurst on the Nile, Diary of a Victorian Traveller in Egypt by Marianne Brocklehurst, Millrace, Disley, Cheshire, 2004

Egypt 1879–1883 by the Rt Hon. Sir Edward Malet, John Murray, London, 1909

The Colonial Wars Source Book by Philip J. Haythornwaite, Arms and Armour, London, 1994

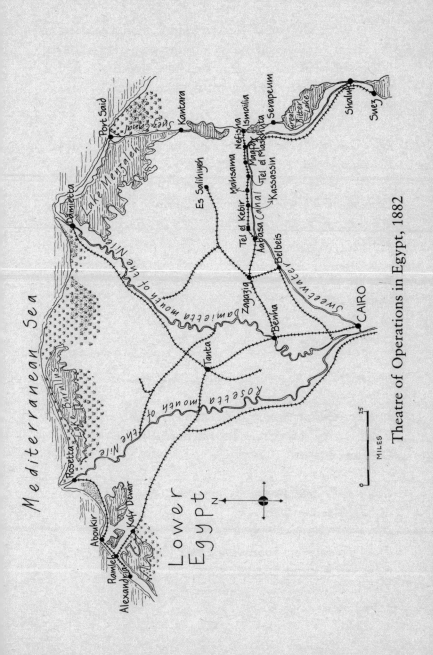

Theatre of Operations in Egypt, 1882

Chapter 1

Simon Fonthill shrugged on his tweed jacket and strode down the stairs, adjusting his tie and smoothing back his hair as he went. For his mother, breakfast was almost as formal a meal as dinner and she insisted that everyone was properly dressed for it. Simon wished to avoid any further confrontation with Mrs Fonthill; there had been enough of these already since he and Jenkins had arrived at his parents' home three months ago.

'Morning, Mama,' he greeted as he walked around the long table and kissed the cheek offered to him. 'Father out already?'

Mrs Fonthill dabbed her mouth with her napkin and turned to look behind her through the window at the late winter sky, already beginning to turn a bright blue as the early morning mist stole away. 'He went out while it was still dark, silly man.' She turned back to Simon. 'There's kedgeree under the tureen on the sideboard, but ring for Sarah if you want eggs. You know, Simon, I worry about your father. He's getting no younger, and to go ditching in this piercingly cold

1

weather is really most ill-advised.' She directed a level gaze at her son. 'Really, my dear, you could have offered to do whatever needs to be done in this ridiculous ditch.'

Simon sighed but avoided her gaze as he loaded his plate. 'Would have done, Mother, quite happily, if Papa had mentioned it. But you know he still keeps things rather close to his chest.' He sat at the table, two places down from where his mother presided at the head. 'Anyway, why isn't Williams doing the ditching? That's what he's paid for, isn't it?'

Mrs Fonthill sniffed. 'He's sick. Estate workers are allowed to be sick, it seems, but not the Major.' She paused for a moment and then spoke in a lower, even more disapproving tone. 'Your man Jenkins has gone with him to help.'

Simon paused, his fork halfway to his mouth. 'Oh, capital. Good for 352. I'll go and find them and give them a hand as soon as I've finished breakfast.'

'Oh, for goodness' sake!' Mrs Fonthill threw down her napkin. 'Why on earth do you call the man by that ridiculous number. Doesn't he have a name like decent Christian folk?'

'Of course he does, Mother. It's a Welsh thing. You will remember that when he was in a holding company at the regiment's depot in the town, there were three other Jenkinses with the same initial, so they were all called by the last three of their army numbers to differentiate them and I suppose it has just stuck. Anyway, he hates his Christian name and prefers 352. Everybody calls him that.'

His mother pursed her lips but remained silent, picking up her discarded copy of the *Morning Post* but covertly watching her son round the edge of the page as he ate. Mrs Fonthill, a handsome figure in her stiffly bodiced gown, the blue of it setting off her perfectly coiffed white hair, was a woman of strong opinions and was noted in the county for her hatred of Mr Gladstone and of all things radical. She disliked the unconventional – and her son *was* unconventional. He continued to avoid eye contact as, head down, he tackled his kedgeree, so she was able to rest her gaze on him and contemplate his . . . his . . . what? His stubborn refusal to conform? His dislike of tradition. His cussed independence? His reluctance to take up a profession or – more acceptably – stay at home and help his father manage the estate? Was it the oxymoronic and seemingly quite unpredictable contradictions in behaviour? In a rural economy that relied on horses, he disliked riding. Born into a military family, he had willingly taken a commission in his father's old regiment, but left the army early. There was that terrible business of the court martial for cowardice in Zululand, and yet he had been found not guilty and even commended for bravery in later campaigns in South Africa and Afghanistan. He had refused the chance to resume his commission, with guaranteed promotion, but still stayed working for the army as a scout in the field with Jenkins.

Ah, Jenkins . . . ! The two seemed inseparable and it was unquestionably a close relationship. Mrs Fonthill sniffed. Much closer than master and servant should be. It was quite unhealthy. Of course, it was a manly friendship, born of serving together and of risking their lives together – Simon had said that Jenkins had saved his life many times. But it didn't do to cross the divisions of class. It just didn't do.

She pushed her reading glasses down her nose the better to regard her son. He was really quite good-looking, she noted, particularly now that, at twenty-seven, he had filled out a little, and campaigning had even, it seemed, broadened his shoulders. It was his face, however, still brown from the African sun, that commanded attention. The cheekbones were high and the lips, unfashionably unframed by whiskers, were thin and sensitive, though the jaw was firm enough. The nose had sustained a blow that had clearly broken it at some stage – a Pathan's musket barrel in the Hindu Kush, he had said, or something like that – and left it slightly hooked, giving him a predatory expression. The brown eyes, though, still retained that uncertainty of his youth, as though they were searching for something or someone.

Simon looked up, caught his mother's gaze and flushed a little. 'If you'll excuse me, Mama,' he said, 'I will go and change and see if I can go and do a bit of honest ditching. Where did you say they were?'

'I think they've gone to the big field by Wellard's Cross. Take my hunter if you wish, but be careful. The ground's hard.'

Another peck on the cheek and he was gone. She watched him leave and slowly shook her head. God had been merciful in finally allowing her to have a son – their only child – but why had He decided to test her maternal instincts with such an awkwardly unorthodox boy? She sighed and picked up the *Morning Post* to resume her anxious reading about the unrest in Egypt.

Simon strode away from the house with a sense of relief. It was good to be out in the clean, crisp air – he had decided to walk rather than take his mother's brute of a hunter – and he felt a sense of physical satisfaction as his boots crunched through the crust of frost to the grass beneath. Far away, he heard the plaintive note of a hunting horn. Ah, his father wouldn't like that! It was distant, but near enough to set a protest of crows fluttering up from the twisted branches of a winter oak. A good day for hunting.

His father's estate was not large and it took only half an hour's sharp walking to crest the hill above Wellard's Cross. Down below he could see the figures of his father and Jenkins, bent beside the hedge as they shovelled away the detritus of winter to clear the ditch. Hedge and ditch care were important parts of estate management in this country, where the wind marched from the west throughout the year, driving the rain before it. Clear ditches were vital if good grazing land was not to be turned into bog and mud. The two men looked up, their breath rising like steam, as Simon approached.

'Good morning, my boy,' nodded the Major.

'Afternoon, bach sir,' said Jenkins. ''Ad a good lie-in, then?' His voice carried the mellifluous inflection of the Welsh valleys.

Simon ignored the sarcasm but grinned at the pair. At five feet nine inches, his father was of a similar height to his son, but with a much stouter build. He wore his greying hair unfashionably long and his face, too, was free of beard or moustache. His resemblance to Simon was not marked, except for the wide-set brown eyes, which seemed to carry a similar look of doubt and caution.

Jenkins, on the other hand, standing shovel in hand, his feet wide apart and perfectly balanced in the ditch, had the bearing of a cheerful labourer. He measured no more than five feet four inches, but he seemed almost as wide as he was tall, so broad were his chest and shoulders. His face was tanned like Simon's but his eyes were as button black as his short, spiky hair and the great moustache that seemed to curve from ear to ear. Perspiration poured down his face to mingle with the hairs that poked above his collarless shirt.

Major Fonthill nodded towards him. 'I thought a bit of digging might help to rid him of the beer he consumes at the Black Dog,' he said with a wry smile. 'But I must say, he works damned hard and he's cheerful with it.'

Jenkins had the grace to look crestfallen at the mention of the pub. Simon had long ago discovered that the Welshman had many talents, some of them surprisingly arcane. Brave as a bull, he was a superb horseman, a crack shot and possessed a happy disposition that remained undiminished by danger. Incongruously, he also had a sensitive nose for champagne and fine wine. Yet his predilection for beer and public houses was a weakness that often led him into trouble, for too much ale could turn the cheerful Jenkins into an irascible fighting machine. Twice since their return Simon had had to intervene with the local constabulary to rescue the Welshman from an overnight cell after a set-to at the bar of the Dog.

'I'm 'appy to lend the Major an 'and,' said Jenkins, gazing at his shovel, then, looking up directly at Simon, 'Can't stand doin' nothin', look you.'

Simon frowned and nodded. Neither of them quite fitted into the ordered, almost smug routine of the red-brick house on the Borders. After sharing in the horrors of the defeat of the British by the Boers at Majuba Hill in the recent Transvaal War, Simon, at least, had been glad to return to his family home for a while, to readjust and decide what next to do. And Jenkins, of course, had come too. But the disapproval of the Welshman shown by Mrs Fonthill – particularly after his pugnacious behaviour in the village pub – and Simon's growing restlessness had introduced a feeling of general unease into the house. Simon sucked in his breath. He couldn't stand doin' nothin' either. But what to do? Where to go?

The hiatus was broken by the hunting horn again, a little nearer now. Simon instinctively looked at his father. The Major had concluded some years ago that hunting was cruel and had given up riding to hounds. More to the point, he had banned the local hunt from crossing his land.

Major Fonthill shook his head at the unspoken question. 'They know better than to come on to my estate,' he said. 'They won't follow on to my land. Now,' he handed his shovel to Simon, 'I would be grateful if the gallant army scout would spell me with this damned thing for a while.' He picked up a pitchfork. 'I'll pile up this bracken, and if we don't get snow or more rain, Williams can come and burn it when he recovers.'

The three men bent to and worked in happy companion-ship for a while, the silence broken only by Jenkins's tuneless whistling – the little man was the only Welshman Simon knew who couldn't carry a tune. The horn, however, was heard again and it was clear that the hunt was approaching. Above the baying of the hounds, they could now hear the thud of hooves, although no horsemen could yet be seen through the thick hawthorn hedge.

'Dammit all,' cried the Major. 'The fox is heading this way. Why on earth couldn't they have headed him off after they'd raised him? They *know* I won't have them on my land.'

As though on cue, a fox sped like a greyhound through a hole in the hedge less than six feet away from them. Ears laid back and brush in an elegant but terrified line parallel to the earth, it gave them an expressionless glance, then turned sharply to the right and raced away, alongside the hedge up the hill towards a group of trees.

Within seconds, the pack of hounds hit the hole in the hedge and struggled to get through, wedging themselves together in the effort, for the hedge itself was too high for them to leap and too thick to penetrate except by the route taken by the fox. Immediately, the Major leapt to the gap and thrust his shovel across it, denying exit to the lead hound, who was halfway through and who immediately let out a howl of frustration. Within moments, the huntsmen arrived. The leader could not rein in in time and was forced to take the hedge at full tilt, as did the second horse. The rest, as they arrived at the formidable obstacle, milled about on its other side.

The leading horseman, a large man wearing mud-splashed pink and riding a magnificent bay, had cleared the hedge well, and now he skilfully wheeled his mount around as the second rider, taking the jump less ably, nearly pitched over his horse's head. The two rode up to George Fonthill, who was now firmly wedging his shovel across the gap.

'What the hell do you think you're doing?' shouted the bay's rider, his face flushed a shade deeper than his coat.

'Morning Colonel Reeves,' answered the Major equably, making sure that the shovel was firmly fixed before turning to face the rider. 'I am just making sure that there will be no further trespassing on my land.'

'Dammit, man. The hunt doesn't trespass. It clears the land of vermin.'

'If I want to clear the land of vermin, I will do it in my own way, thank you.'

'Look here, Fonthill.' The second rider, much younger and slimmer than the MFH and displaying an extravagant frill of lace at his throat, spoke in a high-pitched voice. 'We try to avoid your land because we know your views, but sometimes we just have to follow. Now which way did our fellow go?'

Fonthill ignored the younger man and held the Master's gaze coolly. The big man jerked the reins in exasperation as his bay fretted to be off again, and turned his gaze on Simon and Jenkins, who were watching the turn of events with some dismay. Involuntarily, Jenkins shot a quick glance up the hill, the direction taken by the fox.

'That's it, Evans,' shouted the Master across the fence to his huntsman, 'set the hounds up the hill to the right. They'll be able to get through the hedge higher up and pick up the scent. We'll follow from this side.'

He hauled his horse's head round to start up the hill, but George Fonthill caught the bridle to prevent him. The bay shied and half reared, causing the Master to sway perilously in the saddle.

'Don't grab my bridle,' snarled the rider, the veins standing out in his neck above his stock. 'Let go, damn you. Let go.' He swung his whip up and brought it down across the elder Fonthill's shoulder, and then lashed him across the head, causing the Major to fall away, one hand held up to his face to protect himself.

At this, Simon sprang forward but slipped in the mud.

Jenkins was quicker. The Welshman leapt to the far side of the rider, pushed the latter's boot out from the stirrup in one quick movement and heaved the leg up and over the saddle, causing the Master, flailing desperately to regain his lost hold on the reins, to pitch on the ground with a thud. Jenkins nipped around the startled horse and held out a hand to assist the Master to his feet, but the big man cracked him across the wrist with his whip and struggled upright, raising the whip behind his head to bring it down again on the Welshman.

Major Fonthill moved to intervene, but Simon put a restraining hand on his chest. It was some time since he had seen Jenkins in action, and he was not to be denied this opportunity.

Perfectly balanced, as always, the Welshman skipped aside to avoid the lash, seized the Master's wrist to whirl him round and then, with cool precision, kicked him in the groin. With a gasp like air escaping from a balloon, the big man sank back to the ground, his eyes protruding.

'I say, you scoundrel, you've killed him.' The younger rider's jaw had dropped at the speed and ferocity of Jenkins's attack.

'No, I 'aven't killed 'im.' Jenkins pointed to the Master, who was kneeling on the ground, gasping and holding his testicles. 'I just kicked 'im in the balls.' He turned to Simon and his father, as though for support. 'Look, see, 'e's movin' all right. But 'e shouldn't go around whippin' people, now should 'e?' His voice was quite plaintive.

The Major strode forward and bent down by the stricken man, who was now rocking back and forwards on his knees and drawing in deep breaths. George Fonthill looked up at the younger rider. 'For God's sake, Barker,' he growled. 'Get down and see if we can get him to his feet. Straight legs and his head between his knees is what he needs now.'

But Barker showed no desire to dismount in the presence of Jenkins, and Simon went to assist his father. Together, they struggled to help the large man, his face still contorted with pain, to his feet and then pushed his head down and instructed him to take deep breaths. Eventually the treatment seemed to bring some relief and the Colonel was able to stand upright. He shook off the Major and Simon with a gesture that bespoke no thanks for their concern, and pointed a finger at Jenkins.

'That man will go to jail for attacking me in that cowardly way,' he gasped. 'I shall bring charges, I promise you. The whole county will recognise you for what you are, Fonthill – a . . . a . . . lily-livered socialist who employs ruffians of the worst kind. You will both suffer for this.'

'Quite so,' Barker now joined in, having backed his horse well away from Jenkins. 'I saw what happened. I am a magistrate and I will give evidence. It was a cowardly, unprovoked attack.'

'Unprovoked!' Jenkins's indignation seemed to increase the Welsh intonation in his voice. 'The bloody man was whippin' everybody in sight, so 'e was. It's 'im who should go to jail, look you.'

'That will do, Jenkins.' George Fonthill turned to Reeves. 'Would you like to rest in our house for a while, Colonel? It might be wise if you are hurt. We could send for Dr Davies from the village.'

Reeves regained his whip from the ground. 'Certainly not. I shall make my own way to the village: to the police house, to lay charges. Now if you can show me a gate nearby, I *will* leave your damned land, Fonthill. But you will be hearing from me shortly. A warrant will be issued for your man's arrest as soon as I can see the constable.'

George Fonthill pointed to the lower end of the field. 'By the willow there. Please close it behind you.'

The Master gathered his reins and, limping, led his horse away from the little group. With a reproving glance at the three men, Barker followed him.

The Major held out his hand to Jenkins. 'My dear Jenkins,' he said, 'I am not sure that I approve of your method of fighting, but I am grateful to you for coming to my aid. Most grateful.'

The Welshman shook hands and then looked at the ground in some embarrassment. 'Sorry, Major. I don't know any fancy ways of fightin', see, an' 'e was a bit big to muck about with. Particularly with that whip of 'is. Sorry, I'm sure, if I've given offence.'

'Well, my man, I'm afraid that you've given plenty of offence to Colonel Reeves. But the man is a bully and – what can I say? – a most reactionary sort of fellow. If there was one man I would like to see receive a blow in the . . . whatchamacallit? . . . the unmentionables, then I can assure you that Reeves is the chap. However, I do hope he is not permanently injured.'

Simon picked up the shovels and pitchfork. 'I feel that's enough ditching for the day, Father. Perhaps we should get back. I think we may have some preparations to make if Reeves carries out his threat.'

In silence, the three climbed into the little dog cart and, Jenkins taking the reins, made their way back to the house.

As they bounced along the uneven tracks across the small estate, Simon watched the broad back of Jenkins and began to feel growing concern for his friend. Of course the attack had been provoked and, indeed, Reeves had been the aggressor. Technically, he was also trespassing. Simon knew, however, that, should the matter come to court, it would not be as simple as that. Reeves was a large landowner, a member of the county council and a magistrate himself. The hunt was supported by rich men, farmers and workers alike, and it was the custom to cross private land. A counter-charge of trespassing was unlikely to stick. The Master had many highly placed connections throughout the Borders, and in those circles he was a popular man. The main point, however, was that an attack on such a man *by a servant* would not be tolerated, particularly the mode of attack chosen by Jenkins. *So very brutal*, the gossip would insist. *Such a disgusting way to behave and so typical of what happens when a liberal entertains 'modern' ideas!* Simon shook his head.

Surprisingly, however, Charlotte Fonthill took a different view. Sitting around the dinner table that evening with her husband and son (Jenkins, on his own insistence, always dined with the servants), Mrs Fonthill demanded to be told everything. To Simon's amazement, his mother threw back her head and guffawed when the details of the affray – or, as she came to refer to it, the Battle of Jenkins's Boot – were unfolded.

'Serves the man right,' she chortled. Then her face darkened. 'How dare he raise his whip to you, my dear!'

With an inward smile, Simon realised that even if it was the sainted Prince Albert who had attacked her husband, he would receive the same enmity as if the assailant had been an itinerant tramp. The Fonthills' was a love affair that was set in concrete.

'Now, my dears,' she concluded at the end of the story, 'the first thing to do is to summon Jenkins into the drawing room and give him a large glass of the best whisky we have. Then we must discuss his defence. There is no doubt that he will be charged, but he must not – *he must not* – be found guilty. I have an idea, but we must discuss it with him. He is clearly a most resourceful man who deserves our full support.'

Simon smothered a grin. One swing of the boot and dear old 352 had been elevated from the ranks of the boozy underclass to become a friend of the family! Ah well, Jenkins was certainly going to need all the help he could be given.

It was clear that Jenkins considered the summons to join the family in the parlour the prelude to a hanging, at least. As he entered and perched on the edge of the chaise longue, he shot a despairing glance at Simon. This was difficult ground for him. Gone was the easy, free-wheeling relationship between master and servant that had existed on the veldt of Africa and the hard scree of India's North-West Frontier. He had always feared that that warm friendship – not between equals, because that could never be, but between comrades – would end as soon as they entered the family home on the Welsh Borders. And so it had proved, despite all Simon's solicitude. The family, and particularly Mrs Fonthill, had made it clear that in her house Jenkins was just a servant – and an unruly, alcoholic one at that. He had regretted kicking the Colonel as soon as the boot had gone in.

Not because the act was not deserved, but because he knew it would confirm him to be a savage. He should have taken the whip across the face and then punched the bastard hard. Mrs Fonthill's welcome now, then, was all the more unexpected.

'George,' she commanded. 'A very large whisky for Mr Jenkins.'

A huge single malt in a shimmering cut-glass tumbler was presented to him – the first he had tasted since, as officers' mess orderly in the 24th seven years earlier, he had helped himself every evening before clearing up. He sipped thoughtfully. 'Thank you, sir,' he said. 'I think it's an 1873, isn't it?'

'Good lord, so it is. How on earth did you know?'

Simon intervened. 'Oh, 352 is a man of many parts, Father, as . . . er . . . you have seen today.'

'Indeed.' Charlotte Fonthill now took charge. 'Mr Jenkins, I wish to thank you most sincerely for coming to the aid of my husband today. Not that he could not have taken care of himself, you know, but he was most certainly disadvantaged and your intervention was most timely.'

Jenkins shifted on the chaise longue. 'Yes, well. Thank you, my lady.'

Mrs Fonthill's former habitual irritation with Jenkins returned momentarily. 'No. As I have told you so many times. We are not titled and therefore you must not call me your lady. I should be madam or Mrs Fonthill.'

'Right, then. Yes. Thank you, missus . . . I mean madam.'

'Yes, madam is perfectly acceptable. Now, back to this distressing incident of earlier today. We have been talking amongst ourselves and we believe that because Colonel

Reeves has some influence here, you almost certainly will be charged.'

Jenkins shot a quick glance at Simon. 'Does it mean jail, then, miss . . . madam?'

'Not while I have . . . I mean while *we* have breath in our bodies. Now look here, the case will come before the local magistrates. We have no idea whether it might be referred to a higher court or whatever. But I have a cousin in London who practises at the Bar and I intend to call him down here to defend you.'

Jenkins shifted again. 'Very kind of you, madam, but with great respect, I don't see how a barman can 'elp in this kind of situation, particularly a bloke what's still practisin' and learnin' the job, like.'

Simon and Major Fonthill stifled smiles as Mrs Fonthill sat with her mouth open, her brow furrowed. 'What? What? Oh, I see. Yes, they're confusing terms, aren't they? No, he is a barrister – which means he is an advocate and will speak for you – and he is also a QC, a Queen's Counsel. You couldn't do better, I assure you.'

Jenkins was now frowning. He sat silently for a moment and then took a deep draught of the whisky. 'Thank you, Mrs Fonthill,' he said eventually, wiping his moustache with the back of his hand. 'But, you know, I really don't want anybody to speak for me, see. I've always done my own talkin', like, and I'd rather do it now, if you don't mind. I really appreciate the trouble you're takin', though, absolutely.'

The Major leaned forward. 'Don't be silly, man. Sir Roger Chamberlain, my wife's cousin, is probably the best barrister in the land. It would be most impressive to have him down here in a magistrates' court to defend you. He will, of course, do a first-class job and his presence alone, I feel, would score heavily in your favour.'

Jenkins directed another glance at Simon, but the latter, his chin in his hand, staring at his friend, stayed silent.

The Welshman took a deep breath. 'Yes, well, that's just the point, see, Major. Gettin' this great gentleman down from London to handle this piddlin' little local matter – savin' your presence, madam – would show everybody that you're worried about winnin' and that, without this barman chap, I wouldn't stand a chance. In fact, I can't 'elp thinkin' that the local judges, or whatever they are, would get their backs up a bit, what with posh blokes comin' down from London, see.'

Mrs Fonthill opened her mouth to speak, but Simon intervened. 'I think Jenkins has a good point here,' he said. 'But 352, who would you want to speak for you? A local solicitor from Brecon, say?'

'Oh no, bach sir, thank you very much. As I said, I don't want anyone to speak *for* me. I will speak for myself.'

'But you can't defend yourself!' The Major exchanged incredulous looks with his wife. 'A court of law is a sort of ritualistic place, highly disciplined. You have got to know the rules and procedures and to conform to them. You can't expect to just . . . well . . . talk your way out of it, you know. You attacked a highly respected member of our community and we must put up a well-argued case for you. Frankly, my dear chap, I don't quite see you being able to do that.'

The room fell silent for a minute and Jenkins took another draught from his glass, emptying it. Simon stood and refilled it.

'A magistrates' court, then, is it?' asked the Welshman eventually.

'Well, to start with, anyway,' answered Charlotte Fonthill. 'It could be settled there or, if the charge is considered serious enough, it could go to a higher court.'

'Ah well, if it's a magistrates' court, then I shall be comfortable enough.'

'Why is that?'

Jenkins gave a wry, rather shamefaced smile. 'Back 'ome in Wales, I came up before the local beaks twice and got off twice, see. I just spoke the truth an' asked a few awkward questions to the fellers who were tryin' to prosecute me. I must 'ave done well enough 'cos they let me off.'

Simon's mind went back to his early days as a subaltern in Brecon when the quick wits and barrack-room-lawyer abilities of his servant had helped protect him against the campaign of persecution employed by his commanding officer, Lieutenant Colonel Covington.

The Major sighed. 'It won't be that easy here, I'm afraid.'

Jenkins leaned forward. 'P'raps not, sir, but I'd rather you left it to me. Maybe you and the Captain could be witnesses for me about what 'appened an' all that, and you, Major, could give me a bit of background information, like, about this trespassin' business before I go in the dock. But I think I can 'andle it, given 'alf a chance by the judge bloke. You'll see. Anyway,' he sat back with an air of finality, 'I'm very grateful to you all, but that's the way I'd like to do it.'

Simon stood. 'Very well, 352. It looks as though your mind is made up, so we must let you get on with it. Of course, we will be witnesses and give you all the help we can.' He turned to his parents. 'As I said earlier, Jenkins has hidden talents. We'll just have to see if he can deploy them well enough to get himself off this hook. Now, if you've finished your whisky, old chap – and I see that you have – we'll let you get off to bed. We'll meet again when the summons arrives.'

Although his glass seemed empty, Jenkins upended it one more time to make sure, gave the Major and his wife the benefit of his face-splitting beam, nodded to Simon and left the room. The Fonthills stared at each other.

Mrs Fonthill stamped her foot. 'If he defends himself, he won't stand a chance.'

Simon shrugged his shoulders. 'He can be damned stubborn when he wants to be – but he can also be very resourceful. I just hope that his recent fracas in the Black Dog will not be held against him.'

Chapter 2

A week later, they all assembled in the gloomy magistrates' court at Brecon. The summons to attend court had been delivered unusually – and ominously – quickly. Three magistrates sat on the bench.

Simon leaned across to his father. 'Do you know them?' he asked.

The Major nodded. 'The two flanking the chairman are farmers. The chap on the left is a great supporter of the hunt, a dedicated Tory, and has a reputation for sending down almost everyone who appears before him.' He sniffed. 'The one on the right is a bit more balanced, from what I hear. He farms further west but sits on the county council with Reeves, so is likely to support him. The chairman is new to me but I understand he is some sort of industrialist just outside Brecon. Not a good show, my boy, I'm afraid.'

The usher motioned for Simon and his father to leave the court because, as witnesses in the case, they were not allowed to hear previous evidence. Once in the busy entrance chamber outside, however, Simon left his father, who would be called first, and slipped away up the stairs to the public gallery, where his mother had already taken her seat. He was anxious to hear the prosecution's case and he had asked Mrs Fonthill to sit at the back and to save him a seat at the end of the row.

He was in time to hear the clerk of the court open the proceedings by reading the charge against Jenkins, who stood in the partitioned box reserved for defendants, looking rosy-cheeked and freshly scrubbed. Simon's heart went out to him, for the Welshman had donned his only suit and made every attempt to plaster down his stubbly hair. He bore the appearance of a collier at Sunday morning chapel. But would this air of innocence prevail?

The charge accused Jenkins of assault and attempting to cause actual bodily harm. It was short and to the point and was taken up by the solicitor who appeared on behalf of Reeves, a small, birdlike man who wore his pince-nez on the end of his nose and who, when he spoke, did so with a sniff.

'May I begin,' he intoned, 'by revealing to the bench a little about the defendant's background.' He examined a document in his hand and turned to Jenkins. 'Is it true that you joined the army in 1874 and achieved the rank of corporal?'

Simon's heart sank. This man had done his homework.

Jenkins beamed and nodded. 'Yes, sir.'

The solicitor's thin nose rose into the air and he addressed the ceiling. 'But you were reduced to the ranks, I think, some two years later. Why was that?'

The smile had left Jenkins's face now. 'I was forced to 'it a colour sergeant, sir.'

'Forced! Forced! What do you mean?'

'I was forced to 'it 'im because he 'it me on the 'ead with 'is swagger stick, sir.' A murmer of laughter ran round the public gallery, causing the chairman of magistrates to scowl upwards in disapproval.

'And because hitting someone of superior rank is a serious offence,' continued the lawyer, 'you were sentenced to one year's detention in the army's detention centre in Aldershot, were you not?'

'Yes, sir.'

'Mr Jenkins, is it not true that you have always been of a rebellious and violent nature?'

'Well, I don't know about that, sir, though I don't like bein' put upon, like.'

'Indeed. And is it not true that you often imbibe alcohol to the point that it inflames this violent nature of yours and you get into fights? Eh?'

'No. Well . . . not often, see.' Jenkins was now visibly squirming. 'P'raps once or twice. But it always takes two to start a fight, you know.'

'Is it not true that since you came to live under Major Fonthill's roof only three months ago, the police have twice been called to eject you from . . .' the lawyer referred to his notes, 'a public house called the Black Dog because you were involved in an affray?'

'Yes. But I wasn't the only one, you see . . .'

'That will do, Mr Jenkins. Now, I want to turn to the events of the morning of the second of March last. If I may, your worships, I would first like to call the Honourable Tobias Barker,' he gave the magistrates a dry smile, 'no stranger, of course, to this Bench.'

The elegant second rider came forward and, under careful prompting, gave his account of what had happened in the field near Wellard's Cross. The facts as he related them were not specifically inaccurate, but they skilfully shaded the evidence against Jenkins. Major Fonthill had almost unseated the Colonel, who had merely tapped Fonthill on the shoulder with his whip, while Jenkins had moved in as quickly as an assassin and used a gutter fighter's tactics to wound the Colonel.

The beginning of Reeves's own testimony was delivered with the Colonel leaning heavily on a stick, until the chairman insisted that he sit. From his chair, Reeves spoke in a voice that seemed to thunder back from the wood panelling cladding the walls. The charge of trespassing was ridiculous. All landowners around Brecon allowed the hunt to cross their land. It was a matter not only of tradition but also of good housekeeping, because the huntsmen kept down the fox population and so protected the sheep flocks. As for his so-called attack on Major Fonthill, it was really the other way around. Fonthill had grabbed his bridle so violently that he was virtually unhorsed and he had merely gestured with his whip to ward off the Major. The attack by the much younger Jenkins had been unprovoked and vicious. As a result, Reeves was still limping and forced to walk with the aid of a stick.

At the conclusion of the Colonel's testimony, the lawyer turned to the Bench. 'I intend to call no further witnesses, your worships. I could call the landlord of the Black Dog if my references to the defendant's behaviour there are challenged, but I have no wish to waste your precious time.' He turned to regard Jenkins for a moment and sniffed. 'For the same reason, I don't even intend to cross-examine Major Fonthill. You have heard enough already to realise that this gratuitous attack on a respected member of our community by a violent man must result in a custodial sentence, of as severe a nature as the law allows.'

He sat down and a murmur of − what? Appreciation, dissent, agreement? − ran round the old courtroom. For the first time, Simon realised that the public benches were full. His mother grabbed his hand. It was clear from the frown on her face that she felt the prosecution had made a strong case. She leaned towards her son. 'Sir Roger should have been here,' she whispered. 'He doesn't stand a chance, the silly man.'

Jenkins, however, seemed unfazed. He gave his broad beam to the chairman of the magistrates as the latter asked, with some puzzlement: 'I understand that you have no one to represent you, Mr Jenkins?'

'That's right, your honour.'

'You will address the magistrates as your worship,' interjected the clerk testily.

'Sorry. No. I would rather speak for myself.'

'Do you have any witnesses you would wish to call?'

'Yes, your worship, Captain Simon Fonthill and his father, the Major. Then, after that, I would like to ask a question or two of the Colonel, if that's allowed, like. Might as well get all the ranks in, eh?'

His grin was not returned by the chairman. 'That is quite in order,' he said. 'Now please call your first witness, but,' he raised a warning finger, 'I urge you to stay with the point and desist from making facetious remarks. This is a serious court of law. Pray do not waste our time.'

The usher called for Simon, who, swearing at his unreadiness, slipped out of his seat and plunged down the stairs. Luckily, the hall was echoing with the buzz of conversation as lawyers met clients and witnesses and he was able to stride forward and apologise to the usher for 'taking a walk'.

In the witness box, facing Jenkins, Simon realised that the Welshman was not as composed as he appeared from the back of the court. He was perspiring slightly and his eyes betrayed his anxiety. 'Now, Captain,' he began, 'much 'as been said 'ere about my character. Would you like to explain 'ow we met?'

Taking a deep breath, Simon related how the two had met in the holding company of the 24th Regiment at Brecon, and how Jenkins had offered to be his servant and been gladly accepted. After leaving the army, they had been together for six years, acting as scouts through the campaigns in Zululand, Afghanistan and Sekukuniland, and had been offered permament positions, Simon as major and Jenkins as warrant officer.

Jenkins's beam had now returned. 'Difficult to see, sir, that rank bein' offered to an 'abitual drunkard, eh?'

'Quite impossible, I would think.'

'Thank you, bach . . . er, sorry. Thank you, sir. That will be all. That is . . .' Jenkins whirled round to beam at the prosecuting solicitor, 'unless this gentleman would wish to chat to the Captain, like?'

The lawyer raised his eyebrows in disdain and shook his head.

Simon left the court, and as his father was called, took advantage of the usher shepherding the Major into the courtroom to double up the stairs and regain his place at the back of the public gallery. His mother patted his hand. 'Well done, dear,' she whispered.

As planned during their week-long preparation for the trial, Jenkins now turned to the question of trespass. Was the Major aware of the custom in the county for land to be crossed by the hunt when in pursuit of a fox?

'Of course,' said Fonthill. 'That is why I wrote specifically to the MFH to explain my position. I took a copy at the time, and if the bench will allow, I will read it.'

The chairman nodded. The Major's letter was short but polite. It requested the members of the hunt to refrain from riding across his land, asked that if a fox was raised near his estate, it be headed off and that if this was impossible, the chase should be abandoned. Reeves's reply had expressed his surprise at the request but promised to do his best to accede to it.

'Ah.' Jenkins turned to the bench. 'P'raps your worships would like to hear from the Major why 'e so dislikes 'untin'?'

'No we would not,' growled the chairman. 'Irrelevant. Get to the point.'

Mrs Fonthill turned to her son. 'They're against us,' she said. 'Anyone can see that.'

But Jenkins was unabashed. He asked the Major to relate exactly what had happened on that morning by the hawthorn hedge. He had not, Fonthill explained, pulled the bridle; merely held it to prevent Colonel Reeves from galloping away up the field. The whip had been used offensively and certainly not with a gentle tap on the shoulder. He had been hit severely across the shoulder and also across the face.

'Oh,' enquired Jenkins innocently, 'enough to leave a mark, then?'

'Yes. A small one, but enough to sting. Across the forehead, here.'

The Major pulled back the lock of hair that hung over his forehead to reveal a red weal running above the right eye. 'Here.'

'Would you care to show their worships that, please?'

The Major turned towards the bench. The three magistrates leaned forward and gazed intently. The chairman made a note.

'One to us,' hissed Mrs Fonthill. 'Don't remember that showing up before, though, do you?'

'No, Mother. But damned good point.'

The Major finished his evidence, and to Simon's surprise, the prosecuting solicitor made no request to cross-examine. 'Arrogant devil,' muttered Simon. 'He thinks he's got it in the bag.'

Jenkins, with ponderous deference, offered to recall Simon to give his version of events in support of the Major, but again the chairman felt that it would not be necessary and the prosecutor did not demur. Simon bit his thumb. Now came the key element of the trial, Jenkins's cross-examination of the Colonel. Would the little man have the forensic skill to counter Reeves's bluster and innate air of superiority – not to mention the obvious bias against him shown by the three magistrates?

It was a surprise, then, when the Welshman took a completely different tack.

''Ow tall would you be, then, Colonel?' he asked.

'What? What? What on earth's that got to do with anything?'

'Oh, come on, sir. It's a simple question. 'Ow tall are you? Five foot eleven? Six foot?'

Reeves pulled back his shoulders and sat very straight in his chair. It was obvious, from the care with which he was dressed and the careful grooming of his side whiskers and moustache, that his appearance was important to him. 'No. Six three.'

Jenkins nodded. 'Ah, a big man. An' what weight would you be, then, Colonel? Thirteen stone or something like that?'

Reeves turned to the bench. 'Look here, this is ridiculous. What's the point of these silly questions?'

The magistrate on the chairman's right nodded in agreement but the chairman held up his pencil. 'I think I might glean a point,' he said quietly. 'Unless you specifically wish to avoid the question, Colonel, perhaps you would answer it?'

'Very well. I'm just under sixteen stone, about two hundred and twenty pounds, for whatever that's worth.'

'An' 'ow long in the army?'

'Nineteen years.'

'Cavalry or infantry?'

'Cavalry. Dragoon Guards.'

'Ah yes.' Jenkins nodded his head sagely, for all the world as though he was an ex-comrade chatting with the Colonel in their club. 'The 'eavy stuff. Big 'orses.' He paused for a moment. Simon began to sense that Jenkins was beginning to enjoy himself. If he became overconfident it could be dangerous. He had only the most tenuous hold on the chairman's patience.

'Now,' Jenkins resumed. 'Would it be right to presume that you 'ave 'unted all your life?'

'Course I have.'

'Good. Now, take your mind back to when you used your whip on the Major. We've 'eard that you just tapped the Major on the shoulder to make him let go of the bridle. Is that right?'

'Something like that, yes.'

'But in actual fact you lashed him twice, didn't you? Once across the shoulder and once across the face?'

'No, nothing as bad as that. Just a couple of taps.'

Jenkins's eyebrows rose histrionically. 'A couple! I thought you said you touched him only once.'

Reeves's face darkened. 'Oh, I can't remember exactly. Once, twice, what does it matter?'

'Well, with respect, sir, it matters a lot to the Major, 'cos you 'urt him, see, and now you're sayin' *I* attacked *you*. But more of that in a minute. If you only tapped the Major, 'ow did he get that nasty mark across his forrid, then?'

'What? I don't know. Perhaps the end of the whip caught him. I didn't intend to . . .' He turned to the bench. 'I didn't intend to cause harm, you know. The man was being damned infuriating.'

But Jenkins was continuing. 'So let's see. We know now that you gave the Major two bashin's with that whip of yours. Then, to stop you 'ittin' 'im again, I tipped you out of your saddle. Do you remember what 'appened next?'

'What are you driving at?'

'What 'appened next, Colonel, was that I nipped round when you were sprawled on your arse and put out me 'and to 'elp you to your feet, but you 'it me across the wrist with that bloody whip and then, when you were standin', you raised it to whip me again, didn't you?'

'Yes.' The big man's eyes were now blazing. 'And I'd do it again, damn you. How dare you throw me off my horse? And then you kicked me in the . . . er . . . groin. A cowardly, swinish thing to do.'

Jenkins seemed quite unmoved. 'Right, then. We've

established that I tried to 'elp you get up but you wouldn't let me, slashin' me with the whip. An' then you were goin' to whip me again until I defended myself with me boot an' stopped you.' He turned to the bench. 'So the picture is this, then, your worships. 'Ere's this big man, on 'is 'orse, who attacks my master, then, when I 'elp the Major, 'e turns on me. Now . . .' Jenkins sighed for effect. 'The Colonel 'ere is six foot three and I'm just five feet four, as you can see. 'E's sixteen stone and I'm eleven stone when I've 'ad a scrub-down, like. 'E's a big man and 'e's as fit as a fiddle 'cos 'e's ridden horses all 'is life, 'unts twice a week and carried a big sword in the 'Eavy Dragoons when 'e was servin'. Now, 'e's got a whip and I am unarmed. Was I goin' to stand there and let 'im whip me? Of course not. We're both ex-soldiers. 'E must 'ave known I would defend myself, and I did it in the only way I know 'ow, when faced with a really big man, see. In those circumstances, look you, you just 'ave to use your natural faculties, like. An' that's what I did.'

As Jenkins paused, the court stayed silent. The Colonel's jaw had now dropped and his eyes seemed quite protuberant. Simon smiled. The bench were now regarding Jenkins with, if not sympathy, at least careful attention. Was his rough but logical marshalling of the facts beginning to win them over? Simon was conscious that his father had joined him, standing at the back of the gallery. They exchanged grins. Mrs Fonthill, however, was unaware of her husband's presence. Her eyes remained fixed on Jenkins as she leaned forward, fist supporting her chin.

The little man had not finished. 'Now,' he said, 'let's consider this terrible injury I inflicted on you.'

Reeves blew out his cheeks. 'I won't have this sneering,' he shouted. 'I was in extreme pain and I can hardly walk, even now.'

'What about ridin', then?'

'I find it incredibly difficult to stay in the saddle.'

'But Colonel,' Jenkins's eyes were now wide in mock astonishment, 'you can hardly walk or stay in the saddle. Yet you went out 'untin' last Wednesday and stayed in the field all day. I know, and I can call witnesses to prove it.'

'What? Well . . . I am recovering a bit, I suppose. I felt I had to stay out, you know . . .' he turned to the bench again, 'to set an example. Yes. To set an example . . .' His voice tailed away and somehow he seemed smaller.

But Jenkins did not wait for his adversary to recover his bluster. Quickly he turned to address the bench. 'The facts are, your worship, that the Colonel 'as admitted that he struck the first blow or blows – and they weren't just gentle taps either, 'cos they left their mark. It's true I tipped 'im off 'is 'orse, but that was to stop 'im further 'urtin' the Major, an', of course, I kicked him in self-defence. 'E's a big man and you can all see 'e 'as a temper, and if I'd let 'im, 'e would 'ave near murdered me.'

He took a deep breath. 'Now, my lords, we can't 'ave blokes goin' round whippin' other people in this day an' age, now can we? Whoever they are. It's the sort of thing that causes . . .' he cast his eyes up to the ceiling in search of the right phrase, 'revolutions an' that. We saw this in Italy. Let them eat cake, wasn't it? Well, we can't 'ave that sort of thing in England, or Wales, look you. What I did I did in self-defence.'

Jenkins's face now adopted a lugubrious air of abject confession. He went on: 'One last thing: I do 'ave too much to drink sometimes. It's when there's no soldierin' to be done with the Captain an' just nothin' to do. But the lads at the pub will be the first to say that it's six of one an' 'alf a dozen of the other, 'cos it always takes two to cause a fight and no one would ever think of bringin' charges, see. An' my army record over the last six years 'as been . . . er . . . impecunious; no, impeccable, so it 'as.

'Sorry, there is one more thing, your worships. The Major showed by writin' that 'e didn't want the 'unt on 'is land and the Colonel knew that. So it was a clear case of trespassin', so it was.' He stopped, rather like a steam locomotive coming to the station buffers, and looked around as if in desperation. 'That's it, then. I rest my whatsit . . . I rest my case, see.' And he sat down.

A soft sigh, as if in relief, seemed to rise from the public gallery. The chairman of the magistrates raised a questioning eyebrow at the prosecuting solicitor, but the latter merely polished his spectacles and stared back blankly. He made no attempt to rise. Simon realised that the man was clearly out of his depth. A solicitor, not a barrister, he did not possess the skill to cross-examine. Jenkins's skilled unravelling of the Colonel's story in the witness box had left him with no ground on which to make a counterattack. He had carefully prepared his case, as a good solicitor should, and given the standing of his client, had expected to win. The wind had turned against him, but he lacked the expertise to trim his sails. He was defeated!

The chairman of the magistrates, the arm of his spectacle frame in his mouth, leaned to his right and consulted his colleague. The latter was frowning and arguing strongly but the chairman was shaking his head in disagreement.

The other magistrate, however, was clearly in concord with his chairman, for their conversation lasted no more than half a minute. The chairman scribbled a note and then cleared his throat. He spoke with a distinctive Midlands accent.

'We find that the defendant,' he said, 'acted in self-defence and is therefore not guilty of the charge of assault and of attempting to cause actual bodily harm.' A hum of approval rose from the packed benches of the public gallery. Simon saw that the Colonel had risen to his feet, on his red face an expression of disbelief and then fury. Jenkins sat quite impassively, nodding his head slowly, as though in approval of the work of a young student.

'However . . .' The chairman had not finished and waved his hand to indicate that everyone should remain seated. He addressed Jenkins. 'My colleagues and I feel, Mr Jenkins, that we should administer a warning to you as to your behaviour in future. It is clear that you have skills in combat that, if deployed in anger and, more to the point, perhaps under the influence of alcohol, could cause harm to anyone who opposes you. You are cleared of this charge and I very much hope that we shall not see you in this place in future. Now, clear the court.'

Mrs Fonthill stood, her eyes blazing. 'What an unfair thing to say! That rider was gratuitous.'

'Never mind, Mother,' said Simon. 'We won – no, *Jenkins* won – and that's all that matters. Come, let us return home.'

The four of them rode back in the carriage, with the newly recovered Williams sitting outside, up ahead, holding the reins. Jenkins seemed to take their effusive congratulations imperturbably, even shyly.

'How on earth did you know that Reeves had gone out hunting?' asked Simon.

Jenkins's eyes sparkled. 'Ah, I popped into the Black Dog durin' the week, just to show that there was no 'ard feelin's, like. Some of the regulars there work on Colonel Reeves's estate an' 'ave no love for 'im. They told me. They're a good lot really, when they can 'old their liquor, see.'

Simon shot a quick glance at Jenkins, but the Welshman's face looked blandly innocent. His eyes dropped for a moment then they engaged Simon's gaze once again. 'I just felt,' he said quietly, 'that I wanted them people in the courtroom to know that workin'-class folk like me, who've never 'ad an education, see, are not stupid. That's why I worked so 'ard at preparin' what I was goin' to say and 'ow I was goin' to do it.'

'Well, you certainly proved your point, old chap.' Simon looked out of the window at the cold black hedgerows and realised that Jenkins was not just trying to impress the court. The house they were riding towards also contained his targets.

Mrs Fonthill leaned towards her husband. 'George, I hadn't realised that you had been so marked by that infernal whip. Show me now. Ah yes, I see it. But it's not much of a mark, is it? I'm amazed it stood out so clearly in the courtroom.'

George Fonthill coughed. 'I must confess, my dear, that we used a touch of artistic licence there. I borrowed a little of your rouge to heighten the mark. Jenkins's idea. I wiped it off a minute or so ago. Bit of a risk, I suppose, but we sensed that Reeves would lie about using the whip and we had to show the man's depravity.' He chuckled. 'I don't mind fighting dirty, if I have to. We old soldiers know a thing or two in that line, eh, 352?'

The three men chuckled, while Mrs Fonthill shook her head in disbelief.

The Major and Fonthill insisted that Jenkins join them in another glass of malt whisky before he retired to the servants' quarters for dinner, and the mood of congratulation continued throughout the meal.

As Simon was about to retire, Mrs Fonthill suddenly snapped her fingers in irritation. 'Goodness, I forgot in all the excitement of the day.' She pointed to the sideboard. 'There, on the tray. A letter from Alice, Alice Griffith, although we must remember to call her Alice Covington now, of course. It arrived this morning. She didn't know you were home but asked after you. Take it and read it. You were such good friends, and I know you will be interested to hear how she is getting on with helping Covington to run that estate of his in Norfolk.'

Simon paused and then stood stock still. Alice! He realised that, consumed as they all had been with Jenkins's problems, the last week had been the first time that a day had passed without him thinking of her. Alice, with her fair hair, her enquiring grey eyes, her soft skin – and her honourable but self-sacrificial marriage to Colonel Ralph Covington. She and Simon had finally declared their love for each other on the borders of Mozambique as Wolseley's campaign against Chief Sekukuni's bePedi tribe neared its apogee. But the injuries sustained by Covington in that final battle and the subsequent ending of his army career had resulted in Alice's decision to honour her previous commitment to the Colonel. She and Simon had vowed never to meet again. The wedding had taken place more than a year ago now, here on the Borders, and had been the reason why Simon had stayed in South Africa, sublimating his anguish by fighting with the British against the Transvaal Boers. Now he forced himself to look unconcerned.

'Splendid,' he said. 'Ah, how is she?'

Mrs Fonthill sniffed. 'Well enough, it seems, though they've had no children yet. And she is getting on now, rather, you know. She's about your age, isn't she?'

Simon nodded, not trusting himself to speak. He felt his father's direct gaze on him.

'Well, it's jolly well time she was pregnant. These young girls think they can leave everything to the last minute. It's not as easy as that, you know. Anyway, I shall write and tell her that you are here and invite her and Covington over for a weekend. You would like that, wouldn't you, dear?'

'Well – I'm not sure, Mother. Covington and I never got on, you know. He was behind the . . . er . . . court martial in Zululand. I don't hold him in high regard, you know.'

'Oh, stuff and nonsense. That was long ago, and you and Alice were so close. I don't see why—'

Major Fonthill cleared his throat. 'I am not sure it would be a good idea, Charlotte. I don't think you should push Simon on this.'

'It's very kind of you, Mother.' Simon gave his father a wan smile of gratitude. 'Perhaps we could talk about it over the next few days? I'll read Alice's letter in the morning, if I may. I am rather tired now and I need to put my head down. Good night.'

The softest of pillows, however, could do little to help Simon banish the vision of Alice that kept dancing before his closed eyes. This talk of her conceiving a child by Covington tortured him, and although part of him yearned to see her again, that, he knew, would only give the rack a couple of extra turns. He was doing his best to forget her, for God's sake, and here was his mother dangling her before his eyes and talking of her as though she was a breeding mare! He must get away before his mother brought them together again. But away to where?

He did not drift off into sleep until just before dawn, and almost immediately, it seemed, he was being shaken awake by Sarah, the housekeeper who had been his nurse as a child. 'Telegram for you,' she said, her voice showing that she was impressed. 'Looks as though it's from the army, so I thought it would be important and you must have it first thing.'

'Thanks, Sarah.' He tore open the brown envelope. The address at the top merely said, 'Horse Guards, London'. The telegram ran:

ARE YOU AND YOUR WELSHMAN FREE FOR IMPORTANT CONFIDENTIAL WORK IN EGYPT IMMEDIATELY STOP CAN YOU DISCUSS HERE AT THREE PM 11TH STOP REPLY BY RETURN STOP WOLSELEY

Simon read it through again, then slowly let his head fall back on to the pillow. He smiled at the ceiling. A way out, at last?

Chapter 3

Simon nodded to Admiral Nelson, looking down Whitehall from his column in Trafalgar Square, and turned under the white stone archway into the Horse Guards, the command centre of the Queen's army. He was early but he was not kept waiting and was ushered immediately into the presence of Lieutenant General Sir Garnet Wolseley, the Adjutant General and virtual number two in the military chain of command.

'Good of you to come, Fonthill.' The General sprang from behind his desk and came forward, hand outstretched, almost bouncing rather than walking. Wolseley was just below middle height, perhaps five feet seven inches, and smartly suited in mufti, but he looked every inch a soldier: his back ramrod straight, his shoulders squared and a scar running from above his sightless left eye to his cheek, the result of a Russian shell exploding in a trench before the Redan during the Crimean War. His one good eye was bright and bulbous – the other was obviously made of glass – and he had a lofty forehead topped by wavy brown hair. His pleasant features were enhanced by a soft, full moustache and only marred, perhaps, by a receding chin. This, however, betrayed no lack of guts. Wolseley had proved himself time after time as a brave and astute commander of men in both peace and war, and had long ago been lauded as 'the very model of a modern major general' by those lions of British light opera, Gilbert and Sullivan.

'Congratulations on your appointment as Adjutant General, sir.'

'What? Yes, well, thank you.' The General grunted. 'It carries with it more frustration than satisfaction, I can tell you.'

Simon tried to conceal a smile. The whole army – no, the whole country – knew of Wolseley's ongoing battle with the Duke of Cambridge, the army's commander-in-chief and the Queen's cousin, whose views on military procedure, strategy and tactics had changed little since they were established by the Duke of Wellington after Waterloo, sixty-seven years ago. Sir Garnet's reforming zeal was constantly running foul of the C-in-C's conservatism. 'Sorry to hear that, sir.'

'Hmm. Rather be chasing Sekukuni out of his holes in those hills any day than sitting here counting beans.' He gestured to a chair. 'Sit down. Cigar?'

'No thank you, sir.'

'Right. To business. Of course you know a bit about Egypt because you were there in '80, just before you went down to help out poor old Pommery-Colley in the Transvaal. Went across the desert from Cairo to Suez, I hear?'

Simon shifted uncomfortably. Wolseley was always so damned well informed! Would he also know about the affray in the back streets of Cairo when he and Jenkins were attacked by thieves and were forced to leave one of their assailants with a stab wound to the heart? They had slipped away from the city before the anti-British authorities could find the body. 'Yes,' he said, 'decided to go by camel train. Rather more fun that way.' Even to Simon, the reason sounded unconvincing.

A slow smile spread across Wolseley's face. 'Hmm. And on the way, I gather that you were attacked by desert bandits and that you organised the traders to defend themselves and so brought off a victory previously unheard of in those sort of affairs. Right? Eh?'

'Something like that, sir, although I wouldn't go quite that far.'

The General gave a grin that lit up his good eye. 'I must say, Fonthill, one of the things that intrigues me about you and your man – 428, is it?'

'Three five two, sir.'

'Ah yes, 352. Yes, one of the things that intrigues me about you and your Welshman is your ability constantly to get into trouble and equally constantly to get out of it. You do seem to be a most resourceful pair.' The General drew on his cigar and watched the blue smoke curl up into the air. Simon remained silent. Better not argue or intervene at this stage. There was more to be gained by listening. 'And that was one of the reasons,' Wolseley continued, 'although only one of them, why I wanted to talk to you. I presume that the fact you are here indicates that you are currently not employed and that you have some interest, at least, in what I may have to offer you?'

'That is so, sir, on both counts.'

'Good. Now tell me what you know about the present state of affairs in Egypt.'

Simon drew in a deep breath. 'Well, I know that when the

country went virtually bankrupt in the late seventies, just after we'd bought the Egyptian shares in the Suez Canal and so gained control of it, we gained permission from the Turkish overlords of the place to appoint commissioners, with the French, to oversee the country's public and financial affairs.'

Wolseley, his eye narrowed, squinted at him through the cigar smoke. 'Right enough so far. Pray continue.'

'Our presence there has not exactly pleased the Egyptian underclass, who are not enamoured anyway of what I suppose one could call the rather indolent suzerainty administered by the Turks from Constantinople. The fact that the French took possession of Tunis last spring hasn't helped, in that it looks as though the French could have ambitions to take Egypt too and extend their North African empire, though we don't believe this.' Simon paused for a moment to gather his thoughts. It was typical of Wolseley to test him in this way, and he was damned if he would flounder. 'Now, it seems to me from what I've read in the newspapers that things are beginning to get a bit out of hand: the Egyptian army is adopting nationalistic postures and a formerly obscure colonel named Arabi – a *fellaheen* or member of the peasant classes . . .'

Wolseley nodded his head in approval. 'Glad you know the terminology.'

'. . . is putting pressure on the Khedive, the chap in charge, to change the Egyptian government to make it more, er, radical and representative of the peasants, and also to reduce the number of Circassian or Turkish officers and promote Egyptians. A few months ago, I think it was, he and some of his fellow colonels marched his troops on the Abdin

Palace in Cairo and demanded a change of government, some sort of new national constitution and an increase in the army. I believe he has got his way more or less, and he is obviously a dangerous man, given our investment in Egypt. From what I know, though, he seems to be more or less well disposed to the two great powers, ourselves and France, who are still holding most of the purse strings. Frankly, it all sounds a bit of a mess, but I presume our government is keeping a close eye on things.'

Wolseley nodded slowly and then smiled. 'Not a bad résumé for an army scout. I can't see that you could be expected to know more. However, there has been one other development that has muddied the waters further. We – that is the French and the British – recently put our foot in it by issuing some stupid joint note, stressing our determination to preserve the Khedive on his throne and to oppose together any movement that threatened the stability of Egypt. The idea was to cool things down a bit and show that the poor old Khedive has powerful backing, even if he doesn't get much from the Turks, who put him on the throne. But that act has been interpreted by everybody in Egypt, from the Khedive downwards, as a threat to intervene militarily if this nationalistic movement grows stronger. The fires are being fanned, of course, by most of the other European powers, who are only too delighted to see the French and the British, with their fat fingers in the Egyptian pie, being thoroughly embarrassed. Now Arabi has been appointed Minister for War and is controlling the whole army, if not the country, and the Khedive is becoming a virtual prisoner in his own palace.'

At this, Wolseley laughed so loudly that Simon was forced

to grin, although he couldn't quite see the joke. 'So,' he began, 'is invasion on the cards, then?'

The laughter died. 'This country has huge investments in Egypt,' said the General, stubbing out his cigar. His voice took on a mocking element as he continued: 'From its lofty position on the high moral ground, Mr Gladstone's government concerns itself very much with the plight of the poor *fellaheen* and wishes to retain influence in Egypt so that it can improve the lot of those poor devils – keep the lash off their backs, reduce the high burden of taxation they carry, perhaps even spread Christianity, that sort of thing. Of course, it wants to protect the capital that the City has put into the place, but far more important than any of these things is that ditch that links the Mediterranean and the Red Sea: the Suez Canal.'

Wolseley sprang from his chair and began to pace the room, one hand thrust deep into the pocket of his jacket, the other gesturing to make his points. 'That bit of water cost us nearly four million pounds seven years ago, but dammit, it was a bargain and we got it at that price because the Egyptians were bankrupt and had to sell. Now it's our lifeline to India and to the colonies in Australia, New Zealand and the Pacific. Saves our merchant trade and the government millions in terms of time and fuel. If there were to be another mutiny in India, for instance, we would be able to ferry troops out in days rather than weeks and stamp it out in far less time than it took us thirty years ago. Same thing if the Russian threat in Afghanistan flares up again. So if this Egyptian nationalism got out of hand and the Egyptians took the Canal back by force – and it would be easy to do – we would be in real trouble. D'you follow, Fonthill?'

Simon nodded. 'Of course, sir. So . . . you *are* planning to invade?'

The General stopped his pacing, walked back to his chair and sank slowly into it. It was as though the air had gone from a balloon. 'No, I am not. And that's just the point. The Liberal Party that now rules this country dislikes foreign intervention. You will have seen some of this for yourself in the Transvaal.' He scowled at his blotter. 'They so procrastinated in their support of Pommery-Colley – one of our army's best men – that the poor chap was forced to occupy that accursed hilltop at Majuba and lay himself open to the massacre that followed and get himself shot. Disgraceful!'

Simon thought of that general's failure to post vedettes down the hillside to warn of an enemy advance and to erect even the most basic fortifications on the summit to defend his position. He opened his mouth to make the point, then thought better of it. He was here to listen, not to argue.

'No,' Wolseley continued. 'Gladstone will do all he can to avoid armed intervention and so will the French, despite this silly warning we have jointly issued. What's more, the Duke and my political master won't allow me to make contingency plans yet, although I feel that view will change soon if things continue to get worse in Cairo.' He looked hard at Simon. 'And this is where you come in, Fonthill.'

Simon swallowed hard. 'I must confess, I don't quite see how, General. You must be receiving constant diplomatic and military information from our people in Cairo, all of them far more au fait with the position and better able to interpret it than I.'

'That's where you're wrong.' Wolseley put his head on one side and regarded Simon in silence for a moment, long enough to cause the young man to colour in embarrassment. 'Oh yes,' he resumed. 'We get plenty of information through the normal channels. In fact, our political agent there, Edward Malet, is young, industrious and considered to be good. But he too is anxious to avoid armed intervention, and I can't help feeling that he occasionally looks at the situation through rose-tinted spectacles. As for military information, well, we've got no one there I consider good enough to give a balanced assessment. Anyone in uniform or known to be a serving officer of the Queen, anyway, wouldn't get very far in picking up the sort of detail I want.'

He pulled at the end of his moustache. 'Now you, Fonthill, have certain very definite advantages. I shall save your blushes, but you certainly have brains, and a tactical awareness in military terms far in advance of most serving officers much older and more experienced than you.' Simon stirred on the chair and opened his mouth to speak, but Wolseley held up his hand. 'Your appreciation of the way to attack Sekukuni's stronghold helped me win that battle. In addition, until his sad end, I was in constant communication with Pommery-Colley during his campaign and he sang your praises in terms of the value of your scouting for him and, in particular, your advice on attacking the Boers at Laing's Nek. In fact, he admitted you were right and he was wrong.'

Simon gave an inward nod of thanks to the memory of a gentle, intelligent officer whose only fault lay in his lack of experience of command in the field.

The General smacked two fingers into the palm of his hand. 'The second point is that, as I mentioned earlier, you can handle yourself if and when you get into trouble – and given the fact that Egypt at the moment is a bit of a melting pot, this could be important.' He shot a hard glance at Simon. 'In this context, will 352 be coming with you?'

'Definitely, sir.'

'Good. You may well need him, but you'll need to keep him well under control. No gratuitous killing, you understand?'

Simon frowned. What did Wolseley know?

'Of course not, sir.'

'Very well.' Three fingers now slapped into his palm. 'The third advantage . . .' he paused and gave a grim smile, 'and you must understand and accept this, Fonthill, if you wish to undertake this mission: the third advantage is that, if things go wrong, you are dispensable, in that you can be cut off without any acknowledgement from us of any kind. Do you understand?'

Simon raised his eyebrows. 'I think so, sir. No links back to the Horse Guards?'

'Quite so. If I have to, I shall deny that this conversation ever took place. That is why I need you. You are not a serving officer, nor a member of our diplomatic or civil service. You will be a freelance, doing whatever it is you are apprehended for on your own initiative completely. Understood?'

'Understood.' How ruthless these successful generals were! He had served under two of them, Roberts and Wolseley, and they both shared the same attribute of determining what they wanted and then going for it, irrespective of who stood in their way. At least Wolseley never dissembled. Simon appreciated that, and his spirits lifted for a moment at the thought of being completely cut off from official control to be free to act to do . . . to do what? 'What exactly is it that you want of me, sir?'

The General leaned back. 'Yes, the important part. Sure you won't have a cigar?'

'No thank you, sir.'

'Right. What do we want of you?' He let his chair come crashing back and leaned across his desk. 'First, I want to know as much as you can feed me about the Egyptian army. Of course, I know its numerical strengths. Arabi would be able to put far more men in the field than whatever I could summon in terms of an invasion force. But that's of comparatively little importance. It's quality that counts. From the information I have, I sense that the *fellaheen* who comprise most of the infantry are not that impressive – their performance in the recent Egyptian–Abyssinian war was not good – but they could perform with far more backbone if they perceive that they are fighting to set their country free, don't you know.'

Simon felt a pang of sympathy for the rank and file of the Egyptian army, paid a pittance, treated badly by their Turkish officers and living in what was virtually an occupied country. But he nodded.

'From what I hear,' the General continued, 'the artillery is a different matter, and I believe that Arabi has recently been buying decent ordnance from Krupp. This could be a hard nut to crack. I would like to have it confirmed. Most importantly, however, I would like you to scout the country and give me your assessment of my options in terms of invasion, as well as how you think Arabi would react and where he would set up defensive positions to stop me. Let's look at a map.'

Wolseley strode to a table at the far end of the wood-panelled room and Simon followed him. The table was placed under a large portrait in oils of the Duke of Wellington, Napoleon's conqueror. Simon couldn't help feeling that despite Sir Garnet's reforming energies, the Iron Duke and his practices of long ago still permeated the corridors of the Horse Guards.

'Now.' The General unrolled a large map of Egypt and pinned the corners to the edges of the table. 'There are really only two ways I can go in if I am going to march on Cairo. From here, in the north,' he tapped the port of Alexandria in the eastern Mediterranean, 'or from the south, here.' His finger rested on the Red Sea entrance to the Suez Canal, at Suez itself. 'Nowhere else will do to land an invasion force.'

Simon frowned. 'Can't you do both? Come from the south, presumably with troops from India, and also with a force from home, landing in the north, and catch Arabi in pincers, so to speak?'

Wolseley shot him an appraising glance. 'I've considered that. Good idea in theory but difficult in practice, and it would take time to organise the logistics. It might be on, though. Have a look at the Canal and the landing facilities at, say, Ismailia. But be careful. I hear there are marauding gangs of Arabs ranging up and down the banks now. In fact, lawlessness is growing throughout the whole country, so you'd better have your wits about you.'

'Can we have rifles?'

'No. You're not in the army. Take pistols and, if you must, maybe a couple of hunting rifles for sport; for shooting crocodiles on the Nile, that sort of thing. It depends what identity you are going to adopt.'

'I will have to think about that, sir, and decide when we get there how we can best fit in.' Fowling pieces or sporting rifles would be no good against Egyptian soldiers or, for that matter, the armed Bedawis they had encountered on their last crossing of the northern desert.

The General looked up from the map. 'This question of identity or cover is important. There are still plenty of English gentlemen taking their holidays along the Nile, hunting for archeological finds and so on, but as things warm up there, as I am sure they will, these people will be forced to leave the country, so you could be quite exposed unless you can adopt some credible disguise or other. You will need to think about that and set up your baggage accordingly.'

'Hmmm. Whatever we do, or whoever we are, we shall travel light, sir. We may have to move fast.'

'Absolutely right. Of course,' Wolseley smiled waspishly, 'you could apply to join the Egyptian army. I understand there are quite a few mercenaries in their ranks already.'

Simon shook his head firmly. 'Jenkins and I are basically scouts, sir,' he said. 'We are not spies. I intend to lie as little as I have to.'

Wolseley frowned. 'Well, that's as maybe, Fonthill, but if we are to serve the Queen to the best of our ability, then we all sometimes have to do things we dislike. But I am not directing you on this matter. You must find your own cover and stick to it. To repeat: you will be on your own.'

'Yes, I well understand that.'

'One more point, though. Speaking of mercenaries, there is a fellow right at the top of the Egyptian army who could, perhaps, be useful to you. They call him Stone Pasha. He's an American who was a divisional commander in the Civil War – don't know whose side he was on. He's a rather shadowy figure who has, or had, the title of Chief of Staff of the Egyptian army, and I suppose his role was to knock them into shape as a modern force. Now, of course, Arabi will be in charge. I don't know if Stone's nose has been put out of joint by all this promotion of the Egyptians and, indeed, the rise of Arabi. He just might be useful, so bear him in mind.'

'Thank you, sir. I will.

'Now.' The General was gesturing to the map again. 'I want to hear from you within five weeks at the latest. Give me the options on going in and some idea of where Arabi might stand to fight at each place. Use your soldier's eye to assess the ground. I won't expect you to dot the I's and cross the T's, but if things move as I think they will, I shall have to make plans very quickly – and that means that to help me, you will have to move equally fast.'

'Who do I report to, sir?'

Wolseley looked at him in surprise. 'Me, of course, and only me. At this point there is no question of invasion, and if anyone knew I had sent someone into a country with whom our relations are strained to help me plan just that, then there would be hell to pay.' The General gave his grim smile. 'Sorry, my boy, but you will be on your own. You will not make contact in Cairo or anywhere else with representatives of Her Majesty's Government.'

'Very well. But how do I report to you?'

'Here.' Sir Garnet produced a small scrap of unheaded white paper carrying two names. 'These chaps, Mr Roberts and Mr George, work as clerks for Thomas Cook, the travel agency, which as you must know has tremendous commercial power in Egypt. Roberts is in Alexandria and George in Cairo. They can be trusted completely and will relay cables to me directly. You can't use code because that could be counterproductive and attract attention. Pretend that I and my family are planning a holiday in Egypt and tell me where to go and what the problems could be. Eh? Got it?'

Simon smiled ruefully. 'Got it, sir.'

'Good. Now, as soon as we have landed or I tell you otherwise, I want you to report to me personally on the spot, because there will be further work for you once hostilities have begun. This means, my boy, that the pair of you could be away for some time. Does that cause you problems?'

Simon's mind flew to Alice and her possible visit to Brecon. He must *not* be there. 'No, sir. On the contrary.'

'Splendid.' Wolseley walked back to his desk and opened a drawer. 'While you are in service, you will be paid at the level of major and your Welshman at that of warrant officer second class.' He withdrew an envelope and gave it to Simon. 'This is a draft for two hundred guineas for your initial expenses. It will help you to equip yourselves for the trip and, at least initially, to get about the country. Mr George in Cairo can provide further funds when and if needed, but be discreet.' He gave a smile that didn't quite reach his eye. 'This comes from a confidential budget I have here that is by no means limitless, so don't go about buying elephants or such like. Understood?'

Simon gave an answering smile and nodded his head.

'Now, Jervis and Hawsbury, just off Piccadilly, can kit you out and will be expecting you this afternoon. They know the country and will be able to advise.' He handed Simon another envelope. 'Here are two tickets for the Indian mail *wagon lit* to Bologna and Brindisi, from which you will board the P & O steamer *Cathay* for the three-day voyage to

Alexandria. You leave the day after tomorrow and you should be in Egypt seven days from then.' He gave another smile, gentler this time. 'You see, my dear boy, time is of the essence.'

Simon gave an answering smile and shook his head, almost in disbelief. 'You seem to have been pretty sure of me, sir.'

Wolseley raised his eyebrows. 'I trust my judgement in men, Fonthill. I was sure that once you had decided to come and talk to me, you would not resist this request to serve your country in a way that,' he smiled again, 'I rather felt would suit you and your man. I remember you telling me in bePedi country that you did not have too high a regard for the regular army after your experiences in Zululand, and indeed, you rejected my offer of a regular commission and promotion. Something *irregular*, however, I thought would suit your style. I do hope that I am not wrong?'

'No, sir. I suppose Jenkins and I are destined to be "irregular" for the rest of our lives. For better or worse, as they say.'

'So you'll go?'

'Of course.'

'Capital. Now, off you go. You have much to do before you set off, and I must apply myself to the pressing question of the quality of the brass buttons being supplied to the Household Cavalry. Goodbye, Fonthill. Thank you, and good luck.'

He held out his hand and Simon shook it. 'Goodbye, sir.' Simon had reached the door when he was called back.

'One more thing – forgot all about it. You remember Covington?'

The name made Simon stand stock still. 'Of course. What about him?'

Wolseley rose from his chair and sauntered across to Simon with a look of, could it be mischief, in his eye? 'Well, he has applied to me for permission to rejoin the army, damn it all. He's only got one arm and one eye, but he wants to come back in to serve and fight. What d'you think of that, Fonthill?'

Simon regarded the General intently. Wolseley knew full well that Simon had knocked Covington down before Rorke's Drift in Zululand and been court-martialled for it. He might even have received an inkling of Simon's regard for Alice, now Covington's wife. Yes, he was playing games, all right.

'Full marks to him, sir. But it'll be difficult for him to serve, won't it, with his disabilities?'

'Depends. There are precedents. If he can ride, shoot and hold a sword, then I must confess I am tempted to let him come back. I know you had your differences with him, Fonthill, but he was a damned good soldier, y'know. Served me well on the Ashanti campaign. Yes, I'm inclined to give him back his commission. Gad!' He began to chortle. 'You might even meet him in Egypt.'

'That will be a pleasure, General.'

'Yes, I am sure it will. Goodbye, Fonthill, and good luck.'

Simon paused outside by the iron railings and took a deep breath. Hansom cabs were lined up along Whitehall, nose to tail, interspersed here and there with a few delivery drays. The line seemed to be at a standstill. An elderly gentleman in top hat and smartly cut overcoat stood waiting for a gap so that he could cross the road. He caught Simon's eye and gestured with his stick. 'Gettin' beyond a joke, this damned traffic,' he said. 'Average speed of about seven miles an hour now, I read somewhere. Disgraceful.'

Pulling a face in distant sympathy, Simon began to walk away slowly towards Piccadilly, deep in thought. London's traffic problems did not occupy his mind, however, nor did the difficulties and dangers facing him in Egypt. They were real enough, but for the moment, they could wait. It was Ralph Covington who loomed before him as he picked his way along the crowded pavement on that March afternoon: Covington with his cold courage and arrogant bearing, his chilling blue eyes and sweeping moustaches; Covington, the husband of the woman he loved; Covington, cruelly disfigured by a bePedi spear, his left arm shattered by an elephant gun – it seemed that he now wore some sort of hook. Simon bared his teeth in anguish. It would be unthinkably cruel if this man who had been his persecutor and competitor for Alice should once again be about to cross his path. Wolseley had seemed to take delight in the prospect. What was it the General had said? 'No gratuitous killing.' Of course, he would have been thinking of Jenkins and his fierce reputation as a fighter. And yet . . . Simon shrugged his shoulders. If, during this difficult assignment, Ralph Covington stood in his way, then there would be nothing gratuitous about the result. He strode on, trying now to concentrate on the requirements for the journey ahead.

Chapter 4

'Don't look now,' said Jenkins, 'but I think we're goin' to be in trouble in a minute. Behind you, on the right, out in the desert.'

Instinctively Simon turned, and putting his hand above his eyes to shade them from the white glare, saw five faraway black figures, mounted on camels. They were shimmering in the heat haze but it was clear that they were approaching fast. They were coming from north of Ismailia, now just a smudge of buildings on the horizon behind them, but linked by the arrow-straight line of railway that ran back to the town and then, to the west, ahead of them, across the desert to Zagazig and distant Cairo. Menacingly, the riders were now fanning out to cut off their retreat to Ismailia, although, in truth, there was no way that Simon and Jenkins on foot could have outdistanced the mounted Arabs.

'Damn,' said Simon.

'Yes, well, with respect, bach sir, I thought it was a bit daft to go marchin' out into the bleedin' desert in this 'eat an' without an 'orse, a camel or a Martini-Henry between us.'

'I'm not saying you're wrong, but I wanted to get a feel for the terrain. If Wolseley's going to march this way – as he will probably have to, because the rail line will almost certainly be cut – then I must know how difficult it will be.' He shielded his eyes again. 'What the hell do they want?'

Jenkins sniffed. 'I'd say they want us. That's what they want.'

The two men had been in Egypt now for three weeks. They had landed in Alexandria to find that elegant town, with its palm trees and gentle sea breezes, throbbing with sullen but tangible anti-English and anti-French resentment. The streets had been strangely quiet and the few Europeans forced to be out on them hurried along, their heads down, as though they had contracted some strange disease and were anxious not to pass it to the indigenous population. Twice Simon and Jenkins had been spat at in the streets, and Simon had been forced to restrain Jenkins from reacting. He had no wish for them to be the spark that would ignite the tinder keg. They had trudged past the big forts – Ras el Tin, Ada, Pharos and Cobra – that commanded the bay with their old but still serviceable ten-inch Armstrong guns. Egyptian troops in white cotton uniforms were manning these positions, which, though run down, could easily be restored, it seemed to Simon, and pose a big threat to a seaborne invading force. While taking coffee in the fashionable public gardens by the Mahmoudieh Canal, Simon had fallen into conversation with a young Turkish officer of artillery anxious to practise his French, and learned that the Egyptian army was indeed receiving shipments of modern German cannon from the Krupp factory and was distributing them to units throughout the country.

Alexandria, of course, was the obvious point of entry for an invading force, if the forts could be put out of action. Its port and Aboukir Bay had deep anchorages and were near to the British possession of Cyprus, which formed a convenient base in the eastern Mediterranean for imperial troops. But a brief excursion along the railway line south towards Cairo had revealed to Simon several positions of strength where the Egyptians could hold up an invading force and leave them with leisure to sabotage and close the Suez Canal. He and Jenkins therefore had taken passage to Port Said, the northern entrance to the Canal, and boarded a boat sailing south. They had disembarked at Ismailia, situated some fifty miles along the Canal, just where it debouched into Lake Timsah.

The little town was not much more than a village and owed its existence solely to the construction of the Canal. It nestled in an amphitheatre bordered by low sand hills and consisted principally of the houses of M. de Lesseps, the French engineer who had led the construction of the Canal, and other officials, the Khedive's palace, the railway station and a native quarter with two or three thousand inhabitants. A pleasant, green, well-watered spot, it had hardly existed ten years before and its landing stage was small. But it was the nearest point on the Canal to Cairo, the railway between Alexandria and Suez (from which a branch line broke off to the capital) ran within two miles of it, and the Sweetwater Canal passed along some two hundred yards back from the lake. This canal carried fresh water from the Nile to north-eastern Egypt, and whoever controlled this water supply in Cairo controlled the Suez Canal, or at least the towns at its head, its length and its base. As he and Jenkins walked through the sleepy, wide lanes of Ismailia, Simon began to formulate the beginnings of an invasion strategy for

Wolseley. A short stroll out into the desert, following the railway line for a way to familiarise himself with marching conditions and the approaches from the west, seemed to Simon all that was necessary to put flesh on the bones of his idea.

Until, that was, these grim riders materialised out of the desert to cut off their retreat back to the town.

Simon unslung his field glasses and focused on the nearest of the riders. From the blur a face emerged, swathed in black to shield it from dust, so that only the dark eyes and the nose emerged. 'Blast,' breathed Simon. 'Bedawis!'

'What, like those gents we 'ad trouble with crossing the desert a year or so ago?'

'The very same. Desert bandits.' He swung the glasses to take in the other riders. 'Except that these chaps aren't carrying old muskets. It looks as though they've got reasonably decent rifles.'

He put down the binoculars and looked around. The desert was flat and completely barren, with not even the short scrubby 'devil plant' bushes to break the monotony of sand and gravel until it merged with the deep blue of the horizon. The twin railway lines ran straight ahead and back towards Ismailia, like black scars across the soft ochre of the desert, and there was no sign of another living thing.

When going ashore at Ismailia, Simon had been warned of the armed bands that increasingly were coming out of the desert to take pickings from passengers unwise enough to stretch their legs on the banks of the Canal; ships were often forced, because of the one-way system of the Canal, to moor at the *gares* or stations cut into the canal sides while priority traffic came through. There was a strong contingent of

Egyptian troops stationed at Ismailia, but perhaps because of the general air of tension that hung over the country, it seemed reluctant to leave its billet in the town. As a result, the Bedawis were becoming increasingly bold. Simon cursed his own arrogance. Jenkins was right. How stupid to walk out into the desert with only two Colt pistols for protection!

The Arabs were now some quarter of a mile away and had slowed the trot of their camels to an insolent walk. They had spread out into a crescent and rode with the stocks of their rifles pressed into their thighs, the barrels pointing skywards. Simon pointed along the railway line, where, about a hundred yards away, a small linesman's shed hunched by the side of the track.

'We'll wait for them there,' he said. 'It's not much cover but it will have to do. Do you have your Colt?'

Jenkins nodded and drew from the band of his trousers a long, silver-barrelled, pearl-handled revolver. It looked more like an ornament than a weapon, but its barrel size indicated that it carried a man-stopping .45 slug. A pair of these American handguns had been given to them in the Transvaal. They would be needed now. 'Glad to get it out,' he said. 'It's been stickin' in me, like, since we began this daft stroll. What's the plan, then?'

Simon withdrew the Colt's twin, inspected its six chambers to ensure that each one carried a cartridge and tucked it back inside his shirt. 'Put it away inside your shirt,' he said. 'I will try and talk us out of this, so only shoot if I do.'

'Good job we've got these little babies, then, isn't it?' said Jenkins companionably as they strode towards the hut. 'Though I'd rather 'ave me rifle and a lunger. I'm not sure, look you, that I can 'it anythin' with this.'

They reached the hut and found its low door only closed on a latch. Inside were a couple of shovels and a huge one-ended spanner, presumably used for adjusting the bolts attaching the rails to the timber sleepers. Simon tossed a shovel to Jenkins and took up the spanner. 'We've got to have a reason for being out here, so we'll say we're line workers. God knows we look filthy enough.'

Indeed they did. Each wore thin cotton trousers tucked into large boots. Their shirts were of light flannel and were now deeply stained with perspiration and covered in dust. Tied around their necks were equally stained cotton handkerchiefs, and they had both elected to wear wide-brimmed South African-type slouch hats, rather than English pith helmets. While Jenkins dug to clear sand away from the sleepers, Simon made a great show of tightening the bolts. As the riders drew near, the pair leaned on their tools and waited for them.

Simon held up a hand in greeting: '*As-salaam alaykum.*'

The five riders gently urged their camels forward until they faced Simon and Jenkins in a semicircle. Five pairs of black eyes stared down at them and the rifles stayed braced against their haunches. There was no traditional response to the greeting; no one spoke. A black crane, foraging abortively far from the waters of Lake Timsah, wheeled high overhead. The breathing of the camels and the buzzing of a distant fly hardly broke the silence.

'Not very sociable, like, are they, bach?' murmured Jenkins.

Simon tried again. 'Good morning,' he said.

Eventually the central figure in the quintet loosened the *esharp*, the black cloth around his mouth, and spoke. 'English? French?' he asked.

Simon shook his head. 'Neither. Americans.' Jenkins looked at him sharply. 'We are railway engineers. Here to maintain the line.' He held up the spanner to indicate the work.

The Bedawi spoke in Arabic to his fellows, presumably translating. One of them indicated Simon and replied derisively. The first man eased his camel forward and gestured to Simon with the barrel of his rifle. Simon noticed that it was an American Remington and had a brief moment to wonder how a desert wanderer would find such a modern weapon before the man spoke again. '*Baksheesh*,' he said, pointing to Simon's midriff with the barrel of the gun. 'Money. Your money.'

Simon looked the Arab firmly in the eye. 'We have no money,' he said. Then he put his hand in his pocket and pulled out an assortment of Egyptian coins. 'Only this change. You can have this, but we have no big money. We are workers, not rich tourists. Here.' He offered the coins. 'Take it. It's all we have.'

The Arab leaned down, took the coins, examined them and then with a curse hurled them away into the sand. 'Dollars,' he shouted. 'Dollars, pounds, pounds.' And he pushed the muzzle of his rifle into Simon's chest.

'Careful, bach,' murmured Jenkins.

Holding the Bedawi's gaze, Simon reached inside his shirt with his right hand, as though to produce his wallet, while with his left he held the rifle barrel and gently moved it away. From the corner of his eye he noticed that the other Arabs were watching intently, although their rifles remained pointing skywards. Jenkins's hand had moved to his own shirt button.

Without hurrying, Simon withdrew the big Colt, clicked back the hammer with his thumb and pointed it directly at the Arab's chest. 'I said,' he murmured, 'no money. No money.' He sensed, rather than saw, that Jenkins had also produced his revolver.

The tableau remained perfectly still for a moment, the crescent of Bedawis, their rifles couched on their hips, looking down on the two Europeans, who stood defiantly, revolvers raised. Simon, perspiration now pouring down his face, kept his eyes locked on those of the Arab leader, watching for the slightest flicker of intent. His brain told him that at the first aggressive move he could kill perhaps two of the bandits, and Jenkins could certainly do the same. That would leave one Arab with a chance of levelling his rifle and firing. Who would he select . . .?

The stalemate was eventually broken when the central Bedawi slowly lifted his rifle and, still holding Simon's gaze, nodded and smiled. He gave a brief command, and one by one the Arabs wheeled their camels and loped away, leaving only the leader. Without a word, he turned his beast's head and followed the others.

'Bloody 'ell,' breathed Jenkins. 'That was a close call an' all. I thought we was done for.'

'So did I.' Simon took out his handkerchief and wiped his brow. 'Five against two are not odds I fancy. Nor Remington rifles against hand guns. I wouldn't want—'

A bullet slapped into the side of the hut at his elbow. He looked up. With a shriek, the Arabs had manoeuvred their camels into their crescent formation and were now thundering down on the two men, splitting two and three to take them from either side, firing from their saddles as they came.

'Kneel!' shouted Simon. Both men went down on one knee to make a smaller target and, crouching back to back, levelled their Colts. Through Simon's mind flashed the thought that they only had twelve rounds between them and that every bullet must count. He just had time to marvel at the skill of the Arabs as they dropped the reins of their galloping camels, firing their rifles from the shoulder as they came.

Their skill as riders, however, was not matched by their marksmanship, and none of the bullets from the Remingtons found their mark. Simon released two shots as the three Arabs on his side galloped by, but as far as he could see, they too missed. Not so Jenkins. After the charge had passed and the Bedawis wheeled round to form up, Simon realised that one of the Arabs on the Welshman's side lay coiled on the sand, his camel loping away disconsolately.

'In the shed now, 352,' gasped Simon. 'It will give us a bit of cover. Use the shovel to make loopholes. Let's hope they charge again. At least it gives us a chance.'

Using shovel and spanner, the two men smashed holes in opposite sides of the shed and waited for the next charge. It did not come, however. In its place came a volley of rifle shots that crashed into the roof of the shed.

'Damn,' cried Simon, 'they're going to stay out of range and outshoot us, the clever bastards. They're firing high. Make smaller holes further down. We'll lie on our stomachs and hold our fire.'

''Alf a mo', said Jenkins, crashing his shovel into the wall of the shed at his feet, 'why are we supposed to be Americans?'

'Thought it might help a bit, since everybody here seems to hate the French and the English.'

'Well, now we know they 'ate the Americans too. This is not a sociable place at all, is it?'

Simon wriggled forward on his stomach and squinted through the hole he had made at ground level. At first he saw nothing, then a stab of flame and a crack as a bullet crashed its way through the thin planking of the hut above his head marked the Arabs' position, some two hundred yards away. They had tethered their camels and now lay prone, using the hut almost as target practice. They were safe enough, for they were out of the effective range of the Colts.

'We can't just lie here,' said Simon. 'These walls are no protection at all and the shed will soon be riddled like a pepperpot. They will adjust their aim lower and hit us sooner than later. Somehow we have to lure them within range.'

'Yes, but 'ow? I've only got four rounds left.'

'So have I. We shall have to pretend that we are hit. After the next shot, let out a shout.'

Immediately four bullets cracked through the flimsy frame of the hut above their heads and they both let out cries of anguish – Jenkins's worthy of a lead part at the Haymarket Theatre in London. Three more shots followed, this time hissing just above them as they burrowed into the soft sand that formed the floor of the hut.

'I can't see them at all now,' whispered Simon. 'Can you?'

'No. 'Ang on – yes, two of 'em are startin' to wriggle forward. Shall I give a bit of a moan?'

'Yes, but not too theatrical. You're not playing in *Little Nell*.'

Jenkins's groan contained all the passion of the Welsh valleys and a musicality that he could never summon to carry a tune. 'Ah,' he murmured, 'it's workin'. They've both got to their feet an' they're walkin' towards us now.'

'Wait a minute,' whispered Simon. 'I can see the other two on my side now. They're lying back to cover the pair walking in. They're clever devils. They really do seem to want us. Hold your fire, 352. Don't shoot unless you're sure you will hit.'

'Right you are, bach sir. Come on, my lovelies. Just a bit closer, there's good little Arabs . . .'

Jenkins held his fire for what seemed an eternity to Simon before the baking hot interior of the hut suddenly exploded with two cracks from the long-barrelled Colt. 'Damn,' shouted the little Welshman. 'Got one but missed the other perisher. Blast these peashooters. 'E's runnin' back now, out of range.'

Immediately two more bullets whistled through the hut close to their heads as the Bedawis lying back opened fire.

'Out of here now, before they reload,' shouted Simon. 'Out behind the shed. Come on.'

He crashed open the door and hurled himself to the back of the shed, putting the little building between himself and the Arabs. Jenkins followed, thumping into the sand beside him.

'What now then, bach sir? I'm buggered if I know what we do next.'

'Nor do I. We've got six rounds between us. But they're down from five to three. These thieves are usually cowards who run when they're opposed. I can't see them hanging about much longer. Cartridges are precious to them, too . . . Hey, what's that?'

Faraway, from the west, came a sound completely alien to

the desert. Indistinct, it sounded almost musical on the still, heavy air. If it was a bird, it was giving a cry neither of the two had ever heard before: a distant *poop poop*.

''Ere, bless you, bach,' exclaimed Jenkins, peeping around the corner of the hut, 'it's a bloody train, that's what it is. Must be the ten twenty from Aberystwyth, late as bloody usual.'

Simon ventured his head around the corner of the hut. Far away, down the track to the west, he could see a black dot with a white smudge of smoke above it, gradually getting larger as he watched. 'A train it is,' he shouted. 'And the Arabs are going – they probably think there are soldiers on board.'

The two now stood, revolvers in hand, and watched as the three Bedawis mounted their camels. Instead of riding away, however, they came trotting towards the hut.

'Bloody 'ell,' said Jenkins, raising his Colt, 'they're comin' again.'

Simon held up his hand. 'No. Don't shoot. They want to collect their dead.'

The leading rider raised both his hands and indicated the two bodies. Simon stepped from behind the hut and nodded. Immediately the two other Arabs slipped down from their camels and carefully slung the bodies of their comrades on to their saddles. Then the sad little cavalcade turned back, picked up the reins of the riderless camels and peeled away to the north, whence they had come.

'Well blow me down,' said Jenkins. 'At least the bastards 'ave got some Christian instincts.'

Simon tucked his Colt back into the trouser waistband inside his shirt and wiped the perspiration from his face with his sodden handkerchief. 'Well, I don't think they'd thank you for calling it a Christian instinct. As a matter of fact—'

Before he could complete his sentence, a bullet crashed into the shed at his side. A puff of white smoke came from the leading camel as the little trio headed off into the desert.

Simon grinned. 'I guess he wanted to have the last word. He had guts, that man, I must say. Would have made a good soldier.'

'Bugger 'im,' said Jenkins. ''Ow about tryin' to cadge a lift on the train? I don't fancy walkin' 'ome, with them three still out there.'

'Good idea. Get the shovels.'

They hurriedly picked up the shovels, found two scraps of red rag from within the hut and tied them to the ends of the shovels. Then they stood in the centre of the track, waving the shovels, as the train approached. It pulled to a halt with a great hissing of steam and an anxious face appeared from the side of the cabin.

'Do you speak English?' asked Simon as they approached the footplate.

'No I bloody don't,' said the driver. 'I'm a Scotsman, I'll have you know.'

'Thank goodness for that,' grinned Simon. 'Can we get a lift with you into Ismailia? We have been attacked by Bedawis and your arrival has probably saved our lives.'

'Och, the devils are strong hereabouts. They're all right in the north, where they're peaceable out in the desert. But not here. They come up from the Sudan. You're lucky: I wouldna have stopped for any Arabs wavin' bits o' rags. Climb up on the footplate and let's be off before they come back. I'll no be chargin' ye for the ride, laddie. What the hell are you doin' oot here anyway, on foot? You must be mad.'

'Tell you later. We don't want to hold you up.'

Carefully concealing their Colts, the two climbed aboard, and with much clanking and hissing, the great locomotive got under way again, as Simon explained how they were studying the flora and fauna of the banks of the Canal and had wandered too far out into the desert. He was not at all sure that the canny Scotsman – thank God for the great diaspora of Scottish engineers that had spread around the world under Victoria's rule! – accepted the story. He merely grunted, but they arrived at Ismailia within the half-hour, and Simon and Jenkins extended their thanks and slipped away before any railway officials could question them.

Back in their hotel, they bathed and then took a congratulatory whisky together. Jenkins shook his head. 'I still don't know why we 'ad to walk out into the desert like that. Why not 'ire a couple of 'orses or camels or whatever? I know you can't ride for toffee, but it would 'ave been better, wouldn't it?'

Simon took a deep draught of whisky before replying. 'Point one,' he said, 'I bloody well *can* ride now. Not as well as you, but well enough. I have improved. Second, I had to know about marching conditions for Wolseley. I reckon the surface sand is about nine inches to a foot deep either side of the railway track. Now, that makes for difficult marching for an army and would slow it down considerably. If the General is to attack Cairo from this side – and I think he should – then this fact must go into his calculations and affect his timing.'

Jenkins pulled a face. 'Just occasionally, only occasionally mind you, I forget that you're clever. Sorry, bach sir.'

'Right. After the whisky, get down to the railway station and book us two tickets to Cairo, leaving tomorrow. It's time we had a sniff around the capital city – and it's also time I cabled the General.'

The train journey was uneventful, but it gave Simon time to consider their next step and also the contents of his cable to Wolseley. By the time they had reached Cairo, he had made his decision on both counts. Strategically, he knew exactly what he would recommend to the General regarding his landings if he had to invade, but he knew little about the Egyptian army. It would be difficult to dig deep in this area in the time available without using subterfuge – and he had sworn not to be a spy. But he had also promised to serve the Queen, and he would gain no one's sympathy if he pussy-footed about in Cairo merely to salve his own conscience. He would have to find a pretence to call on the American at the heart of the Egyptian command; what was his name? Ah yes. Stone Pasha. But first they had to find lodgings.

Emerging from the station in Cairo, with its cacophony of sounds – the hiss of steam, the deep-throated puffing of the engines, the cries of the porters and the pleas of the fruit vendors – Simon and Jenkins's senses were assailed anew by the familiar smells of the great city: a mixture of old dirt, incense, spices and bad drains. The streets teemed with a multi-ethnic stew of humanity, seemingly drawn from every corner of North Africa. Urchins in turbans and little else led camels laden with brushwood or green fodder; grey-bearded elders nodded along on donkeys; coal-black Nubians from the south strode through the multitude with primitive elegance, their heads held high; ragged water-sellers bent their backs under the weight of their sodden skin sacks; European-suited grandees sat back in their two-horse carriages preceded by breathless runners, who cleared the way for their masters with shrill shouts – 'shemalak, ya weled' '(to the left, oh boy!'); and everywhere – this a new element – Egyptian soldiers, clad in white cotton uniforms that looked more like pyjamas, sauntered along with a new-found arrogance.

'Blimey,' mouthed Jenkins. 'Gone quiet again, isn't it?'

The two had remained dressed in their desert wear, and with their burnished complexions and wide-brimmed hats could have come from anywhere in the Dark Continent. Eschewing a carriage, they hired three donkeys, one to carry their modest baggage, and with their boys running ahead, took their place in the swirling tide and headed for the unfashionable Metropolitan Hotel in Bourse al-Gadid Street, Old Cairo, where they had stayed on their last visit to the city some eighteen months earlier.

Bourse al-Gadid sat on the edge of a labyrinth of narrow lanes leading down to the bazaars. The upper storeys of its houses leaned towards each other, like those of Elizabethan England, so that it seemed a leap could take one across the gap, giving the added advantage of avoiding the coagulated traffic in the street below. The two men paid off the boys and, shouldering their bags, climbed the stairs to the second floor of the building, which contained a large and surprisingly cool reception area. Their entry provoked a jerk of the head and an appraising stare from the white-gowned manager behind the battered reception desk. Europeans – if they *were* Europeans – rarely visited his hotel.

'Hello, Ahmed,' said Simon, and removed his hat.

The little Egyptian's frown immediately disappeared and his eyes lit up. He gave a little bow and then took Simon's outstretched hand. '*Effendi*. Mistair Fonteel and Mistair Jonkins. I am so sorry. I did not recognise you. Welcome. Welcome.'

'I am sorry, Ahmed, we had no time to cable you. Do you have two rooms we could take for a few days, please?'

'Two rooms! No! You shall have the best in the hotel. I throw people out immediately.' He threw his hands up in emphasis.

'No, no. That's very kind, but two ordinary rooms will be fine, thank you.'

'You will have them. Give me three minutes. Sit. I bring you whisky.'

'No thank you. It's a little early for that.' Simon put his hand on Jenkins's shoulder to stifle the inevitable protest. 'How is your brother?'

Ahmed's white teeth flashed beneath his small, elegant moustache. 'Ah, Mahmud is well. He always talk of you. He is still very grateful.'

'Any more trouble on the camel train with the Bedawis?'

'No. They not come again. You frighten them off, I think.'

'Good.'

Ahmed looked around him and leaned towards Simon, lowering his voice and tapping his finger against the side of his nose. 'You on important government business again, yes?'

'Yes, Ahmed. Perhaps more important than last time.'

'Ah. Of course. I help you, if I can.'

Jenkins intervened. 'Very kind of you, I'm sure, Amen. Perhaps just the one whisky while we're waitin', eh?'

'Of course. Sit. I am back in several jiffies.'

They were soon installed in two adjoining rooms, sparsely furnished, whitewashed and perfectly adequate, and while Jenkins unpacked their few belongings, Simon began the tricky task of drafting his cable to Wolseley. It was hard enough to couch his advice without sounding patronising to a man twice his age who was soldiering before he was born; but having to put it into a code that sounded juvenile whichever way he read it aloud made it doubly difficult. It took him an hour to scribble the following:

RE YOUR HOLIDAY EGYPT STOP YOUR AUNT ADA WILL PROBABLY WAIT FOR YOU AT ALEX STOP IF YOU WANT TO AVOID HER AND HER FAMILY SUGGEST YOU FEINT ALEX AND TRAVEL QUIETLY SUEZ EMBARKING AT ISMAILIA STOP FROM THERE DIFFICULT ON FOOT IN SAND TO CAIRO FOR YOUR CHILDREN BUT TRAIN COULD BE AVAILABLE STOP UNDERSTAND AUNTS BOYS HAVE MANY GERMAN TOYS STOP HOLIDAY COULD BE NOISY STOP MORE LATER STOP COUSIN SIMON

Changing into white drill jacket and trousers, which Jenkins had carefully pressed, Simon made his way by foot to the new Cairo, an enclave of modern buildings and wide thoroughfares built on swamplands by the Nile in a magnificent reproduction of Haussmann's Paris. It had been created by Khedive Ismail, whose spending had brought Egypt to virtual bankruptcy and led to French and British fiscal control and his own abdication in 1879. Simon took pleasure in strolling once again through Ismail's twenty-acre

Azbakiyya Gardens, with their expensively imported Madagascan flame trees, banyans from India, and Australian bottle trees, before finding the offices of Thomas Cook by the Shepheards Hotel.

Mr George proved to be a small, bespectacled Englishman, prematurely balding, whose resemblance to a London bank clerk was lent credence by his toothbrush moustache and polished celluloid collar. Simon introduced himself and handed over his cable.

The little man read it and gave a brief smile. 'That will be quite satisfactory, Mr Fonthill,' he said, as though messages about General Sir Garnet's aunt were commonplace currency at Cook's. 'It will be in London within the hour. Now,' he leaned across the counter, 'may I ask how you are for funds? Do you need a — what shall I call it? — a little topping up, perhaps?'

'Well, that's a kind thought. I think fifty pounds would be useful.'

Mr George scribbled on an orange-coloured form. 'Let's make it a hundred, shall we, sir?' He gave a wan smile. 'Better to be safe than sorry, eh? These are difficult times in Egypt. Now, how would you like it? What currency?'

'Ah. I think perhaps twenty pounds in gold sovereigns if you have them, as a kind of reserve, you know. The rest in piastres, if you please.'

'Of course, sir. Would there be anything else?'

Simon stifled a smile at this curious transaction, rather like dealing with an unctuous grocer in London. 'Yes, there is, actually. I am in need of getting some visiting cards printed, rather quickly. Could you help me there, and how long would it take?'

'That will be no problem, Mr Fonthill. We have our own small printing plant at the rear of the building. Please write here what inscription you would like and I can have them with you within, oh, forty-five minutes. How many would you like?'

'Oh, only half a dozen or so, thank you.'

Simon scribbled on a piece of paper, and if Mr George was surprised at the small number of cards required or the identity they were to convey, he gave no indication of it.

'Perhaps,' he said, gesturing to a chair in a corner of the reception area, 'you would care to wait there and read this copy of *The Times*. It is only a week old, but events have not moved on here very much since it was published in London. I will have some tea sent to you. Indian or China?'

'Indian, thank you.'

Simon was glad of the opportunity to read a British report of the Egyptian situation, which was carried on page two of *The Times*, the paper's main news page. It seemed that Colonel Arabi now had the army fully under his control and a botched attempt had been made on his life. The perpetrators, all of them of Circassian or Turkish origin, had been arrested and tried in secret, without being allowed formal defence pleas. All had been sentenced to exile in southern Sudan – a virtual death sentence. The Khedive had refused to confirm the sentences and this had led, for the first time, to outright confrontation between him and Arabi, so that he was now a prisoner in his own palace in Cairo. How long, *The Times* wondered, would it be before the Great Powers would be forced to intervene to restore order in Egypt?

Simon put his chin on his hand. How long indeed? He

was glad that he had been able to dispatch his cable, just within the time stricture that Wolseley had stipulated, although he couldn't help wondering how useful his ramblings about aunts and toys would be to the Adjutant General. His musings were interrupted by a gentle cough from the nearby counter.

'Very well, sir,' said Mr George. 'Here now is your money: originally eighty pounds in piastres and twenty pounds in sovereigns, but I have taken the liberty of reducing the amount by the charges for the cable and the cards. These are two pounds, seventeen shillings and sixpence. Would you please be so kind as to check that everything is correct.'

Simon did so.

'Thank you, Mr Fonthill. Now here are your visiting cards. I have given you a dozen. I hope this will be sufficient. Kindly ensure that these are in order.'

Simon read:

> *Captain Ethan Williams II*
> *Late 7th Cavalry, US Army*
> *47, Bishop Street*
> *Cape Town, South Africa*

He looked up. 'Everything is very much in order, thank you, Mr George. I am most grateful to you.'

The clerk inclined his head, a faint smile on his lips. 'Not at all. I am always here at your disposal, Captain . . . er . . . Williams, sir.'

Simon returned the smile. 'Tell me,' he asked, his voice low. 'What exactly is this arrangement Mr Cook has with Sir Garnet?'

George's face became inscrutable once more. 'It is a personal matter, sir, and does not concern the company. Will there be anything else, sir?'

'Ah, no thank you. Good day.'

Carefully depositing the notes and coins in his small valise, Simon stood at the door of the offices for a moment in thought before striding out on to the thoroughfare and making for the impressive stone edifice that was Shepheards Hotel. He climbed the steps between the stone lions at their base, and with a nod to the turbaned doorman made his way to the elegant lounge, where he sat at a small writing desk in a corner. The lounge was empty except for a few elderly, linen-suited Englishmen and a sprinkling of Turks and Egyptians dressed in European clothing and talking in quiet tones. The atmosphere was that of a gentlemen's club in St James's.

It had been very different the last time Simon had taken a drink at Shepheards. There was always something of the grand railway station about this hotel, because it was the halfway house between home and the outer reaches of the British Empire in the East. Eighteen months earlier, Shepheards had been full of Englishmen on the way out to or back from Malaya, Singapore, Australia and, mainly, India. Fresh-faced young men out to take their first posting swam against the home-going tide of sallow-complexioned memsahibs and their whisky-ruined husbands. Sometimes the women were on their own, perhaps widowed, or accompanied by young children whom they were taking back home to the misery of some public school in the shires. Saddest of all, however, were the 'returned empties' of the ladies' Eastern Fishing Fleet, who, as bright young things, had journeyed out a year or so earlier in the hope of finding a husband and were now sailing back home, their hopes shattered. The present crisis, it appeared, had swept all of this flotsam away.

Sighing, Simon reached out, took a pen from the inkwell and a sheet of fine headed hotel notepaper and began to write.

General Stone Pasha,
Headquarters, Egyptian Army,
Cairo

23 April 1882

Dear General,

Please forgive this approach to you from a stranger, albeit a fellow countryman, but I would be most grateful for your help, or, at least, your advice.

As you will see from the enclosed card, I am an ex-officer of the 7th Cavalry, US Army, and I am anxious to investigate the possibility of finding employment in the Egyptian Army. I left the 7th about six months ago because I wished to see a little of the world and have been living in the Cape.

I know that many American ex-officers have worked with you to help build the Khedive's forces and I would dearly like to join them, for I am sorely sick of doing nothing. I appreciate that you would need references before offering me employment, if you are able to do so, that is, and I would be happy to supply them, given a little notice. At this stage, however, I would merely beg a little of your time for an exploratory talk.

I would welcome an early reply to this address – the

hotel – and would once again beg your indulgence for intruding upon your valuable time.

I am, sir, your obedient servant,
Ethan Williams II

He read it through once, and then, shrugging his shoulders, slipped the letter and his card inside the envelope and sealed it. He was taking a risk in pretending to an American to be a fellow national. But his proficiency in French and German had always owed more to his keen ear for dialect than to scholarship, and he gambled that he could maintain a Yankee accent long enough to eke out at least a few morsels of information about Arabi's army from Stone. He was also chancing his arm in professing to be a member of the 7th Cavalry, arguably the most famous US regiment after its mauling under Custer in the great Indian battle at Little Bighorn in 1876. But for the life of him, Simon could not think of another American regiment, and he knew enough about the encounter with the Indians to be able to talk about that, at least, if he was asked. He didn't even know if Stone's rank was indeed that of a general, but he guessed that the Egyptian title of Pasha was roughly similar. Anyway, how was he, just a recently discharged American cavalryman, supposed to know these things?

He selected a small roll of Egyptian notes from his valise and took the letter to the reception desk. He waited until the concierge was free and adopted his American accent. 'May I request a favour of you, please?'

The concierge, flattered at being addressed in such polite tones by an American, smiled and gave a half bow. 'At your service, *effendi*.'

'I would like this letter to be delivered today, by hand, to Stone Pasha, at the Egyptian Army Headquarters here in Cairo. Do you think you can arrange that?'

'Of course, *effendi*.'

'One more thing. For once I am not staying at Shepheards but with friends here in Cairo. As this is a personal matter, I do not wish to involve them and so I have asked for the reply to be delivered to me at the hotel. Now, would you be so kind as to hang on to that reply until I call in for it in, say, a coupla days' time? Here's my card.' And Simon presented his card wrapped in the bundle of notes.

Without looking at the notes, the concierge gave his half bow again. 'Of course, *effendi*. It will be a pleasure . . .' he looked at the card, 'Captain Williams . . . er . . . the Second.'

Chapter 5

Stone's reply came with pleasing celerity, if couched curtly: *I can make no promises but call on me at 3 p.m. the day after tomorrow, Wednesday. I can give you five minutes.*

Simon and Jenkins used the intervening time to walk the streets of Cairo, absorbing the atmosphere in the alleys and bazaars. During their previous visit they had been aware of a certain underlying tension between Europeans and native Egyptians, caused, Simon had presumed, by the control over the state's finances exercised by the French and British 'commissioners'. That muted enmity had been expressed with surly glances and frowns. Now, however, the tension had heightened and was manifested, as in Alexandria, by muttered curses and the occasional jeer or expectoration. The most obvious change was the presence of so many Egyptian troops in the city. Colonel Arabi had moved at least a couple of his regiments into town, and the unaccustomed favoured status bestowed on them by their leader – the troops were almost all low-born *fellaheen*, like Arabi himself – had given them a self-confidence bordering on arrogance. When off duty, they now swaggered rather than walked through the crowded streets. Seeing a group of whitecottoned young men approaching, Simon and Jenkins would stand deferentially aside. The city, Simon was now sure, was on the verge of revolt. The pressure could almost be tasted in the air, along with the bad sewage and the dust.

As the time came for his interview, Simon became increasingly uncomfortable. So much for his posturing to Wolseley about not acting as a spy! Here he was, adopting a false identity and wrapping himself in a festoon of lies, to extricate military information from a senior officer. How mendacious could one be! Even Jenkins was disapproving.

'You'll be found out, as sure as God made little apples,' he warned. 'If an American tried to pretend to me that he was Welsh, I'd know. An' what if 'e's from the same bleedin' regiment, eh? Knows the Colonel an' all that. Then where will you be?'

Simon sighed. 'It's a risk I've just got to take. I think Stone has been here for some time, trying to build the Khedive's army, so I must just hope that's he's out of touch with things back home. In any case, I can't just walk up and ask him what I want to know. I must have some reason for quizzing him. I've got no choice.'

He decided to forsake his white ducks and dressed for the interview in his travelling clothes of flannel shirt, khaki cotton trousers and wide-brimmed hat. It was, he felt, what an ex-American officer knocking about Africa would wear. He was proved right.

Stone was a tall, bony man with a wide moustache. The glance he gave Simon as he stood behind his desk with outstretched hand seemed almost to be one of approval. 'Envy you not having to wear damned uniform, collar and tie and all that, in this infernal heat,' he said as they shook

81

hands. Simon, who had decided to adopt a southern accent because it was the easiest to assume, was relieved that the General's clipped tones were undoubtedly those of the northern states. It would have put him in double jeopardy to face a man who knew the south.

'Sorry, General,' said Simon. 'I've bin travellin' kinda light.'

'Take a seat, son. Tell me what you want of me.'

'Thank you, sir. Well, as I explained in my note, I resigned my commission 'bout six months ago because I wanted to see the world, you know? Thought that South Africa might offer a bit of excitement – Zulus an' all that. But I got there too late for the Zulu campaign, an' what I saw of the British Army I didn't like too much – all that brass-polishin' an' salutin' – even if they'd have accepted me for somethin' like a bit o' scoutin', which they wouldn't anyways. So after doin' a bit of huntin' an' . . .' he attempted a wan smile, 'spendin' all my money, you know . . . I knew back in the States that you'd bin setting up the Khedive's army for him, an' recruitin' ex-officers from home, so I thought I'd try my luck up here. I'd like to know if it's possible to take somethin' like a short-service commission, maybe. What d'you think, General?'

Stone looked at him coolly. 'Can I see your passport, son?'

Simon's heart dropped for a second, but he had anticipated this. 'Now damme, sir. Sorry. I've left it back in Shepheards with my discharge papers an' all. Precious stuff. Didn't wanna walk through the streets with all that documentation with the city in the state it's in just now. But I can drop 'em in here later today if you like.'

'We can see about that later. You say you were in the 7th Cavalry. Where are you from originally?'

'Texas, sir. Sam Houston's town. My folks had a bit of a ranch just outside town. Flat country. My daddy raised longhorns, sir. I was born in the saddle' (*Oh the lies, the lies!*) 'so I wanted to join the cavalry. Missed the Little Bighorn, o'course, because I was still at West Point, but got in later, when they was recruitin' after the massacre when we lost the General an' mostly five companies. P'raps I wouldn't have gotten into the 7th if'en it hadn't been for the Sioux an' Cheyenne an' what they did on that day in '76. No, sir.'

Simon shifted in his chair and wondered if he was overdoing it. But Stone seemed convinced – or almost.

'Who was your commanding officer when you got into the 7th?'

'Well, sir.' Simon took a deep breath. This was the kind of questioning on detail he had dreaded. As a young subaltern he had studied Custer's tragic campaign against the Indians and before the interview he had dredged his memory for fragments to give his story verisimilitude. 'After we lost General Custer there was a great inquest, you'll remember, sir. Major Reno got most o' the blame for the massacre, but I can't help feelin' that was a touch unfair. Anyways, when I got in, Mr Reno was commandin' us, on a kind o' temporary basis. After that we had a succession o' gentlemen in command. Back in the hotel I've got a reference from my last commandin' officer, Colonel, er, Bennet, which I can show you, sir.'

Stone wrinkled his brow. 'Bennet, Bennet. Don't recall the name. Where's he from?'

Simon plunged on. 'He was a southerner too, sir, so maybe you wouldn't have known him. Joined the army just after the war and did real well, sir.'

'Hmmm. So you're a Johnny Reb, eh?' But the tone was not unfriendly.

'Guess so, General. Though, o' course, I was far too young to have fought. Just as well, I guess. But we're one country now, sir, ain't that so?'

'I guess so, son.'

Simon decided to take the initiative before he plunged into any deeper quagmires. 'Mind if I ask you a coupla questions, sir?'

'Go ahead.'

Simon breathed an inward sigh of relief.

'If I could get into this here army, I would wish to be a cavalryman. But I guess these Egyptians don't have no cavalry much, do they, General?'

Stone frowned and looked almost offended. 'That's not so, Williams. I've worked hard on building a fine body of cavalry for the Khedive. There are more than twelve regiments of cavalry now and I reckon they're as fine as any set of men on horseback anywhere in Europe. They can ride horses or camels, depending upon the terrain, and they're damned good at what they do, particularly in terms of reconnaissance.' His face relaxed into a smile. 'Although perhaps not quite as good as your 7th.'

Good! He was accepted! 'Is that so, sir? Gee! Would I fit in? Any Americans servin' as officers, or are they all Turks?'

The General shook his head. His face had become animated now, and it was clear that talking of the army he had virtually created appealed to his vanity. Simon knew that the Egyptians had performed badly in their recent war in Abyssinia. This was a rare chance for Stone to extol his troops' virtues. 'The Yankees I enrolled after the war were mainly for training purposes and they've virtually all gone back to the States now. But we've trained up the Turks to become first-class squadron and troop leaders – probably the best in this part of the world. They would fight for Egypt because it's part of the Turkish empire. If you've served in the 7th, that means you can ride and shoot, and there could be a place for you if you could pick up the lingo.' His face wrinkled again into a frown. 'But there's one problem I ought to put to you before we go any further.'

'Sir?'

'I don't know how long you have been in Cairo, but you will know that the political situation here is unsettled, to say the least.'

Simon nodded, putting his face into earnest mode.

'These are difficult times.' Stone pulled at his moustache. It was obvious that he was unsure how much to tell this young man. 'There is a growing movement throughout the country against Turkish occupation and, with it, the support that the French and the British give to Constantinople. The fact that the British now control the majority shareholding in the Suez Canal is a particular cause of unrest here. There have been demonstrations against the Europeans and they may get worse – particularly in Alexandria. It just could be that the French and the British will invade.'

'Gee! How would they come in, sir?'

'Almost certainly from Alexandria and then down the railway line to Cairo. But if they do,' Stone Pasha allowed his features to relax into a grim smile, 'they will get a bloody nose. Colonel Arabi is erecting some damned good defensive positions on that route and even the mighty British Army could get a shock.' The smile gradually faded away. 'But the point is that, if you joined the Khedive's army, you could end up fighting against the British and the French. How would you feel about that, son?'

Simon shrugged. 'Well, sir, it's only just over a hundred years since we were fighting the Brits. It wouldn't worry me too much if I had to ride at 'em – particularly if your cavalrymen are as good as you say they are. But General: wouldn't the Brits come up the Canal way, from the south?'

Stone shook his head. 'Doubt it very much. They'd never get down the Canal from the north before we blocked it. One dredger sunk in the right place would do the trick. And if they invaded from the south, they'd have to bring troops from India and we would have plenty of advance warning to do the same down there.'

'But General, this wouldn't be like fightin' tribes of Indians out on our western frontier. The Brits have good artillery. You would need some pretty damned good ordance to match 'em, wouldn't you?'

The General held up a dismissive hand. 'We've been buying from Krupp for months now, ain't no secret really. The Germans have been delivering with great speed and we are well equipped with the latest and best cannon.' He smiled. 'As you can imagine, old Bismarck is only too delighted to do anything to embarrass the great British Empire.'

'Ah can see that, sir. But tell me. What sort of man is this Colonel Arabi? I guess he's in charge now and not you?'

Stone's eyes veiled for a moment, and Simon sensed that perhaps all was not well between the new head of the Egyptian army and the experienced mercenary who had built it. But he smiled again. 'Interesting fellow. He's a *fellaheen* himself, from peasant stock in the south. And he looks it. Big man. Not exactly elegant. Got promoted to colonel quickly by Said, the old viceroy, who was well intentioned towards the *fellaheen*, but his successor, Khedive Ismail, was not, so Arabi got stuck as colonel for sixteen years.'

The General waved his hand. 'Then it all got terribly complicated. With the abdication of Ismail, Arabi's stock rose and fell with the appointments of various ministers of war. But he's a good orator and he began to gather the support of the *fellaheen*. I guess he wants the Turks out, a lessening of foreign influence and a new constitution. Anyway,' the hand waved again, 'he's now Minister of War and virtually controls the country.'

Stone's smile held for a moment and then slowly faded as he realised that perhaps he had been indiscreet. 'Very well, son,' he said. 'I reckon that's enough. You get yourself off to your hotel and let me have something that backs up what you've told me, and I'll consider what I can do to help. Now you'd best be on your way, because I have much to do.'

He rose and Simon took his hand. 'Sure am obliged for your time, sir,' he said. And he meant it.

Back at the hotel, Simon told Jenkins what he had heard and then began drafting a second cable to Wolseley. It read:

AUNT ADA DEFINITELY PLANNING TO MEET YOU ALEX STOP SUEZ PROVING BEST FOR HOLIDAY IF YOU AVOID HORRIBLE FAMILY STOP ADA'S CHILDREN HAVE TWELVE HORSES CAMELS AS WELL AS GERMAN TOYS SO HOLIDAY SHOULD BE FUN STOP AM TRAVELLING ALEX STOP COUSIN SIMON

Jenkins read it over. 'So we're goin' back to Alexander, then. Why?'

'First, I don't want to be around when Stone finds out there isn't really an Ethan Williams II. But the main reason is that I have a feeling Alexandria is where trouble could break out and I want to be around when it does. Also, if Wolseley is given the job of invading, and if he decides to take my advice – though I am sure he has many other sources of information – he will land a force at Alexandria and pretend to advance from there, thus tying down a large section of Arabi's forces. Then, if he handles it smoothly and quickly, he could send a second force to take the Canal and advance on Cairo the easiest way, from Ismailia. I want to be in Alex when he arrives. And, anyway,' he shrugged his shoulders, 'there's very little we can do by staying on in Cairo, other than keeping our heads down to avoid Stone.'

The cable duly delivered to the ubiquitous Mr George, Simon returned to the hotel to find Jenkins deep in conversation with Ahmed, over a large whisky and an orange juice respectively.

'	'Ere, bach sir,' called Jenkins. 'Old Amen 'ere 'as a sort of proposition.'

Simon's heart sank. Had Jenkins been indiscreet?

'Perhaps, *effendi*,' said Ahmed, 'we could go to your room to discuss? I get another whisky first, this very, very minute.'

'No whisky, thank you – oh well, perhaps just a small one. Bring it along and we will talk.'

As soon as the two of them were alone in Simon's room, the latter whirled on Jenkins. 'What have you been saying to him about why we're here?'

Jenkins held up a hand. 'Nothin', bach sir, I promise. But

whatever 'e thinks we're up to, 'e wants to be part of it. 'E wants to come with us, wherever we go, see.'

'Oh lord! We can't have—' Further discussion was ended by the arrival of Ahmed carrying probably the largest small whisky ever seen in Cairo. He was a diminutive man, even shorter than Jenkins, and much slimmer. His hands were finely shaped and his fingernails delicately manicured. That element of fastidiousness was present in his narrow, high-cheekboned face, for his small moustache was always well trimmed. He wore the anonymous dress of most Arabs, a loose white cotton garment, the *glabya*, gathered at the waist by a cord and worn outdoors under a voluminous *burnous* or hooded cloak. He had been of service to Simon and Jenkins on their last visit, and his brown eyes now glowed with excitement as he set Simon's drink before him.

'That's a bit big for you, bach sir,' murmured Jenkins. 'P'raps I can 'elp you with it, like?'

'I can manage, thank you, 352. Now, Ahmed. What can we do for you?'

Ahmed ignored the chair Simon offered him and instead sat cross-legged on the floor. 'Well, *effendi*,' he said, leaning forward, 'I understand that you engage yourself again in highly important, very special, confidential work for government, et cetera, et cetera. Yes?'

'Why do you ask, Ahmed?'

'When you last graced my very fine but really very humble hotel, you wished me to find you Arab clothing and camel train to take you across desert to Suez. And I did that, with my brother Mahmud, did I not?'

'You certainly did, and we were very grateful.'

'Thank you. It was pleasure. In the desert you fought the robbing Bedawis and, as result, Mahmud has no more trouble with them. Wonderful!'

'Well, we were glad to help.'

'Now, I want help you.'

'That's very kind of you, Ahmed, but I'm afraid—'

'No. Mr Jonkins say that you will leave for Alexandria soon.' Again he tapped the side of his nose with his finger. 'This is not a good place for Europeans to go, I can say. I do not know what you do but I know you cannot speak Arabic and you do not know ways of Egyptians and you could be in danger there. Ahmed can help with the . . .' he sought the appropriate word, 'translations and where you stay for nights, et cetera, et cetera, et cetera.' His words came more quickly as the value of his offer became apparent to him. 'I am *fellaheen* from the country by the Nile, but I came to Cairo and was young man in bazaars. I am familiar with the, er, dirty things, you know?'

Jenkins's smile was matched by Simon's frown and Ahmed hurried to correct the misapprehension. 'No, not those dirty things . . . ladies and such like. No. I mean,' the finger went to the nose again, 'those things you cannot buy in shops. I know the dirty men who can get things not legal, like guns, et cetera, et cetera, et cetera, you know?'

'An' whisky?' enquired Jenkins.

'Oh whisky, most definitely.'

Gradually the worth of Ahmed's proposal began to grow on Simon. They were travelling in a country of which they had little knowledge and which was quite likely to go to war with their own. They did not speak the language and knew little of the customs of the Egyptians. They would probably have to go into war zones, even perhaps behind enemy lines. Ahmed could be invaluable. But there were dangers.

'It really is most kind of you to offer to join us,' said Simon, 'but perhaps we might have to do things with which you would not agree. May I ask you how you feel about Colonel Arabi and his movement?'

'Ah.' Ahmed frowned and rocked slightly on his haunches. 'Because I am *fellaheen*, at first I support Ahmed Arabi. There is too much taxation of *fellaheen*. But he goes too fast, too far. He is peasant and does not understand business like I do.' He waved a deprecatory hand. 'He want to throw out Turks and British business. If he take over government, what do we do? We lose nice British people coming here for Nile. He wants big Canal back. How? We sold it, so we must buy it back. But we have no money. No. Arabi is soldier. Soldiers cannot run governments. Mr Gladstone like poor people and want to help *fellaheen* and pushes Turks that way, so I support Khedive now. I think you do too, yes?'

Simon exchanged a grin with Jenkins. There seemed no doubting Ahmed's sincerity, his thinking was shrewd and he had proved resourceful and helpful in the past. He decided to trust him.

'Yes, Ahmed,' he said. 'We do. We work for the British government and the Khedive. We do not want Colonel Arabi to depose him. The British do not want war but they may have to invade, perhaps with the French, to stop Arabi from causing a revolt throughout Egypt. We are working to prepare the way for the British to come in if they need to do so. That is our task and it is difficult and dangerous. I am not sure that you would really want to be part of it. After all, it could lead to loss of Egyptian lives.'

Ahmed's eyes lost their sparkle for a moment. 'Ah yes, that would not be nice.' He thought for a moment and then looked up. 'But sometimes it is necessary to chop off finger to save leg – no, arm. Yes? I do not want this big colonel to bring his troops into Cairo and . . . what is the word? Ah yes, bully, is the word. I do not want him to threaten to remove head of Khedive, et cetera. He goes too far and must be stopped. British only people who can stop him. I read Mr Gladstone's speeches and like what he says. I help you, I think.'

Simon's thoughts flashed for a moment to someone else, far away, who also admired the liberally minded British Prime Minister. Someone with fair hair, steadfast grey eyes and skin the texture of . . . He coughed. 'But Ahmed, you have a fine business here. What about your hotel? We could be away for several months, you know.'

Ahmed waved his hand again. 'That is not a problem, *effendi*. I have brother-in-law who will manage the hotel while I am away. You see,' his eyes grew sad, 'my wife she died a year ago now. I am very sad. I am also very, er, mono-tonous – no, that is not the word. Bored, that is the word. I am bored. I have money. I would not want you to pay me, but I would like to do . . .' his eyes flashed again and the white teeth appeared under the neat moustache, 'exciting things. Yes. Exciting things. I think you do exciting things, yes?'

'Blimey,' said Jenkins, 'you've come to the right place, all right.'

Simon made up his mind. 'Right,' he said, standing and holding out his hand. 'Ahmed, you have just become part of the team.' Grinning, they shook hands. 'Also part of the family. From now on, there is no more *effendi*. You will call me Simon, and Jenkins 352 – no,' he held up his hand, 'don't ask, it's too complicated. Just call him that. We cannot pay you, I am afraid, but I will bear all the costs we incur and, yes, you will be a great help. Now, to be practical. We need to leave for Alexandria as soon as possible in the morning. Can you do that?'

'Oh yes. When we go, we have to go, I think. Yes?'

'Oh blimey, bach,' said Jenkins, 'that's about right.'

'Very well. Now, 352, go off to the station and buy us all tickets for Alexandria by the first train. Oh, all right then. Here.' He handed Jenkins his half-full glass. 'Finish it off. But straight back, mind you.'

The next morning found them comfortably seated in a first-class carriage on the 8.15 for Alexandria. Ahmed had changed his Arab dress for a white cotton suit, impeccably pressed, and he looked the very epitome of an Egyptian businessman – so much so, in fact, that Simon felt distinctly scruffy sitting beside him in his desert travelling slacks and shirt. The train was billed as an express, but in fact it made several unscheduled stops at the little two-storey wooden buildings where railway officials both lived and worked and where the driver smoked a cigarette and took coffee with his friends. Here Arab boys ran along the trackside calling up to Simon: 'I say, John. Buy orange?' It was not unpleasant, rolling along, watching the flatlands of the Nile pass outside their window. Ahmed had insisted on providing provisions for the journey, and they contentedly munched cold chicken and delicate cucumbers stuffed with forced meats, followed by ruby pomegranates, washed down by a bottle or two of Hadji Hodson beer, although Ahmed, of course, abstained from the latter. Simon exchanged a glance of approval with Jenkins. So far, Ahmed was proving to be an undoubtedly fine addition to the partnership.

Inevitably, Ahmed knew exactly where they should stay in Alexandria. It was a little hotel, a few streets back from the harbour, not quite in the native quarter but certainly not smart enough for most Europeans. 'My cousin's hotel,' explained Ahmed. 'She very confidential lady. She don't want to know anything. Good, eh?'

Once installed, Simon decided that he should check with Mr Roberts for cables, and the three walked through the streets to the Thomas Cook offices in the heart of town. Once again the absence of Europeans from the streets was noticeable, and an air of menace hung over the wide avenues – much more apparent than in Cairo, where the crowds in the narrow streets and their noise seemed somehow to dilute the promise of danger. Alexandria, however, shared with the capital the presence of Egyptian soldiers, lolling in doorways, sitting smoking outside cafés and sauntering along the pavements. To Simon, it seemed that their numbers had increased considerably since they had landed here a few weeks before.

Mr Roberts confirmed this. He was the antithesis of Mr George in Cairo, although he obviously shared the same strange personal relationship with General Wolseley. Broad as an ironclad, and with a waxed moustache that seemed to project past his ears, he had been, he freely offered, a sergeant with Wolseley in the latter's Ashanti campaign, and owed his job to the General, although how long he would keep it with revolt around the corner he would not care to say.

'What's the latest then, Mr Roberts?' asked Simon.

Leaning on his counter, Roberts looked proprietorial. 'The latest, my dear sir, is that a British and French fleet is on its way and will anchor in the bay. The idea is to face down Arabi and his lot and make sure that British and French nationals here – who all have the wind up, I can tell you – are protected if violence breaks out.'

'Has there been any trouble so far?'

'Yes. Europeans have been stoned in the streets and others more directly attacked. Representations have been made to the Khedive, but that poor bugger can do nothing about it. He's a prisoner in his own palace in Cairo. The Turks are supposed to be sending somebody important from Constantinople to restore order, but I can't see that stopping Arabi. He wants the Turks out anyway – or a new constitution to protect native Egyptians. It'll be war, I'm afraid.'

He selected a small key from his jacket pocket and inserted it into a box set into the wall behind him. From within he produced a folded piece of paper. 'From Sir Garnet, for you, sir. Came this morning.'

Simon read:

THANKS YOUR ADVICE AND INFO STOP FATHER HAS GIVEN PERMISSION TO PREPARE HOLIDAY STOP WILL GIVE YOUR VIEWS CAREFUL THOUGHT STOP WILL INFORM YOU VIA COOKS STOP GIVE MY LOVE TO AUNT ADA STOP COUSIN GARNET

Carefully pocketing the cable, Simon grinned. He was beginning to enjoy this new intimacy with England's Adjutant General. How he wished he could flaunt it before Colonel Ralph Covington!

Mr Roberts leaned across his counter and gazed at the three of them in turn. 'Now, all you gentlemen must be very careful walking home. It's really quite dangerous now at this time of the late afternoon, just when it's getting dark. Take care, sir.'

'Thank you, Mr Roberts,' said Simon. 'We will be careful.'

'Bit of an old windbag, wasn't 'e?' growled Jenkins as they walked away. 'Looks quiet enough to me.'

But it was not. They had just turned into a street parallel to the harbourside when the first stone took Jenkins squarely in the back. He staggered for a moment – as much from the shock as from any injury sustained – and they all turned to see four Arabs running towards them, throwing stones as they came.

Ahmed threw up his hand. 'Go into doorway,' he said to his companions. 'I tell them you Americans and stop throwing.'

'No, Ahmed,' shouted Simon, but the little man was already running towards their assailants, waving and shouting to them in Arabic.

Ahmed's approach halted the stoning for a moment, and Simon and Jenkins, huddled in a doorway, watched as the little man argued with what seemed like great eloquence, turning and pointing towards them, then spreading his hands as though in supplication. At first he seemed to have gained an audience, but suddenly the largest of the Arabs pushed him in the chest, so strongly that he fell on to his back. Then all four began kicking him.

'Right,' said Simon. 'Don't use your knife except as a last resort. Run straight at 'em, fast. Go!'

The two sprinted as quickly as they could to the little group, some twenty yards away. At first, the Arabs were so intent on kicking Ahmed that they did not notice that they in turn were being attacked, and Jenkins's lowered head took the largest of the four squarely in the midriff as, too late, he turned. Simon had no time to see the sequel, for he now crashed into two of the others, his arms outstretched, taking each of them around the waist and bringing them down.

Unencumbered by a long gown, he gained his feet first and kicked the nearest man in the face as he attempted to rise, then swung his boot into the other's midriff. As he did so, he felt a blow on the head that sent him staggering. Another and then another rained on to his shoulders as he turned to face his assailant. The fourth Arab had produced a stave and had it raised in both hands to bring it down again when Ahmed, his beautifully pressed white suit now covered in mud and dust, caught him behind the knees, like a spaniel harrying a bull. The two went down together, but again Simon had no time to witness the outcome, for the man whom he had kicked in the stomach was now upon him, enveloping him in a bear-like hug and lifting him off the ground. He crashed Simon against a wall and pulled back his head to butt him in the face, but he had telegraphed the action and Simon was able, at the last minute, to lean his head to the right so that the blow caught him on the side of the cheek. At the same time, he was able to slip his hand down to the Arab's groin, grab his testicles through the loose folds of his garment and squeeze them tightly.

The man howled and loosened his grip so that Simon was able to knee him in the groin and push him away. A glance to his right showed that the Arab whom Ahmed had tackled was now on top of the little Egyptian, both hands round his neck and, judging by the colour of Ahmed's face, attempting to strangle him. Simon swung his boot again – what it was to have Jenkins as his dirty fighting mentor! – and caught the man high on the cheekbone. It was enough to send him rolling away from Ahmed. Simon saw a sizeable stone on the ground, obviously from the arsenal the Arabs had been using; he grabbed it quickly and swung it down on the man's head. A second blow was enough for him to subside on to the ground with a grunt.

Wearily, and panting to get his breath, Simon turned just in time to take evasive action as a knife swung at his face. He lowered his head, ducking under the man's arm, and swung a succession of short-armed punches into his midriff, forcing the man back by sheer aggression until the Arab's heel caught the inert form of the stave-wielder and he too went sprawling.

His breast heaving, blood trickling down his cheek on to his chin and then his shirt, Simon surveyed the scene. A grinning Jenkins was wiping his knife on the *burnous* of one of the two Arabs lying on the ground. Ahmed – dishevelled but grinning – was on his hands and knees trying to regain his feet, and of the other two Arabs there was no sign.

'Oh God,' panted Simon to Jenkins. 'You didn't kill anyone, did you?'

'Good lord, no, bach sir. You told me not to. So I just stuck a couple of the perishers who drew knives on me in the arm, look you, an' they was off like rabbits when they saw that two could play that game, see. Anyway, most of the time I was just standin' back and watchin' you two fightin' like tigers. Most impressive, I must say. Good old Amen.'

'Thank you, *eff* . . . 352.' The Egyptian wiped dust from his eye and tried to adjust his tie, but failed. He looked up again with a smile. 'I did not know this would be so exciting so soon. Does this sort of thing,' he waved his hand, 'et cetera, et cetera, et cetera, happen often?'

'Every Tuesday, Amen,' grinned Jenkins. 'Every Tuesday.'

'Are these two all right?' asked Simon, gesturing to the prostrate Arabs.

'Yes,' replied Jenkins. He pointed. 'That one – the one you punched in the belly so nicely – is just fakin'. The other one I tapped on the 'ead with a bit of stone just to discourage 'im from gettin' up, see.'

'Sure? I don't want to leave any corpses.'

'Absolutely, bach sir. No lastin' 'arm done – although by golly they deserve it.'

'Right.' Simon extended his hand to Ahmed. 'You did marvellously, Ahmed, and I am so sorry that you got involved in the mess. Three five two was just joking. We don't usually get caught up in this sort of thing. And I am particularly sorry about the suit.'

The little Egyptian tried to brush the stains from his once white jacket. 'Ah yes. It is a pity. It was my best. Still,' the grin came back, 'I shall brush when it is dry and then it will wash clean again.' A sudden thought struck him and the smile was lost again. 'Unless, that is, we shall be fighting again tomorrow. Should I leave it dirty, do you think?'

'No, old chap. I don't want to get involved in this sort of brawl again, thank you very much.' Simon winced as Jenkins attempted to clear the blood away from his face with a soiled handkerchief. 'Come on. Let us get away from here back to the hotel to clean up.'

Darkness had fallen as they moved away, but a backward glance from Simon showed that both the inert Arabs had miraculously come to life and stolen away. They all felt conspicuous in their bloodstained, soiled clothing, but the darkness helped to shroud them, and within five minutes they had gained the refuge of the little hotel. Ahmed's cousin was, indeed, 'confidential', for if she was surprised at their condition, she gave no sign. Baths for the three of them stretched the hotel's resources, but it was managed somehow. Jenkins and Ahmed had walked away from the fight with only light bruises, and Simon's wounds to the head and face were found to be comparatively superficial, demanding only the application of a little antiseptic and a light dressing.

'We were lucky,' said Simon as they gathered together that evening for a meal of kebabs beautifully cooked by Ahmed's cousin in a sauce of plums and herbs. 'Things are hotting up here and I don't think we should go parading about like that again. Given that we've caused a bit of damage, what's left of that gang could be looking out for us.'

Jenkins sucked his fingers. 'Well, if Amen's auntie or whatever she is is goin' to carry on cookin' like this, I don't mind lyin' low for a while.'

'Hmmm.' Simon frowned. 'But I don't want to be holed up here. I want to see what Arabi is doing to the city's defences.'

'Ah, er, Simon . . .' Ahmed still found it difficult to address Simon by his Christian name. 'Perhaps I make a suggestion? Yes?'

'Of course.'

'You both dark people. I dress you before like Arabs and you look very well. Let us do that again. I find *glabya*,' he

100

indicated the long, loose garment he was wearing, 'for you, and also *burnous*, et cetera, et cetera, et cetera. You will be good Arabs, I think. Yes?'

Simon smiled. 'Ahmed, you are worth your weight in gold. I should have thought of that. Can you do it tomorrow?'

'Of course. Then we go, er, strolling again. Yes?'

'Yes,' said Jenkins. 'Let's 'ave a good stroll in our nighties. Why not?'

Chapter 6

Alice Covington threw down her copy of the *Morning Post* in disgust and put a hand to her brow. There was no doubt about it, Gladstone was going to invade Egypt! Gladstone, her radical, anti-imperialist, caring hero was about to don the mantle of Disraeli, the great jingoist, and send troops to occupy a patch of gravel and sand in northern Africa. Oh, he was talking of 'reintroducing stability' to the country, but once in, she was sure the troops would not leave. The City demanded that Britain protect the great ditch that was the Suez Canal, and so another piece of foreign soil would be added to the British Empire. Gladstone was showing that he was really just like the rest of them: political aggrandisers anxious to placate the merchants and financiers who grew rich from the pickings of empire. Oh, how she hated them all!

She picked up the newspaper again and propped it up against the breakfast condiments. The British and French squadrons that had been sitting in the bay off Alexandria had been sent to provide a symbolic warning shot across Arabi's bows and to reassure the European residents in the town. But, it appeared to Alice from her reading, both purposes had failed. The Khedive had fled Cairo and had taken refuge in his palace in Alexandria, under the protection of the French and British guns, but Arabi had followed him and was now in the northern port with a large part of his army camped outside its walls. The Sultan of Turkey had sent a representative, Dervish Pasha, to his colony in an attempt, it seemed, to restore some kind of order. But an appeal to him from the British diplomatic representatives in Cairo to guarantee the lives of the many British in Egypt had been met with the reply that neither he nor the Khedive could give that guarantee, for they did not have the troops to do so. Within the last two weeks, some fourteen thousand Europeans and their dependants had fled Egypt, and thousands more were ready to go. Riots were expected to break out in the streets of Alexandria. Gladstone was saying that Colonel Arabi had 'thrown off his mask' and was now openly working for the deposition of the Khedive and the expulsion of all Europeans from Egypt. What a mess!

And Simon, she was sure, would be right in the middle of it.

Alice let the paper fall from her hand and stared at the wall of the breakfast room. Simon, who was supposed to be out of her thoughts but who was forever in them. In the last eighteen months, since they had parted on the eve of Wolseley's attack on King Sekukuni's stronghold near the Mozambique border, she had received just one, simple letter from him, expressing congratulations on her wedding and regretting that he could not be there. She knew from Charlotte Fonthill that he had recently left Brecon on some confidential mission for General Wolseley. Oh God – if he should be killed in some sordid street fracas in Egypt! She put her hand to her mouth and then let it fall again, for Jenkins, the great 352, would surely be with him and protect him.

Her reverie was interrupted by the sound of her husband descending the stairs, and she pushed the paper away. It took him a while every morning to fit and adjust the hook that served as an artificial hand – he insisted on doing it himself – so she always breakfasted alone but waited for him so that they could discuss the day's programme. There was much to do on their estate in Norfolk, particularly now that the summer was approaching.

Colonel Ralph Covington, Companion of the Bath, strode into the room with his customary air of command. 'Kedgeree or bacon, my dear,' he cried. 'What shall I have?'

'Kedgeree. The bacon is rather too fat.'

'Very well.' He looped his hook under the handle of the tureen and deposited it skilfully on a serving plate. 'I always follow orders, as you know.' Now nearing the middle forties, almost twenty years her senior, Covington was still an imposing figure. Well over six feet tall, his wounds had not affected his erect bearing. His shoulders were broad, and the corpulence that had begun to mar his posture a few years ago had now been more or less banished by careful eating and good tailoring. A touch of grey coloured the sideburns that led to his great moustaches, and the black patch that covered his sightless eye – worn as much to hide the scar left by the bePedi spear across his eyebrow and high cheek as much as to conceal the false eye itself – gave him a piratical air that, Alice suspected, he deliberately cultivated.

With his good hand, Covington scooped the kedgeree on

to his plate and strode to the table. He nodded to the paper. 'What's happening in Egypt?'

Alice sighed. 'Things seem to be going from bad to worse. There has been some rioting in the streets of Alexandria, our ships are obviously lying there itching to fire their broadsides into the town and Arabi seems to have taken complete control of the country. Gladstone is rattling sabres in a manner worthy of Beaconsfield himself.'

'Well, bloody man's a revolutionary. Probably have to be put down.'

'Who, Arabi or Gladstone?'

Covington grinned. 'Both of 'em, if I had my way.'

Alice summoned up a return smile. They had long ago agreed to disagree on their politics, although Covington could be surprisingly liberal on certain issues. The threat posed by Arabi, however, was not one of them. She decided to change the subject.

'How did you get on in London yesterday?' she asked. 'I am sorry that I had retired when you came back, but I had had rather a long day and I was tired.'

Covington's jaw clenched slightly. His wife often 'retired early' these days, and he could not avoid the fear that she found his lovemaking distasteful. The subject, of course, had never been broached, and he had no intention of doing so. He had always undressed in his own dressing room and took care that she should not see the stump of his arm or the eye without its patch. Nevertheless, the problem seemed to be growing. There was no sign of Alice becoming pregnant, and if things continued as they were, she never would be. He had no idea what to do about it.

'Thank you, my dear. I had a pleasant day.'

'What exactly did you do, Ralph?'

'Oh, saw one or two old friends from the regiment, lunched at the club. That sort of thing, you know.'

Alice gave a sweet smile. 'And did you pass, my dear?'

He looked up sharply. 'Pass? What do you mean?'

'Oh really, Ralph. You must think me no end of a fool. I know that you have been receiving letters from the Horse Guards, one of them at least from the Adjutant General's office. And Jackson packed your riding jodhpurs and boots yesterday; not quite the things to take to London, my dear, now were they? You can have much finer riding here in Norfolk than on Rotten Row. No. You were being tested by the army to see if you could serve again, weren't you?'

Covington reached across with his good hand and took hers in it. He gave a rueful smile. 'You are too smart a girl to deceive, aren't you? Just as well I am not having an affair; you'd sniff me out in no time.' He shook his head. 'I was going to tell you, of course. Just waiting for the verdict and the right time.'

'Good. Well I think that now is the right time, don't you?'

'Very well.' Covington carefully put down his fork, clipped carefully to his hook. 'I wrote to Wolseley some time ago and enquired if there was any chance of regaining my commission. Just a shot in the dark, really. I told him that I was fully fit again, that the sight in my good eye was perfect for shooting and that I was riding without trouble every day. Told him that I had been practising and could swing a sword from the saddle, and that, in fact, this damn thing,' he held up his hook, 'had given me an extra weapon. Right as rain again really.'

There was a plaintive note of appeal in his voice, and

Alice felt a conflict of emotion rise within her. Part of her pitied this fine man whose career had been so tragically ended and yet who was determined – as he always had been – to fight back. That pity and admiration, of course, had been behind her decision to honour her commitment to him, despite the development of her deep love for Simon Fonthill. She now felt also, however, a sense of guilt that she could not give him the kind of love for which he yearned. Above all, he wanted an heir. She had tried – God how she had tried! – but so far she had failed him. Another part of her, however, a despicable, shameful part, thrilled at the thought that, if the army accepted him, he would be away and could make no further demands on her, for a time at least.

To hide a blush, she looked out of the window behind her, at the perfectly cut lawn, the early roses and the laurel hedges that shielded this end of their large garden. 'Oh, Ralph,' she said, turning back, 'I am so sorry that you want to go back.'

His hand tightened on hers. 'Ah, nothing to do with you. It's just that . . . Well, I enjoy running the estate, and indeed, there is plenty to do, although, in fact, you could run the place on your own and make a better job of it than me. But I miss the active life of the army so much and I can't stand the thought of Wolseley, my old commander, going into action again without me.'

'Are we definitely going into Egypt then, and will he command?'

His good eye seemed to light up. 'Well, this is very confidential, of course, but it looks as though we *will* invade. Wolseley will be in charge. He's the obvious choice, of course; the man's hardly ever lost a battle. Almost as good a record as Wellington. I understand the plans are already drawn up. Gladstone is pussy-footing about, of course, as long as he can, but it looks inevitable to me.'

Alice slowly withdrew her hand. 'So,' she said. 'Did you pass your test?'

Covington sat back and seemed to grow in his chair. 'With flying colours, of course. They put me through all the drill in some indoor riding school back of Whitehall: galloping, turning, charging and swinging with the sabre from the saddle, firing with the old Martini-Henry rifle – couldn't reload the bloody thing quickly enough, of course, but I was fine with a revolver, the officer's weapon, so that was all right. Felt like I was a subaltern again. They told me I was as good as new. Haven't heard from Sir Garnet yet, of course, but I know he'll give me a job.'

Alice smiled. 'I am glad for you, Ralph, if it's really what you want. I just want you to be happy.' It was as true a statement as she had ever made to him.

He rose, put his good arm around her shoulders and kissed her. 'Knew you'd support me. And anyway,' he gave her a strong, almost brutal hug and returned to his chair, 'I wanted to be sure I could pass the bally test. Knew I would, though.' He gave a self-satisfied sigh.

'What are your plans for the day?' Alice rose. 'You can hardly spend all morning sharpening your sword, can you?'

He grinned. 'As a matter of fact, I did that three days ago. No, I am riding into Norwich with Watkins. The blade on one of the ploughs has broken and we need to have it replaced. Watkins could do it, I suppose, but I want to make sure that everything's shipshape before I go. What about you?'

Alice looked out of the window for a moment, her brow creased. 'Oh, I have some letters to write,' she said. 'I would like to catch the midday post, so please excuse me, my dear. Finish your breakfast.' She brushed his brow with her lips and left the room.

Alice waited until she heard him leave the house before sitting down in the morning room and pulling a sheet of paper towards her. She sat for at least three minutes before beginning to write. It was, after all, a most important letter.

The reply came three days later. As usual, she was up before her husband and was able to retrieve the envelope before he came down. Since revealing his secret to her, Covington had become a new man. He seemed to have found a new source of energy, and hardly relaxed at all during the long days he spent out of doors, beating the bounds of the estate to ensure that everything would be in order, enabling him to leave as soon as the call came. Wolseley had confirmed the offer to him of a lieutenant colonelcy in his old regiment, the 24th of Foot. He could not be reinstated in his rank of full colonel, it was explained, but Covington cared nothing for that. Should the expedition to Egypt be mounted – and it was growing more likely by the day – then he would join Wolseley's staff. It could not be better.

Alice had plenty of time to digest her own letter in the quietness of the large house. Written on *Morning Post* headed paper, it was short and to the point:

My dear Alice,

How splendid to hear from you. Of course we miss you, and I would be delighted to meet and discuss your proposal. That would be appropriately reminiscent of a previous occasion, would it not?

Let us have lunch on Thursday 27th, if you are free. That should give you time to come up from Norfolk and return in the day. Shall we say 12.15 at the Writers' Club?

Please confirm or otherwise by telegram.
Yours most sincerely,
Charles Cornford
(Editor)

Alice immediately sent off a telegram of acceptance, read the letter again and smiled at the reference to 'a previous occasion'. More than four years earlier, as a freelance writing from her parents' home on the Brecon Beacons, she had penned a series of articles on current affairs for the *Morning Post*. Some of them had been published, and this had encouraged her to write to the editor, asking for an appointment as a foreign correspondent. Cornford, under the impression that 'A. Griffith' was a man, and impressed by the perspicacity shown by her articles, had agreed to meet her. His shock at seeing a young woman in her early twenties walk through his door had, after much argument from Alice, been replaced by a sense of intrigue. As a result, he had reluctantly agreed to give her a temporary trial posting in the quiet backwater of South Africa, where Alice claimed she had contacts, through her brigadier father, with the 24th Regiment, both of whose battalions were serving there. From a clear blue sky, the Zulu War had broken out, and Alice's coverage of it had made her reputation. This had been cemented by her subsequent reporting from Afghanistan and the Transvaal, before she had resigned on her marriage to Ralph Covington.

To tell Ralph, or not? She pondered for a moment. No. She would have her own secret for a day or two and, like her husband, if she failed then it would remain her secret. In any case, she was not used to failure and would not contemplate it.

Covington needed a new uniform, and she persuaded him to take an early train to London on the 27th to see his tailor. She followed him on the next train and made her way leisurely, for she had plenty of time, to the Writers' Club, just off the Strand. Arriving there early, she visited the ladies' room and carefully made her toilet, studying critically the image that stared back at her from the large gilded mirror. It was that of an attractive, though perhaps rather strong young woman, for the jaw was a little too square and the grey eyes seemed to invite challenge and even confrontation. Making her professional way in an almost completely male environment had stiffened an already strong backbone, and the Alice Covington, née Griffith, who had experienced enemy fire in Zululand, Afghanistan and the Transvaal had already shown in the genteel drawing rooms of East Anglia that she took no prisoners in debate. Nevertheless, her overall appearance was feminine and pleasing, for her fair hair was full and soft and her skin was as clear as a sunlit day. Studying it now, she thought no rouge was needed but perhaps just a trace of face powder, for she had acquired a slight tan from her days out of doors in Norfolk – and she so hated looking like a country bumpkin!

Charles Cornford was waiting for her in the ladies' lounge – the Writers' Club was one of the few such institutions to have one, reflecting its rather bohemian position in London's

Clubland – when she entered, and he stood to receive her, looking more than ever like an elderly Prince of Wales, with his neat beard, and his grey morning jacket emphasising, rather than concealing, his considerable paunch.

He bowed over her hand and kissed it. 'My dear Alice,' he said. 'It is so good to see you again. Do sit down. I think the occasion calls for a little champagne.' He beckoned the waiter. 'A bottle of the Bollinger '70, George, please. Now. How is married life in the shires suiting you, my dear?'

Alice smiled. 'As a matter of fact, Mr Cornford . . .'

'I think it's time you called me Charles.'

'. . . Charles, it is not suiting me at all. I have become, I have to admit, very bored. Oh, there is plenty to do on the estate – we farm a little, you know – but we have people to look after it, and although I try to become involved, they know much more about it than I do. It is almost driving me to submit androgynously signed freelance articles to *The Times.*'

He threw back his head and chortled. 'Good lord, that would never do! Can't have you writing for the opposition. Do you know,' he leaned forward conspiratorially, 'I do miss your pieces. We don't seem to have anyone these days who can upset cabinet ministers as you did. I always enjoyed receiving their apoplectic letters, sent by special messenger, usually by about ten a.m. Such fun, such fun.'

'Oh Charles,' she put her hand briefly on his, 'I was always so grateful for the way you supported me. I know I caused you more trouble than anyone else on the *Post*. I was always running into trouble with generals and such.'

He shook his head and took a sip of the Bollinger. 'Freedom of the press is vital,' he said. 'You will remember that, as a Tory newspaper, we had to tone you down a bit when you were writing what I used to call "colour pieces" and boosting our present dear Prime Minister when he was in opposition, but your reportage from the campaigns abroad was always factual, informative and vivid. Now, tell me, what do you think about the present position in Egypt?'

She realised that Cornford, with his suave skills, was gently testing to see if her sabbatical in rural Norfolk had reduced her knowledge of current affairs or, indeed, blunted her ability to analyse them. Drawing on the champagne, then, she presented a well-rehearsed critique of the government's seeming opposition to the Egyptian people's right and proper desire for independence from the Turkish yoke and British and French interference in their affairs. An opposition, indeed, that had impelled it to send a squadron to menace the Egyptians and persuade them to accept the suzerainty of the Turks – the most backward and barbaric of all the imperial powers.

'It's both hypocritical,' she concluded, 'given that this is supposed to be a Liberal administration, pledged to people's rights to self-determination, and unwise, in that it will end in another expensive war – just think of that seemingly "easy" Zulu campaign – and we could lose the very thing we are trying to protect, the Suez Canal, for it would be so easy for its defenders to blow it up or block it.'

'Hmmm. I see that you haven't lost your radicalism. I fear that things are never quite as black and white as you paint them, Alice. I genuinely don't think the government wants war. What it would prefer, of course, is a return to the status quo, but with the Turks assuming more responsibility for the damned place and, of course, easing the taxation lash on the backs of the poor labouring *fellaheen*. But I fear that Arabi has got the bit between his teeth now. I also don't see Constantinople easing itself off its sleepy backside, if you'll pardon the expression. It looks as though we will have to go in to protect our people and interests there. Regrettable, I grant you, but probably unavoidable.' He summoned the waiter. 'Come, let us eat. George, please bring the champagne through.'

In the panelled dining room, Cornford tucked his napkin into the top of his waistcoat and picked up a spoon to dip it into the turtle soup. As he raised it to his mouth, he looked up at her. 'Now, my dear, tell me what you want of me.'

Alice sighed. 'Oh, I think you have guessed already, Charles. I want to come back. I want you to send me to Egypt to cover the coming campaign. This life in the country is not for me, at least, not all the time. I suppose that by now I must have printer's ink running through my veins. I miss journalism so much: the excitement, the competition, yes, even the occasional danger. I know that people still think it is a most unsuitable, even disgraceful, role for a woman to play but you know there are precedents and I believe I can say that I have served you well in the past. Please, take me back on. I don't need much money, you know, although,' she corrected herself quickly, 'I will expect to be paid, of course.'

'Ah,' he grinned. 'That's more like it. Shades of the old Alice.' He dabbed his moustache with his napkin. 'I remember that when we had a rather similar conversation some years ago, I said to you something like, "That's all very well, but will your family let you go?" I must say something similar to you now: what of your husband? What will he think?'

Alice frowned – it was more like a scowl. 'He will not oppose me. First, he is rejoining the army. Despite his injuries he has wangled his way back into the regiment and on to Wolseley's staff. I presume he will go in with the invading troops. What is good enough for him is good enough for me. Second, I am a mature woman and do not need the permission of my husband to do what I wish. I am both financially and sociologically independent. Times are changing, you know, Charles.'

Cornford held up both hands, as though in self-defence. 'Oh my goodness. Please don't think that I am unaware of that. Telephones, gaslight everywhere and now women going off to war. Whatever next?' He replaced his napkin on his lap and smoothed it down. Then he leaned forward. 'Alice, I am delighted to offer you the post of special correspondent in Egypt. I shall write to you about remuneration and so on as soon as I have had time to consult with my colleagues, but I don't think we shall fall out over that. Conditions for travelling expenses and suchlike will be the same as before.'

He paused. 'But I make two conditions. First, you must not endanger yourself by going into the firing line. Even seasoned male reporters like Russell don't find it necessary to do that. Second, I do not wish to come between a woman and her husband. You must reconcile your going with Colonel Covington. Is that understood? Do you agree?'

Alice sat still for a moment as her mind whirled. To hell with not going into the firing line! She could not do her job without taking risks. But a white lie – a white promise – would not hurt anyone. As for Ralph, well, she felt she could handle him. She smiled and held out her hand. 'I agree,' she said. 'Thank you for having me back.'

'Now,' Cornford relinquished her hand and settled back in his chair, 'I shall want you to go to Egypt immediately. I have a man there, of course, but he is not up to scratch. You will replace him. I don't want to wait until the invasion starts. I would like you filing stories on the conditions there as soon as possible. Try and see Arabi, of course; our man has failed so far, but I have a feeling you will succeed. I will see that you are accredited to our forces as and when they go in. When can you leave?'

Alice thought for a moment. 'Today is Thursday. I can leave on Monday.'

'Splendid. Now: what about a little claret with the lamb?'

Alice's confrontation with her husband that evening did not go exactly as she had expected or planned. Contritely, she confessed to her assignation as they sat together over dinner (lamb again, dammit! She had forgotten). With care and in a soft voice, she explained the reason for her desire to return to cover this campaign and her joy that Cornford had accepted her. He heard her out to the end without interruption, and then carefully laid down the fork from his good hand.

'I absolutely forbid it,' he said. 'There is no question of you going and I am amazed that you have carried out this deception behind my back.' He threw back his head and gazed at her, his blue eye blazing with indignation.

Alice drew herself up in her chair and tried to keep her voice level. 'Deception? Deception? Do you mean having an appointment in London that I kept from you for three days? Doesn't it sound familiar, somehow, Ralph? Didn't you have a secret – of a similar nature, as it happens – that you kept from me for much longer? Why does one rule apply to you and another to me?'

'Don't be ridiculous. That's beside the point. I mean you resuming your career. When we married, you promised that you would give up all this . . .' he gestured dismissively with his hook, 'scribbling. Your place is here, where your home is, particularly now that I have to go away.'

Alice sighed. 'That is just the point, Ralph. You are going away again, after giving up your career, and I wish to do the same. This is not the end of our marriage; in fact, I shall see more of you on campaign than if I had stayed here. We are both talented people who have something to contribute in these troubled times. I wish to make a contribution, as you do.' She reached across and put her hand over his, and her voice softened. 'It is not as if we have children, my dear. If we did, then of course I would not leave them. But the estate does not need me. Watkins is probably the best estate manager in the whole of East Anglia, and I shall certainly not be missed.' She decided to make a concession. 'I promise I shall return when the campaign is over.'

They sat in silence for a time. Then Covington, as though receiving a new source of energy, flared up again. 'No, dammit, no. It is not right. What will people think?'

It was an unwise tack for him to try. 'Don't you know me well enough by now, Ralph,' she said, her voice now ice cold, 'to understand that I don't care a damn what people think? The opinions of the county set around here or of your friends in the club in London matter to me not at all. Most of their brains seemed to have atrophied anyway. You will not *forbid* me, Ralph. You can try and persuade me –

although I don't think you will succeed – but you will not, I repeat *not*, forbid me. I am of age and an independent, free-thinking human being, and although I am married, I am no one's slave or servant.'

The silence descended again and Alice stared at her husband in cold fury. Gradually, however, she saw the handsome face begin to crease. Then he threw back his head and the dining room was suddenly filled with laughter. 'My God, woman,' he cried, slapping his thigh, 'I'd forgotten for a minute or two why I fell in love with you in the first place. You're a feisty thing, Alice Covington, and although it makes you difficult to live with sometimes, I admire you for it. Love your spirit. Always have. Pack your damned bags then, but come here and kiss me first.'

They embraced awkwardly at the table and Alice cradled his good hand in hers. She, too, remembered what had first attracted her to him when they had met before the invasion of Zululand. He was a man of his time: reactionary, high Tory, jingoistic, a traditionalist, but he was also brave and could show remarkable flexibility and good will at the most unexpected times. She kissed him again. 'Thank you, Ralph,' she said.

It was not until Covington was fast asleep at her side – he had not attempted to take advantage of their reconciliation by forcing himself upon her – that she allowed herself to think of Simon. Where was he? Was he out there in Egypt, that inhospitable, volatile foreign land? Would their paths cross again out there? And was that the *real* reason she was resuming her career? She sighed and turned over, but sleep proved elusive.

Chapter 7

Ahmed's cousin seemed to have bottomless resources, and the day after their affray in the street she produced two sets of garments for Simon and Jenkins that were both authentic and suitably anonymous. Their shirts were replaced by two simple cotton garments, buttoned to the neck and sufficiently voluminous not to demand niceties of sizing, worn under the ubiquitous long gown, gathered at the waist by a sash. They were given head cloths of undyed cotton, kept in place by plaited cords tied around the crown of the head, and soft slippers for their feet with upturned toes that seemed to Simon to have come out of the pantomime *Ali Baba and the Forty Thieves* that he had seen as a boy at Brecon.

Ahmed regarded them with satisfaction, as did Fatima, his cousin. Then his approving smile was replaced with a frown. 'The problem is if you talk,' he said. 'You look Egyptian, or, at least, like Arabs. But you speak no Arabic. Ah,' he clicked his fingers, 'I know. If people talk to you, shake head and say, "Sudan". They think then that you are from deep south, with different tongue. Or . . . I hope.'

'Blimey, so do I,' said Jenkins. 'Pity we don't know Welsh, now, isn't it?'

Under the anonymity of their disguise, the three spent the next few days walking the perimeter of Alexandria while Simon surreptitiously marked the depositions of the troops that Arabi had brought up to surround the town. It was clear that the Egyptian commander was preparing for war and that he had made the presumption that the invasion would occur at Alexandria. It was an obvious assessment. The city had a deep harbour, with lying-off anchorage in Aboukir Bay. It was the nearest point of disembarkation to the mainland of Europe and near to the newly occupied French territory of Tunisia and also to the British military base in the eastern Mediterranean at Cyprus. Simon made a rough estimate that Arabi had something like twenty thousand troops already based around Alex, with others in fall-back positions at his strong base at Kafr Dewar, some fifteen miles south-east of the city. Fatima reported that the town was full of rumours that the soldiers were poised to storm Alexandria and take the European possessions within it.

Ahmed had learned that the gun emplacements defending the port were now being considerably reinforced, and Simon turned his attention towards assessing these. On their previous brief stay in Alexandria, they had been allowed to saunter along to inspect the forts, but now they were turned back by Egyptian troops as they attempted to get close. The problem was solved, after waiting a day, by buying sacks of camel fodder, heaving them upon their backs and joining the lines of similarly burdened *fellaheen* who wound their way up to the fortifications, where work was continually in session. No one gave them a second glance as they plodded along the coastline. The forts and major gun emplacements were scattered along some four miles of the shore, before the city itself and on either side. It was obvious that Arabi had ordered considerable reinforcements to the individual forts. Long lines of earthworks were being erected to cover the entrance to the harbour, and Simon noted that the old Armstrong cannon were being supplemented here and there by new Krupp ordnance. He decided that it was time to make a full report to Admiral Seymour, in command of the British squadron lying in the bay, and, via him, to Wolseley in London.

Back at the hotel, he wrote a full signal to Wolseley, relieved at last of the strictures of using the 'family' code, and leaving the others behind, he hired a boat in the harbour to take him out to the Admiral's flagship, the *Invincible*, so that the message could be relayed immediately to London. The ironclad – its armour-plated sides were said to be eight to ten inches thick – was lying near to the city and seemed to dominate it with its massive armament of two 25-ton guns and ten others of 18 tons each. It was with some apprehension that the Egyptian boatman steered his small vessel alongside the bobbing landing stage at the bottom of the mighty vessel's companionway. Gathering his *burnous* about him, Simon transferred to the slippery landing stage with some difficulty.

'Oh no you don't,' shouted a voice from above. 'Get orf that gangway, you dirty A-rab.'

Simon looked up at the aggrieved Chief Petty Officer of the watch. 'Would you ask the Officer of the Watch for his permission to come on board, please?' he demanded in his best Sandhurst voice.

'Wot?'

'I am Captain Simon Fonthill, with an urgent message for

General Sir Garnet Wolseley in London, and I would like to see the Admiral as soon as possible.'

'Blimey. 'Alf a mo' ... er ... sir.'

Very quickly, the Chief Petty Officer's head was replaced by that of a young man, resplendent in navy whites. 'Do come on up, ah, there's a good fellow,' he called. 'Watch your step.'

In less than two minutes, Simon was sitting in the Admiral's day cabin at the stern of the ship, facing the considerable figure of Vice Admiral Sir Frederick Beauchamp Seymour, Commander of the Mediterranean Squadron. The Admiral, white-bearded, bluff-browed and with shoulders seemingly as broad as his ship, had joined the navy as a boy and was not to be fazed by a young man in Arab fancy dress.

'Why the hell are you dressed like that, and what do you want?' he demanded.

Resisting the urge to say that a cup of tea would be welcome, Simon shrugged off his *esharp* and decided to be amenable. 'Sorry to look like an Arab barrow boy, sir,' he said, 'but I have been working for some time in Egypt directly for Sir Garnet Wolseley, the Adjutant General at the Horse Guards. It's getting a bit difficult for Europeans to move freely around in Alex just now, so I had to go native. I have been communicating with Sir Garnet on open cable by code, but this has restricted me and I have reached the point where I need to report more fully. I would be grateful if this could go to him as a signal.' He pushed forward his report. 'Actually, sir, perhaps some of the content could be useful to you – although, of course, I am sure that you have your own sources of information from the shore.'

Simon had gone into some detail, amplifying his previous

messages about Arabi's artillery strength and his allegedly strong regiments of cavalry, which gave him flexibility and reconnaissance competence in the desert – quoting Stone Pasha as the source – and reporting on the Egyptian concentration around Alexandria and the repair of its forts. He repeated his view that invasion was expected from the northern port and his advice to the General to feint at Alex and then move speedily to block both ends of the Suez Canal and land at Ismailia to strike at Cairo. Although the signal was formally addressed, he had decided, on a whim, to sign it 'Cousin Simon' once again.

The admiral read it slowly and with a frown that seemed to entwine both bushy eyebrows. He looked up. 'Yer not Wolseley's cousin, are yer?'

'No, sir. It's my code signing.'

'But yer not usin' code now, so why be impertinent?'

Simon sighed inwardly. 'No impertinence intended, sir. It's the signature I have been using and I thought for the sake of continuity and to give verisimilitude to the signal I would continue to use it.' He coughed. 'Sir Garnet signs himself to me as "Cousin Garnet".'

'Umph!' The Admiral returned his gaze to the signal, then looked up again. 'How old are you, young man?'

'Twenty-seven, sir.'

'Don't you think you've got a bloody cheek giving military advice to the Adjutant General, eh?'

'No, sir. I don't. I am merely carrying out my orders. The General has asked for my advice. He has used it before.'

'How do I know you are who you say you are? It all seems a bit far-fetched to me.' He gestured to the signal. 'This business of the Egyptians improvin' their defences here. The

Khedive himself has assured me that the only work goin' on is routine maintenance stuff. Am I to take your word against his, eh?'

'If that is what the Khedive has said, sir, he is either lying or has been lied to by Arabi – and I would think that the latter is the case. I have seen the work being done myself. May I suggest, sir, that tonight, after dark, you train a couple of searchlights on the shore by the lighthouse at the entrance to the harbour. I know the Egyptians are working through the night there, throwing up earthworks. You will see them doing it.'

The great eyebrows lowered again as the Admiral considered the proposition. Then he slammed down the paper and pushed it back across the table to Simon.

'Don't believe a word of it. I don't know what you are up to, young man, but I don't like it and I won't be part of it. I will not send this rubbish to a man who is already up to his eyes working hard. Now, I would be grateful if you would get off my ship.'

Simon rose slowly to his feet. Fighting back anger, he kept his voice level. 'Admiral,' he said, 'I do not wish to be disrespectful to you, not least because I know you have many years of very fine service behind you. But you *must* send that signal. I may seem very young and inexperienced to you, but in the last three years I have fought at Rorke's Drift and Isandlwana in Zululand; Kabul and Kandahar in Afghanistan; and Sekukuni and Majuba in the Transvaal. I know what I am talking about, and General Wolseley is expecting me to report.' He paused for a moment. 'If you do not promise to send that signal, sir, then I must immediately go to Cook's offices on shore and cable him, explaining that you have refused to pass on my report. The choice is yours, Admiral.'

For a moment the two men, the old and the young, stood gazing at each other, their horns locked in metaphorical combat. Eventually it was the older man who gave way. 'Very well,' he looked down at the paper and spoke with heavy irony, ' "Cousin Simon". I shall send your report. But I shall preface it with my own comment saying that yer a cocky young man and that I doubt the truth of much – if not all – of what you say.'

Simon took a deep breath. 'You have no right to do that,' he said, 'because you have no evidence that I am wrong. But,' knuckles on the table, he leaned towards the Admiral, 'there's one way of proving which one of us is right. Shine your bloody searchlights on that wall after dark tonight. That will show. Good day to you, sir.'

He swept out of the cabin, flouncing his *burnous* behind him and stalking across the deck, ignoring the smiles of the Officer of the Watch and the Chief Petty Officer. Luckily, his boatman had obeyed his instructions to wait, because the dramatic effect of his leaving the ship would have been completely sabotaged by having to stand about on the deck until another boat was summoned.

Sitting in the stern as the boatman hauled on the oars, his mind seethed at the stupidity of the senior officers serving the Queen. He had had experience of it before, with the army, but not with the so-called Senior Service. He had come up against dunderheaded colonels and generals: specifically in the Transvaal with General Pommeroy-Colley (although not, definitely not, with Wolseley), and in Zululand. Had not Colley decided that the digging of trenches on top of Majuba

Hill would not be necessary, even though the Boers had proved that they were the finest marksmen in the world? Had not Lieutenant Colonel Covington, his former commanding officer, refused to accept that the column of British infantry left at Isandlwana could be overwhelmed by the Zulus? And had not the brave officer left in command under that terrible hill failed to heed Simon's warning that the camp was comparatively undefended against the Zulus, who were out in force and moving fast? Why could the unusual and the unthinkable never be faced? And why was being young so unforgivable? Simon clenched his fist. The decision to invade might already have been taken. Indeed, Wolseley might now be on his way, with his army. It was imperative that the signal be sent, otherwise the work of the last seven weeks would be made completely redundant. What fools these people were! So bloody inflexible!

It was, then, with anxiety that Simon, Jenkins and Ahmed walked that evening just after dusk to the highest point behind the town. And with huge relief that they saw first one, then two searchlights spring into life from the *Invincible* and play their beams on the scurrying, ant-like figures working on the embrasures and earthworks. So elephants could be moved, after all!

There was now little that Simon and his companions could do except wait. He attempted to keep in touch with affairs in Egypt by buying a week-old copy of *The Times* every day from a small French bookshop near the harbour, but the headline 'Heightened Tension' above reports of continued diplomatic activity between London, Paris, Constantinople and Cairo seemed to be a daily constant, with little hard news to support it. If the Admiral had taken action as a result of the activity shown by his searchlights, there was little to show for it. The great ironclads, with their French consorts, still rode out in the bay, mute, immobile and threatening.

'Y'know,' said Jenkins, 'I've been thinkin' about it, see, an' if I was the Egyptians, I would bloody well start rebuildin' *my* forts, if them bloody great guns was pointin' at me. It's very threatenin' an' very provokin', that's what it is. What would we do if Gyppo gunboats were anchored up the Thames, and were pointin' their guns at our pubs, eh? Well, we'd point a few guns back at them, that's what we'd do, isn't it? So why should old Admiral Blunderguts make a fuss, eh?'

Simon looked sharply at Jenkins. First the lawyer, now the anti-imperialist. The man was coming on! He nodded his head. 'I have to agree,' he said. And they both looked at Ahmed, who shrugged his shoulders and made a lugubrious face.

On the third day after his visit to *Invincible*, Simon slipped through streets that were now semi-deserted to the Thomas Cook office to see if Wolseley had cabled him with further instructions, perhaps to return to Ismailia, Cairo or even London. But Mr Roberts shook his head gloomily. 'Nothing, sir. And I would keep right off the streets if I were you. Trouble's coming, I can smell it. You make a very good Arab, but if you're out and about when it blows up, you'll get caught up in it. I'd stay indoors if I was you, sir.'

Leaving the offices, Simon glimpsed a figure approaching that made him finger the handle of the Colt tucked into the cummerbund under his *burnous*. The man was similarly dressed to Simon, except that he had raised the hood of his cloak, and by the look of it was wearing European trousers and boots. He had something awkwardly large that he was carrying under the folds of the cloak. The two were set to pass on the same side of the street, and Simon felt that he would attract attention if he crossed to the other pavement, so, head down and right hand on his revolver, he moved forward. As they passed, he glimpsed under the hood a familiar small moustache, round spectacles and celluloid collar.

'Mr George,' he called, in surprise. The little clerk jerked his head round and his eyes widened as he recognised Simon. 'Oh, hello, sir,' he half whispered. He was clearly embarrassed and clutched the large object closer to him under his cloak.

'What on earth are you doing in Alexandria?'

George looked around, obviously anxious not to be seen. 'Sorry, sir,' he said. 'Didn't recognise you in that get-up. Just on an errand for the company. You'll excuse me if I don't stop. In a bit of a hurry, you see. I hope you are well, sir. Now good day to you, excuse me please.' And he hurried away, pulling his hood further down over his face.

Simon looked after him with a puzzled frown. Why was the clerk so far from his post in these dangerous times? And what was he carrying? He shrugged his shoulders and hurried back to the hotel.

Three days later, Simon was woken in the morning by Jenkins shaking his shoulder. The Welshman was obviously himself fresh from his bed, for he was stripped to the waist, his chest a mass of tangled black hair. 'Trouble in the streets, bach sir,' he said. 'Listen.'

Simon could hear distant shouting and occasionally the

sound of gunshots. He threw back his covering and pulled on his pantaloons and Arab shirt. 'Have you any idea what started it, and are any British involved?'

Jenkins pushed open the wooden shutters and hung his head out. 'Can't see anything,' he called back. 'But it's from the direction of the harbour. Old Amen says that a crowd is attackin' some Europeans, but 'e don't know 'ow it started. Best to keep out of it, eh?'

'No. Not if British people are involved. We must help. Come on.'

Hurriedly dressed, the two men ran to the door of the hotel, where Ahmed was waiting. From somewhere he had found a fearsome curved scimitar, which he had pushed into the sash around his waist. 'A little bit of fighting today, I think, Simon, eh?' His eyes were bright and Simon noticed that he had begun to grow his moustache military style, so that it looked like a weaker version of Jenkins's.

'Looks like it. Where is the trouble?'

'Fatima says corner of Sister Street. Something to do with British consul. Big riot.'

'Show us the way. Quickly now.'

Winding their *esharps* around the lower part of their faces, Simon and Jenkins ran behind the scurrying figure of the little Egyptian. As they did so, the noise grew louder until they turned a corner to find a crowd of Arabs, including, Simon felt sure, some black-shrouded Bedawis, jostling around an open carriage so that it was completely surrounded. The single horse in the shafts was wide-eyed and rearing, keeping some parts of the crowd at bay. An elderly European stood in the middle of the carriage, attempting to keep his balance while flailing away with his driver's whip at the hands attempting to pull him down. As the three arrived, a shot rang out and the European's Egyptian driver, who was also standing and shouting at the attackers, crumpled and fell.

Simon quickly pulled Ahmed to the side, handed him his revolver and shouted something in his ear. Then, Jenkins at his side, they thrust their way through the crowd as best they could towards the man in the carriage. Suddenly behind them a shot rang out, and then another. Turning, they saw Ahmed firing around the corner, into the street from which they had come. Ahmed wheeled round – he had now drawn his scimitar and was waving it – and screamed something in Arabic at the top of his voice. Then he fired one more shot around the corner and ran towards the crowd, waving his arms.

' 'As he gone mad?' demanded Jenkins. 'What's 'e up to?'

'Don't talk. Run and wave your arms. Point ahead.'

Suddenly the crowd began to panic and, ushered by Simon, Jenkins and Ahmed, left the carriage and began running up the street. One man – obviously the one who had shot the European's driver – stayed behind and began reloading his rifle.

'Kill him,' panted Simon.

Jenkins drew his Colt, aimed with care and brought the man down before he could reload. The crowd, now in full flight, did not seem to notice. The elderly man in the open carriage, however, immediately, and with great courage, lashed at Simon with his whip.

His hand across his face, Simon shouted, 'Get down, you fool. Lie flat in the carriage.' And he leapt up on to the driver's seat and began gathering the reins.

'Who the hell are you?' demanded the man, his face and grey whiskers drenched in perspiration, and, Simon noticed for the first time, his left arm bleeding from what seemed to be a gunshot wound.

'Never mind,' shouted Simon, gaining control of the horse. 'Lie flat. If they see you, they'll pull us all down.'

'No. I'm not leaving without my driver. Can you put him in the carriage?'

'Jenkins?'

The Welshman tucked away his Colt and lifted the inert figure of the driver as though he was thistledown, depositing him gently on the floor of the carriage.

'Best lie down, bach,' he said to the elderly man. 'Do as the Captain says, there's a good gentleman.'

The man's jaw dropped – whether from the control being taken by the hawk-nosed Arab with the reins who spoke like a young subaltern, or from the Welsh accent coming from his fiercely moustached companion – but he obediently lay down next to his driver. Jenkins stretched down an arm to pull aboard a breathless but exultant Ahmed, and with a shake of the reins, the carriage began to move.

'Take the next siding, that way,' shouted Ahmed.

'What?' It had been some time since Simon had driven a carriage, and the combination of a terrified horse and quite inexplicable instructions shouted from behind him combined to make the carriage sway fearsomely from side to side.

'I think 'e means take the next left,' shouted Jenkins. ''Ere, let me do it.' Simon happily surrendered the reins to the Welshman and, taking his Colt back from Ahmed, who was brandishing his scimitar over the side of the carriage like some medieval Saracen, knelt beside the elderly man.

'Keep your head down, sir,' he said. 'We will probably have to drive straight through the crowd if we can. I don't want to shoot again, but we may have to.'

The carriage rocked as Jenkins hauled on the reins to take it around the corner. But they had not completely escaped the mob. Most of the Arabs had certainly sprinted ahead, towards the harbour. But a minority had swung around the corner and were now coming back. Seeing the carriage again, they hurled derision and began to stretch across the narrow street. Simon levelled his revolver beside Jenkins's hip and dispatched two rounds into the air above the line of the crowd. At the same time, Jenkins, his left hand holding the reins skilfully and his right brandishing the whip, let out a Celtic scream and urged the horse and carriage straight towards the front line of the mob. Like magic it parted and the fugitives galloped straight through, Ahmed hanging over the rear, abortively swinging his sword and hurling imprecations at everyone within sight.

'Keep galloping,' shouted Simon. 'There are plenty of them still about.'

As if to underline his words, two shots rang out from a doorway and Simon glimpsed two smoking *jerzails* as they thundered by. The musket balls hissed harmlessly over their heads, but several gowned figures attempted bravely to grab the carriage's harness as they passed, one of them gaining a cut on his shoulder from Ahmed's scimitar for his efforts.

'Where to, sir?' asked Simon, realising that they could be galloping into further trouble.

The elderly man looked up, his face waxen. 'Head for the public gardens by the Mahmoudieh Canal,' he gasped. 'European quarter. My house is near there and we should be safe. I'm the British consul. Name of Cookson. I owe you my life. Who are you?'

'Just a minute, sir.' Simon stood to shout in Jenkins's ear. 'Next right, and right again on the main highway. Keep galloping if the horse can take it.' He turned back to Cookson. 'Simon Fonthill, sir. Late of the 24th Regiment and the Queen's Corp of Guides in India. This is Sergeant Jenkins, same regiments, and this is Ahmed, without whom we should all probably be dead.'

Jenkins waved his whip in airy greeting and Ahmed tried to bow in the bouncing carriage but failed and sprawled back on to the seat. '*Enchanté, effendi*,' he said.

Simon took off his *burnous* and bundled it into a pillow for the consul's head. 'Let me take a look at that wound, sir.'

'Oh, it's only a scratch. Bullet's gone through the fleshy part of the arm, that's all. They pulled me from the carriage and banged me about a bit. But Ali here,' he gestured to his driver, who lay depressingly still, 'hauled me back in. I do fear that he may be dead. Splendid chap. I'd rather you took a look at him.'

Simon did his best to examine the wound in the Egyptian's chest and felt for his pulse. 'I fear he has gone, sir.'

'Ah.' Cookson dropped his head back and closed his eyes.

The horse was now blown and Jenkins let him walk. But they were near to the gardens, and here the thoroughfare was much wider and quite empty. Eventually, they found the British consulate, without bothering Cookson further. He had relapsed into unconsciousness, although he was breathing evenly. Simon wondered what had made him set out in his open carriage in the narrow streets at such a dangerous time.

The consul's wife greeted them anxiously, and Mr Cookson was lifted with care into his house and a doctor summoned. Mrs Cookson, a stout, competent woman, showed the imperturbability of a colonial officer's wife, for she asked no questions about why they were wearing disguise, but declared that it would be unsafe to return that evening and insisted they stay in the consulate overnight. She fed them well, and by morning the consul had recovered sufficiently for Simon to visit his bedside. The reason for Cookson's drive, it seemed, lay with Admiral Seymour.

'The Admiral has threatened Arabi that he will open fire on the forts unless the defences are dismantled,' confided Cookson. 'I was visiting the leading Europeans still left in the city, warning them of this to give them one last chance of getting out or boarding up their houses.' He raised himself on one elbow. 'I don't know how accurate these naval big guns are, but there is bound to be widespread damage to the town itself, I would have thought.'

'Don't distress yourself, sir,' said Simon, gently pushing Cookson back on to his pillow.

'No. I'm well recovered now. Managed to get round most of them until that mob caught me and you and your strange friends saved me. I really am most grateful to you, for I am sure that you saved my life. But you must tell me what you are doing here, at this difficult time, disguised as Arabs. Are you still serving in the army, then?'

Simon decided to dissemble. The consul was the senior representative of the British government in Alexandria, and, as such, was one of the main sources of information to the government, via the British agent in Cairo. He would not take lightly the fact that the army's Adjutant General had set up his own line of intelligence in Egypt. Simon recalled Wolseley's warning that he was on his own.

'No, sir. Here really on a bit of a holiday – Jenkins is my servant and Ahmed our interpreter. I am interested in archaeology and have been looking to see what I could buy to take home.' He indicated his dress. 'Got Ahmed to kit us out like this so that we could move around the streets more easily. I didn't realise how bad things had become here.' He decided to move off the shifting ground his lies were taking him towards. 'But do tell me, sir, why has the Admiral gone so far? If he fires on Alexandria, that is tantamount to a declaration of war. Has he had instructions from London to do so, do you know?'

'No. He says that his squadron is threatened by the shore defences, and that it is his duty to protect it.'

'Good lord. The man must be mad.'

Cookson frowned in disapproval at the condemnation of such a senior figure by one so young. 'Well, he has heavy responsibilities, you know. Nevertheless, you make a fair point, and I have begged him to wait while we continue to negotiate with the Khedive – who is here, of course – and Colonel Arabi. But Seymour is talking of putting a time limit on his threat; in other words, of issuing an ultimatum.'

'What time will he put on that?'

'I don't know. It depends upon whether the Khedive and Arabi continue to prevaricate. I gather they have been doing this for the last few days – still promising to stop the work on the emplacements but not doing so. However, I feel that time is now running out. It is significant that I have had a message this morning to say that the French squadron has weighed anchor and sailed, leaving Seymour here on his own. I fear that the Admiral is no diplomat.'

Simon grinned at the thought. 'I can imagine that, sir.'

Cookson frowned again, and the head that lay on the pillow now seemed older. 'Look here, young man,' he said, 'er, forgive me, I've forgotten . . .'

'Fonthill, sir.'

'Ah yes. Look here, Fonthill. I owe you a great debt. If I did not, I would look very severely upon your presence here, dressed as you are and carrying very military-looking revolvers. You have expressed an interest in archaeology, and I am sure you know that the Egyptian government set up the Antiquities Service to ensure that all new archaeological finds were registered and a licence granted before they could be exported.' He was now looking at the ceiling, as though embarrassed to catch Simon's eye. 'Inevitably, this has resulted in a thriving trade in smuggling such things out of the country, of which Alexandria is the main port of exit. As a result, I am sure – although I cannot prove it – that this town is full of such precious objects, most of them having been brought here from Cairo.'

He turned his gaze back to Simon. 'There will be treasures here behind many doors, Fonthill. Now, if the British Navy fires on Alexandria – as it looks as though it will – there could be widespread destruction, either from British shells or from Egyptian gangs who will take advantage of the chaos to attack buildings and loot them.'

Simon nodded slowly. 'Would you like us to stay here and help protect you, sir?'

Cookson gave an irritated shake of the head. 'No, no. We have our own defences, and Seymour knows the position of the consulate; we are far enough away from the forts not to be in danger from the guns. No. I am talking of you, Fonthill.' He raised himself on one elbow again. 'Do not – I repeat – *do not* stay here. Do not become involved. Get away while you can.'

Simon realised that this good man suspected him of being a smuggler of ancient Egyptian artefacts – and even, perhaps, of hoping to take advantage of the shelling and to engage in the consequent looting. He smiled. 'Thank you for the advice, Mr Cookson. I will take it.'

'Good man.' Cookson held out his hand. 'You should still be able to get a ship in the harbour, or even a train south to Cairo, although I wouldn't advise that. Thank you again for your intervention on my behalf back in Sister Street.'

Within minutes, Simon and his companions had left the consulate. They had to do so by the back gate, for a small crowd had gathered outside the tall railings that fronted the building. It seemed peaceable enough, for the moment more sullen than angry, but Simon feared for the consul and his quiet, able wife. She assured them that they were quite capable of looking after themselves, and gestured to two tall Nubian servants. 'We have rifles,' she said, 'and they can shoot. If things get really out of hand we can signal to the Admiral from the roof and he will land marines, I am sure.' To Simon's amazement, she pressed a small box of Colt .45 cartridges into his hand. How resourceful were these women working in distant lands! 'My husband tells me you expended quite a lot of ammunition on his behalf yesterday. Now go, but do be careful, all of you.'

The three of them slipped away, through the palms and sycamore fig trees at the back of the consulate, and eventually made the safety of their hotel without incident. Once there, Jenkins turned to Ahmed.

''Ere,' he said, 'I knew there was somethin'. Why did you suddenly start shootin' round the corner, and what were you yellin' that made them fellers run for it?'

Ahmed grinned, and his chest seemed to swell by a couple of inches. 'Simon tell me to shoot up empty street,' he said, 'and then say that sailors were coming. So I shot and shouted, "British sailors are coming with bloody great bayonets, et cetera, et cetera." Good, yes?'

'Bloody marvellous, bach. Bloody marvellous.'

Chapter 8

The next morning, promptly at seven a.m., the bombardment began.

It commenced with a deep boom, as though a sighting gun was being used, then immediately the warm, soft morning exploded into a hellish cacophony as the rest of the squadron opened fire. At first the Egyptian gunners seemed to have been taken by surprise, despite the fact that the ultimatum had obviously been delivered. Then, however, their response began, and the deeper note of the guns on the forts and at the newly dug positions along the shoreline mingled with the more distant crashes from the ships, so that the port of Alexandria – hitherto an idyllic haven, its tree-lined avenues fringing the bluest of seas – became an inferno of noise, smoke and, increasingly, collapsing bricks and masonry as the huge naval shells crashed in from the sea.

Despite their years of active service, Simon and Jenkins had never before experienced such a bombardment. Nothing that the Zulus, the Pathans, the bePedis or the Boers had unleashed could match the terror of these mighty shells exploding only a couple of hundred yards away from their fragile hotel. The three of them, with Fatima and her terrified Egyptian staff, crouched in the little dining room as the explosions seemed to creep closer. Dust filled the air, and particles crunched between their teeth.

'Right,' shouted Simon, 'let's move out. Ahmed, tell Fatima and the rest to take their valuables – wrap them in blankets or something – and we will escort them to the hill above the town. Quickly now, and lock up the hotel. We should be safe on the top, and we can come back when the bombardment has finished. It can't go on all day.'

But it did. The shelling continued for more than ten hours. It was as though Seymour was determined to reduce the forts to rubble. Looking down from the heights – they were, in fact, little more than a swelling in the ground, but they gave the fugitives some perspective on the battle being waged below – it seemed as though the whole shoreline was being destroyed. The parts of the city that fringed the sea were marked by a cloud of black smoke that was constantly being illuminated from within by flashes of orange flame as the big shells landed. But it was clear that it was not one-way traffic. The Egyptian gunners seemed to be putting up a courageous fight, for the distinctive flare of their own guns could be seen, showing like intermittent white sparks through the smoke. Whether they were having an effect on the vessels out in the bay no one could tell, for the smoke had now taken on a kind of permanence, hanging like an oleaginous mantle over the town, preventing the viewers on the hill from seeing the ships.

Simon and his group, rendered silent by the noise, sat glumly watching the battle, chewing oranges as the day wore on. They were by no means the only witnesses to the artillery duel; there must have been hundreds of natives who had fled the town and were now waiting for the resolution of the bombardment. There seemed to be no Europeans among them, however, and Simon wondered if they had all fled the city, or if they were huddled in their houses, praying that a wayward shell would not land on them – and also waiting perhaps, guns in hand, to repel any looters who would attempt to take advantage of the end of the shelling. This prompted a thought, and during the afternoon, he and Jenkins left their companions and walked to the Egyptian army's positions, spread out somewhat to the rear of the town in a vast semicircle. They found nothing except rubbish and other military detritus. The troops had all been withdrawn, probably to their previously prepared positions to the south and east. It was obvious that Arabi was not going to defend the town.

'It also means,' said Simon as they trudged back, 'that he won't make any effort to prevent looting. If Seymour wins this artillery battle – and so far there's no evidence that he will – then I hope to God that he puts ashore a strong landing party to stop looting and organise some sort of clearing-up of the damage.'

The guns fell silent at last in the late afternoon. It had been clear for some time that the Egyptian reply had been diminishing, and the distinctive bark of the shore-based guns had disappeared long before Seymour called a halt to his bombardment. As the black cloud eventually began to drift away, the ships in the bay came into view again. Simon counted them: eight ironclads and five gunboats. None had been sunk, and as far as he could see through his field glasses, none had suffered severe damage. He ranged his glasses along the shoreline. In contrast, the devastation to the forts and the newly thrown-up emplacements along the shore was clear. Guns could be seen torn away from their mountings and thin grey smoke rose from the rubble of stone and brick that had once been stout bastions. It was amazing that the Egyptians had been able to continue their defiance for so long. Simon recalled from his Sandhurst days the debate about whether modern vessels, with their huge long-range guns and armoured sides and tops, could at last tip the balance away from guns firing from fixed emplacements on shore, an imbalance that had existed since Nelson's day. The gun battle at Alexandria had settled that debate. The new ironclads were the masters.

Simon swept his glasses along the rooftops of the town. It was obvious that the navy's gun-layers had not been as accurate as had been hoped, for fires were now springing up away from the forts, particularly in the European quarter. Was it, though, collateral damage from the shelling, or were looters already moving in?

Simon turned to Jenkins and Ahmed. 'We must get down into the town quickly,' he said. 'First we will take Fatima and her people back to the hotel, then we must go and help any Europeans who might be in danger. Come on. Quickly now.'

At first the streets of the town seemed deserted, and it appeared that the native quarter had been spared any damage. Fresh fires, however, could be seen springing up towards the European sector. The hotel had survived the shelling, apart from the thick layer of dust that lay over it, and Fatima and her staff were safely reinstalled.

'Tell her,' said Simon to Ahmed, 'to lock the doors and admit no one until we return, which may be tomorrow, I don't know. Now, we need ammunition for the Colts. Sorry,

Ahmed, but I think you should stay here. Fatima may need protection, and anyway, you don't have a weapon.'

Ahmed's eyes widened. 'No, no. I come with you. It is a fighting day again, yes? Then you need me. Fatima has old shotgun she can use if people come. But I don't think so. So I come with you, for the fighting again. I have my father's sword.' His teeth gleamed through his now quite luxurious moustache.

'Oh, very well. Three five two: the ammunition. Thank God for the consul's replacements. Let's go.'

Once outside, they realised that the street was now full of running figures. A new sound had replaced the booming of the bombardment: the noise of shouting people. The mob had taken to the streets and the looters were out. Dusk was falling, but the sky was now lit a swollen red by the gleam of the burning fires. The biggest lay to their right. 'What is there, Ahmed?'

'Anglo-Egyptian Bank, maybe.'

'An obvious target. Let's go there.'

In fact the bank was not alight, for it was a solid building, laid in stone. But it was clear that it was being besieged. A mob was milling about at its front, hurling stones and burning brands through its smashed windows. More seriously, gunfire had now opened up from the edge of the crowd, and Simon saw that four Bedawis were firing their *jerzails* from the protection of a half-shattered building virtually next door to it. Although the bank building was occupied – frightened faces could be glimpsed through the shattered windows – there seemed to be no sign of an organised defence.

Simon nodded towards the gunmen. 'Let's take those four

first,' he said. The three of them slipped through the crowd to the edge of the still smouldering building next to the bank and clambered through fallen stonework to where they had a clear view of the gunmen.

'Do we . . .?' asked Jenkins.

'Afraid so. We have no time to ask them to lay down their arms – and we know they wouldn't anyway.'

Simon and Jenkins carefully sighted their long-barrelled revolvers, and two shots rang out. Immediately two of the Arabs fell, for even Simon could not miss at that range. Jenkins's second shot brought down the third man, but Simon missed with his and the fourth Bedawi immediately levelled his musket and fired. The ball crashed into the stonework above Simon's head, but before he could cock his revolver to fire again, Ahmed had leapt to his feet, sword in hand, and run across the rubble towards the man.

'Don't shoot,' shouted Simon to Jenkins, as the Welshman levelled his Colt. 'You might hit Ahmed.'

The danger was clear, for Ahmed was now blocking the eye line to the Arab and was swinging his scimitar around his head like some primitive Marmaluke. The Bedawi had had no time to reload his *jerzail*, but he was no coward. With the barrel of his gun, he parried the little man's sword and swung the stock back to plunge it into Ahmed's face. But the Egyptian, half slipping in the rubble, half ducking, saw the butt of the musket pass over his head, and punched the other man in the stomach with the hilt of his sword. As the Arab let out a wheeze and doubled up, Ahmed swung the scimitar back and brought the blade down on his opponent's neck. Alas, the old sword was blunt, but the force of it was enough to break the man's neck, and the crack could clearly be heard by Simon and Jenkins. The Arab fell without a sound. Simon ran to Ahmed.

'You all right, old chap?'

The little man looked up at Simon, his eyes wide and his mouth open. Then he began to shake.

'Quick, bach,' said Jenkins, 'sit down. The first time's always the worst.'

In fact there was no time for rehabilitation, for they had been seen by some of the mob at the rear, who immediately began hurling stones at them. Two more musket balls pinged off the wall nearest to them.

'Round the back of the house!' shouted Simon. 'Let's see if we can get on to the bank's roof. It looks as though the houses are almost joined and the back looks solid enough.'

'Oh bloody 'ell,' groaned Jenkins. 'You know I don't like heights. You go on up, look you, and I'll protect the rear, like.'

'No. You'll get picked off on your own. Ahmed, are you all right to climb?'

The little man seemed to have recovered, for his eyes were bright again and he nodded his head.

'Good. You go first. See if we can get across to the bank's roof and through a skylight or something down to the interior. I'll push Jenkins up from behind.'

'No, bach sir, it's all right, see. I'll just . . .'

'Get on with you. It's not difficult. Look, Ahmed's halfway up already.'

Somehow the trio, with Jenkins perspiring and not daring to look down, and Simon with a hand on his bottom, managed to scramble up the loosened brickwork at the back of the building to where only a small gap separated it from the flat roof of the bank. A hunched wooden structure seemed to promise entry to the floors below, and even Jenkins was persuaded to leap across the gap. The shed was, indeed, the entrance to a stairway and a shot from Simon's revolver shattered the lock, allowing them entry.

Clattering down the stairs, their arrival on the first floor, where most of the occupants seemed to have gathered, created great consternation and cries of horror. A portly Englishman came forward with his hands raised. 'No, no,' he cried. 'Don't shoot. We can open the vaults.'

'No need for that,' said Simon, slipping his Colt into his waistband. 'Are you in charge here?'

The man was visibly shaking and perspiring. 'Yes. I am the manager. But who are you?'

'It doesn't matter.' He turned. 'Three five two, go back up the stairs and block that entrance we have opened. Others could follow us if we've been seen. You,' he gestured to a young man in European clothing, 'go and help him. Now . . .'

His words were drowned by a thumping from below. A quick look out of the window showed that a large blackened rafter was being used as a battering ram to crash against the door.

Simon turned back to the manager. 'Do you have any weapons here?'

The man nodded, wide-eyed. 'We have one shotgun and a fowling piece. I did not want to use them because I thought it would inflame the mob. Surely the navy will arrive soon?'

'I've no idea, but this mob is well and truly inflamed already, and if they break in I wouldn't give a farthing for our lives. Get the guns quickly.' He looked around him. Perhaps fifty people were crammed into the open-plan first floor, above what was obviously the reception area of the bank below. They seemed to be mainly Europeans, including some dozen women. One mature woman was eyeing him steadily. 'Madam,' he said, 'do you know if there are cooking facilities here?'

If she was surprised at being asked such a question, she showed no sign. 'Not really,' she said. 'But there is water and we have filled buckets and pans in case the building was set on fire by the shelling.'

Simon realised that the bank must have formed a refuge and rallying point for families living nearby. Down below he could hear the tempo of the battering ram's blows increasing. 'Splendid,' he said. 'Get the rest of the ladies and boil as much of the water as you can. Make fires from any wood you can find. Quickly, now. Where are those two guns?'

A young man appeared. 'Here, sir. I have loaded them. Only buckshot, I am afraid.'

Simon shot him a grateful glance. 'That will have to do. Can you shoot?'

'Yes, sir.'

'Anyone else?'

'Of course.' A tall elderly man with a crisp beard and still immaculate in his white ducks strode forward. 'About time we fought back, dammit.'

'Right. To the windows and fire on the men holding the battering ram. Shoot at their heads and faces if you can. Make the buckshot count. I will get you help.' Simon turned. 'The rest of you men go downstairs and shore up the doors and windows with whatever you can find. And stamp out those burning brands they have thrown through the windows. Ahmed, you go with them. I'll join you in a second. Don't stand there gawping, all of you: GO!'

Two loud reports from the windows showed that the marksmen had begun their work. Simon ran back to the stairway and shouted up, 'Three five two, you're needed down here. Can you come?'

'On my way, bach sir.' And Jenkins, Colt poised, arrived with a clatter.

'You take that far window and shoot down on the leading ranks of the mob. We have to deter them. Don't waste ammunition, but shoot to kill. I'm going downstairs to make sure they can't break through there.'

'Careful, bach. Shout if you need me.'

Simon took the stairs two at a time, and a disturbing sight met his eyes as he reached the ground-floor reception area. The fire from the upstairs window had indeed halted the attack of the battering ram – for the moment at least. But the windows had now become a target for entry. Two men had already climbed through, and Simon was just in time to see Ahmed bring down the first with a blow across the knees with his scimitar. Blunt or not, the sword was as effective as a tackle from a two-hundred-pound rugby footballer, and the man went sprawling across the floor, cracking his head on the tiling. The second intruder was being incongruously but bravely faced by a young clerk from upstairs who held a chair before him like a lion-tamer. Simon shot the Arab before he could circumvent the clerk's awkward defence and released a second shot at a form that presented itself at the same shattered window. Cocking the Colt quickly, he fired again at a head that had appeared at the second window.

'You four,' Simon shouted to a group of the refugees who

were standing indeterminedly watching the action, 'grab those tables and wedge them into the windows. You two, push these desks against the door. Ahmed, are you all right?'

The Egyptian was standing, almost forlorn, fingering the edge of his scimitar. 'Very all right, Simon. I think this is a good fighting day. But I am afraid my father's sword is damned blunt, look you.'

Simon could not keep back the grin at the acquired Welshness of the little man. 'You seem to be doing pretty well with it so far. Well done. Now stand by the windows, and if anyone tries to climb through before the tables are in, whack them with your blunt sword.'

Above the howling of the mob Simon could hear the crack of Jenkins's Colt and the firing of the buckshot from the first floor. The blows of the battering ram had not been renewed but the tables now being awkwardly thrust into the windows were being met with a hail of bricks and stones, and the occasional musket ball was still thudding into the thick timber of the front door. Even so, the flimsy defences seemed to be holding for the moment, so Simon ran back up the stairs and across to Jenkins.

'There's a couple of them still with muskets or rifles,' he said. 'Can you see 'em?'

Jenkins peered out. 'No, but we've stopped the bastards bangin' away at the door . . . oops, no we 'aven't.' A crash from below confirmed his words.

Simon looked down. The Arabs had taken advantage of a pause in the defensive fire, as the shotgun, the fowling piece and Jenkins's Colt were reloaded at the same time, to pick up their ram and relaunch it against the door. Simon turned. 'Ladies. Where the hell is the boiling water?'

'Now, young man. There is no need to use such language. We are doing our best.' The mature lady was staggering towards him carrying a huge bowl of steaming water.

Simon leapt to her aid. 'Sorry, ma'am,' he said, relieving her of her load. 'Is there more to come?'

'Boiling now.' As she spoke, two more women emerged from a corridor at the back of the room, carrying another steaming pannier between them.

'Jenkins,' shouted Simon, 'open the window wide and grab the other pot.' With care, he positioned himself on the edge of the windowsill. Looking down, he waited until the Arabs with the battering ram shuffled forward once more, and then tipped the boiling water on to their heads. The screams were as satisfying a sound as Simon had heard since arriving in Alexandria. As he watched, he heard Jenkins intone from the other window, 'One, two, three, go!' And the contents of the second, larger pannier showered down in all its hissing menace.

'Well done, young man.' The matronly woman patted Simon on the shoulder. 'I had a feeling you had something in mind at this juncture other than making tea. We will get you some more water.'

He grinned his thanks at her and immediately put her into the same category as the counsul's wife: brave, calm and resourceful. Where would the British Empire be without women like that?

The elderly man with the shotgun beckoned across to Simon. 'I think the varmints have had enough,' he said. 'They're getting thinner down there. They probably think we're too tough a nut to crack and they're slipping away to find easier game elsewhere.'

And so it seemed. The musket fire had stopped, and by the light of the red glare, figures could be seen moving away. Certainly the battering ram had been dropped and the ring that had formerly been pressing up to the door and windows had melted away. Two more shots from Jenkins's revolver seemed to hasten the exodus, and within a couple of minutes, the street in front of the bank had become completely deserted, except for seven prostrate figures marking the accuracy of the defenders' fire. Three more lay on the ground, clutching buckshot wounds.

Simon turned to the bearded man. 'I think we should get them inside and see if we can tend to their injuries.'

The man gave him a quizzical glance. 'If you think so, although I'm not sure they deserve it.'

'Will you organise it, sir, perhaps with the ladies' help? We ought to be on our way, in case we can give a hand to others.'

'Of course.' He put his head out of the window and then turned back to Simon. 'But are you sure you want to go roaming around the streets through the night? There are lots of fires burning now and it looks as though the mobs are out in force. They can be quite frightening.' He smiled apologetically. 'They knocked the wind out of us here, I can tell you. Feel quite ashamed, in fact. Thank God you came and put a bit of backbone into us.'

'We'll be all right. It looks as though we are passing for Arabs well enough. Do you know if there are any Europeans nearby who have stayed in their homes?'

'Must be a few. Not everybody wanted to clear off in the boats and just leave their houses to the mob. Those of us in here felt that we couldn't put up a fight on our own and that we would have greater security in the bank.' He smiled wryly. 'Just shows you that banks are never as safe as you think they are.' He put out a hand. 'But if you must go, God speed to you and take care.'

'Goodbye.' Simon grinned. 'If the symptoms return, repeat the dose of buckshot and hot water.'

Outside the bank, the three men stood guard for a while as the wounded rioters were carried – none too gently – inside. Then the big doors were bolted behind them and they set off, picking their way over the rubble, to where the sky seemed to be glowing the deepest red.

'We can't take 'em all on, bach sir,' growled Jenkins. 'That'll just be askin' for trouble, look you.'

'I know. We can't stop the looting but we might be able to help one or two families holed up in their homes. We've got to try. We can't just stand by.'

Simon looked around in despair as they turned a corner and saw a line of once elegant houses, all with their fronts torn open and displaying the most intimate details of their domesticity: beds with their sheets torn and hanging, pictures askew on fire-ravaged walls, chairs spilling out their soft fillings like intestines torn from corpses. These were obviously all victims of the shelling, but further along, more sinister sights met their eyes. Houses spared the bombardment had obviously been deliberately set afire. Men were tossing burning torches into their interiors while others ran in and out, dodging the flames and carrying away ornaments, paintings and pieces of furniture. Worse still, the bodies of men, women and children, some wearing night clothing, lay strewn across the pavement. Simon and Jenkins wrinkled their noses in disgust.

'Bastards,' said Jenkins, and drew out his revolver.

'No.' Simon shook his head. 'There's nothing we can do here. Let's go where there is gunfire. Listen. Yes, here.'

They turned into a side street at the end of which a small crowd had gathered in front of a white stucco house. Three in the mob had rifles and they were firing them at a half-open tall window behind a small wrought-iron balcony, from which a man, incongruously wearing a white pith helmet, was attempting to return the fire with a pistol. Others in the crowd were trying, so far abortively, to set fire to the wooden door.

'What . . . ?' asked Jenkins.

'Straight into the middle and kill the ones with guns,' said Simon. 'Short range. Shock tactics. You, Ahmed, stay on the edge, and if we get into trouble, shout again that the sailors are coming.'

Jenkins frowned but nodded, as did Ahmed.

Simon and Jenkins edged their way along the wall of houses until they were immediately under the balcony and facing the mob. They did so unnoticed, for they appeared to be just two more from the desert or the town anxious to join in the pillaging. Then, backs to the wall, they drew their Colts and fired at the riflemen. At such short range they could not miss, and all three fell. Coolly cocking their hammers, the pair turned their fire on to the front row of the Arabs, bringing down four more. At this, the rest turned and fled, their sandals making a despairing flapping noise on the cobbles as they ran for their lives. Within seconds the street had been cleared.

Simon stepped out from underneath the balcony. 'Are you all right up there?' he called.

Cautiously the man in the helmet peered over the edge, his revolver at the ready. 'Who on earth are you? Are you English?'

'Half Welsh. Anyone injured up there?'

'No. Sent my family off in a steamer three days ago. Stayed on to defend the place. I don't intend to let the buggers have it. God bless you for turning up like this. Can you stay?'

'No. Do you have ammunition?'

'Yes. Plenty.'

Jenkins appeared. 'If they come back, bach, try pourin' boilin' water over 'em. They 'ate it.'

'What?'

'Never mind,' said Simon. 'We'll call back later, if we can. Good luck.'

Several times during that long night the same scene was repeated, as the three men intervened crucially to disperse would-be pillagers attacking homes in the town. They had to exercise care, for of course in every case they were outnumbered, but they had the advantage of surprise, and Simon's shock tactics always prevailed. As dawn broke, the trio, soot-stained and weary, made their way back towards the haven of Fatima's hotel. But before they reached it, Alexandria, battered, smoking and bleeding had one more surprise for Simon.

They had long ago decided against attempting to prevent looting, and so, as they passed one more empty building with its attendant pillagers swarming over it like ants, they walked on by. But the presence of one seemingly familiar figure, who looked as though he was in charge of the looting, in that he was directing the loading of objects on to a cart, made Simon pause. He walked across.

'Mr George again, isn't it?' he enquired.

The little man started and pushed his spectacles back up his nose. His face was smoke-blackened and the celluloid collar glimpsed from under his Arab *burnous* was filthy, but his features were unmistakable.

'Oh, hello, sir,' he said, and gave a weak smile. 'Fancy seeing you again.'

'What on earth are you doing, Mr George?'

'Oh, er, this, you mean?' He gave a sweep of his hand, as though Simon might be referring to something else. 'Just trying to save a few *objets d'art* from the house of one of the company's clients, you know.'

Simon's jaw dropped and he looked at the Arabs running in and out of the house. They appeared to be no different from any of the other looters they had seen during the course of the long night. 'What? Are these your chaps?'

'Oh, yes, sir. Got to find help where we can. Now, if you don't mind, sir, I'd better be getting on. There are plenty of others about this morning who would like this stuff. Nice to see you again, sir.'

Simon shook his head. Thomas Cook certainly seemed to look after their customers. Then he joined the others and walked away. It had been a long, fraught night and he was very tired.

Chapter 9

At approximately the time when Simon was entering Alexandria for the second time, Alice Covington sat waiting for Colonel Arabi. It was proving to be a tiresome and time-consuming business, and with a toss of her head, Alice consulted the little watch on her fob. The dashed man had kept her waiting now for nearly an hour and a half. She tapped her foot on the mosaic floor of the corridor – the army headquarters in Cairo used to be a palace, and traces of its noble ancestry shone through the prosaic nature of its usage now. Still, she was inside the HQ at last and she was damned if she was going to leave until she had seen the Colonel. He had refused all previous requests from the foreign press for an interview, and to get this far was a triumph. She must hang on!

She dipped into her handbag and read again the rough copy she had made of the letter to him that, to her surprise, had resulted in his agreeing to meet her. It had been a gamble, of sorts, but it had worked – at least, so far:

...If I may say so, we share certain features in common. You are a member of the fellaheen who has

156

made his way to the top of a profession dominated by Caucasians purely on merit, and I am the only woman currently serving as a foreign correspondent on a British daily newspaper staffed almost completely by men. I hope that you find the comparison neither impertinent nor inappropriate, for I have much personal sympathy with your cause and would like to record your point of view.

I must confess that that sympathy is not shared completely by the British people nor by the main newspapers in England that serve them — including, I am afraid, my own. This is because your viewpoint has never, to my knowledge, been presented fairly to them. This I would like to do through the medium of an interview with you. I cannot promise to convey outright propaganda but I can promise to articulate your views as fairly as I possibly can. Enquiries will show that I have a reputation for empathetic and accurate reporting from conflicts in which Britain has been recently involved in Zululand, Afghanistan and the Transvaal . . .

'The Colonel will see you now, madam.' Alice looked up into the impassive face of a tall Egyptian wearing a *fez*.

She pushed the letter back into her bag, rose and, resisting the temptation to say, 'About time,' murmured instead, 'How kind of him.'

She was ushered into a surprisingly small room, very plainly furnished, containing only one desk and two chairs and dominated by a large man, in a plain uniform, who rose to greet her. Alice looked at him keenly. Now in early middle age, he had the build and appearance of a peasant: tall, broad and running to corpulence, with a large fleshy nose and great sweeping moustaches. It was his eyes, however, that held her. They were black, of course, and they seemed to contain a sadness that spoke of hardship and disappointment. She knew that he had the reputation of being a great orator – the Tories in England, of course, called him a 'rabble-rouser' – and she quickly sensed how he could sway an audience, for he had an air of charismatic command that strangely reminded her of Gladstone. He had joined the army as a boy and had been raised by Ismail Pasha, the previous khedive, to commissioned rank and then colonel, an almost unheard-of progression. Then, as he languished without promotion for years under the present khedive, he had begun to agitate for better conditions for the army and been cashiered for insubordination, only to rejoin again with a short-service commission. His agitation had met with some success in that he had secured an increase in pay for all ranks, and he had gradually become acknowledged as a spokesman for the army, making further demands and not being afraid to march with his regiment on Cairo with drawn sabres to enforce them. Now he was Minister for War and, it was widely assumed, plotting to remove the rule of Turkey and the influence of the Great Powers.

He smiled at her and gestured to one of the two chairs. 'Welcome, miss,' he said, in a voice deep and rich – she could see how he could hold a crowd. 'My English, not good. This man talk for me.'

Alice noticed for the first time that a small Egyptian in a white suit was standing deferentially in a corner. He smiled at her and she nodded to him and then held out her hand to the Colonel. He paused for a moment and then took it, holding it limply. Alice presumed that this was probably the first time he had ever touched a white woman. She sat.

'Please tell the Colonel,' she said to the interpreter, 'how honoured I am that he has agreed to see me. I realise how busy he is and therefore, with his permission, I will begin immediately by asking him some questions.'

Arabi nodded, although Alice felt that his sad eyes assumed a rather apprehensive expression. She took a deep breath. 'Do you wish to depose the Khedive?' she asked.

She sensed the interpreter almost wince at the directness of the question. The Colonel was probably more used to the sycophancy of those beneath and around him and to the more pliant modes of address used by the diplomats and statesmen with whom increasingly he had to deal these days. But he answered it directly enough, talking fluently in Arabic, using his huge shoulders and his hands in emphasis.

No, he replied, the Khedive was his master and he was loyal to him and to the Turkish empire, of which Egypt would forever be a part. Similarly, he did not wish the removal of British and French influence in Egypt. It had been proved that their financial expertise was necessary for the continued economic growth of his country. British residents, in particular, had nothing to fear from him.

Why, then, was the country in a state of unrest and near revolt, with foreigners being jostled in the streets? Ah, that was because the justified demands of the people were not being met and, regrettably, some of the ordinary people blamed high taxation on foreign demands. A new constitution was needed that would give all Egyptians more say in their affairs, and the army needed to be strengthened by the promotion of more people, like himself, from the *fellaheen* class so that it could be more representative.

And so it went on. As Alice asked her questions and laboriously wrote down the answers – oh, how she wished she had mastered shorthand! – she became increasingly aware that she was dealing with a man who was probably sincere in his radical view of the need for greater liberalisation of the Egyptian people but who would stop at nothing to get it, including force, once he had moulded the army to his satisfaction. He was, after all, a soldier. Was he being duplicitous in some of his more contradictory answers, or was he merely displaying the ingenuousness of the peasant? Difficult to tell. A strange and not unlikeable man on the surface, but also a potentially dangerous one.

She ended the interview, as she had begun it, with a direct question. The British government had bought the Egyptian shares in the Suez Canal and was now the majority shareholder. Would Arabi attempt to regain the Canal by force if present negotiations between the Egyptian government and its Turkish overlords failed?

The big man smiled. Of course not. Except under certain conditions, which were highly unlikely to arise. What conditions? Ah, only if an attack was launched on his country by the foreign powers, Britain and France. Then the smile disappeared. He had just heard that a joint British and French fleet had arrived and anchored off Alexandria. This seemed to him to be a gratuitous attempt to put pressure on the Egyptian government to resist the legitimate demands of the people. He would shortly journey to Alexandria to attempt to defuse any misunderstanding there. But he was certain that there would be no war. He knew that Mr

Gladstone, the British Prime Minister, had long argued against any interference by Britain in the domestic affairs of other nations, and he could not believe that such an honest and distinguished statesman would change his policy now. And with that, he held out his hand again – gripping hers more confidently this time – and indicated that the interview was at an end.

Alice took an open carriage back to Shepheards Hotel, and despite the strange noise and colour of Cairo all about her – scenes that would normally have delighted and intrigued her – she sat frowning as she went through her infuriatingly inadequate notes and attempted to digest what Arabi had said. In fact, it seemed he had told her nothing particularly new, nothing that had not been written in dozens of newspapers already and analysed so many times. Yet she had *met* him and would be able, under her author- itative if anonymous byline, 'by our Special Correspondent in Cairo', to give her balanced view of the man by reporting his words and, er, yes, adding just a touch of colour. Then there was that sting in Arabi's tale: the threat of reprisals against the Canal should there be an invasion. Now *that* was something he had not said before. She put her pencil to her teeth and looked out on the multicoloured streets of Cairo and grinned. On only her second day in Egypt she had a – what was it the Americans were now calling an exclusive? Ah yes. Scoop. She now had a scoop after all!

Back in the hotel, Alice settled down and wrote her story. Afterwards, she reduced it to cablese, gritting her teeth as she did so because she was not good at this. Then she sat in thought for a moment. What to do next? Stay in Cairo with the rest of the journalistic pack and attempt to keep in touch with events from the centre? Or go to Alexandria? If Arabi was heading there, that was where events would be, not least because the British and French had sent squadrons to intimidate the Egyptians. She frowned. How stupid and typically jingoistic of the British to do this! Palmerston had been dead for years, but his adage of 'if in doubt, send a gunboat' lived on. The other reason for heading north was that Alex would almost certainly be the point of entry for Wolseley, if he did invade, and she would be on the spot. Yes, she decided. She would go to Alexandria and leave the other plodding scribblers behind here in Cairo. She added a postcript to Cornford to this effect in her cable.

Waiting for her carriage on the terrace of Shepheards, Alice resolved to go to the offices of Thomas Cook to send her cable. In these troubled times, she would rather trust them than the Egyptian post office. And, of course, she could ask them to arrange her travel north to Alexandria.

At the travel agent's office, she was served by a rather unctuous little man wearing spectacles and a celluloid collar. He read through her cable first, before counting the words, which she thought odd, but handled it expeditiously enough. He could not help her, however, with the journey north.

'I am sorry, madam,' he said, 'but it is not possible to book railway tickets to Alexandria. Colonel Arabi has forbidden civilian traffic from going to that city until further notice.'

'How very inconvenient.' Alice frowned. 'But there must be some other way to go north. I know that the Nile can only take me as far as Desouk. Can you arrange transport for me by road? I can pay whatever is involved.'

The clerk shook his head. 'I am afraid not. The company cannot attempt to contravene the Colonel's orders.'

'But the man is not the Khedive yet, is he? Is Egypt a police state now?'

The clerk gave a mirthless smile and Alice had the impression that he was rather enjoying being obstructive. 'I am sorry, madam, but I am afraid that for the time being, the company cannot help you.'

Back at Shepheards, she immediately singled out Mustapha, the Turk who was the hotel's urbane concierge. On her arrival two days earlier, Alice had followed her invariable practice of making herself known to this most important member of the hotel's staff and asking him to look after her as best he could during her stay. She was, she explained, a journalist with the United Kingdom's greatest newspaper, and it was quite possible that she would need his help. She sugared the conversation with her sweetest smile and a golden sovereign. Now it was time to redeem his pledge of support.

Reproducing the smile, Alice leaned across the reception desk and asked, 'Mustapha, is it true that you are all-powerful?'

The concierge gave his elegant little bow and with only a flicker of a smile replied, 'Of course, madam. Everyone considers that to be true, except my wife, of course.'

'How sad. But now I need your help. I understand that all civilian travel to Alexandria – at least conventional travel – is temporarily suspended by order of Colonel Arabi.'

He inclined his head. 'I believe that is true, madam.'

'But Mustapha, I need to go there urgently. Can you arrange for me to do so?' She slipped three sovereigns across the desktop.

The sovereigns disappeared as if by magic. 'I will do my best, madam, but you may have to wait a little. Ah, one other point. Do you mind if the travel is, what shall I say, a little uncomfortable?'

'Not at all. Just get me to Alexandria, Mustapha.'

'Very well, madam. Thank you, madam.'

But it seemed that Mustapha was indeed all-powerful, for the very next day Alice found herself sitting astride a rather scruffy pony outside the walls of Cairo, waiting to fall into line with a mixed string of load-bearing camels and donkeys heading north towards Alexandria, some hundred and forty miles away. She was the only woman in the caravan, and also the only European. The latter was a source of relief to her rather than concern, for she harboured a worry that her competitors might have resorted to the same device to reach the northern city. But she did not wish to draw attention to herself and had therefore eschewed obviously European clothing for the journey and now wore androgynous pantaloons, the *esharp* and *burnous*. If, as seemed likely, they had to pass through the lines of the Egyptian army just south of the city, it was as well to be as inconspicuous as possible. It would be galling to be turned back after coming so far.

The road between the two cities, while unmetalled, of course, was well trammelled and by no means as difficult as crossing the northern desert. The discomfort that Mustapha had referred to, however, quickly proved to be an understatement. The Muslim camel drivers paid virtually no attention to her and she was left to fend for herself. The terrain was a mixture of soft sand and hard gravel, and as the sun beat down on her small beast, she was often forced to dismount and lead him and the swarms of flies that beset them all. Her biggest problem, however, proved to be the donkey that trailed behind carrying her small tent, bedding and other baggage. He quickly proved to have his own agenda, and terrified of being left behind, she was forced to beat him and pull his ears several times a day to persuade him to keep up with the cavalcade.

Nevertheless, the strange rhythm of desert travel began to impose upon her a sense of tranquillity that she had not experienced for some years. For many miles at first the road followed the railway and the Nile itself, and she marvelled at the new birdlife the river introduced to her: ibises, cranes, black kingfishers, hoopoes and white hawks. She glimpsed white lanteen sails, saw camels pulling primitive ploughs, and, once, a camel and an ox incongruously yoked together, with the half-naked *fellah* behind struggling to control the unequal pull on the plough. Sometimes they passed a small village and she was able to buy eggs, a chicken or two and native bread made of Indian corn and *durra*. When the cavalcade camped for the night, she busied herself making her own fire, brewing coffee and cooking the one good meal of the day. If the days were hot, then the nights were often toe-numbingly cold, and the panoply of stars revealed after sunset entranced her. She took to rolling herself in her blankets and sleeping out of doors – the desert's tranquillity allayed any fears – and attempting to identify the main stars that she remembered: Polaris to the north; Sirius, the dog star, to the east, hunting at the heels of Orion; and, if she awoke before dawn, Venus, the morning star.

If tracing the stars did not bring on sleep, then she would lie wide-eyed, her thoughts tumbling about like garments in a washtub. She tried to focus on Ralph, her husband, her committed partner in life. Would he have sailed by now? She had left him waiting for Wolseley's call, practising shooting with his revolver and sabre sweeps from the saddle as he attempted to control the horse with his hook. At least he would be happier now, knowing that he *would* be called and that he could resume the life he loved. And perhaps it would take his mind off the nagging urgency of producing an heir. And Simon . . . Ah, Simon! No, no, she would not go down that route.

Alice had managed to establish a friendship of a kind with a camel driver who could speak some English. It was he, about three-quarters of the way along the route, who told her of rumours that the English ships had fired on Alexandria and that the town was ablaze. The news shattered whatever peace of mind she had managed to acquire on the journey and set her brain seething with frustration. Here was the biggest news story in Africa and, although only a few miles from it, she could not report it. She was like a fly caught in amber, out on this seemingly endless road, condemned to travel at a snail's pace, away from the action. But there was little she could do about it, for although the road seemed well marked, there were deviations that tempted the ignorant and she dreaded getting lost. In any case, there was little hope that her pony and lethargic donkey could be made to travel faster. She must master her impatience.

Three days later, the party began to meet patrols of Egyptian soldiers, and then passed through fortified lines of some sophistication: trenches and gun emplacements backed by rows of tents. Keeping her head down and her fair hair well tucked away behind the *esharp*, Alice made surreptitious notes. This was a large and seemingly formidable army, straddling the main route to Cairo at Kafr Dewar, just before the road followed the narrow isthmus across Lake Mareotis to the coast and then swung to the west and Alexandria, fifteen miles away. If Arabi had abandoned the city itself, then this was obviously where he was preparing to make his stand. It was, she could see, a strong position indeed.

As they crossed the lake via the isthmus, she could make out distant traces of smoke still rising from the west and she somehow managed to prod and cajole her mule to make her way towards the head of the convoy. There she met her English-speaking friend.

'Are Egyptian troops still in Alexandria?' she asked.

'No, missy. Soldiers come back to here and by railway.'

'But is there fighting in the city?'

'I do not know, miss.'

She frowned. If the Egyptian soldiers had gone, surely British sailors and marines would have been landed to keep the peace and to extinguish the fires? Why, then, was smoke still curling up? She decided to give up the questioning and allowed her pony to fall back a little, although maintaining her new position at the head of the column. She really *must* be patient.

The caravan reached the walls of the city as dusk was beginning to fall and wound its way through the native quarter at the edge of the town. Alice left it there and made her way towards the harbour. It was then she saw the results of the bombardment and the fires that had followed it. She sat on her pony and looked around in awe.

The seaward side of the city looked as though an earthquake had torn it apart. Smoke still rose from the piles of rubble and blackened timber that lined the thoroughfares and marked where substantial houses had once stood. It seemed as though the shells and the conflagrations had followed no consistent pattern, for untouched buildings stood between the demolished houses. Following the little map Mustapha had given her, she made her way towards the European quarter. It was here that the damage was worst. It was clear that fire had been the greatest destroyer here, for the skeletons of the houses remained standing but the walls were smoke-blackened and the remains of the doors lay splintered where they had been thrown. Remnants of furniture were scattered in driveways and on the pavement, and Alice wrote 'looters' in her notebook. More horrifying were the red stains that still marked the roadway and showed where bodies had lain.

Darkness was now descending, and it was with great relief that Alice met a party of blue jackets under the command of a young midshipman who looked all of fifteen years of age.

'Good evening,' she called down from her pony, and pulled off her *esharp* so that her fair hair tumbled down. 'Can you tell me if the Victoria Hotel is still standing?'

The young man's jaw dropped and one of the sailors gave a low whistle. Desert dust still covered Alice, her pony and her donkey, and until she removed her headdress she had looked like a desert trader coming in from the interior to take advantage of the disruption of commercial life in Alexandria to set up a stall amidst the rubble. The transformation brought about by her drawing room voice, the flaxen hair now around her shoulders and the white teeth flashing against the gold of her tan was charismatic.

'Sorry, er, madam,' he said, belatedly saluting her and blushing. 'I don't think so. Most of the hotels have been stormed by the looters and set afire.' His voice sounded as though it had only just broken. He cast a puzzled eye over the pack strapped to the back of her donkey and to the tent, with its poles, lashed to its side. 'Are you looking for accommodation, then, madam?'

'Well, I am very much afraid that is so, if my hotel has burned down.' She gave him her best smile. 'I would be so grateful if you could help in any way. It looks to me as though Alexandria is not the safest of places just now to spend a night out in the open. Do you patrol through the night?'

'No, miss, er, madam. We haven't got the men to do that.' He put a finger to his mouth. 'Perhaps if I took you to the Anglo-Egyptian Bank . . . It is still standing and I know that some people who have lost their homes are sleeping there. Would that help?'

'That would be most kind. Thank you very much, but first tell me, what is your ship?'

'The *Invincible*, the flagship.' He sounded proud.

'Ah, splendid. So Admiral Seymour is flying his flag from her?'

'Yes, madam.'

'Then perhaps you would be so kind, on your return, to give the Admiral this card.' Alice fumbled in the cloth bag hanging from her saddle pommel and extracted a pencil. She scribbled on the back of a card and handed it to the young man. 'Perhaps you would explain how we have met and that

I have ridden overland from Cairo to interview him.' She hoped the Admiral was susceptible to flattery. 'I will take a boat out to the flagship tomorrow at nine o'clock in the hope that he can grant me a few moments. Will you tell him that?'

'Oh yes, mi – madam.'

Surrounded by her new bodyguard of grinning blue jackets, Alice was escorted to the bank, where she bade farewell to her rescuer and was met by a tall, grey-bearded man in soiled white ducks who welcomed her gravely. There was not too much room, he explained, but if she had her own bedroll they could surely find a corner for her on the first floor, and her pony and donkey could be tethered safely at the front, for an all-night watch was being kept in case the mob returned, although the threat now seemed remote, since the sailors had landed and begun putting out the fires and patrolling the streets.

Much as she had been looking forward to a hot bath, a soft bed and a hotel meal, Alice was delighted to join the little community in the bank. She looked round with interest and sympathy at the tattered remnants of the original defenders. They now numbered a little over a dozen; many, she learned, had been able to return to their homes, but those that were left were virtually homeless and were in the process of arranging to leave Alexandria. Alice shared out what remained of her food and, more importantly, her bottle of cognac, and set about picking up invaluable details about the attack on the bank during the terrible hours following the bombardment.

The bearded man, who, it seemed, had become de facto leader of the group following the defection three days earlier of the bank manager, took her through the stages of the ultimatum, the opening of the bombardment and their shelter in the seeming security within the bank's stone walls, the attack by the mob and the defence through the night. It was riveting material for Alice and began to compensate her for the fact that she had not been present herself.

'Of course,' said the bearded man, 'we would have been lost without those three fellows.'

'Oh,' Alice paused, her pencil poised, 'who were they?'

'Never did find out. Mysterious lot. All dressed very convincingly as Arabs but they were really two Englishmen and a little Egyptian. Actually, it was only one Englishman, because the other was Welsh.' The man blew out his cheeks. 'Gad, they were fighters, the three of them! The English chappie organised the defence completely. Gave us backbone, got the women boiling water so that we could tip it down on the Arabs. And the little Welshman – strong as a bull, he was, and a crack shot. My word, they were splendid chaps. Even the Egyptian was swingin' about with a sword. Saved us, I'll tell you. Put the guts back into us.'

A slow flush had crept over Alice's face as she listened, forgetting even to take a note. Eventually she said, very quietly, 'You obviously didn't get their names, but can you describe them?'

The bearded man pursed his lips as he concentrated. 'The leader was quite a young chap, probably ex-army because he knew what he was doing. Strange face. Broken nose, I think. The Welshman had a bristling black moustache, and though he was much smaller, he had shoulders as broad as a barn door. The little Egyptian . . .'

'No, don't worry about him. Do you know where they came from or where they might be now?'

'Sorry, I don't have the faintest idea, I'm afraid. They did come back in the early morning to see if we were all right, but I haven't seen hair or hide of them since. Pity. They should all get a medal.'

'Thank you,' said Alice. 'You have been most helpful. I think I will retire now. It's been a long day.'

Alice crept back to her corner and found that her hand was shaking as she poured into the bottle cap what was left of her brandy. Simon and 352! It had to be. They were here! – or, at least, they had been in the city a few days ago. It could only be them: the young one with the broken nose taking charge of the defence; the Welshman with the barn-door shoulders. There could not be such a distinctive pair anywhere else in the world. She slipped into her bedroll and lay there, hugging herself with joy. Oh, how she prayed that they had not left Alex! The thought of seeing Simon again – and genuinely by accident, without her losing pride or respectability by seeking him out – sent a shiver down her spine. Then she frowned and knuckled away the moistness that had crept into her eyes. This would never do. She was a married woman and she would not, she *must not*, go back on the pledge that she had made so many months ago. No. There would be no question of that. But it would be *so* good to see them both again. Of course it would. She settled herself down to sleep and the aches in her bones soon prompted a dream that she was riding on a camel across a stone-hard desert, towards a distant church in an oasis where Simon was waiting to marry her.

At eight thirty the next morning, Alice made her way down to the inner harbour and found that life there was beginning to re-emerge after the hostilities. A boatman agreed to take her out to the *Invincible*, and she sat in the stern making notes as she passed each of the ironclads. The *Alexandra*, the *Penelope*, the *Monarch*, the *Superb*, the *Temeraire*, the *Sultan* and the *Invincible* all seemed to have come through the gun battle with the shore batteries comparatively unharmed, although there were gashes on their super-structures and indentations on their hulls where the thick armour plating had resisted the Egyptian shells. The smaller gunboats showed more evidence of the fight, but she had little time to take further notes, for the boat was now approaching the flagship's companionway.

Alice had dressed as well as she could for the interview with the Admiral, for she had discovered many months ago when first she had arrived on the overwhelmingly masculine scene at Cape Town that her appearance was a distinct asset when it came to opening doors with the military. But the bank had provided no facilities, of course, to enable her to clean or press the few garments she had been able to roll into her pack on the donkey. Nevertheless, she had made an effort. Her long hair had been tied back with a soft wisp of silk, and a matching shirt of green cotton, looking fresh in the morning sun, if a little wrinkled, was tucked into her jodhpurs. As a mark of professional intent, she wore her long riding boots, from which she had managed to wipe much of the desert sand. She smiled radiantly up at the startled face that appeared at the top of the gangway.

'Permission to come aboard, please? I have an appointment with the Admiral.'

The face above broke into a grin. 'I should rather say so, miss. Very much so. Come aboard.'

She had half expected to be turned away by the Admiral, for she had read somewhere before setting out that he was a gruff sea dog of the old order and she doubted if he would take kindly to being bearded without invitation in his lair by a woman journalist. She had written down his full name: Vice Admiral Sir Frederick Beauchamp Paget Seymour. Looking at it as she dressed that morning, her radical lip had curled. The very name sounded like a roll call of privilege. In fact, however, the Admiral proved to be charm personified. Perhaps the hyperbolic flattery had worked. It wouldn't have been the first time.

'Sit down, dear lady,' Seymour said as she was ushered into his day cabin. His face positively beamed behind his fearsome whiskers. 'This is an unexpected pleasure.' He looked at the card in his hand. 'The *Morning Post*, indeed. My daily reading when I am at home. And yes, I have heard of you. You seem to have established quite a reputation in a short time. But I am amazed to find you here. No British journalists came out with my squadron, and as far as I know, there were none in Alex when this . . . this mess began.'

Alice smiled. As an expert in the field, she knew flattery when she heard it. 'No, Sir Frederick. As I expect you know, Colonel Arabi has closed down the rail route to Cairo, so I came by horseback, with a camel train.' She looked down and then back up at him through her eyelashes. 'I came alone and it was a question of roughing it. That is why I look such an awful mess, I'm afraid.'

'How intrepid of you! But goodness, you look perfectly delightful to me, madam. Now, how do you take your tea?'

They chatted inconsequentially and half flirted as they took tea and some excellent muffins, both of which Alice accepted with gratitude, for she had had no breakfast. Then she began gently probing the Admiral, starting uncontentiously by asking him about the damage inflicted on his ships by the shore batteries and the effect that his guns, in turn, had had on them. She learned that he had taken the decision to issue the ultimatum when his searchlights had shown that, despite assurances, the Egyptians were expanding their defences and he felt that his squadron was under threat.

'Perhaps,' she said ingenuously, her eyes wide, 'they felt that your squadron, with all these magnificent ironclads anchored out here off the port with their huge guns, was threatening *them*.'

'What?' Seymour looked at her sharply, but the question seemed to have been asked in all innocence. 'Good lord, no. They knew that we were just there to protect British nationals in case trouble broke out.'

'I see.' Alice sucked her pencil, rather like a schoolgirl attempting to find her way through a difficult problem of mathematics. 'But why, then, did the French squadron sail away when you issued the ultimatum? Didn't they have nationals to protect? I understood that the two powers were supposed to work in concert.'

'Good lord. You know what the French are like. They're off at the first sniff of grapeshot.'

'Ah yes. The French . . .' She left unsaid her obvious agreement with him on the question of France's typical perfidiousness. 'Sir Frederick, it must have been quite brave of you to fire first. Did you have orders from the Admiralty to do so?'

'What?' The great eyebrows came down. 'No. Had full

powers granted to me here to do what was necessary to protect my fleet.'

Alice put down her pencil and, tilting her head on one side, gave him her sweetest smile. 'So I suppose we are at war with Egypt now, then, Admiral. Is that so?'

'At war . . . no. Well, not exactly. No declaration has been made. No. Of course we're not at war. Well, not yet, anyway. Soon will be, though. Wolseley's on his way.'

'Ah yes, of course.' Damn! This must have been announced while she was on the road with those blasted camels. 'General Wolseley and I are old friends. When, pray, is he due?'

'Pretty soon now. But General Sir Archibald Alison will be here any day with an advance force from Cyprus.'

'Then we *are* at war with Egypt, and so, presumably, with the Turkish empire?'

'No, dammit. Ah, I beg your pardon. You must excuse the quarterdeck language. No. We shall be invading to put down this revolt by Arabi and restore the Khedive, who reigns, of course, on behalf of Turkey, to his throne. And also, naturally, to protect our main investment here, the Suez Canal, and the many British who are working and living in Egypt. We will invade to restore order. We shall not be attacking the Egyptian nation.'

It was clear that Sir Frederick was uneasy on these issues, so Alice led the conversation back to the bombardment, the attack on the European quarter by the mob and the subsequent looting. The Admiral had to admit that the damage and loss of life were regrettable. It was estimated that between fifty and a hundred Europeans had been killed. He had been unable to land a force to subdue the rioting and begin clearing up the damage until he had been reliably informed that Arabi's considerable army had retreated from the city.

Alice took a deep breath. Had the Admiral heard of two Britons who had worked through the night of the rioting, saving the lives of dozens of Europeans who were under attack? They were, she had heard, dressed in Arab clothing.

This time the eyebrows rose. 'Two of 'em, you say? No. Not heard a thing.'

'One of them is an ex-British officer, I understand. Quite slim, with a broken nose.'

'Ah, *that* feller! Yes. Came on board nearly two weeks ago, on his own, though. Said he was working for the AG – Sir Garnet, don't you know – and asked me to pass on a signal to him. I did so, but under protest.' He scowled. 'He was of some small service in terms of providing information from the shore, but he seemed an arrogant young chap to me. However, if he's been some use during the rioting, then good for him.'

'I don't suppose, Admiral, that you would know where I could contact him?'

'No idea. I understand that he had previously been cabling Wolseley via Cook's office, so you might try them. Near the harbour. Anyone will direct you. Why do you want to track him down?'

Alice felt a blush coming on and looked down. 'Oh, it's just that I thought he might make good copy.' She returned her gaze to the old seaman and smiled. 'Now I really must go and let you get on with your important work. Thank you very much indeed. You have been very helpful. Ah, one more thing. I must find a hotel. Are there any left standing?'

'I think so. My major of marines should know.'

A few minutes later, Alice was being ferried back to the shore in the stern of the Admiral's steam pinnace, escorted by three blue jackets and the same young midshipman, now exuding a proprietorial air. They took her to a modest hotel in the European district, blessedly untouched by either the shelling or the mob, where she was able to hire a bedroom and a small sitting room in which to work. Here she began drafting her cable to the *Post*. She led it with her interview with Seymour, confirming that he had ordered the bombardment on his own initiative and that up to one hundred Europeans were thought to have died during the shelling and the consequent rioting. She then developed the story into a colour piece on the devastation caused and the terror unleashed when the mob took to the streets, going into detail on the siege of the bank and the intervention of the three unknown men who had organised the defence and then disappeared. On completion, Alice read it through with satisfaction. It was a good piece: a mixture of hard news and feature-style colour. Had she been hard on the Admiral? She went back to the beginning and checked. No. She had let the man's arrogance be reflected in his own words. Let the Tory sub-editors tamper with this at their peril!

Alice put her copy into her bag, tied back her hair and strode down the stairs. At the reception desk a small man who was somehow familiar was just leaving. He caught her eye for a second, then bent his head and hurried away. She paused on the bottom step and frowned. Now, who *was* that? She had caught a glimpse of spectacles and a small moustache. Shaking her head in annoyance, she dismissed the problem and asked the clerk to direct her to the offices of

Thomas Cook. Thanking him, she walked to the door, then stopped and turned back.

'That man who just left,' she said. 'I am sure I know him. Do you mind telling me his name?'

'Ah,' the clerk smiled, 'that was Mr George from Cairo, madam. He is a regular guest here. An English gentleman.'

'I see.' Alice shook her head. 'I don't know him. I must have been mistaken.'

'He is employed by Thomas Cook in Cairo,' the clerk offered helpfully.

'Ah, of course. Yes. Thank you. That's where I met him.' She smiled her gratitude, glad to have the puzzle solved. He was the unctuous clerk at the desk who had seemed happy to be negative. Then the smile was replaced by a frown. George had told her that Arabi had stopped all non-military train travel between Cairo and Alexandria. She had had this conversation with him some nine days ago in Cairo. How, then, had he travelled to Alex?

She turned back to the desk. 'Is it now possible to travel by train from and to Cairo? Has the track been opened?'

'No, madam. It has been closed for about two weeks and, given the circumstances, I am afraid it will remain closed for some time to come now.'

'I see.' She summoned up her radiant smile. 'I am so sorry that I missed Mr George. Has he been here long and is he staying on for a few more days, do you know?'

'He has been with us for about a week, but he has just left us rather unexpectedly, I am afraid. I do not know his destination but perhaps the people at Cook's office here can help you, madam.'

'Yes, of course. I will ask them.' This minor mystery

deepened. So Mr George could not have travelled by train – unless, of course, he was allowed to do so by the military, and that seemed most unlikely. He could perhaps have come up the Nile to Rosetta and then travelled along the coast westwards, or even disembarked at Desouk and travelled overland. But she knew those routes to be slow and difficult. Obviously he had come along the same road that she had travelled. Yet he had been here a week. He could not possibly have come overland all the way within three days! She shook her head and tried to put the mystery of the phantom Mr George out of her mind. She had far more important things to think about.

Nevertheless, after she had handed over her cable at the office of Thomas Cook, had her words counted and paid the cost of transmission, she enquired of the genial employee there if Mr George was within.

'Who, miss? Old Georgie of our Cairo office? No. He's in Cairo. Haven't seen him for some six months, when I last went down the line. He's not here, miss, that's for sure.'

'I see. Thank you.' Well, that was that. Perhaps there were two Mr Georges. Anyway, it was of no importance. She smiled her gratitude and turned towards the door. There, she bumped into a slim young Arab man. His eyes were a melancholy brown and he had a broken nose.

'Simon!' she gasped. And burst into tears.

Chapter 10

Simon's jaw dropped in amazement and instinctively he started forward to put his arms around her. Then he stepped back and coughed. 'Alice, he said, 'what on earth ... You were the last person I expected to see in this place.'

'I am so sorry.' Alice fumbled for her handkerchief. 'I just ... so sorry ... I am so glad to see you. Oh dear, please forgive me.' She turned away and put the handkerchief to her eyes.

'My dear, dear ...' he began, and then coughed again. 'Here. Take my handkerchief.'

She accepted it, dabbed at her eyes and then blew her nose. She smiled at him through her tears. 'I must look a mess. I am sorry, and now I've ruined your handkerchief. Let me keep it and I shall wash it and return it.'

'No. There's no need. Just keep it.'

They stood awkwardly in the doorway of Cook's and an uneasy silence descended on them. Simon became aware that Mr Roberts was watching them from behind his desk. He took Alice by the arm and led her into the street. 'We can't stand here,' he said. 'Look – I know somewhere in the square where they still serve coffee. Would you care to . . . I mean, do you have the time . . .'

'Oh yes.' Alice dabbed her eyes again. 'Of course. I have just filed my story. Of course I have time. How nice, Simon. Thank you.'

'Story? Ah.' Simon nodded his head. 'I see. You are reporting again, then, for the *Morning Post*?'

'Yes. I arrived yesterday.'

'I see.'

A sudden embarrassment had descended upon them and they walked along in silence, each looking straight ahead and being careful not to touch the other. When they reached the little café, Simon carefully pulled out a chair for Alice in the shade. Without thinking, he ordered two dark, sweet Turkish coffees.

'Oh, I'm sorry, Alice. Is that how you like . . .'

'Yes, thank you. That will be ideal.'

After studying the tablecloth for a moment, Simon forced himself to look into those well-remembered grey eyes. They were still brimming with tears and he fought back the desire to cup her face within his hands.

She smiled. 'How is dear 352? You see, I know he is with you and I have heard about your exploits during the riots. Oh Simon, I am so proud of you.'

He looked away. 'The old devil is fighting fit, very much so, in fact. As usual, he took the lead in the awkward business we have had around here. I presume that you were not in Alex then?'

'No. I only arrived yesterday.'

'Of course. You said so.' He addressed the next question to her right ear. 'And how is your husband? Is he with you?'

The two questions came like a blast of cold air to Alice – a reminder of her position and her duty and a cruelly effective puncturing of any hope she might have cherished that there could be a rapprochement for them. What nonsense. She tightened her lips. 'He is quite well, thank you. At least, I think he is. I left him back in England. He has regained his commission and Wolseley has promised to take him back on the staff. So I expect he will be in the invasion force and, of course,' it was her turn to cough, 'I am looking forward to seeing him again.'

'I see.' Simon sipped his coffee and made a decision. He leaned across the table and took her hand. 'Oh, Alice,' he said. 'This is nonsense. I have thought about you so much. Please tell me all about yourself and your life since we parted. I presume that you have no children? I want to know everything.'

Alice sighed. 'Oh, that's better, Simon. And yes, I have thought of you, too. And no, we have no children.' She allowed her hand to remain in his, and slowly began to recount the details of her life in Norfolk: the work on the estate, the social round, Covington's unrelenting attempts to overcome his disabilities, his efforts to regain his commission, Wolseley's acceptance of him and her consequent successful application to rejoin the *Morning Post*.

'And tell me, Alice. Are you happy?'

She looked at him steadily. 'No, my dear, I am not. But there is nothing, absolutely nothing, I can do about it.'

He stared across the square. 'I see. Yes, of course. I quite understand.' He cleared his throat and smiled at her. But a little of the warmth between them, regained with such difficulty, had suddenly slipped away, and he released her hand. 'Very well. Now tell me everything that has happened since you landed here.'

'Only if you reciprocate.'

'Agreed. You first.'

So they began talking again, quite formally, as though they were merely old friends who had just encountered each other. Alice told him of her interview with Arabi – he was impressed that she had broken through his defences to see him – of her journey overland to Alex, of her stay at the bank and then her interview with Seymour.

'Reactionary old devil.'

'Yes. He thought you were an arrogant young pup.'

They both laughed quite genuinely, and Simon began recounting his recruitment by Wolseley but she stopped him there. 'No,' she said, 'start first with your work for General Pommery-Colley in the Transvaal. I know you were at Majuba.'

He took her through that campaign, his and Jenkins's return to Brecon, his growing discontent at the boredom of life there, Jenkins's magnificent performance in the magistrates' court and the call from Wolseley that had come just in time. Then he traced their adventures in Egypt to the point where they were now waiting in Alexandria for Wolseley to land.

'So you are kicking your heels here?'

'Absolutely. We have filled the time over the last few days scouting Arabi's positions to the south-west. He is well entrenched and, of course, would have to be dislodged before Wolseley could use the railway for his advance south, if he intends to go that way. Wolseley has thanked me for my reports but has given me no idea of his intentions, except that he will sail to Alex and that I must wait for him here because he has plans for me. It sounds as though he will not take my advice about going directly to Port Said and Suez and protecting the Canal before marching over the northern desert to Cairo.'

'Of course.' Alice lowered her voice, stuck out her chin and gave a reasonable imitation of Seymour's gruff tones: 'What right have you, young man, to lecture the General on his strategy?'

They both laughed and the tension was eased a little. 'Oh, Alice,' said Simon. 'It is *so* good to see you again.'

'I feel the same, Simon. We don't have to stay at arm's length, do we?' Then, realising that the question could be interpreted too literally, she flushed and looked embarrassed. 'I don't mean . . . you know . . . that would not be right. But we can see each other, can't we. Please, Simon?'

He smiled at her confusion, but the smile did not quite reach his eyes. 'Of course. Good friends. Let's have some more coffee.' He gestured to the waiter. 'And then I must go back to Cook's. I was about to check to see if I had any further cables from Wolseley.'

'Ah.' Alice leaned across the table towards him. 'That reminds me.' She related the mystery of Mr George. Simon was immediately intrigued, and told her of meeting him in the street and then of their encounter during the looting.

'There is something strange about that little man,' said Alice. 'Even sinister.'

'Oh, I wouldn't say that. There is probably a perfectly good explanation for how he was able to magic himself up to Alex so quickly when the only obvious route was closed to him. After all, he does work for the greatest travel agency in the world and one that practically owns Egypt – well, it did until Arabi came along. If *he* couldn't find a way of getting here speedily, then nobody could.'

Alice frowned. 'I am not sure. There is the strange matter of him saying that he was on company business here when his colleague had not seen him for six months.' Then her face brightened. 'Since we are both virtually kicking our heels until Wolseley arrives, why don't we work together to try and solve the mystery of how Mr George got here and what he's up to?'

Conflicting emotions ran through Simon's brain. Part of him wanted to clutch at any straw that would allow him to be near Alice, to see her regularly and even perhaps to persuade her that she still loved him. The other, more rational part, however, argued that this would be a dishonourable course to pursue and would only lead to more pain and distress.

'What?' he said, disapproval seeping into his voice. 'Conduct a sort of intellectual exercise, a kind of game?'

'Yes, why not?' Enthusiasm had taken hold of Alice. Her eyes were bright and her face glowing. 'We have nothing better to do – I can't see any action breaking out again here that I can write about until the General arrives – and it would be fun. In fact, it could help us both. If the little man has found a way of slipping through Arabi's lines easily, then it could be more than helpful to us both to know about it. What do you think?'

Simon looked into Alice's sparkling eyes and was immediately lost. 'Why not?' He grinned. 'It would be fun to solve the puzzle, as long as we don't harass the little fellow.'

'Of course. Now,' she leaned across the table conspiratorially, 'where do we start?'

Simon thought for a moment. 'I suppose we could begin by checking whether George was telling me the truth when he said that he was acting for a client when I saw him directing the removal of the contents of that house during the riots.'

'How do we do that?'

'Well, I could call on the municipal authorities here and discover the name of the owner . . .'

'And we could check with Cook's to see if the owner is, indeed, a client of the company.'

'Quite so.' Simon thought for a moment. 'On second thoughts, perhaps you had better do that. I can remember the address. Also, see if George has called on the company since first you checked this morning. You say that he left your hotel only today?'

'Yes, about an hour ago.'

'Good, then he might not yet have left the city. I will harness Jenkins and Ahmed and the three of us will split up and see if we can check the main routes out, particularly the way you came in, through Arabi's lines. Perhaps, somehow, he does travel by train and has the military's permission to do so. It is not going to be easy, but there is comparatively little movement in and out of the city now, so it is not so hopeless a task as it might seem.' He frowned. 'In fact, the more I think of it, the more I am beginning to agree with you. There is something strange about the man. What was he carrying when I first saw him up here? And why was he so anxious to slip away and not speak to me? He could not have been more obliging and talkative in Cairo.'

'Yes, and perhaps there could be a story in there for me.'

They exchanged the names of their respective hotels and agreed to meet at the same place at the same time the following day to report progress. As they stood, Alice half leaned forward, offering her cheek to be kissed, but Simon had already turned away.

Jenkins was amazed and delighted when Simon returned and told him of his meeting with Alice, but less than impressed when he heard of the plans they had made to pin down Mr George.

'But bach sir, it will be like looking for a needle in a bleedin' 'aystack,' he growled. 'An' why bother, look you? The bloke's not important to us, is 'e? 'E's got a perfect right to move about the country, 'asn't 'e? This is a nice little billet 'ere. Old Fati's cookin' suits me fine. Why do we 'ave to go poncin' around the town lookin' for a little bloke in a celluloid collar? I just don't understand it, see.'

Simon had to confess that Jenkins had a point, but he attempted to rationalise the 'game'. 'Look,' he said, 'until General Wolseley gets here, we are more or less bottled up in this place. If we can find a quick way out, that could be invaluable to us.'

Jenkins grimaced but did not pursue the argument. Ahmed, on the other hand, was delighted at the prospect of an end to their days of inaction.

'Fatima can help,' he said. 'She know everybody here. She can – what you say? – put out the words, et cetera, et cetera, et cetera. Will it be fighting?' His eyes lit up. 'I should sharpen sword?'

'No – well, perhaps you should. One never knows. By all

means see if Fatima can help us.' He gave Jenkins and Ahmed a very detailed description of Mr George and handed the latter three gold sovereigns for Fatima to offer as a reward to anyone who could lead them to the clerk. Then the three of them set out.

It proved to be a most frustrating day. There were, of course, many exits from the city, but only two main routes: one along the coastal road to Rosetta in the east, and the other to the south-east, by the isthmus across Lake Mareotis, to where Arabi's lines crossed the railway. Ahmed took the first and Simon and Jenkins the second. It was true that traffic in and out of the city had been reduced since the bombardment and the riots, particularly on the exit policed by Simon and Jenkins. But there were sufficient pedestrians for it to be difficult to distinguish between small, genuine Arabs and a particular Englishman in Arab dress. The three gathered together later that evening in Fatima's kitchen to report failure. Even Fatima confessed that she and her informants knew nothing of a little foreigner who might meet George's description.

Their failure, however, did little to depress Simon, for he was elated at the thought of meeting Alice again the next morning. It was, after all, only a game they were playing.

He arrived early for the rendezvous and so was not surprised to find that Alice had not yet arrived. He ordered coffee for them both and sat idly speculating on the plans that Wolseley might have for him. Most likely out into the desert to wheel around Arabi's lines to see what sort of reserves the Egyptian had down the line; or perhaps a spot of sabotage on the railway line behind the Colonel, to prevent him retreating by rail towards Cairo? That would be fun.

The coffee arrived, and it was as he took his first sip that he saw the envelope lying on the table, secured and partly obscured by the ashtray. He picked it up. It was addressed to him in a firm, schoolmasterly hand – a clerk's hand. The letter inside read:

> Dear Sir,
>
> I am afraid that your lady friend will not be able to meet you this morning, because she has, it seems, encountered a little trouble.
>
> If you wish to see her again, then come tonight to 23a Ismail Street at 8 p.m. You will come alone and unarmed. If you inform the authorities, then she will be shot. You are under constant watch.
>
> G. George.

Simon's mouth went dry and he instinctively looked around him. There were several couples taking morning coffee at the table but they seemed innocuous enough and quite uninterested in him. Conventionally dressed Egyptians and one or two desert Arabs ambled by. He looked up at the houses fronting on to the square. Most of them had shutters across or blinds down to keep out the flies and the heat, but dozens of eyes could be observing him from behind them. He licked his lips and put his hand to his brow. This was no longer a game. Who was George, and what was he up to? Was he an Arabi spy? Yes, most likely. Then Simon's heart sank further. If so, then he was in a perfect position at Cook's in Cairo to report to his master on the contents of all cables – including Simon's own – that passed across his desk.

But why capture Alice? There was no obvious reason why Arabi would want to harm her.

His mind in turmoil, he paid for the coffees – one of them, alas, untouched – and stood for a moment undecided. Yes, his first point of call must be the offices of Thomas Cook, here in Alexandria, to talk to Mr Roberts. But wait. Was Roberts in on the game? He conjured up the picture of the tall, stout ex-soldier, with his waxed moustache and stolid Englishness, and shook his head. He was poles apart from the unctuous Mr George. He had served with Wolseley and, for God's sake, not *everybody* could be a spy! Nevertheless, he decided that he would not confide in Roberts. Not yet, anyway.

Roberts was not on duty at the desk, for once, but was soon fetched.

'Nothing for you, sir, I'm afraid,' he said, like the village postmaster at Simon's home outside Brecon.

'Thank you, Mr Roberts. Tell me, you may remember that I met a lady here yesterday – an old friend?'

A broad grin spread under the waxed moustache. 'Oh yes, sir. She seemed a bit upset at first, but I'm sure you soon cheered her up.'

Simon forced a grin in return. 'Yes, indeed. But I half promised to meet her here this morning. Has she called in yet, do you know?'

'No, sir, and I've been on the desk until a couple of seconds ago. She did come back yesterday, though, in the afternoon. Asking about a Mr Ahmed Kamul, to see if he was a client of ours. I had to tell her I'd never heard of him. Oh, and she also wanted to know if Mr George from our Cairo office had been in since her previous visit. Blimey, I don't know what old Georgie's done to deserve all this attention, I'm sure.'

'And *has* Mr George been into the office?'

'Lumme, now you're doin' it. No. Haven't seen him for six months. He rarely comes to Alex.'

'Thank you, Mr Roberts. Sorry to be a nuisance, but I wonder whether I could use your toilet?'

'Of course, sir.' He lifted up the flap on the desk and pointed. 'Down that corridor and you'll find it on the right, by the back entrance.'

'That's very kind of you.'

Simon walked to the door of the lavatory, glanced behind him to ensure that no one could see him and then opened the door giving on to a yard at the back of the offices. It was deserted and he was able to slip through another gate to find himself in a back street behind the office. He doubled along it and took a circuitous route back to the hotel, frequently turning suddenly up side streets to ensure that he was not being followed. There was no obvious reason for him to have been watched before he met Alice and she began her enquiries, and so hopefully George would not know where he was staying. If he did, then he would surely have delivered the note to the hotel. In turn that meant, equally hopefully, that he would not know of the existence of Jenkins and Ahmed, for neither of them had accompanied him to the Cook offices. He had also been alone when he met George the first time in the street in Alexandria, and when he encountered him during the riots, there were sufficient Arabs milling around for 352 and Ahmed not to be noticed. Hopefully . . .

On his return to the hotel, he summoned a council of war

with the others. Jenkins, of course, was all for storming 23a Ismail Street. Ahmed remained quiet, fingering his moustache.

'No,' said Simon, 'we cannot take the risk that they will carry out the threat to harm Alice. I must go alone. Perhaps I can buy her release.'

'Yes,' muttered Jenkins, 'but p'raps it's you they want. 'Ave you thought of that?'

'Yes, I have. If George is in the pay of Arabi, then they could well want me as a spy and attempt to get me to tell them all I know of Wolseley's intentions. After all, George will have seen my original cable from Cairo and I don't suppose that code would be difficult to decipher, dammit.' He turned to Ahmed. 'Would you ask Fatima where this address is and in what sort of area. I presume it will be in the native quarter. Ask her if, by some chance, she knows who lives there or anyone who lives nearby.'

'Of course.' The little man looked up with fire in his eyes. 'It is a fighting evening all right, I think. Yes?'

'Well, I do hope not. We shall have to see.'

Simon and Jenkins fell silent for a moment. Then Jenkins spoke. 'You know, bach sir,' he said, 'the more I think about this, the more I don't like it. This George bloke obviously lied to you when we met 'im unloading stuff from that 'ouse, see, because Miss Alice found that out when she checked at the travel place. It's pretty obvious, then, that 'e's one of old Arabi's lot an' 'e will want to know what you know, like – an' that could be messy, bach.'

They stared at each other, and a small, unconscious shiver ran through Simon. Jenkins was talking about torture, of course, and Simon's mind went back to red-hot coals in a high mountain pass in the Hindu Kush. He shook his head to clear the memory.

'I don't intend to let them torture me, 352,' he said. 'I intend to free Alice – and with your help. Now, I've got a plan of sorts and I will explain it when Ahmed returns.'

The little Egyptian was back within minutes. 'Yes,' he said, 'place is in native quarter. Teemings with peoples. Egyptian peoples, that is. She don't know nothing of peoples there. Sorry.'

'Never mind. This is what we will do. I am not sure whether they know of your existence or where we are staying. I hope not, but we must take precautions. I will leave well before the time and find this place. You will leave the hotel by the back door and through the garden, exactly three minutes after me. We will plan the route so that you know where I am going. It might be that 23a is just a first port of call, to put off any people, like you, covering me. If that is so, then I will try and leave a clue about the next destination.'

Jenkins was clearly unimpressed. 'Then what?'

Simon sighed. The thought of Alice in the hands of that strange, obviously ruthless man made his mouth go dry and fuddled his thoughts. He tried to concentrate. 'I am afraid we must play it intuitively to some extent . . .'

'What does that mean when it's at 'ome?'

'React to circumstances as they occur, but the basic plan is this. I will follow their instructions and give myself up, so to speak. I am sure it is me they want, so I will try and buy Alice's freedom. I estimate that this will take about ten minutes. Follow me to wherever I go, taking care not to be seen, and then hide outside for ten minutes. If Alice is not released within that time, it means that my negotiations have failed and we must use force, although,' he frowned and shook his head, 'I hate taking that risk, with Alice in their hands.'

'What sort of force? Just blast in?'

'Not quite. You, 352, see if there is a back entrance. If, as Fatima says, this place is in the native district, then it won't be a grand stone edifice, so you should be able to get round the back. Ahmed, give 352 three minutes to do this – do you have a watch?'

Ahmed, his eyes bright, nodded.

'Good. Give him three minutes and then make a hell of a row at the front, knocking hard at the door and shouting in Arabic that you are the police. Take one of the Colts – you have the other, 352 – and if the door is not opened right away, shoot the lock away, but do not enter. Do you understand: *do not enter.*'

'Understand. Do not enter. Hold back, yes?'

'Exactly. Because they might shoot you as you go in. Wait until you hear Jenkins firing and creating a diversion. Then, once you are in, start shooting and create all hell. But Ahmed, be careful when you fire that pistol. I don't want Alice hurt. Now, 352, if you have not been able to get into this place quietly by the time you hear the commotion at the front, then you shoot your way in at the back, through a door or a window. Once in, shoot to kill. Understood?'

'An' what will you be doin' all this time, without a gun to your name?'

Simon gave a weary grin. 'To be honest, I don't bloody well know. But I won't be completely unarmed. I can't take a revolver because they will undoubtedly search me, but give me that knife that you're so good with and I will tuck it inside the top of my boot and hope they don't find it in the search. With you two coming in from different directions, there should be enough noise and confusion for me to grab Alice, at least, and put her out of harm's way.'

There was a moment's silence as the other two considered the plan. Ahmed's eyes showed that he considered it an excellent idea, but Jenkins's face was gloomy. 'What if we lose you some'ow? 'Ow will we know where they've taken you to?'

'I've thought of that. I'll take a couple of pocketfuls of rice and try and leave a trail. Just watch for it.'

Jenkins sniffed. 'All right, bach sir. But, with great respect, I 'ave to say I don't think it's one of your better ideas.'

'I agree, but can you think of a better one?'

'No, but that's not my department, you know that.' Then he grinned slowly. 'But, bach, by God we'll do it. We'll get that lass out of there. Don't you worry.'

They spent the remaining hours in their various ways. Jenkins showed Ahmed how to load the Colt and pull back the hammer with his thumb, and then he sharpened his fearsome knife. The little Egyptian similarly honed his sword, from which he would not be parted. Simon wrote a letter for General Wolseley, explaining all that had happened, and asked Fatima to have it delivered to the Admiral if he did not return. He also penned a very short letter to his parents and left that too in Fatima's care. Then he studied a rudimentary map that Ahmed had procured and found that Ismail Street was only some twenty minutes' walk away. He memorised his route there. Jenkins and he then changed into Arab dress and Simon carefully tucked the Welshman's long knife down into his riding boot.

'Now you remember,' said Jenkins, 'if you do get into a knife fight . . .'

'I know. Watch his eyes.'

'Absolutely. Don't watch his knife, watch 'is eyes. They will almost certainly tell you what 'e's goin' to do.'

'Very good, sir.'

They grinned at each other, gripped each other's shoulders and shook hands. Then Simon set out alone, through the darkened streets, his fingers nervously sifting through the rice in the pockets of his *burnous*. It was the longest, most frightening walk of his life.

He found 23a Ismail Street well enough. It was not a residence, just a small shed next door to a wooden house that seemed to be unoccupied. As he half expected, there was a note pinned to the door:

Dear Sir, (what ridiculous formality!)

Walk further along Ismail Street and take first right into Abdullah Row. Knock on number 17. Bring this note with you. Your every move is being watched.

G. George.

Simon made a great show of pocketing the note and took advantage of the action to grab a handful of rice. He looked around him. There was no one, absolutely no one to be seen. The 'teemings of peoples' that Ahmed had talked about were either a figment of Fatima's imagination or else everyone was indoors, watching him. He turned around to scan the street the way he had come but there was no sign of Jenkins or

Ahmed. He began walking slowly along Ismail Street, dribbling the grains of rice as he went, his heart in his mouth. It was not so much the obvious presence of danger that made his heart beat faster and his mouth taste of sandpaper. It was the eerie emptiness and silence that hung over the street, like a blanket of humidity, a cloak of evil.

He turned into Abdullah Row. It was a repeat of Ismail Street: the same empty wooden houses, the same smell of drains and stale spices, the same pregnant silence, as though the world was waiting for an explosion. Was Pompeii like this before the eruption?

Number 17 was a little larger than the other houses, although, like them, it was single storeyed. Built of timber, it boasted a small veranda, and up a side passage, he glimpsed what was presumably a small patch of garden. Simon drew in his breath. Good, that meant a rear entrance. The windows were boarded up, but he thought he could detect a chink of light through one of the cracks. He looked around him. Nobody, of course. Making sure that his rice trail showed exactly where he had turned off, he approached the door, half expecting to see further directions pinned to it. But there was nothing. Taking a deep breath, he knocked.

Immediately a key turned in the lock and the door was flung open. The gratuitous violence that ensued shocked him. Two pairs of hands grabbed him, hauled him inside and threw him to the floor. He was kicked heavily in the ribs and a blow on the shoulder set his head singing. Then a slippered foot was placed on his cheek, pressing his face to the floor, so that all he could see was a wooden wall and a small table on which two candles were guttering. The smell of unwashed feet was overpowering. He lay like that for perhaps thirty seconds, his arms spread-eagled and other feet standing on his wrists so that he could not suppress a whimper of pain. He could hear also a muffled sound, as though someone was attempting to cry out but could not.

Then a dry voice spoke in Arabic and he was hauled to his feet as roughly as he had been thrown down. Hands ran over his body to ensure that he was unarmed. He blinked in the candlelight and then bellowed in anger and anguish at what he saw.

Immediately in front of him, on a low table, stood Alice. Her legs were bound around the ankles, her hands were tied behind her back and the fresh green silk scarf that had so beguilingly tied back her hair was now thrust into her mouth and secured behind her head with a cord. Around her neck was a noose of coarse rope, which was tied to a beam above her, so tightly that her head was tilted to one side and she was forced to stand on tiptoe. Her face was bruised and one eye was almost closed, but the other glared defiance, and the noise he had heard was that of her muffled voice.

Mr George sat in front of her in a small cane chair. His cotton suit was heavily creased, as though he had been sleeping in it, and his small round glasses gleamed in the candlelight. Incongruously, however, he seemed to be wearing a new celluloid collar.

'Good evening, sir,' he said. 'Thank you for coming. I knew you would.'

Simon looked quickly around the room. Two tall Egyptians – those who had hauled him inside – stood one on either side of him. They seemed to be unarmed but they were too big to grapple with. One other man, in Arab dress, stood to the side, a long *jerzail* crooked in his arm, the muzzle pointed at Simon. But there was more. The room was a bizarre storage chamber. Artefacts of all kinds lined the walls and were set atop wooden crates: canopic jars; gold scarabs and amulets, glinting in the yellow light; vases and jugs of porcelain and alabaster set down in a jumble on a succession of tables; necklaces of amber and gold, looped from nails driven into the walls; several long, narrow boxes bearing ancient inscriptions that Simon presumed were mummy cases; funerary figures in plaster and wood – the room was clearly a repository for the pickings of dozens of ancient graves along the Nile. Sawdust and wood shavings on the floor showed how the objects had been protected on their long journey in wooden cases from the south.

But Simon had little time or care for these treasures. How long had Alice been forced to stand like that – on tiptoe, with a rope cutting into her throat? He struggled to keep his voice level. 'I will say not a word to you, George,' he said, 'unless that rope is slackened and she is allowed to stand properly.'

'No, sir,' said the little man. 'Not George. *Mister* George, if you please. Let us retain the courtesies.'

'Mr George, relax that rope, or you will hear nothing at all from me from now on.'

George shrugged. 'I don't particularly want to hear anything from you, sir, and it doesn't matter to me if the bitch remains in discomfort until she dies, but just to indulge you for a moment, we can relax the rope, although it remains around her neck – to save time, you understand.' He spoke in fluent Arabic to the man on Simon's right, who immediately stood on the table and eased the knot around the beam, so that Alice's heels were allowed to touch the tabletop. He then fondled her breasts for a moment and dug a finger between her thighs before stepping down.

Simon felt an icy calm descend on him. He *must* stay cool. George and his henchmen were not rational employees of Arabi. They were clearly some kind of psychopaths intent on . . . intent on what? He did not know. But he must play for time until Jenkins arrived. His brain raced. How long had he been in here? Perhaps three minutes. Jenkins and Ahmed were three minutes behind him, say five. If they managed to follow the rice trail, they would be here in two or three minutes. Then they would allow ten minutes . . . ah, in the event, far too long! So, if everything went according to plan – which it never did – he had to keep them talking for thirteen minutes.

Simon swallowed. 'Now, Mr George,' he said, 'I presume I have information that you want from me. I am quite prepared to divulge that information if you let Miss Griffith – Mrs Covington – go free.'

A muffled snort came from behind Alice's gag. George removed his spectacles and polished them. He looked genuinely puzzled. 'Information, sir? What sort of information would I want from you, then?'

It was Simon's turn to look puzzled. 'Why, details of General Wolseley's plans for invasion, of course. I am privy to his plans, you know, and they will be extremely valuable to your master.'

'My master? Who is my master?'

'Colonel Arabi, of course.'

'Pah! I do not work for Arabi.'

Simon's eyes wandered round the room. The two candles on the table he had first seen were perched just above a pile of wood shavings on the floor. If he could only . . . The silence of the room was suddenly broken by the sound of gunfire. It carried from some distance away but was near enough to be distinguished as six separate shots.

George took a silver hunter from his pocket and clicked it open. 'Ah yes,' he said. 'On time. That will be the end of the two friends who have been following you since you left Nashwa Fatima's hotel. My people lay in wait for them and have shot them. It was planned.'

Simon felt his heart lurch again. Jenkins and Ahmed dead! His only real hope was gone. He shot a quick look at Alice. Her one open eye was staring at him in anguish. He had to keep talking.

'If you are not working for Arabi, how did you manage to travel from Cairo to Alex so quickly? The railway was closed.'

'Not to me.' The man's voice was now a purr and his conceit was obvious. 'You see, sir, I am not some cheap little spy. I am a businessman, and a very good one. Many people are in my employ, and they include the military who run the railway. I can come and go as I wish. I bribe, you see.' He waved his hand. 'This is my business. I smuggle priceless artefacts from the burial sites out to my friends, mainly in Greece. Working at the travel company provides an excellent base. But you knew that, of course . . .'

Involuntarily, Simon shook his head.

'Ah, then I overestimated you. When you saw me emptying that house after the bombardment, you probably thought I was taking part in the looting, but I was not. I own that house – or what is left of it now that the damned British have half destroyed it – and I was moving my possessions here, to a much safer storage place. You see, I am also known here as Ahmed Kamul.'

Simon frowned and took half a step forward. Immediately, two large hands gripped him by the upper arms. Keep talking . . . 'But your connection with Sir Garnet Wolseley? I don't understand.'

'I don't have any connection with the General, except that, as a clerk at Cook's, I handle an account for him there. It is company business, not mine. Ah, old Roberts up here has some sort of sentimental attachment to the man, but I do not. Of course,' his voice resumed its self-satisfied note, 'I doctor the accounts, and you will be on record as having received far more of Wolseley's money than you actually took. That, of course, is just good business.'

'Of course.' Simon felt the Egyptians' hands on his arms slacken slightly and he made a deliberate attempt to relax his muscles. They must not think he was tensing to break away. 'But why have you captured Mrs Covington and now me? What harm have we done you? We pose no threat to you.'

George's lip curled. 'You toffs take us working-class blokes for fools, don't you? Just little clerks there to serve you.' He hunched his shoulders and rubbed his hands together in a Fagin-like parody. ' "Will that be all, sir? Would you like a copy of *The Times*, sir?" Well, I'm no fool. I am a businessman. When, after we met twice in the streets here, it was reported to me that your whore was asking at the town hall about my property, and also enquiring about me at the hotel where we both stayed, and then when you followed up with more questions at the company, I thought you were on to me. Maybe I was wrong, but I think not. I don't usually make mistakes. Anyway, it makes no difference. You know

now about my affairs, and I am not going to have the very good business I have built up over the years ruined by you. I am a rich man, but I want to be richer, and you will not prevent me. I shall hang you both now.' He gestured with a nod of his head to where Alice stood behind him. 'I have been keeping her alive long enough so that I could see you both strung up and kicking together.'

'No,' said Simon. His voice quickened as he began his last ploy. 'Look, I can pay you. There is plenty of money in the Cook account for me here that I will sign over to you if you let her go. And I have brought one hundred pounds with me, here in my boot. Look.'

He held up his hand in supplication, and George nodded to the guards. Slowly Simon bent down and drew up his right trouser leg with his left hand. He held it up quite high for a moment, so that his elbow was bent, and straightened his fingers, holding up the trouser leg with his bent thumb. At the same moment, he slowly inserted his right hand into the top of his riding boot, as though searching for the money. Then, in one swift, flowing movement, he withdrew the knife, swung his left hand up and round, and caught the guard on his left just under the chin. At the same time, he ducked down round and low, breaking the grip of the man on the right and plunging the knife into his stomach.

'Shoot!' screamed George, and the *jerzail* boomed within the confined space. The musket ball, however, shattered the head of the first guard, who, clutching at his throat, had staggered directly into the line of fire. Simon sprang to the table bearing the candles and swept them on to the wood shavings piled at its base. Flames leapt high immediately and crackled along the line of shavings and sawdust that fringed the wall. He heard a shriek of anger or terror from George, and swung round towards Alice only to see George kick away the low table on which she perched, so that she swung from the neck, her legs jerking.

'No,' shrieked Simon. He ran to Alice and caught her around the knees, taking her weight. Holding her with one arm, his knife hand extended in a hopeless act of defence, he faced the two men. George was desperately trying to stamp out the flames, but the Egyptian with the *jerzail* was calmly pouring powder into his pan and then ramming home a ball down the long muzzle. Simon tried to cut the rope around Alice's neck, but he could not quite reach without loosening his grip around her legs. He was powerless as he stood watching the Arab calmly cock the hammer on the ancient weapon and begin walking forward to make certain of the easy target before him. The choice before Simon now was desperate: release Alice so that she would die of strangulation – if she had not done so already, for her body felt inert – and rush at the Egyptian; or stay as a sitting target.

It was then that a thunderous hammering sounded on the front door and Ahmed's high-pitched voice began shrieking something quite unintelligible from outside. Simon saw the man with the gun look questioningly at George, who had given up his attempt at putting out the flames and was now trying to pick up as many of the precious amulets as he could.

'Kill him!' shrieked the clerk. He repeated it in Arabic, and gestured angrily towards Simon.

The killing was quickly undertaken, but not by the Egyptian. As he raised his musket, Jenkins's bullet took him squarely in the chest, spinning him round until he sank slowly to the ground, his *jerzail* falling away with a clatter.

'Thank God,' shouted Simon. 'Quickly. Help me with Alice.'

Jenkins, the mouth of his Colt still smoking, ran from the corridor doorway, climbed on to the cane chair and, with Simon's knife, sawed through the tough rope. At that point, further pistol shots sounded at the front door and Ahmed, Colt in one hand, his scimitar swinging from the other, burst into the room.

'Get after that swine,' yelled Simon, desperately trying to undo the great knot above Alice's throat and gesturing with his head towards the open corridor leading to the rear.

Ahmed stood for a moment. 'Ah, sorry,' he said. 'What swine? I don't see nobody.' George had obviously fled from the smoke-filled room before the little man had entered.

'I'll go,' shouted Jenkins. He gently handed Alice's slumped form to Simon and, pistol in hand, disappeared up the corridor.

The flames were now ravaging the wooden wall against which the shavings had been strewn and creeping along toward the main entrance. 'Help me lift her,' said Simon. 'We must get her out of here.'

Together the two men picked up Alice and, stepping around the corpses, half ran, half shuffled with her towards the doorway, which was now ringed in flames. They ducked through it into the blessed air outside to find that a throng had gathered. Fearing attack, Simon grabbed Ahmed's Colt. But there was no danger. The Egyptians held back in awe at the flames and amazement at the sight of the European woman lying on the ground, a noose around her throat and her arms and legs bound.

Simon was now able to slip the accursed rope over Alice's head, and he cradled her in his arm while he desperately sought to feel her pulse with his other hand. He was conscious that an elderly Egyptian lady was kneeling at his side. Without thinking, his eyes wide with relief, he shouted at her, 'She's alive, I think. I can feel a pulse. She's alive!'

The woman smiled at him, turned her head and shouted something in Arabic at the crowd. 'We fetch water,' explained Ahmed, 'and damp things for forehead and throat.'

'Thank you,' said Simon. 'Where's my knife? Let's get these bloody things off her legs and wrists. No. We'll have to carry her away first. The whole building is aflame.'

They did so, with the crowd making way for them. Two women now appeared, and as Simon and Ahmed hacked away at Alice's bonds, one of them poured a little water from a goatskin on to her lips. She did not stir and her face looked waxen by the light from the leaping flames. Cloths were then soaked in the cool water and gently applied to her forehead, cheeks and throat, where the rope had left an ugly blue mark.

'Oh God, she's not dead, is she?' Simon asked of the women. Ahmed, his face sombre, translated. But the first woman shook her head and spoke quickly.

'Unconscious is all,' said Ahmed. 'We told to rub her hands and feet to get blood circu . . . circula . . . going round. Yes?'

'Thank God for that.' And the two men began rubbing Alice's feet and hands vigorously.

They were still doing so when Jenkins reappeared. Inevitably, he had lost his *esharp*, and was perspiring and puffing. 'Lost the bastard, I did,' he confessed. 'Little bugger was as slippery as an eel, look you. Lost 'im in the lanes. 'Ow is the little love, then?'

It was Alice herself who provided the response. Her eyes flickered and then opened. Simon put his arms around her and lifted her towards him, and then sat rocking her gently. The crowd, who had been silent, now began chattering and some of them ran to help the men who were relaying buckets of water to sluice down the walls of neighbouring buildings and so restrict the fire to the guttering house.

'No, don't try to speak,' said Simon, cradling Alice's head. 'Here, take some more water.' She tried, but the effort of swallowing made her gasp in pain. Simon bit his lip in sympathy. 'Stay still for a while,' he murmured, 'then we will get you out of here. Don't try to talk.' He wiped her lips gently with the damp cloth and then looked up at Jenkins. 'I heard shots and thought you'd both been done for. What happened?'

Jenkins sniffed. 'I'd got a feelin' that we'd been spotted and that someone was goin' to try an' take us. So I split us up, to spread the target, so to speak, old Amen on one side of the street an' me on the other. Brainwork, see. You'd 'ave been proud of me, bach sir.' He grinned. 'They fired a couple of shots at us and missed, see. Terrible shots they are. Then they ran at us with swords, four of 'em. I got two straight away and dear old Amen, bless 'im, got one with 'is Colt before nearly shootin' 'is own foot off with the second round. But I finished off the last bloke. That delayed us a bit, see, an' I'm sorry if we was a bit late arrivin' like. Mind you, it looked as though you was lookin' after yourself quite well, though,' his brows came down, 'it was terrible to see Miss Alice strung up like that. Nearly put me off me shot.'

'Yes, the swine. The man is obviously a sadist, but I am not going to worry about him now. That can come later. You arrived just in time, and thank you both.' Simon summoned up a grin for Ahmed, who was now standing abjectly, his sword dangling from his hand, looking down at Alice. 'Well done, Ahmed. For a hotel keeper, you fight like an old soldier.'

The little man gave his hotelier's bow and rolled his eyes. 'Thank you, Simon. But I hope we finish with the fighting for a while. I nearly shoot my foot off.'

'I hope so too. Now, be a good fellow and thank these ladies. Then see if someone in this crowd has a cart or something on which we can lay Alice, so that we can take her back to Fatima's.'

Eventually, a cart pulled by a donkey was produced and Alice was laid in it, wrapped in Simon's *burnous*. Then they set off, Ahmed leading the donkey and Simon and Jenkins walking either side, their Colts at the ready, in case George still had underlings who had the stomach for a fight.

The journey back to the hotel, however, was uneventful, and Alice was found a room, where Fatima fussed over her and put her to bed, after persuading her to sip some milky substance that she had warmed and applying cool poultices to her neck and swollen eye.

The next morning, a Greek doctor was found to visit Alice. He commended Fatima on her treatment and prescribed more of the same, together with rest. He clearly thought it none of his business to probe too deeply into why this English lady had so narrowly escaped hanging but he attributed her good fortune to the fact that the table on which she had stood had not been high, the rope had been taut, and consequently the drop had not been long enough to break her neck. Her throat would be swollen and painful for a few days, he explained, but no lasting harm had been done to her vocal cords.

A relieved Simon paid a quick visit to the consul, and, after having given the briefest of explanations, gained permission for Alice to move into the consulate under the care of Mrs Cookson. He felt it was not safe for her to remain at Fatima's hotel – given that George knew of their presence there – nor to stay at the Victoria Hotel. Alice was now able to whisper and she tried to protest, but Simon overrode her demurral.

The two had a moment together before the consulate carriage, with the two armed Nubians as guards, came to take her away. Simon knelt by her stretcher as Alice related how, on the way back to her hotel, she had been waylaid by George's men, bundled into a covered cart and taken to the wooden house. With tears in her eyes, she whispered that she had stupidly revealed her assignation with Simon the following day, as a threat to show that she would be missed and a search begun. It was, of course, just what George wanted to hear. In despair she had fought with her captors and been beaten as a result.

'Simon,' she breathed, 'I have never been so frightened as when they put that noose around my neck. And then, when you appeared, I thought we were both going to die. How I wished I had never started that stupid game . . .'

Simon gripped her hand. 'I am glad you did, despite all your agonies. At least we have flushed the man out.'

She summoned up a smile. 'I don't think he likes women, somehow. Where is he now, do you think?'

'I would guess that he has slipped back through Arabi's lines and bribed his way on to the train to Cairo. With British forces due to land here any day, and with us still alive, he knows he couldn't last an hour in Alex now. I will report all that has happened to Wolseley when he gets here and see that the people at Cook's know exactly what sort of viper they have been employing. One way or the other, I shall make sure he doesn't survive this war.'

Alice nodded and held Simon's gaze for a moment. Then she frowned, looked away and began to speak, as though addressing the far wall. 'Simon, I am so ashamed of myself for getting you into this terrible situation and so grateful to you for saving me. Seeing you being thrown through that door raised such a conflict of emotions in me . . .' A half sob came into her voice, and she paused. 'It was such a relief to know that you had found me, and then when they began hitting you . . .'

'Don't say anything more. It is all of no consequence now.'

They fell silent but held each other's gaze again. Simon realised that he was still holding Alice's hand. Awkwardly, he withdrew it and Alice turned her head away. She did not turn it back to say goodbye to him as she was lifted into the carriage.

Chapter 11

Troops from Sir Archibald Alison's force from Cyprus, Wolseley's advance guard, had landed in Alexandria, and they combined with the marine and blue-jacket patrols now regularly policing the streets to ensure that further rioting was discouraged. They also began the task of cleaning up the city, organising gangs to take away rubble and clear the streets. Their presence finally removed any lasting fear that Simon might have had that George remained in Alexandria, so posing a continuing threat. He visited the shell of the house in Abdullah Row and found nothing there of George's treasures. If any had survived the blaze, they would not have lasted long in a city still pulsing with looting fever. Nor could he detect any sign of the three men who had been killed there. Fire, he reflected dourly, was a great cleansing agent. There had been no repercussions from the city authorities or the British patrols. One more blaze in a city that had sustained so many was obviously of no concern to anyone.

Arabi still showed no sign of moving on the city, and General Alison had begun to probe the Colonel's defences some ten miles away. Accordingly, Simon felt it his duty to call upon Alison with his report of the scouting he and

Jenkins had already carried out around the Egyptian lines. He was not allowed to see the General, however, and was forced to leave his report with a stout little major who seemed quite unimpressed with – or, more accurately perhaps, disbelieving of – Simon's explanation that he was working in Egypt directly for Sir Garnet Wolseley. He did, however, find a young subaltern who was able to update him with the latest news from England.

Wolseley, it seemed, was well on his way and was expected to arrive in Alexandria any day now with an expeditionary force. In the House of Commons Mr Gladstone had asked for and received a vote of credit for £2,300,000 to fund the invading force, which he proposed to meet by an increase in income tax. The force would include a contingent from India. The Prime Minister had denied that Arabi was a national leader and charged the ruin of Egypt upon 'lawless military violence, aggravated by wanton and cruel crime'. Egypt, he said, would be retaken for the Khedive. If this was so, then it would be done, it seemed, without the aid of the French, whose chamber had refused to vote funds for the protection of its Egyptian asset on the grounds that this might be prejudicial to French interests in Tunisia. Turkey also was reported as being happy merely to hold an insouciant watching brief. England would have to invade alone.

Simon's visit to General Alison's headquarters, abortive as it was, at least enabled him to take his mind off Alice for a few hours. After much thought, he had decided that he would not visit her at the consulate. At least he knew that she would be safe enough there, and he could not bear the agony of renewing a relationship that, it was quite clear, could only be platonic. Now that she was secure and had, it seemed, suffered no lasting injuries, he must leave her to herself and, more to the point, her husband, who would be arriving soon.

Lieutenant General Sir Garnet Wolseley, indeed, sailed into Alexandria three days later. The fleet that filled the harbour and the bay was prodigious. In all Wolseley had brought with him fifteen thousand men, plus horses and ordnance, to add to the two battalions of infantry, one battalion of marines and assorted contingents of sailors now under the command of Alison. Admiral Seymour's nose had been tweaked and the British lion had roared. But was the force large enough to engage the twenty thousand troops that Arabi had ranged across the isthmus at Kafr Dewar, plus the many thousands he had in the hinterland of Egypt?

Simon was now making daily calls at Thomas Cook, and the summons to meet Wolseley came via that route gratifyingly quickly. The same afternoon he was being ushered into the Commander-in-Chief's stateroom aboard the flagship of the newly arrived fleet. His first reaction was one of dismay. The General had, it seemed, suffered a recurrence of a fever contracted in Africa many years ago, and it had left him thin in the body and white in the face. He had now taken to waxing the ends of his moustache, but his fashionable conceit did nothing to take away the impression of a man recovering from a serious illness. Yet his good eye still glowed with inward drive and determination and his voice retained the bounce lacking from his thin frame.

'Good morning, Cousin.' He smiled. 'Take a pew.'

'Thank you, sir.'

'First-class stuff you sent me. As a result, I added extra

troops of cavalry and four more batteries of artillery. I didn't get that sort of detailed advice from our political people in Cairo.'

'I am glad to hear it, sir. I have written a full report, filling out the bare bones I was able to give you in the cables.' He handed the document across the desk. 'But you still plan to advance south from Alex?'

Wolseley smiled and sat back in his chair. 'What? My dear fellow, ignore your advice? I wouldn't dream of doing that. Whatever would you think of me?'

Simon stirred uncomfortably. He had always disliked irony. Was he being mocked? 'What *do* you intend to do, sir?'

The General leaned forward, the smile gone. 'I have every reason to trust your discretion, Fonthill, so I am asking you to keep this under your hat – and your collar stud, for that matter, my boy. All of this lot,' he waved his hand airily, 'will be out of here in a few days. I am making a feint, as you recommended. I want dear Colonel Arabi – dammit, whoever heard of a colonel taking on a lieutenant general, the very impudence! – I want him to hang around here with his twenty thousand men across that isthmus and protecting his precious railway line. I shall leave General Hallam here with sufficient troops to harass him and persuade him that the main thrust will come from Alex. Then I shall slip away with the majority of the force to Port Said, at the top end of the Suez Canal, and occupy it. At the same time, a considerable number of troops from Bombay will land at Suez and seal the southern end. We shall then join up, disembark the force at Ismailia and march across the northern desert to take Cairo. There!' He sat back in his chair. 'Just as you recommended. Don't know why you're not the general, Fonthill, bless me if I don't. Mind you,' he grinned, 'if it goes wrong, it'll be this general who will get the blame, not you.'

Simon grinned back. 'Sounds a fine plan to me, sir. Congratulations on thinking of it.' He pondered for a second or two. 'At the moment, Arabi has few troops at Ismailia, and I doubt if he is a good enough field commander to get an army together and move it quickly enough to oppose your landing, if you strike quickly. After all, he has had little battle or logistical experience. But the march across the desert won't exactly be easy for you in midsummer. Arabi has plenty of infantry, cavalry and artillery around Cairo. He will march east to stop you and he will obviously cut the railway line.'

'Quite so. It will take me time to disembark, of course, and to assemble the army for the advance. He will be able to pick his spot. I want you to get down to Ismailia right away – before we enter the Canal – and scout the desert and let me know where you think he will make a stand. I want to be ahead of this game all the time, Fonthill. The rest of Europe, particularly the French – who, of course, have walked out at the last minute – will have its eyes on us, willing us to get this wrong. I don't intend to give them that satisfaction. I am relying on you again, my dear fellow. Of course, I can have cavalry out scouting as soon as we land, but they won't be able to range far without support. I want you there early, as my eyes. Understand?'

'Of course, sir. How do I contact you?'

'You'll have to use your wits for that.' He pushed a slip of paper across the desk. 'Here is the cable address in Port Said. Our people there will make sure that whatever you say is forwarded to me, wherever I may be. There are cable facilities, I understand, at the pilots' offices in Ismailia. But de Lesseps – you know, the Frenchman who planned and built the Canal?'

Simon nodded.

'His base is there and he's very anti-British, so I am told.' He chortled. 'Probably hates us because old Dizzy bought the Canal from under French noses. Anyway, you will have to be careful. I suppose it will be back to the family code, although under the circumstances, I should think anybody could see through that. I will just have to leave it to you. Use your initiative, I know you have plenty of that.'

'Very good, sir.'

'You must be running out of funds by now, so go and see my paymaster here.' He scribbled a note and murmured as he wrote. 'Were the arrangements I made for you satisfactory?'

Simon sighed. 'Satisfactory in every way but one, sir.' He took a deep breath and began relating the story of Mr George. He was careful, however, to remove from the tale any implication that the pursuit of George by Alice and himself was some sort of intellectual game to while away their time in Alex. Their object, he explained, was to try and establish how the clerk could move so easily between Cairo and Alexandria, in the hope that the information could be valuable. As the story unfolded, Wolseley, who had at first seemed only politely interested, listened with increasing incredulity, and as Simon related the attempted hanging of Alice and the shooting in the blazing house, he became positively agitated.

'Good God, man!' he exclaimed. 'You seem to leave dead bodies behind you wherever you go!'

'I think that's a little unfair, sir. I—'

'Never mind. You're right, of course. I must inform the people at Thomas Cook in Cairo about this immediately. I don't suppose he will show up back there or that, given the present situation, we would have the muscle to compel the authorities to arrest him, but at least we can ensure that he never gets employment there again. Now, you had better tell Colonel Covington all about this . . . Ah, no.' He shot a hard glance at Simon. 'I'd better tell him. I don't think he would particularly welcome this news coming from you. Now, where did you say Mrs Covington is staying?'

He scribbled the address on his pad. 'Right.' He looked up. 'No more clerk-chasing. You have more important work to do. The gunboat *Shalimar* is sailing for Port Said tonight, and I want you and whatsisnumber, Jenkins on it. At Said, take the first boat sailing down the Canal and get off at Ismailia. My intelligence on the landing facilities there is, I hope, more or less adequate now, but I will need to know the size of Arabi's troops and, most importantly, what you can discover about where he will make his stand in the desert. Both of my forces will be hot on your heels, so you won't have much time.'

'Very good, sir.'

'Two more things, Fonthill.'

'Sir?'

Wolseley rose, and Simon realised anew how hard the recurrence of the fever had hit the General, for he was forced to lean on the desk as he moved around it. 'Sorry about this.' Wolseley smiled. 'Getting better every day, though. Sea air has helped, you know. Now, two last points. First, armed bands of desert tribesmen – what d'yer call 'em?'

'Bedawis.'

'Those are the fellers. As I told you in London, they are reported to be marauding up and down the Canal banks, and Arabi, of course, is doing nothing to stop 'em. So be careful.'

'Yes, sir. I have had some experience of them already.'

Wolseley's eyebrows rose. 'Have you now? My word, Fonthill, you do sniff out trouble, don't you? But never mind that. The second point is about secrecy.' He leaned back against the desk and a mischievous grin lit up his pale face. 'You're not formally in the army, my boy, so I can be a touch indiscreet with you, and I know I can trust you. General Hallam, bless him, does not know that it is my intention to withdraw my main force from here and sail for Port Said. I shall even disembark some of my men to fool Arabi – and then load 'em back again. Poor old Hallam thinks he's going to lead the main attack, but he ain't, dear cousin.' His grin widened. 'He will be on shore planning to open his offensive opposite Arabi at Kafr Dewar when, after I have sailed, he opens my sealed orders telling him that his job is just to create a diversion. I'd give my eye teeth to see his face.'

Wolseley's grin turned into a guffaw. Simon summoned a sickly smile, but he could not help but be shocked at this deliberate deception of a senior officer and the General's schoolboyish delight in it. Why could *he* be told of the feint, but not Wolseley's deputy, the man who was to play a crucial part in the charade?

Some of his disapproval must have shown, for Wolseley's jollity immediately disappeared and he grabbed Simon by the arm. 'This is all to show you, Fonthill, how desperately important it is that my real intention does not leak out. It would be easy for Arabi to block the Canal at many points before I can seal it at both ends. Secrecy must be maintained. It was only fair to tell you, not only because this strategy was originally a concept of yours, but also because you are going to play a vital part in helping me to carry it out. But . . . you must keep the secret. Is this understood?'

'Of course, sir. Well understood.'

'Good. Now be off. Don't worry about Mrs Covington. Alas, I have a large press contingent with me, and if she is fit enough, I shall scoop her up and she can join it. She will be glad to see her husband again, anyway, and I shall make sure that he gets off to see her right away.'

'Splendid, sir.' Simon felt a knife twist in his stomach.

'Ah. One very last thing. You will end up being in the thick of it, so you had better get yourself a couple of Martini-Henry rifles. Here's a chit. The armourer's on board. Right?'

'Right, General.'

They shook hands. 'God speed, my boy, and good luck.'

Simon went ashore with his head buzzing. Alice was to be reunited with Covington, and that sent a little shaft of misery shooting through his brain. She was lost to him, of course, but that did not stop him loving her. Yet . . . best to move on, and now, at least, to get away from Alexandria, which had become synonymous in his mind with violence and depravity. At last he and Jenkins had a clearly defined job to do and one that moved him away from spying and into the desert, where the air was clean and one knew who one's enemies were. The thought put a spring in his step.

The news was welcomed by Jenkins and, slightly wistfully, by Ahmed. This caused Simon to think about the little hotelier. He had almost certainly experienced more violence in the last few weeks than in the whole of his life up to this point. And the fight would now escalate into a fully fledged war against his own people. Was it fair to involve him further? He put the question to him.

Ahmed listened carefully and hunched his narrow shoulders. 'Am I not useful no more?' he asked.

'Of course you are, Ahmed. We could have done very little over the last few weeks without you. But the real battles will soon start and we could be involved in them. Do you really want to fight your own people? I don't think it fair to ask you.'

The little man nodded. 'I don't think I kill Egyptians no more,' he said slowly. 'But I still come with you, if I am useful. I enjoy excitement. Much better than running hotel, et cetera, et cetera, et cetera. What you say: in for penny, in for shilling, eh?'

Simon grinned. 'In for a penny, in for a pound. Thank goodness for that. We would be lost without you. Right, let's pack our things. I am told that the *Shalimar* sails at six tonight.'

There were tearful farewells with Fatima, into whose hands Simon pressed more money than she had ever received before. Simon decided against writing a note to Alice – whatever he said would have to be stultifyingly formal and therefore quite hypocritical. They shouldered their packs, Simon and Jenkins carrying their new Martini-Henrys at the sling, and set off for the harbour. At the quayside, they had just hailed a boatman to take them out to the gunboat when Simon heard his name called. Striding towards him was Ralph Covington, ramrod straight and resplendent in his new uniform.

'A word in private with you, Fonthill, if you please.'

Simon's jaw sagged. Covington was the last person he wished to see at this juncture. He could not deny the guilt he felt about Alice, the bloody man's wife. Oh, his actions had been chaste enough, but not his thoughts. And he could not deny that he had willingly accompanied her into danger, leading to her being assaulted and very nearly killed. He faced Covington, then, carrying a mixture of resentment, guilt and slow-burning anger. He tried to suppress it.

'Of course.' Simon indicated to Jenkins and Ahmed to board the *filuka* that now drew up to the harbour wall and stepped aside with Covington. 'Have you been to see Alice?' he asked. 'How is she?'

'She is recovering well.' Covington's tone was cool and even. 'She is up and about and can speak properly again, and she insists on joining the press corps that is travelling with the General. She will join the ship tomorrow.'

'Good.'

Covington's face was as though set in stone, but his good eye gleamed. 'I must thank you for saving her life, Fonthill, and this I do. However,' the fearsome hook now tapped lightly on Simon's chest, 'you were completely responsible for the terrible danger you led her into. I always thought that you were a contemptible cur, and you have proved me to be right once again. How any man could embark upon such an irresponsible caper with a woman in tow, I do not know . . .'

Simon opened his mouth to speak.

'Do *not* interrupt me. I know that Alice is strong-willed, but any man worth his salt would have dissuaded her from partaking in this ridiculously dangerous adventure. You did not, for reasons I cannot begin to comprehend.'

'It was not like that, Covington. When we began investigating George, we had no idea that he was a dangerous man . . .'

'Rubbish! This whole city is dangerous. Now listen to me, young man. Wherever you go, it seems to me you attract trouble. In future, you will not, I repeat, you will not have anything to do with my wife. If you do, I will use every means at my disposal to bring you down. Do you understand?'

Simon took a deep breath. 'I would have thought that over the last six years, you have already used every means at your disposal to bring me down, and have failed. Your threat, therefore, carries no weight with me. You should know that I have not the slightest fear of you, and the contempt in which you seem to hold me is returned a hundredfold. However, Alice is your wife and I promise you that I will not approach her in any way if our paths do cross in the future. But just stay out of my way.'

For a moment, the two men stood glaring at each other. Then, with a last admonitory tap on the chest with his hook, the Colonel turned on his heel and strode away.

'Hey, what was that all about then?' asked Jenkins, as Simon climbed aboard the *filuka*, his cheeks flaming.

'We were just discussing the price of fish, that's all.'

Jenkins knew better than to pursue the matter. A puff of the evening breeze filled the lanteen sail and pulled them away from the quayside towards where the *Shalimar* lay waiting to take them to Port Said and the Suez Canal.

Chapter 12

The three men delayed at Port Said only long enough for Simon to note the situation of the Egyptian barracks there, although he felt sure that this would already be known to Wolseley. They took passage on a small Turkish coaster bound for Hodeida in the Red Sea, and their progression down the milky green waters of the Canal was hot, uncomfortable but uneventful. During the voyage, Simon thrust all thoughts of Alice away as he concentrated on the task ahead.

At Ismailia, they took rooms in the modest hotel where they had stayed before and where the management's seemingly complete lack of interest in its guests enabled them to don Arab clothing without attracting comment. Simon was depressed to note, once again, the size of the single landing stage, which looked incapable of coping with the disembarkation of an army the size of the British expeditionary force. There was also the potential bottleneck of only one bridge across the Sweetwater Canal just outside the town. He was glad to see, however, that Arabi had not increased the size of the tiny garrison at Ismailia, although some two thousand troops were stationed just outside the town, to the west in the village of Nefisha. The latter, though, was well within heavy guns' range of the Suez Canal, and Simon felt that it could be taken easily enough under the guns of a ship or two moored there. The question was: had Arabi established a position out in the desert well beyond Nefisha, and if so, how many men did he have there?

Simon realised that this expedition, of course, would have to be planned with more care than their last venture out on foot into the desert. 'Now, Ahmed,' he said shortly after their arrival in Ismailia. 'Do you know the ways of the desert, and can you ride a camel?'

'Ah. Every *fellaheen* can ride camel, Simon, but my brother, he knows desert much better than me. I do not find my way well there. Sorry.'

'Oh, blimey,' said Jenkins. 'That makes two of us. Now I know we're goin' to get lost.'

Simon shook his head. 'No we won't. Not while I have a compass. I presume, Ahmed, that it would be better to hire camels to go west rather than horses?'

'Of course. Horses no good on sand, and if we go deep in desert there is little water and horses need more water than camels.'

'Right. Please go and hire three riding camels for us, with a fourth for our baggage. We will also need a small tent. Get what you need for desert travel; 352 and I are already equipped. We will also need food for four or five days. I don't know for sure how long we shall be out there.'

Jenkins's nose wrinkled. 'See if you can get a drop of whisky, Amen, there's a good chap.'

'No. No whisky, Ahmed. It will just increase our thirst. Now, at the camel market, see what you can pick up about where Arabi might be establishing lines to fight the British. If he has dug in anywhere, the desert traders should know. We will set off at dawn tomorrow.'

Studying the map, Simon realised that in fact there was little chance of them getting lost, for there were two clear highways linking Ismailia with Cairo: the railway and the Sweetwater Canal. The two meandered parallel and close to each other for roughly half the seventy-five miles between town and city. Then the canal looped to the south-west to Cairo. The railway continued for a further twelve miles before hitting a junction at Zagazig, where a branch line headed due south before meeting the Sweetwater again and following it virtually into Cairo. From what he had heard, the terrain either side of both railway and canal was more or less flat, although it undulated once both were left behind. More importantly, if the canal was not blocked, then it provided drinking water all the way to Cairo. Railway and canal pointed the way to the city for any invading army from the east as clearly as any metalled road.

It seemed to Simon that if the Egyptian leader had taken precautions already to stop an invasion from the Suez Canal, then there were two obvious sites at which to set up his positions, given that he would want to lure the invaders into the desert some way to stretch their lines of communication and let the predations of Egypt's midsummer climate work their effect on white-skinned troops. The first was some thirty-five miles inland at a place called Kassassin, probably no more than a village, and the second at Tel el Kebir, very little larger according to the map, and about eight miles further west.

Simon pondered over the map, pencil in mouth. 'If I was

Arabi,' he mused to Jenkins, 'I'd set up an advance point at Kassassin, to test the waters, so to speak, and my main fortifications at Tel el Kebir, here.'

'Ah, but you ain't old Aunt Ada, are you? 'E ain't as clever as you, is 'e?'

'Well I don't know about that, but we must find out pretty quickly, because if I'm right, it's just possible that Wolseley might want to launch a two-pronged attack, off-loading some of his men twenty miles or so down the Canal from Port Said, at this place, Kantara, here, marching 'em through the desert and taking Arabi from the north, as well as the east.' He traced his pencil across the map. Then he shook his head. 'No. No landing facilities there and it would be very difficult to march across the desert and synchronise the attack, even if he could disembark. No. It's this way or nothing. Depending upon what news Ahmed brings us, that's the way we go tomorrow.'

Ahmed did bring news. 'Arabi Pasha has small people at Kassassin,' he said, 'and big people at Tel el Kebir. A lot of holes in desert there, guns and trenches, et cetera, et cetera, et cetera, you know. But Arabi himself, they say, is still at Alexandria.'

'Good. That means the General's bluff is working. Show me the camels.'

Simon's heart sank when he saw them. In fact, he smelt them before he came upon them. The odiferous beasts were kneeling, with a small boy standing on the doubled foreleg of each camel. The animals were chewing grass that they had already pre-digested, and as the three men approached, they turned their heads and belched, sending green slivers oozing over their loose lips to the ground.

'Bloody 'ell,' said Jenkins. 'I'd forgotten about the smell.'

'Ah, this is why they good desert horses,' said Ahmed earnestly. 'They eat grass and bring it back to chew again. You know how to ride them, yes?'

'Oh, I'm all right,' said Jenkins, 'but you'd better show the Captain again. 'E's liable to fall off when the thing starts movin', see.'

'Nonsense,' sniffed Simon. 'I did quite well when we crossed the desert with your brother, Ahmed. But just, er, show me how to mount the thing, there's a good fellow.'

'Ah. Is easy. Look.' Ahmed seized the cantle at the front of the saddle, dug his left knee into the side of the camel and nodded to the camel tender. As the boy stood aside, the beast lurched to its feet and Ahmed pivoted on his left knee and swung his right leg over the saddle. He coiled his left leg around the front cantle of the saddle and gestured with the small stick he had taken from the boy. 'Ride like this,' he called, 'and use stick to give directions. Tap like this on neck to go right and this way to go left, and so on, et cetera, et cetera, et cetera. Tap on back of neck to go down. So.' The camel slowly collapsed like a concertina and Ahmed alighted. 'Easy, yes?'

'Oh, impeccably easy. Right, we will load the pack animal and you pay the boys, Ahmed. I want to be well into the desert before the sun gets too high.'

They set off within the half-hour. Once installed in the curved wooden saddle on top of his swaying but oddly graceful mount, Simon experienced again the lolloping, somnambulistic rhythm of camel riding and, indifferent horseman that he was, almost began to enjoy it. Once clear of Nefisha, the desert was flat and empty, and their only companions were the flies, settling on the wet lips of the camels and hovering around their own faces, forcing them to draw the tails of their *esharps* across their chins and mouths, so that only their eyes were to be seen. Simon had asked Ahmed to buy cloaks and headdresses of black dyed cotton in the market. They had donned them once out of the town, and now, their Martini-Henrys tucked well out of sight, they presented a passable picture of three desert Bedawi, making their slow passage to Cairo to trade in the capital's street markets. If stopped, Ahmed was to explain that they came from the deep south, over the Sudan border, and that his two companions spoke a version of Arabic inexplicable to the northerners.

They passed the gangers' shed where they had made their stand against the marauding Bedawi, and plodded on, following the railway line to the east, the broad pads of the camels' feet spreading in contact with the sand to gain purchase and then flicking the golden grains behind them in uninterrupted, hypnotic sequence. It was hot, damned hot, and Simon had to force himself to keep awake.

Some seven miles from Ismailia, they reached the tiny village of Magfar, where Simon realised that the low-lying nature of the terrain would make it easy for the Egyptians to break down the banks of the Sweetwater and dam it, so lowering the level of the canal or even drying it up completely, denying the invading force both a source of fresh water and a means of transportation.

They pressed on and camped that night just outside Tel el Maskhuta, another of the hamlets that studded the railway line, providing occasional labour to maintain it and its neighbouring waterway. They erected their low communal tent and used a little camel dung to light a fire, then made coffee and ate some cold mutton. As the sun went down, they were visited by an Egyptian cavalry patrol. While Ahmed spoke to them, Simon regarded them carefully from under his *esharp*. They rode their camels with confidence and were armed with modern Remington rifles. Their commander was a Turk, who spoke to Ahmed with an obvious air of superiority and, it soon became apparent, indifference, for he led his troop away after only a few minutes of conversation.

'Did you learn anything, Ahmed?' asked Simon.

'Little. They are patrolling much desert and are living at Kassassin. But he says the fighting is in north and they are bored. They think they don't ever fight here.'

'Good. The bluff is still holding.'

The village proved to be of little strategic importance, unlike Kassassin, to which they pushed on through the day. Here the Sweetwater curved roughly north–south, and although little more than a collection of huts huddled on the western side of the canal at a bridge across it, the village guarded a lock whose possession would ensure a defending force an easy opportunity to cut off the supply of water for the troops advancing from Ismailia and so deny them the ability to carry stores and provisions up the canal. As Ahmed had originally heard, the village was not strongly defended, but earthworks had been erected that clearly could be supplemented quickly if necessary.

The three rode on the next day, following the railway line towards Tel el Kebir, but Simon's brow was now permanently furrowed. He realised now how vulnerable Wolseley would be to any sabotaging of the railway line and, even more importantly, the Sweetwater. Given the tiny pier at Ismailia and the bottleneck of the single bridge across the canal, which would have to be crossed to march west, the disembarkation of troops at Ismailia would be a lengthy business. Even if most of Arabi's troops were still facing a disgruntled Hallam outside Alexandria, the Egyptian leader could still use his railway to rush troops to the eastern desert to oppose the advance, blow up the Cairo–Ismailia railway and sabotage the Sweetwater Canal, while Wolseley was still slinging his guns from ship to shore. All of this presuming that Sir Garnet would be able to bottle up both ends of the Suez Canal before the Egyptians sank lighters across the waterway to block it and prevent his ships reaching Ismailia in the first place!

Tel el Kebir presented Simon with more reasons to ponder the wisdom of his advice to Wolseley. The village itself, grouped on the southern side of the railway and the canal, boasted a station, a strange tall stone tower (useful for guiding long-range gunfire?) and a small, seemingly permanent barracks for Egyptian troops. It was impossible, of course, to estimate the number of soldiers based here, but the force seemed to be quite considerable and again, of course, could be supplemented by rail at short notice. More impressive, however, were the fortifications dug into the sand and gravel.

These were unfinished, but they stretched due north of the canal and railway out into the desert. Having sauntered into the village, the three men retraced their steps across the single bridge at the station and slowly walked their camels back towards where the entrenchments began to the east of the village. There, they turned the heads of their mounts to the north and began to follow the line of fortifications out across the sand. Simon soon appreciated the wisdom of the choice of Tel el Kebir for the defence of Cairo. Here, the desert was completely flat and there was no cover of any kind for anyone attempting a frontal attack: no dunes, no buildings and hardly a shrub in sight. The trenches were still being dug, but no one was working in that midday heat and the three attracted little curiosity as they plodded along, seemingly only interested in finding a way around the obstacle before rounding it and heading west again. In fact, Simon was making a surreptitious sketch of the fortifications as he rode, his head nodding sleepily to the rhythm of the camel's movements.

A continuous line of earthworks, of course, was being thrown up in front of the trenches. These were high and would pose major problems for infantry attempting to storm them. But it was the artillery emplacements that impressed. These consisted of ten redoubts of varying sizes at intervals along the lines. The strongest sections were in the south, near the canal and railway, where there were ten guns; the centre, with two redoubts a thousand yards apart, one with four guns, the other with five; and the tip of the line in the north, where there was a total of seven guns in two more redoubts similarly spaced. Some thousand yards in front of the entrenchments and sixteen hundred yards north of the canal was an advanced redoubt with eight guns and trenches for infantry.

The whole line stretched, Simon estimated, for at least two miles out into the desert, and when the three riders reached the northern tip, they could see further entrenchments being dug behind the main line, running back for about three and a half thousand yards from the centre of the line and facing north-west to protect the Egyptians' camp, which could be seen shimmering in the distant rear. This line, which also protected the tip of the main line from attack from the north, mounted no fewer than twenty-four further guns.

Simon sat back in his saddle and wiped the sweat from his forehead. Jenkins urged his camel alongside.

'Blimey,' said the Welshman. 'Guns galore.'

'Yes.' Simon recalled Wolseley's estimation back in London of the strength of the Egyptian army: untried infantry but the artillery was good – very good. 'Yes,' he mused, running his eye back down the line to where it disappeared in the heat haze to the south and squinting where the sun reflected from the pewter-coloured steel of the new Krupp cannon. 'Anyone attacking them across this open ground will have to go through an inferno.' He sighed and his gaze fell on Ahmed.

The little Egyptian had not spoken for some while and had dropped a little way behind his companions. He was now slumped in his saddle, contemplating the fortifications. Simon edged towards him and was surprised and embarrassed to see that Ahmed's eyes were moist.

'Are you all right, Ahmed?' he asked. 'Be careful. This sun is damned hot.'

'No.' The Egyptian gave a wan smile, pulled out a huge red handkerchief and blew his nose. 'It's not sun, Simon. It's . . . it's . . .' He blew his nose again and waved his hand. 'It's bloody guns, that's what it is.'

Simon frowned. 'Sorry, old chap. I don't quite . . .'

'Bloody guns.' He stood in his stirrups and gestured. Now he was not tearful but angry. 'All these big guns. All these soldiers. But nobody in Cairo can spare troops to protect my brother and other people crossing desert in caravans from Bedawis. No money for that, they say. Who pay for all this — all these German cannon, eh? I tell you. Poor *fellaheen*, that's who. They pay with their taxes and if they don't pay taxes they beaten with *kourbash*. I see it. My father was beaten. I was beaten as a boy by tax collectors with their whips. Now the money goes to fight British — the British who help us! They stop cheating in government and help the Khedive. They stay at my hotel. Why bloody hell fight them? Silly, silly, silly.' And he blew his nose again.

Simon and Jenkins exchanged glances. The little man was rarely opinionated, usually only anxious to help and, as time went on, clearly a little more apprehensive about 'the fighting'. But this was a new side to him. Simon couldn't think what to say. He patted Ahmed on the shoulder and pulled the head of his own camel round. 'Come on. I've seen enough. Let's go before they start questioning us.'

Simon set the course for their return journey a little further north of the canal and railway, the better to test the conditions to be faced by an army marching in some width across the desert. Here, as he had feared, the sand was deeper, and he realised that it would be difficult for wheeled vehicles to progress and that the British Army's two great beasts of burden, the horse and the mule, would be at a great disadvantage. As, of course, would be marching soldiers. He began drafting his report to Wolseley around the camp fire that night.

The problem of how to communicate with the General, at least, was solved on their return to Ismailia. Half fearing that the Royal Navy would have taken the Canal before their return, Simon was relieved to see that all was still serene in the little town, with the usual procession of steamers of various nationalities making its cautious way between the high banks of the Canal before entering the broader waters of Lake Timsah. Only the presence of an innocent enough Royal Navy gunboat, anchored off the pier head in the lake, provided any possible indication of unusual British interest in the town.

Repossessing their rooms in the hotel, the three men relinquished their Bedawi disguise and Simon completed his report. The hope that the gunboat would have direct Morse contact with the General's HQ prompted him to eschew the use of any clumsy code, but he kept his message terse and factual. He warned Wolseley of the guns of Tel el Kebir, of the entrenchments there, of the problems of advancing across the desert in heat and sand and of the vulnerability of the railway and the Sweetwater Canal. It was vital, he urged, to land a flying column at Ismailia *very quickly* ahead of the main force to strike out into the desert and secure these two 'desert highways' at least as far as Kassassin before they could be sabotaged.

To Simon's relief, he found that the British gunboat not only knew of his identity but had been expecting him. Wolseley thought of *everything*! The young lieutenant in command of the vessel welcomed him aboard and assured him that his report would be immediately telegraphed to the General, who was now, it seemed, steaming towards Port Said with his fleet of transports. As the message was tapped out in the wireless room, and over a large glass of gin and bitters in his small cabin, the young officer, appropriately bearded, brought Simon up to date with plans to take the Canal.

'It's all poised to go tomorrow, old chap,' he confided. 'The navy, thank goodness, is doing the whole job – with the marines, of course. Both ends are to be closed at exactly the same time, and Commander Edwards on HMS *Ready* will steam down the Canal, take over all barges and dredgers between Said and here, and make all ships in the waterway move into the *gares*.' He chortled. 'What's more, *Orion*, *Northumberland* and *Coquette*, plus five hundred marines will be here by daybreak to take over the lock and the Governor's house. By jove, I would love to see the look on old de Lesseps's face when this lot gets in.'

'De Lesseps?'

'Yes, you know, the Johnny who built the damned Canal in the first place?'

'Ah yes. Of course.'

'Well, he built himself a capital mansion here, and he runs virtually all of the pilots who work the Canal. He's very anti-British, and that's already posed a problem, because we know he's likely to withdraw the pilots as soon as the navy goes in. As a result, we've had to allocate a naval officer to every transport to con them down the canal. Tricky business, particularly as our ships haven't got the proper gear to steer in a narrow channel. Another gin?'

'No thanks.'

'This very evening, by the way, old de Lesseps is holding a dinner in his house for the officers of the garrison here in honour of Arabi. Bit of a cheek, eh? Trailing his coat a bit, what?'

Simon frowned. 'I presume he has a telegraph office here?'

'Yes. It's on the quay, just to starboard.' He pointed.

'Do we know the name of the telegraph manager?'

'As a matter of fact, I do. Difficult little bugger called Mahmut Sadat. He's been very unhelpful since we've been here. Why do you ask?'

'When do you expect your ships to berth here?'

'In the early hours.'

'And when will the marines land?'

'At dawn. You've obviously got something in mind.'

'Absolutely.' Simon smiled. 'Could I borrow your wireless operator at first light?'

'Ah. I see where you're bearing. A false message back to Cairo, eh?'

'Yes. In the manager's name, it could cause confusion at the very least. I presume they don't transmit in Arabic, for God's sake, do they?'

'No, French or English. Usually English, I think. That's the main language of the Canal, given the number of our merchant ships that pass through.'

'Good. Ask your chap to be on the quayside just before dawn and I'll tell him what to do. Now I must be off. Thanks for the gin.'

'A pleasure, old boy. I must say, you intelligence chaps are very inventive.'

'Intelligence?' Simon's eyebrows rose. 'Yes, well, I suppose that's what we do. Never quite thought of it like that. We're supposed to be just scouts.' He smiled again. 'Nice to be called intelligent, anyway. Thanks again for the drink.'

Back in the hotel, Simon sat down with Jenkins and Ahmed to tell them of the imminent invasion. Jenkins just grinned and nodded, but Simon's thoughts went again to Ahmed, who was about to see his country attacked by foreign troops. If the little Egyptian had harboured any lingering doubts about continuing to serve Simon and the British, however, the sight of the guns of Tel el Kebir had removed them, for he raised no objection to helping in the takeover of the telegraph shed the next morning.

'I do not want to kill my people,' he explained, 'but I want to push this Arabi down. So I want to help you get on with it. Not too much fighting though, eh?'

'Not too much, Ahmed. I will do my best.'

Jenkins sniffed. 'Oh, it'll be a lovely little tea party, look you. Don't you two worry about gettin' your 'ands dirty for a minute, see. Old 352 will do whatever's nasty, et cetera, et cetera, et cetera.'

Ahmed frowned at first, and then his thin face broke into a smile. 'Ah, 352, you pull my legs. Like you say, all Welshmen have one leg shorter than the other because they live in mountains and walk only one way round. Ha, ha. Very funny . . . I think.'

Jenkins shook his head sadly. 'Oh bloody 'ell. I'd better go an' oil the rifles.'

Simon took the opportunity to lie on his bed and, for the first time, allow himself to think of Alice. If Wolseley had kept his promise, then she would be with him as a member of the press contingent, sailing now with his transports on the way to Port Said and then on to Ismailia. That meant that she would also be with Covington. He stared at the inadequately whitewashed ceiling, seeing but not recording the pieces of plaster peeling away. What a strange situation! Would they live as man and wife on the ship and sleep together? He tossed his head. Surely not. To do so would certainly threaten their respective positions. A man couldn't take his wife with him on active service. But after the campaign, what then . . .? He closed his eyes. They would return to their normal married state, of course, living together, presumably trying to have children and . . . Damn it all! He sat upright. He must stop thinking like this. Alice was not his, she was Covington's and that was bloody well that! He grabbed a pencil and began drafting his *faux* telegraph to Cairo.

Long before the indigo sky to the east was fingered by the new day's sun, Simon and his companions had made their way to the quayside. Ismailia was tucked away on the northwestern side of Lake Timsah, just where the Suez Canal debouched into the lake, so offering sufficient room for ocean-going ships to anchor, and water deep enough for them to do so. Just as the gunboat captain had promised, three ironclads were now anchored off the pier head, looking grey and menacing in the semidarkness, and even though the hour was early, marines could be seen mustering on their decks. Waiting on the quayside was the young wireless operator from the gunboat. Telling him to stand by, Simon availed himself of the gunboat's tender to take him out to *Orion*, which the lieutenant had told him carried the force's leader, Captain Fitzroy. Dressed as he was in his Arab garments, he was not exactly welcomed on the deck of the vessel, where all seemed organised chaos, but he prevailed upon the Marine Major to take him to the Captain, standing aloof on the quarterdeck.

'Captain Fonthill, sir,' said Simon. 'General Wolseley's

intelligence officer' (how much better that sounded than 'scout'!), 'working here in Egypt.'

'Ah, yes.' The Captain's frown disappeared. 'I've heard of you, Fonthill. Now, for God's sake, you've not come to tell me to stop this bloody invasion, have you?'

Simon grinned. 'No, sir. Three things for you, though. First, there are about two thousand Egyptian troops based just over there, perhaps a couple of miles into the desert at Nefisha. You could lay a barrage on the place as soon as it is light. Hopefully that should prevent any attempt to stop you landing in force. Second, I must tell you that I intend to break into Monsieur de Lesseps's telegraph office on the quayside there and transmit a false message to Cairo, exaggerating your strength and warning against attacking Ismailia.'

Fitzroy's lip curled under his grey-flecked beard (was hirsuteness a necessary accoutrement for advancement in the navy? Simon wondered). 'Damned good idea. But don't sign it with de Lesseps's name. He's already proved an awkward customer and we don't want an international incident with France. I know about Nefisha and I shall fire at first light. What's the third thing?'

'A bit more long-term, sir. Arabi has already stationed a considerable number of troops about thirty-five miles away, along the railway and the Sweetwater Canal. A force should go out as soon as possible to protect both the rail line and the canal and prevent sabotage.'

'Very well, Fonthill. I only have a few marines and my orders are to secure Ismailia, but I will see how far I can get into the desert. Now, off you go to get that message off, before this place wakes up. And if all goes well through the day, come and dine with us on board this evening.'

'Very kind, sir, but another time. I have plenty to do.'

'I understand. Off you go.'

Simon landed just behind the first boatload of marines, who looked parade-ground smart in their white pith helmets with their red tunics criss-crossed by white pipe-clayed belts. But he shook his head sadly as he watched them double away, their rifles at the carry, to their allocated targets. When the sun came up, how they were going to sweat in that red serge! The new lightweight khaki had already been introduced in South Africa. Why not here?

Jenkins, Ahmed and the young wireless operator were waiting for him, a trifle impatiently.

'Is the telegraph office occupied?' he asked.

'No,' Jenkins replied. 'An' it's locked and bolted. I didn't like to blast it off, 'cos the place was so nice an' quiet, see. Seemed such a pity to wake everybody.'

'Quite right. Have you got your wonderful sword, Ahmed?'

The Egyptian drew it with a grin.

'Good. Let's see if we can use it to force the lock.'

In the event, neither the lock nor the bolt offered much resistance, and within five minutes the four of them were within the telegraph shed. Simon lit the oil lamp standing on a table and examined the apparatus. 'Can you use this all right?' he demanded of the young sailor.

'Oh aye, sir. I'll have to find the destination in this book. Where do you want to send it?'

'Address it to Army Headquarters, Cairo.' He handed him the message and then, seeing what seemed like a newly received signal scribbled on a message form on the desk, held up his hand. 'Wait. What's this?' He read:

TO COMMANDER NEFISHA GARRISON STOP INFORMER REPORTS THAT BRITISH LIKELY TO ATTACK ISMAILIA SOON STOP BATTALION OF INFANTRY WILL LEAVE CAIRO BY TRAIN AT SIX PM TOMORROW TO REINFORCE YOUR GARRISON STOP MAKE PROVISION ACCORDINGLY STOP FEHMY PASHA END

Simon frowned. An informer? Could Wolseley have a traitor in his camp? No, most unlikely. Somehow, despite all his care, the news of his intention must have leaked. He read out the message to the others.

'Who is Fehmy?' he asked of Ahmed.

'Big man. Number two to Arabi, I think.'

Simon grinned. 'Well, the big man deserves an answer.' He handed the message to the young blue jacket. 'Can you tell when this arrived?'

'Yes, sir.' He pointed to a code at the top of the message. 'About 'alf past five last night. It probably came in just as the bloke 'ere was goin' to shut up shop. So he decided to leave it until this mornin' to deliver it. Lazy bastard.'

'Fine.' Simon scribbled some alterations to his message. 'Now send this in reply.' He read it for everyone's benefit.

ADVISE DO NOT, REPEAT NOT, SEND TROOPS STOP BRITISH HAVE LANDED FIVE THOUSAND SOLDIERS STOP ISMAILIA AND NEFISHA ALREADY TAKEN STOP RAIL LINE DESTROYED STOP EVEN MORE

TROOPS BEING LANDED NOW STOP THIS SENT IN
SECRECY STOP MAHMUT SADAT STOP TELEGRAPH
MANAGER END

He grinned at them all. 'They will learn about the
landings soon enough anyway, but with any luck, this should
stop 'em rushing down here to attack us when we are still
landing troops and supplies and are at our most vulnerable.
Reduce the fighting, eh, Ahmed? Do you approve?'

The Egyptian nodded, his face breaking into his familiar
sad smile.

They waited while the sailor transmitted the message. He
looked up. 'Received all right, sir. Do you want me to wait
here to see if there is a reply?'

'No. I doubt if there will be. They will presume that the
telegraph point has been overrun. Well done. Get back to
your ship and present my compliments and thanks to your
skipper.' Simon opened the door of the hut and listened. He
could hear distant shouting and the crunch of hobnailed
boots on stone as the last of the marines landed and began
doubling away from the pier, but no sound of firing. The
promise of another hot day was now burnishing the eastern
sky, but the town still seemed to be asleep. So far, it seemed
as though Ismailia had been taken without a shot.

'The navy's guns will soon start ranging on to Nefisha,'
said Simon, squinting at his watch. 'We must get over there
and see what the effect is. I have a feeling that Fitzroy may
not have enough marines to put out scouts, so that must be
our job. The Egyptians there certainly have enough troops to
counterattack if they have the guts. If they do, we must give
warning.'

Jenkins wiped his moustache. 'What? Run towards the shells? Blimey, let's be careful, bach sir, eh? A bit cautious, like, eh?'

'Good lord, 352, you're getting to be a proper old woman. What's the matter? Frightened of a bit of gunfire?'

'No, it's just that I want to live to retire and take up the law, see. Now, don't you run too fast, bach sir. I've only got little legs, and Amen's are even littler.'

They began to jog-trot to the west, over the single bridge that spanned the Sweetwater and through palm-tree-fringed boulevards where everyone seemed to be indoors, unaware that sailors and marines of Queen Victoria were occupying their town and beginning the invasion of their country. None of the invading force were venturing this far out of the town's centre, and only dogs observed their progress, some of them following on their heels for a while until they lost interest. The three jogged, rifles and pistol in hand, through the somnolent, whispering quiet of the suburbs. Quiet, that is, until the first gun roared into life from the deck of HMS *Orion*.

The crump came like a thunderbolt from out of the now clear sky, and as they paused at the edge of the town, they saw a V-shaped eruption, black at the top and red at the bottom of the triangle, spring from near the rail track just behind the barrack block immediately ahead of them. As they watched, a bugle sounded and white-clothed men began to double from the barracks. Another shell landed, further out in the desert beyond the block, and then another, exploding harmlessly in the sand.

The shelling stopped and Simon pictured a gunnery lieutenant in the battle-top of *Orion*, focusing his telescope or binoculars on the target, reporting an overshoot and shouting down his instructions to the gun-layers. He noticed for the first time that a steam locomotive and a row of empty trucks were waiting on the rail track behind the barracks. More to the point, however, soldiers were being lined up in loose order in front of the barrack block, hastily adjusting their equipment and shouldering their rifles, as officers doubled up and down their ranks. The soldier in Simon could not resist a nod of approval.

'Good for them,' he murmured. 'They're not running. They're going to attack the town.'

'And us,' growled Jenkins.

'Quite.' Simon looked around. They were on the extreme edge of the town, although it was difficult to know where Ismailia ended and Nefisha began. A low wall ran to their right, indicating the boundary of a rambling garden. To their left meandered a dry *wadi*. 'Right,' he ordered. 'Three five two, you take the wall and Ahmed and I will take the *wadi*. Spread out and double up and down, firing from different positions. We must try and make them believe that an infantry platoon at least is facing them and so make them think twice about advancing over this open ground. If they try to enfilade us, then we will drop back.'

Simon was conscious once again of Ahmed, revolver in hand, looking at him with wide eyes. 'Enfilade means outflank us – get round the side and fire on us from there,' he explained. Then a second thought occurred to him. 'Don't worry, old chap. It is not important to kill anyone; just deter them. Fire your Colt over their heads or, better still, in the ground at their feet. You are almost out of range with that thing from here anyway. It's the noise and gun flashes that count.' He smiled. 'I haven't forgotten my promise. No real fighting, if we can help it. Go now, and keep moving and firing.'

The three split up just in time to see the first detachment of Egyptian soldiers in their baggy white uniforms, rifles at the slope, begin to march in their direction. Simon shouted to Jenkins: 'Don't fire to kill unless you have to.'

'Very good, bach sir.'

The two Martini-Henrys cracked as one and dust spurted up from the sand immediately in front of the leading rank. Simon heard the lighter note of the Colt, and he ran down the *wadi* and let off another round before doubling back again and repeating the exercise. Lifting his head, he saw two Turkish officers, swords in hand, berating their men, who were now lying flat on their stomachs. Reluctantly, the infantrymen began to climb to their feet and, fixing their bayonets, followed their officers towards where Simon, Jenkins and Ahmed were doing their inadequate best to replicate a platoon giving rapid fire.

Simon realised that deterrent fire was not going to be enough to stop the advance of the Egyptians, not least because further troops were now pouring out from the barracks and forming up in front of the building. It would only be a couple of minutes before the first rank were upon them. 'Take out the officers,' he shouted to Jenkins, who nodded, settled his cheek against his rifle stock and dispatched two rounds in quick succession. It was sufficient. Both men, their swords held aloft momentarily, sank to the ground and lay crumpled there. 'Sorry, Ahmed,' murmured Simon to himself. At that moment the shelling resumed.

The lieutenant in his battle-top eyrie had done his work

well, for although the first and second shells overshot into the desert again, the third and fourth hit the barracks, causing black clouds of masonry to spiral upwards and the roof of the building to sag in the middle. It was enough for the leaderless troops in the open. They turned and fled, joining their comrades behind them.

At first, Simon thought that it was a rout. Then he saw officers directing the men round the end of the barracks towards the rail track, where a thin column of white vapour showed that the driver of the locomotive was building steam. As the shells from *Orion* continued to plunge into the now flaming shell of the barracks, the Egyptian troops, showing commendable discipline despite the proximity of the explosions, filed into the rail trucks under the direction of their officers. With a derisive toot on its steam whistle, the train pulled out, to reveal a second locomotive and attendant line of open wagons, which began to absorb the remainder of the troops.

Slowly, Simon, Jenkins and Ahmed stood to watch the evacuation, and Simon wondered idly if their Scottish friend was on one of the footplates.

'Hey, you two A-rabs, put down them rifles!'

Simon whirled round to see a sergeant of marines, his huge moustache spreading out behind the rear sight of his rifle, the muzzle of which was attempting to cover both him and Jenkins. Behind the sergeant a detachment of marines came trotting up, sweat pouring down their cheeks from under their helmets. 'Put 'em down, I say.'

'Very well, Sergeant,' said Simon, in his best Sandhurst tones. He lowered his rifle to the ground. 'You look as though you could do with a drink.'

'Wot? Who the bloody 'ell are you?' The sergeant's head came up, but he still directed the barrel of his Martini-Henry at Simon.

'Captain Fonthill. Army intelligence. This is Sergeant Jenkins and Ahmed, our guide. Now put down that rifle, there's a good fellow.'

'Good lor'! Sorry, sir. You make a bloody good A-rab.'

Simon turned and gestured to where the second train was beginning to follow the first out into the desert. 'It looks as though the Nefisha garrison has departed, so there should be no further threat from that quarter. And it seems, thank God, that *Orion* has stopped shelling. Now, we had to shoot two Turkish officers. They are lying over there. I think one is dead but the other is only wounded. Can you send someone for a doctor?'

'Our ship's doctor is on the quayside, sir. I think we'll 'ave to carry the gennelman back to 'im.'

'Very well. Has the town been taken?'

'Oh yes, sir.' The sergeant grinned. 'Without firin' 'ardly a shot. Looks as though it's goin' to be easy to invade Egypt.'

Simon wiped his brow. 'I wouldn't quite say that. But come along now. Let's see to this wounded chap.'

The senior of the two Turks was, indeed, dead, but the second had sustained a bullet through the shoulder. He was in pain, but the sergeant produced a cigarette and the wounded man was carefully loaded on to a rough litter made from two rifles and crossbelts, and four marines began to carry him to the quayside.

There, Simon met Captain Fitzroy. 'Ah, Fonthill.' The Captain's cap was now set jauntily on his head, tilted to starboard. The light of victory was in his eyes. He could afford to be jocular. 'They tell me that you and your three-man army have sent the bloody Nefisha garrison packing, virtually on your own.'

Simon gave a weary grin. 'Not quite, sir. Had a bit of help from some pretty efficient gun-laying on *Orion*. Congratulations, Captain. I gather the town is taken.'

'Aye. Hardly had to fire a shot. I will push as many marines as possible out along the railway track as soon as I can, but I can't spare many. I gather that things have gone well in closing off the Canal at both Port Said and Suez, and the first of the transports will be here tomorrow and we can begin off-loading. Wolseley himself should be here soon. No doubt you will want to report to him, eh?'

'Of course, sir.' Wolseley and his staff, Covington and Alice . . .

Chapter 13

Alice was grateful for the clean sea air afforded by the passage to Port Said after the heat and pain of Alexandria. The press corps, in fact, were not accommodated on Wolseley's own vessel and Alice was glad of that, for it meant that she would not have to be in daily contact with her husband, who was a member, of course, of the General's staff. Her meeting with him at the consul's house had been difficult. He had been full of concern but also anger at her foolhardiness in pursuing George and, it was clear, he had channelled much of that anger towards Simon. She had felt despair at being the cause of renewing the old hostility, and although the damage to her throat had soon been repaired, a deep depression had descended: a combination of the memory of the terrors of the ordeal she had endured and her realisation that she must, *she really must*, grasp the fact that she had no future with Simon. It was her duty, indeed her only option, to put all her energy into making her marriage work. Wolseley's invitation, however, to join the main press party with his expedition, and a message from Cornford complimenting her upon her reports from Alexandria, had served to lift her spirits, and she left the consulate with a new determination to face the future positively.

The size of the press contingent amazed her. She had had to face little on-the-spot competition in her coverage of the campaigns in Zululand, Afghanistan and the Transvaal – even though the great Willie Russell of *The Times* had been with her on the last. She had always had time and space to slip away and follow her own leads. This war was obviously going to be very different. The press corps now numbered more than forty and was international to an extent that she had not encountered before. The *Toronto Globe* drank on board with the *New York Herald Tribune*; *Figaro* rubbed shoulders with the more familiar Reuters; and *Wiener Zeitung* was to be seen exchanging notes with the bright new *Corriere della Sera* from Milan. The world and its wife, it seemed, was now following the fortunes of Sir Garnet Wolseley. For this was not just the latest in Queen Victoria's little colonial wars. Great Britain was now invading a sovereign country, albeit with the condign, if rather distant, approval of that state's imperial masters in Constantinople. The whole world was watching and waiting for the British lion to flounder and then fall flat on its face in the sands of Egypt. General Wolseley was quite aware of this. Like all his contemporaries, he disliked and distrusted the growing intrusion of the press, but he was worldly enough to know that it was a necessary evil and that he must live with it. As a result, he had set up a special section of his staff to co-operate with and look after the reporters. Alice immediately regarded it as a euphemism for sponsorship, and decided to have as little to do with it as possible.

As always, of course, she was the only woman in this

gaitered, cigar-smoking fraternity. For that and other reasons, she stood aloof and discouraged familiarity. She had no wish to compromise her position as a married woman, of course, but more to the point, she had never liked the practice adopted by some correspondents of working in pairs. This certainly helped to cover the ground more efficiently, but it meant the sharing of information, and this was anathema to Alice, who valued her ability to discover the obscure fact that might illuminate a whole campaign or, more delightfully, reveal the weakness in a strategy presented with pompous confidence by a commander.

There was another reason, however, for Alice's singularity. Despite her youth and her gender, she stood out in that polyglot gathering of much-travelled war correspondents as 'Griffith of the *Morning Post*', an experienced campaigner who had been first into Alexandria and written colourful copy about the bombardment and the riots. Her cold beauty concealed a wily, idiosyncratically skilled professional. She was to be admired but watched, greeted but not courted, respected but never indulged.

All of this suited Alice perfectly. She used the two days' sailing along the coast to set her mind in place, to regain her confidence and her accustomed good health. After much thought, she also penned a background piece to the Alexandria riots and looting, profiling, in more detail this time, the story of the three men dressed as Arabs, two of them, it seemed British, and the third Egyptian, who had toured the city on that first dreadful night. In addition to organising the defence of the bank, they had saved the consul from the mob and also intervened crucially in several other attacks on European residents, before disappearing into the night. They had come to be known, she wrote hyperbolically and quite inaccurately, as 'The Pimpernels of Alexandria'. It was a good piece, she felt, if a little sensational for the *Post*. It was also, she was forced to confess to herself, her goodbye to Simon and her last tribute to him. Finally, it would infuriate Ralph Covington – and she was not averse to doing that at this point in her life.

HMS *Monarch*, the ship carrying the press corps, was allocated the task of leading the attack on Port Said. This was done at three in the morning, under the eager gaze of the correspondents. A small detachment of marines were landed as the town slept and quickly overpowered the Egyptian sentries. Then seamen from *Monarch* and *Iris* strung a cordon across the neck of land on which the town was situated to prevent any escape, and two further companies of marines surrounded the barracks and captured the Egyptian troops in their beds. Very soon after, in response to a request from Captain Fitzroy, a detachment of the Royal West Kent was dispatched by torpedo boat and gunboat down the Canal to Ismailia to secure the railway out in the desert as far as possible.

It was all done, Alice had to admit (and report), with commendable alacrity and efficiency, and with no casualties on either side. Wolseley, of course, at his best.

Monarch was forced to delay her voyage down the Canal as the great convoy of warships and transports mustered at the port and each ship was allocated her own navigating officer for the difficult passage between the narrow, high banks. Alice took advantage of the hiatus to slip ashore. It was still early morning, for the occupation had taken less than three hours, and she was anxious to see how quickly normal life would be restored to Port Said. Would the shopkeepers and street traders in the bazaar huddle indoors, fearful of the invading troops? Would there be, perhaps, residual sniping at the occupying marines from rooftops and high windows? Such early signs could be portents of the way in which the ordinary people of Egypt would regard this invasion, and would make good copy.

In fact, she found what she could only presume to be a healthy normality everywhere. Despite the early hour, the bazaars were a delight of vivid colour and exotic odours, overlaid on a base of humming, burbling noise. As she pushed between the stalls, delighted at the strangeness of it all, she was offered saffron fabrics that sang of the dyers' skills and sweetmeats that made her swallow in anticipation, aggravating her still sore throat. Two patrolling marines, bargaining for curved daggers in elaborate sheaths, started guiltily when they saw her, but she gave them a bright smile and a wave of absolution. She stopped and handled some of the hand-woven rugs and munched a tiny, delicious custard in pastry that was given to her with no demand for payment. She lingered at a silverware stall and eventually bought a delicate filigree bracelet, too entranced to bother with the boring business of bargaining about the price. It was as though she was on holiday.

Then she saw him. Mr George stood behind a stall on the far side of the narrow street, watching her. He seemed to be wearing Arab outer dress, but a glimpse of the familiar celluloid collar, the small, square moustache and the hard eyes behind the spectacles immediately identified him. He was carrying a bag from the top of which a large golden tureen peaked out and gleamed dully in the sun. As she caught his eye, he gave her a little nod of recognition and his eyes seemed to glint behind his glasses.

A sob came to Alice's throat and she immediately swung round to find the marines, but they had gone. Involuntarily, she put her hand to her throat and spun back again, but George had disappeared. She twisted the bracelet around her fist in a pathetic attempt to create a weapon and swept her gaze over the surrounding stalls, but there was no sign of the little clerk. It was as though he had never existed.

Alice realised that she was trembling, but she took a deep breath and forced herself to approach the stall at which George had been standing. 'Do you speak English?' she whispered to the stallholder.

'Leetle bit, missie.'

'That man, the one carrying the dish in the bag, do you know him?'

'What man? I seed no man.'

'He was short and . . . oh, never mind.'

She turned away and began walking, very erect, back the way she had come, keeping her stride long and balanced. But she could not maintain her calm and she soon broke into a frantic run, forcing her way through the crowds until, panting, she eventually reached the boat that thankfully was still waiting for her at the harbour wall. It was not until the boatman had pulled halfway out to HMS *Monarch*, that she was able to relax.

She was still trembling, however, when she lay down on her bunk in her little cabin and began to think. It *was* George, there was no doubt about it – the flash of recognition behind the round spectacles, the almost lascivious half-smile, the tiny bow of the head. Oh, it was him, all right! But what to do about it?

Alice shook her head in frustration. She could not reach Ralph, and in any case, what could he do? George would be lost in the Port Said melting pot by now and she could not exactly demand that a search party be landed to comb the town for a small man with a celluloid collar. Wolseley knew about George, of course, and she had been told that he had sworn to smoke him out after the invasion was over. But, again, she could hardly ask that he put aside his march on Cairo to look for the little swine. Simon . . . Simon would do it. But where was he? And he was no longer her protector, her knight in shining armour, her love . . . Damn! That was enough of that!

She sat upright and tipped a little water – lukewarm, of course – on to her face flannel, then wiped her face and, more gingerly, her neck and throat. George was obviously still in business, presumably trying to acquire bargains or trade his own illicit wares illegally. She tried to remember what he had said in that awful house about his dealings. He exported to Greece, wasn't it? Yes. Presumably he had had difficulty in finding a ship in Alexandria and was now trying his hand in Port Said. The man seemed to have no problem at all in moving around the country, even in time of war. Well, let him be for the moment. He could wait until after the war. In the meantime, though, she resolved that she would buy a revolver. She nodded to herself in the little mirror. No more fear, dammit!

Alice had not long returned to the ship when the great propellers began to revolve and the vessel began to tremble as she made way to fall in line with the convoy setting off down the Canal. A quick dash down the waterway was out of the question because of the absence of trained pilots and the consequent danger of grounding and so blocking the passage completely for the following ships. This danger soon became a reality, and several times the larger ships, *Catalonia* and *Bavaria* among them, ran aground and had to be eased off while the convoy behind waited in the heat and the mosquitoes.

Progress, then, was stately and Alice's mind turned back to the woodcuts she had seen as a child of the great procession down Ismail Pasha's Canal thirteen years earlier, when it had been opened by the Empress Eugenie of France, her steamer leading a line of vessels dressed fore and aft in gay bunting and carrying the royals of Europe. Not quite all of them, though, she reflected with a smile. Queen Victoria had declined the invitation and refused to allow the Prince of Wales and Princess Alex to attend (although Prince 'Tum Tum' and his pretty wife had had their own viewing as Ismail's guests two months before). Standing at the bow rail of *Monarch* watching the high banks slip by, however, Alice's smile soon turned to a frown as she remembered that forty thousand *fellaheen* had been torn from their homes and forced to dig out the ninety-seven million cubic yards of sand, mud, silt and rocks to form the Canal. And how many had died? She shook her head. There were some statistics that even her radical mind forbore to retain.

The landing at Ismailia was chaotic, with vessels queuing to take turns at the solitary landing stage. Alice learned that the transport carrying the two steam locomotives brought to carry much of Sir Garnet's supplies and many of his troops up the line towards Cairo had been forced to sail on to Suez and off-load its cargo there, because the landing pier at Ismailia could not take them. The great engines would have to steam their way north, back up the railway that followed the banks of the maritime canal. She looked behind her at the transports waiting to unload and then forward to the slings laboriously swinging one mule at a time on to the pier. Why on earth, she wondered, did not Arabi attack? It would take days to sort out the embarkation and the priorities of unloading. During this confusion, Ismailia would surely be virtually defenceless?

Then she learned that the marines in the advance party and the guns of *Orion* had seen off the Egyptian garrison just outside the town, and that a clever ruse had been used to telegraph Cairo and mislead Arabi about the speed and strength of the occupation of Ismailia. It made good copy. In the meantime, the only attack on the bustling little town came from the ever-present mosquitoes.

Alice and the other correspondents landed and were housed in a small tented encampment near the Khedive's winter palace, which Wolseley had taken – with the Khedive's permission, it was emphasised – as his head-quarters. A reconnaissance force had been sent along the railway out into the desert, but no fighting had been reported and the journalists were not allowed to accompany it. Alice had to fill her time with reporting on the difficulties experienced in mustering the army and supplying it. Already the heat was taking its toll, for the temperature at midday often exceeded 95 degrees, and Alice made it her business to visit the sickness tents, discovering them full of victims of sunstroke and stomach problems. She learned that medical supplies were proving to be inadequate, with no chloroform, castor oil or carbolic acid and, even worse, precious little rice, the best treatment for the diarrhoea that was sweeping through the camp. She duly wrote about this, but mindful of the censors, modified the implied criticism by reporting that these shortages were thought to be only temporary problems, caused by the difficulties of unloading. To her surprise, these references remained uncensored. Either Wolseley was too busy to be bothered with this sort of detail, or he was becoming more relaxed about press coverage.

Shortly after landing, Alice visited the Khedive's palace to find her husband. She had determined to display more affection to him and astonished Covington by kissing him warmly on the lips. He responded awkwardly – she sensed that his old injuries were causing him discomfort in the heat – and walked her outside into the well-watered gardens, towards the shade of a leaning palm.

'How is your throat, my darling?' he asked.

'Oh, very well, thank you, my dear. Look, no scar, the bruises have gone and I can swallow perfectly well again.'

'Good. I am so sorry, but I can't ask you to mess with us because it wouldn't be right to single out one of the correspondents for this favour.' He smiled. 'Even though she is the wife of a staff colonel.'

'Oh no. I quite understand. Why don't you come to my tent this evening and I will show you how well I can cook over an open fire? It will be rough and ready but quite wholesome, I assure you.' Then she added quickly, 'I am afraid that you cannot stay, for the tent is extremely small.'

He raised her hand to his lips in that well-remembered way and his eye twinkled. 'What a pity, but never mind. I accept and I shall bring champagne, so that we can make the best of it. But you mustn't milk me for information. I don't want to get the sack.'

The meal was a success. Alice had managed to buy a chicken and even find some rice to boil, and with the smoke from the fire keeping away all but the most persistent mosquitoes, they ate adequately and drank well, with the champagne staying reasonably cool in a water-filled leather bucket.

Of course Alice tried to extract as much information as possible from her husband about Wolseley's intentions, but he remained good-humouredly guarded. He did allow, however, that the General had been told that Arabi had about sixty thousand troops at his disposal, plus some six thousand tribesmen, and that Wolseley's bluff had worked, with more than half of that force still deployed along the north coast. Nevertheless, he believed that troops were now being shifted south and that the main confrontation would take place at Tel el Kebir, where the Egyptian cannon would be the main problem.

'He doesn't care whether Arabi has a mob of thirty thousand or a hundred thousand,' Covington confided. 'It's the guns of el Kebir that will be the biggest problem to solve. But he will do it, of course. He has two divisions here and the Indian contingent now being safely disembarked at Suez in the south. He is very confident.'

'Was he ever anything but?' Alice smiled. Despite her dislike of his inbred jingoism, she had a great admiration for the little General, who had been kind to her on the Mozambique border, where Covington had been so severely wounded, and who always knew exactly what he wanted to do and how to do it. She wondered if the intelligence on which he based his confidence had come from Simon. How to ask?

'My dear,' she began hesitantly, 'I know that you dislike Simon Fonthill, but I am concerned about him, for he saved my life in Alexandria and I have no idea where he is. Do you happen to know if he is still working for the General and what he is doing?'

Covington smoothed his moustaches, gave her a quick glance then frowned and gestured over his shoulder with his hook. 'He's out there somewhere, with his little Welshman and this Egyptian he has in tow. Wolseley's sent him out into the desert ahead of Major General Graham's force, to see what's afoot around Tel el Maskhuta and beyond, to Kassassin.'

Involuntarily, Alice drew in her breath. She attempted to conceal her anxiety with a smile. 'Ah well, that means the General should receive reliable intelligence. Whatever you think of him, Simon Fonthill and his Welshman are marvellous scouts, you must agree.'

'Mmmm, though a most unreliable fellow, with a strange streak in him. But I don't want to talk of him. Are you sure I can't stay?' He leaned across and took her hand.

Alice shook her head. 'I am sorry, Ralph, but it really wouldn't do.' She gestured. 'I am surrounded by men, as you can see, and I do think it would be invidious for me to be seen, er, co-habitating with you, even though you are my husband.' She smiled and lifted his hand to her lips. 'Anyway, my dear, there isn't any damned room.'

'Don't need much, as a matter of fact.' He sighed. 'But if you insist, I shall limp away. Sleep well, my love. And thank you.'

* * *

Alice cleaned her pots and plates and put them away. So refreshing to be forced to do things for oneself! To comfort herself, she replenished the fire with another precious piece of dried camel dung as she looked around at the darkened tents. She felt again a little tremble of fear at the thought that George might have followed her down the Canal and could be out there, somewhere, with a noose in his hand, with only the thin canvas of her tent to protect her . . . She shuddered and took the longest of her kitchen knives with her as she crawled under the canvas, into her bedroll, and turned her face to the west on the pillow. Somewhere, out there for certain, was Simon. But she mustn't think of him.

The next morning, she received a call from a sergeant armourer whom she had befriended. ' 'Ere you are, miss,' he said, pressing a small parcel into her hand. 'It's the best I could do. All our stuff would be too big for you, and anyway, it would be a court-martial offence to get you an army revolver. This is actually a French job. A little beauty. Short barrel and small enough to fit into yer bag, but it's eleven-millimetre calibre and can kill at short range. Can't pronounce it, but it's written down 'ere, see.'

Alice took the slip of paper and read 'Chamelot-Delvigne'.

'It's general issue for French officers now,' he continued. 'There's a dozen cartridges with it. Sorry, but I couldn't get more. Don't ask me 'ow I got it, miss, but that'll be ten pounds, please.'

'Thank you, Sergeant. It sounds ideal.' She paid him the money, and back in her tent unwrapped the parcel and weighed the revolver in her hand. It was small and stubby but felt good. She sighed and put it in her bag. Now she would never have to run from danger again.

Chapter 14

Simon, Jenkins and Ahmed rose well before dawn, as was their practice in the desert, and were in the saddle long before the sun came up. Its early rays showed nothing before them as usual but the unrelenting line of the rail track on their right and, on their left, the humped ridges that marked the course of the Sweetwater Canal. A morning breeze, however, had sprung up, though far from being a welcome respite from the early heat, it raised the fine particles of surface sand, causing the grit to penetrate their nostrils and find its way between the squinting slits of their eyes. It blurred their view so that the rare patches of scrub seemed to rise from the surface of a yellow fog rather than solid ground, eerily warranting their Arab name of 'devil plant'. Simon raised his hand and pointed his finger to the left, gently pulling the head of his camel round. The others followed, heads bowed against the swirling sand.

At the canal bank, Simon turned with his back to the wind to enable him to look down at the water level. 'It's gone down,' he shouted. 'They must have erected a dam further up. We'd better locate it quickly and tell General Graham, otherwise the whole canal will dry up downstream and ruin the advance. Top up the water bottles while we can.'

Ahmed scrambled down the bank and filled their bottles from the green water. Then they plodded on, staying close to the line of the canal. Luckily, the sandstorm abated as quickly as it had arisen and visibility was restored to the trio so that, from about a mile away on the flat terrain, they could see the mound of rock and sand that had been piled across the Sweetwater at – as Simon had feared from their earlier reconnaissance – the hamlet of Magfar, where the banks of the canal were low and facilitated the building of the dam. Simon knelt awkwardly on one knee on his saddle and focused his field glasses on the dam. It seemed to be completely unguarded.

It had been the threat of the dams blocking the waters of the Sweetwater Canal that had concerned Wolseley when he had summoned Simon for a meeting immediately on his arrival at Ismailia. The General had seemed preoccupied and pale (as well he might, thought Simon, given the logistical nightmare facing him with the disembarkation of his army and supplies). He had even given up waxing his moustache, so that it now drooped either side of his mouth. His congratulations to his scout on the latter's reports and action in sending the false telegram to Cairo were clearly sincere, but brief.

'What I want from you now, Fonthill,' he had said, 'is to get out there, along the line of the canal and find out where they dam it, as I'm sure they will. Report on how well they're defending the dams. I'm sending Graham out behind you with a considerable force as soon as he can get started. Report back to him and he will clear the dams as far as he can go, even up to Kassassin, if he can. I shall need the canal for drinking water on the advance and as a supply route. Off you go now on your bloody camel, and stay safe, my boy.'

Stay safe. So far on their reconnaissance they had met no danger, only discomfort. The Egyptians did not seem to have put out patrols near to Ismailia, although no doubt they were concentrating in force further up the rail line. Kneeling on his wooden saddle now, Simon could see no sign of troops defending the dam, although beyond it he could see a dark smudge that was the village of Maskhuta. This had been unoccupied when they had previously passed through it, but could well now be a point of defence for the dam and the railway itself. Well, there was only one way to find out . . .

They rode on, trusting to their disguise as Bedawi to protect them from indiscriminate fire, at least. But the dam seemed completely deserted. It had been hurriedly thrown up, that seemed clear, for no attempt had been made to seal the barrier of mud blocks and sand, so that water was seeping through. But it was effective enough to lower the level of water considerably below it. A couple of such blockages could completely cut off the water supply to Ismailia.

Simon levelled his glasses at Maskhuta. Although now much nearer and well within field gun range, a number of sand hills restricted his view. He could see, however, white-clad figures ranging along the hills and dull reflections from what could only be cannon.

He turned to the others. 'We will turn off north out into the desert and see if we can get round these emplacements,' he said. 'Then I shall need you, 352, to ride back to General Graham . . .'

He stopped short. Jenkins, magnificent horseman, shot, knife-fighter, boot-cleaner, shirt-presser and, now, legal advocate, had two great failings: he drank too much and, more to the point now, he had absolutely no sense of direction. Simon frowned. Even with the rail track and the canal to guide him, there was no guarantee that the little Welshman would find Graham's force marching behind them. The look of near panic that had crept into Jenkins's eyes convinced him.

'No', he continued. 'On second thoughts, I would like you, Ahmed, to ride back to the General. I will write you a message when I can see more detail. Let's ride on now.'

Rather shamefacedly, Jenkins grinned his acknowledgement, and the three urged their camels out into the desert. It soon became obvious that Maskhuta was indeed the advance point of Arabi's forces and that the Egyptians had erected a further dam there. The position was a smaller version of Tel el Kebir, with the enemy having dug trenches out into the desert with what looked like twelve guns set in emplacements, all of which also commanded the dam at Magfar. What was more, there was a fringe of cavalry lurking at the northern point of the trenches and a considerable number of white-clad troops manning the line. It looked very much as though Arabi intended to make a stand here, holding up Wolseley's advance on Tel el Kebir.

As Simon made a rough sketch of what he could see of the defences, he was interrupted by Jenkins.

'I don't think we're goin' to be able to get round them lot,' he said, pointing to where the Egyptian cavalry were mustered. As they watched, a detachment of about half a dozen horsemen began mounting and falling into line. It was clear that the trio had been seen.

'Damn,' said Simon. He looked at Ahmed. 'Can horses outrun camels on this ground?'

'Depends. If sand deep, no. If it get hard, yes.'

'Right. We obviously can't get round, so I think we had all better go back and warn Graham. Wait a minute, Ahmed.' He scribbled on a piece of paper, folded it and handed it to the Egyptian. 'If it looks as though they are going to overtake us, you go on ahead and give this to the General. We will try and hold them off while you get away.' He pulled the head of his camel round. 'Let's head out to the north a bit to find the deeper sand. Come on.'

'Oh, blimey,' said Jenkins. 'No racin' now, bach sir. You're goin' to find it a bit precarious up 'ere when we're goin' fast, see.'

They turned round and set their beasts to a lumbering trot. It soon became clear that their camels were made for the plodding walk of desert marathons, rather than short-distance sprinting. Racing camels they were not, and Simon, his left leg hooked desperately round the saddle cantle as he bumped and swayed to the irregular gait, had a horrible feeling that he was edging slowly to the left and an inevitable tumble to the ground. Way ahead of him, Ahmed was flying and had opened a considerable gap on the heavier Jenkins, who, impeccable horseman that he was, was sitting easily, flaying his mount's side with his thin camel stick.

Clinging on for dear life, Simon looked at the ground. The sand certainly seemed deeper here and it billowed up from the pads of the animals ahead. Would it, however, delay horses? He ventured a look behind him. The six horsemen had fanned out but were clearly making heavy going of it, sending up their own much heavier clouds of sand. But were they gaining? He could not tell. One thing was sure, he could not stay on his blasted animal for much longer at this pace.

He called ahead: 'Three five two.'

Jenkins reined in and Simon caught him up.

'Let Ahmed ride on. My animal is not as fast as either of yours. Let's dismount at the top of that rise ahead and put in a bit of rapid fire, to show that we have modern rifles and discourage these fellows.'

Jenkins nodded and grinned but, for once, stifled any jibe about Simon's riding abilities. Together they rode to the top of a high sand dune ahead and, on its reverse slope, dismounted, then hurriedly hobbled their camels and crept to the top of the dune, rifles in hand. Their pursuers were some three hundred yards away, flogging their beasts as they floundered in the deepening sand.

'Rapid fire,' ordered Simon, and the two Martini-Henrys barked together. The lead rider, presumably the officer, immediately threw up his hands and fell from his horse, and the second horse, a bullet through its breast, sprawled in the sand, throwing its rider well clear. The other four cavalrymen reined in and milled around as they attempted to withdraw their carbines from their holsters. Jenkins's second shot brought one of them down and Simon sent a bullet whistling between the remainder. It was enough. With hardly a backward glance, the three men pulled their horses' heads round and galloped back the way they had come.

'Well, bloody 'ell,' said Jenkins, climbing to his feet. 'That wasn't much of a fight, was it? They could 'ave done better'n that.'

'I'm not sure they could. We caught them by surprise.' Simon frowned. 'I don't think we can afford to go back to see if we can help anyone who is wounded, and anyway, those three should return when they've got their nerve back. Come on. I want to see Graham as soon as possible.'

They remounted and Simon set a course further south to regain firmer ground near the railway. They never did catch up with Ahmed, whose speed on the camel belied his earlier claim that he did not know the ways of the desert. They did, however, strike General Graham's force just before nightfall. In fact, the General was not with the advance guard, but Sir Garnet Wolseley and his staff were. Simon was surprised to see the Commander-in-Chief, whom he had supposed to be back in Ismailia, sorting out the depressing conundrum of off-loading his men and supplies and getting them over that narrow bridge across the Sweetwater. He was immediately reminded of Wolseley's contemptuous reference in London to 'counting beans'. He would have been glad of the excuse to get out into the desert to contact the enemy, and he looked all the better for it.

The General and his senior officers was sitting round an open camp fire as darkness descended. They were studying a map, and Simon noticed that Wolseley had his note in his hand. The General looked up as Simon and Jenkins were led into the circle.

'Good Gad, Fonthill.' Wolseley grinned as he looked the pair of them up and down. 'You two make as fine a pair of A-rabs as I have seen since landing in this bloody awful country. You do black up well, I must say. Come in and sit down and have a mug of tea. You too, 374.'

At that, Simon heard a distinct snort of disgust from the circle and caught the disapproving eye of Covington, the scar that stretched from under his patch across the cheekbone standing out blackly in the firelight.

'Thank you, sir. Not shoe-blacking, though. Just sunburn. I see you have my note.'

'Yes. Now fill me in completely. I thought that the Sweetwater level seemed to have fallen. Two dams, you say?'

Simon nodded, and described the results of their reconnaissance, while Jenkins, noisily supping his tea, sat bolt upright on the camp stool at his side, beaming and proud to find himself in the council of war but in no way daunted at being in its presence.

When he had finished, Wolseley nodded. 'Well done, Fonthill.' He looked around at his staff. 'I'm glad we came, gentlemen,' he said. 'I think we would all agree that we need now to move urgently and engage the enemy at the first possible opportunity, to flush them out and clear those dams.'

There was a general murmur of approval, and Wolseley turned back to Simon. 'I've got Major General Drury Lowe here,' he nodded to a heavily moustached officer sitting with his elegantly booted legs thrust before him, 'with the Household Cavalry, a detachment each of the 19th Hussars and the mounted infantry and two guns. General Graham is coming up behind with the 2nd Yorks and Lancasters and some Royal Marine artillery acting as cavalry.' He grinned and pulled at his moustache. 'Bit of a patchwork quilt, but had to take the chaps off-loaded first, don't you know. Now, from what you've seen, have we got sufficient to clear the enemy from Maskhuta?'

'With respect, General.' Covington made his way into the circle of light. 'With respect, I doubt whether Fonthill here has the capacity or the experience to give that sort of advice.

He was in my regiment as a subaltern, you may remember, and I know him well. May I suggest that you go out with a detachment of cavalry tomorrow and take a look for yourself first, before making decisions?'

Simon flushed, and he felt Jenkins stiffen at his side and murmur, 'Bloody cheek.'

Wolseley looked up and spoke coolly. 'You seem to forget, Ralph, that Fonthill has served with me too, and I believe him to have a remarkably old head on his young shoulders.' A testy note entered his voice. 'Of course I shall bloody well go and have a look myself at first light, but if I want to act quickly, I need to send a message back to Graham tonight. Now,' he turned back to Simon, 'pray give me your opinion.'

Simon cleared his throat and avoided looking at Covington. 'I would say you have enough men, sir, to flush the Egyptians out of Maskhuta, but you will be outgunned with just two cannon. The enemy have twelve guns, well emplaced. You will need more guns. And if I may suggest . . .'

'Suggest away, though Ralph here may snort and fume.' Sir Garnet looked up at Covington with a smile to temper his earlier tartness. Simon recalled that the two men had served together closely in the jungle during the Ashanti War.

'Once you have cleared Maskhuta,' Simon continued, 'I think you should strike as far up the railway and canal as you can, sir, with the men you have now and those behind with General Graham, to stop any further damming of the canal and possible disruption to the railway. If you can fetch up more artillery, I think you could clear Kassassin and then pause to build up your strength before making your final attack at Tel el Kebir.' Silence fell on the little gathering, and Simon wondered if he had gone too far. Wolseley sat looking at him.

'Right,' he said finally, slapping his thigh and standing. 'Smithie,' he called to an aide. 'Draft orders immediately to General Graham, asking him to bring forward the 2nd DCLI from Nefisha and the Guards brigade and any cavalry and artillery that are available from Ismailia. Have the orders ready for me to sign within the half-hour, and a rider and escort to take them back. Drury, have your men ready to march out at first light. I shall be with you. And you two Arabs,' he flashed a smile at Simon and Jenkins, 'shall come too. Now, gentlemen, let us muster again at six for something to eat and then it must be an early night.'

He nodded his dismissal of Simon and Jenkins – it was clear that the dinner invitation was not completely inclusive – and strode away, leaving the little group to break up. Without a glance at Covington, Simon led Jenkins away to find Ahmed.

The three men made their own fire by their tent and ate well from the provisions that Jenkins, who had never lost his ability to forage, provided from a friendly army cook. When told that they would be part of the general advance in the morning, Ahmed betrayed a little apprehension.

'It is not that I am afraid, Simon,' he confessed. 'But it will be a killing business, I think. Yes?'

'Afraid so, Ahmed.'

'I would not like to kill my own people, please. I know you understand. And I am a bit afraid of shooting off my foot again, anyway.' His eyes opened earnestly. 'I am good with first shot with your revolver. But it bounces back and I shoot second too soon. I worry I shoot off my toes, et cetera, et cetera, et cetera.'

'Ooh blimey,' said Jenkins, 'you don't want to lose them. 'Ave you tried shootin' with your eyes closed, like?'

Simon sighed. 'Oh, take no notice of him, Ahmed. As you will have noticed, the Welsh are very peculiar. I do understand what you are saying, but I don't think you need to worry. There will be plenty of other people to fire guns tomorrow. But keep your Colt with you at all times. You cannot be in a battle without some sort of protection. Now I think it's time to turn in.'

Before he did so, Simon stood at the edge of the light cast by the fire and looked up at the sky, where the stars hung like sequins on a cloak of the darkest velvet. Only the munching of oats from the nearby horse lines and a stamped hoof disturbed the silence of the desert. Where was Alice on this night of such quiet beauty?

He was joined for a moment by Jenkins. 'The old CO ain't lost 'is charm, bach sir, 'as 'e?'

Simon smiled. 'I don't suppose Covington will ever change. He once believed me to be a coward. I would have thought that enough has happened over the last few years to prove otherwise, but he still hates me and I suppose he always will. One thing's for certain – I have had enough of the bloody man now.'

Jenkins was silent for a moment, and then he coughed. 'Would it be Miss Alice, d'yer think . . .?'

For once Simon did not flare up. 'No. He never knew about us. I am sure that Alice, once she'd made up her mind about honouring her engagement after he was so badly disfigured, would never tell him. I am certain of that.

Perhaps the bastard just needs someone to hate. Anyway, it doesn't matter now. Come on. Let's get some sleep.'

The column set off long before sun-up, with Wolseley and his staff riding in the van and a thin screen of cavalry pushed far ahead. The General gestured for Simon to ride with him. Sir Garnet nodded to the rear.

'The guns and the few carts we've got with us are having difficulty getting through the sand,' he said. 'I know you warned me about this in your cables, but it was just not possible to get sufficient pack camels and their handlers to join us in the time available, so we are going to have to put up with mules and such.'

'Can't be helped, sir. Do you think that Arabi will stand and fight at Tel el Kebir?'

'Undoubtedly. Always thought so. It's the obvious place to try and stop me, once he knew that I wasn't going to push south from Alex.'

This jolted Simon's memory. 'That message we intercepted at Ismailia, sir. It spoke of an informer warning that you would land there. Do you have any idea of who he might be?'

Wolseley frowned and brushed a fly from his moustache. 'No. But it did concern me, of course. Obviously it couldn't be anyone on my staff, and very few people knew of my plans. However, once we were seen off Port Said, the cat was out of the bag. Anyway, we were able to disembark without any interference, so all was well in the end.'

It was Simon's turn to frown. 'Yes, sir, but if we hadn't intercepted that telegram and sent the false one back by return, that extra battalion would have arrived before you'd landed and could have made all the difference to you taking the town.'

'Mmm.' The General's frown was now a scowl. 'Perhaps. Perhaps not.' He seemed to find distasteful the idea that his plans could have been fallible, and looking at the scowl, Simon recalled that vanity so often seemed to accompany ability in the top echelons of the British Army. Wolseley gestured ahead. 'Take your two chaps and range out there well ahead of the cavalry. You might be able to lure the Egyptians to attack you and bring them on to our cavalry. Off you go.'

So dismissed, Simon called Jenkins and Ahmed and they pushed their camels into a trot to join the horsemen a mile ahead and then out through the screen into the empty desert beyond. If the Egyptians had intelligence that a British column was approaching them, then there was no evidence of it, for Simon found that, as before, the first dam at Magfar was undefended by troops, and no screen of skirmishers had been extended before the trenches of Maskhuta.

Simon sent a message to this effect back to Wolseley at Maskhuta via Ahmed and remained with Jenkins observing the enemy's positions until the General and his staff rode up. The little group spent ten minutes examining the Egyptian lines.

Eventually Wolseley put down his binoculars and turned to his advisers. 'Do you think they'll stand, gentlemen?'

There was a general murmur of affirmation.

'Yes, so do I.' Wolseley lifted the glasses to his eyes once more and murmured, half to himself, 'But I don't like the look of those guns . . .' He stayed silently re-examining the entrenchments for a while, and then, his mind made up, he lowered the glasses and turned.

'Right,' he said. 'I don't think we're strong enough, Drury, to attack these lines with those guns with the force we have at the moment, so I will wait until Graham and his extra men from Ismailia come up before I advance on their positions. However, I would like them to attack me. So have Hickman and his two guns come forward. But don't have him open fire on their lines until we've seen if we can induce them to come out across this open ground and be subject to good rifle fire, probably for the first time in their lives.' He turned and grinned. 'Eh, what?'

The decision made, there was an immediate flurry of activity as the senior officers pulled their horses round and galloped away, back towards the British line, which could now clearly be seen, slowly advancing. Simon had a momentary glimpse of Covington's curled lip as he galloped past. Then he and his two companions were left, sitting on their camels.

'Well, that's nice, isn't it now?' said Jenkins, his Welshness seeming to increase with the level of his indignation. 'We're left out 'ere like flies on a mule's arse, with nothing between us and the enemy but bloody sand. It seems we're expensiveable ... expand ... expendable, now, look you.'

Simon pulled his camel's head round. 'No, I don't think so. They'll find another miserable job for us to do soon enough. Come on. Back to the lines before we're chased again.'

It took time, of course, before the British line could be established, but at least Major General Graham and his force had arrived by the time Simon and his companions returned. They watched as Wolseley deployed his men. The infantry of the Yorks and Lancasters were established astride the railway with its left on the canal and the marines on its right, with Lieutenant Hickman's two guns of the Royal Horse Artillery in between, and the line was extended out into the desert by Drury Lowe's cavalry with the mounted infantry on the extreme right. To Simon, the line looked thin but well armed – with the exception of the artillery. Would two guns be enough to take on the dozen Krupps studded into the Egyptian's own line – and would the enemy take the bait and attack?

It did so by mid-morning. A screen of white-clad infantry began to advance along the British left, by the railway and canal, but the attack was hesitant and was soon driven back by the excellent rifle fire of the northern regiments. Then the Egyptians began to probe on the right flank of the British line, but again the marksmanship of the troopers – in this case the mounted infantry – drove them back. To Simon, in the mid-section of the line with his two companions, these tentative attacks seemed only to be a prelude to the main battle. Where were the guns?

The question was soon answered as a cloud of white smoke lined the distant Egyptian trenches and the boom of the Krupp cannon opened up, covering the retreat of the infantry.

''Ere it comes,' murmured Jenkins. 'Get your 'ead down, Amen.'

The Egyptian guns were well and accurately served by their gunners, who fired with speed and precision, so fulfilling their reputations. Their effectiveness was muted, however, as their shells, fitted with percussion fuses, only exploded after burying themselves deeply in the sand. Nevertheless, the barrage was frightening in its intensity and clouds of sand and rock splinters showered the sheltering British.

'Why don't we open up and give 'em a bit of their own medicine?' muttered Jenkins, shaking sand and debris from his *esharp*.

'I think Wolseley wants to lure them to attack him again,' replied Simon, trying to see through the smoke with his field glasses. 'He's hoping they'll think that we've got no artillery and that we can be swept aside by a determined attack.' He looked down. 'Are you all right, Ahmed?'

The Egyptian was lying flat, his cheek pressed into the sand. 'Ah yes, Simon, thank you. I am top hole. Is it long-range killing now?'

'Yes, but not much of that so far, by the look of it. Hello, they're coming again.'

The white-clad figures could be seen emerging from the smoke cloud again, marching slowly across the sand with their long rifles extended, the front rank occasionally dropping to the ground and firing, as the second rank stepped through them to continue the advance. It was all very disciplined, but none of the attacks were pressed home and the attackers faded away long before they reached the British lines. Eventually Wolseley lost his patience and gave orders to the young lieutenant to open fire with his two guns. It could be seen immediately that, although outnumbered, the British shells were being more effective than the Egyptian fire, for Simon could detect through his glasses shell bursts of high explosives and shrapnel erupting all along the enemy trenches.

The Egyptian infantry now gave up their tentative frontal attacks and the encounter between the two forces relapsed into an artillery duel, which continued through the day until dusk fell, marked by the arrival of the reinforcements from Ismailia. In came, first, three hundred and fifty sabres of the 4th and 7th Dragoon Guards, a battery of Royal Artillery and two more battalions of the 3rd KRRC and Royal Marine Light Infantry. At last, after dark, the Guards arrived. They had marched virtually nonstop all day through the hot sun and in temperatures in the mid-nineties, and Simon could only feel pity for them as they slumped into the sand and were issued with full water bottles to replace their long-since-emptied ones. He shook his head in amazement as he noted that they had marched in their home service scarlet and blue serge, carrying their rifles, haversacks containing one hundred rounds of ammunition and water bottles through the blinding heat of the day.

'Och,' confided one young Scots Guardsman, his face bright red under his white cork helmet, as he stretched out beside Simon, 'I don't know 'ow you Arabs do it in this bloody country. Me feet hae slipped back twice fer every forward pace in this bleedin' sand. An' me water bottle was empty after one hour. I don't want to go through that again. Bloody 'ell.' And he immediately fell asleep.

Jenkins grinned across at Simon. 'Serves 'im right for bein' a Scotsman, an' a Guardsman too. Are we goin' to attack now, bach sir, d'yer think?'

Simon shook his head. 'Wouldn't think so. These chaps are all in, and a night attack anyway would be very dangerous. I should think the General would have a go first thing in the morning, though. And some poor devils are going to be put to digging out the dam, so keep your head down.'

'Ooh, I'm a scout. I don't do diggin', see.'

Simon strolled through the lines of the arrivals, wondering if the press contingent had been allowed to come up with the reinforcements. He would keep his promise to Covington, he assured himself, and pull away if he caught a glimpse of Alice. He would not approach or talk to her. A glimpse would be enough – just to assure himself that she was all right, of course. But there was no trace of the journalists. Wolseley obviously did not want to be encumbered, and anyway, he was probably saving their presence to witness his great attack later at Tel el Kebir.

Wolseley moved his troops forward at daybreak, but to everyone's disappointment, it was soon clear that the Egyptians had abandoned their positions during the night and fallen back. To Simon, advancing in the desert for the first time with a large force, the difficulties of keeping the column together to attack as a cohesive unit became quickly apparent. He, Jenkins and Ahmed on their camels were riding in the van with the mounted infantry, who were carried on small, locally bred horses that could move reasonably well over the loose sand. They easily outdistanced the big Household Cavalry troopers on their large English mounts. These beasts, still out of condition after having only recently been landed from their transports, floundered in the sand and were soon left behind. The main guns, too, found difficulty in maintaining any pace at all as the mules struggled to pull their loads across the shifting surface, and the advance was soon spread out over the desert for a mile or more.

Simon nudged his beast alongside that of the General. 'Permission to range ahead, sir, to see how near we are to them?'

Wolseley nodded. 'Get some idea of the strength of the rearguard,' he growled.

The three scouts, glad to be free of the sand dust stirred up by the horses, gently tapped their camels and set them into a loping pace that soon took them away from the column.

'You know,' Simon turned his head and called to the others as they pulled away, 'I think I'm getting better at this riding business. I'm even beginning to grow fond of my camel.'

'Huh,' grunted Jenkins. 'With respect, bach sir, it's all right for you. You've got a pretty one. I don't fancy mine at all.'

Ahmed, delighted as always to be part of this exclusive camaraderie, joined in: 'Oh yes. Camel is good for the desert. Big feet means he spreads weight and load on sand, and so on, et cetera, et cetera.'

Simon and Jenkins exchanged grins.

They found what appeared to be the Egyptian rearguard establishing a defensive position at another little railway hamlet gathered around a station at Mahsama. There seemed to be no enemy cavalry to worry the trio this time, and Simon rode to the top of a sand dune, about three hundred yards from the station, and studied the position carefully.

A large train with, he counted, seventy-five wagons was standing at the station. It seemed to be a supply or ammunition train, for there were no troops aboard.

Numbers of the familiar white-clad Egyptian infantry – too many to count, but perhaps two hundred – were milling about and seven gleaming Krupp cannon were being manhandled into some sort of position to defend the station. No trenches or defensive ditches, however, were being dug.

Simon whirled round. 'Come on,' he said. 'Wolseley can take this lot with his cavalry if he comes up smartly and doesn't let them entrench properly.'

It took them less than half an hour, riding as fast as they could, to come up with the column's vanguard. Simon explained the situation to Wolseley, who took the point immediately. He turned to Major General Drury Lowe: 'Get on, Drury, with your mounted infantry and those two light guns. We can't wait for the regular artillery but I'll come on up behind you with the Household Cavalry as fast as their blasted big drays can move. I don't care too much about capturing these coolies in their nightshirts, but I would like to take their guns and supplies, because I'm thinly stretched for both. Off you go, fast as you can before they settle in. Go with 'em, Fonthill.'

'Very good, sir.'

Somehow, the light horses of the Royal Horse Artillery pulling the two guns and those carrying the mounted infantry were able to summon a trot of sorts, and well within the hour they had reached the large dune from which Simon had made his observation. The scene had hardly changed and the Egyptian infantry were still not entrenched. More to the point, the train was still there, although thin white vapour was rising from its funnel to show that the driver had maintained steam pressure, ready for a quick withdrawal should that prove necessary.

'We've got 'em,' shouted Drury Lowe. 'Throw your shells in behind the locomotive to stop it leaving, Hickman. Then go for the infantry.'

Showing the alacrity for which the RHA were famous, Lieutenant Hickman unlimbered his cannon, laid them on target and opened fire. The infantry dismounted, lay down in extended order and began directing steady rifle fire on the station and the enemy infantry, who were now taking what cover they could or dispersing into the desert on either side. The Egyptians began returning fire from their Remingtons, but it was poorly directed and did little to deter the British fire. Surprisingly, the enemy ordnance was not brought into play, and Simon speculated that the gunners were averse to using their cannon in such unprotected positions.

A trembling of the ground announced the arrival of the Household Cavalry on their big hunters. Both men and horses were perspiring from the intense heat and the pace of their advance, but they paused only long enough to regain breath before drawing their heavy sabres and thundering into the enemy camp, to the cheers of the riflemen, who stood and waved their helmets in exhilaration at the sight.

It was too much for the *fellaheen* who comprised the main element of the Egyptian rearguard. They threw down their rifles and ran, streaming out into the desert like white rabbits fleeing for their lives from foxes. To Simon, watching with his hand to his mouth, it was a relief to see that Wolseley's orders were followed and that there was no pursuit of the fleeing infantrymen. He carried too many unpleasant memories of the Lancers breaking out of the square at Ulundi in Zululand and spearing the running Zulus, even those who begged for mercy. Now, thank God, the cavalry were surrounding the guns to prevent their withdrawal. They were too late, however, to prevent the locomotive from steaming out of the station, towing a few waggons with scores of Egyptian troops clinging to them.

The engagement was over within less than half an hour, and Wolseley stood in his stirrups and looked around with satisfaction. It was clear that the prompt attack by the cavalry had been made well before the Egyptians had had time to establish their line or even unload the waggons. The latter proved to form an ammunition train, and a large number of rifles and a pile of supplies were to be seen stacked against the side of the station building. Just as welcome were the seven Krupp cannon that had not fired a shot against the attackers.

'Damned good morning's work, eh, Ralph?' said Wolseley to Covington. 'I intend to send Graham on to Kassassin to take the lock there. I certainly didn't expect to get that far, and he will have to stop there, because I'm stretching myself damned thin as it is. But I think we should keep the impetus going while we can, and having the railway line and the canal clear up to Kassassin will be a gift in terms of movin' everything up for the main battle. Now, clear that dam behind us, there's a good feller, and I'll move Graham on up once he arrives. Where the hell are my A-rabs?' He turned and shouted: 'Fonthill.'

Simon doubled up.

'Good work, Cousin. Now. Get on your bloody camels and scout ahead to Kassassin. I intend to send Major General Graham on there to take the lock while we have the initiative. But make sure that the Egyptians are not leaving their lines to come to us or that that lot who have just fled are not digging in anywhere. Off you go. I'll send a cavalry troop out to back you up as soon as I can.'

'Very good, sir.'

Simon, Jenkins and Ahmed wearily mounted their camels again and headed due west once more, following the railway line.

'Blimey,' said Jenkins, easing his sore buttocks on the wooden saddle. 'If we come this way again, see, I think we'll just about know the road. We're goin' up an' down this bleedin' canal like three yo-yos.'

'What are yo-yos, 352?' enquired Ahmed.

'Well, they're round things on the end of a piece of string that kids play with and that go up an' down, up an' down. Like us, except that we're goin' up an' back, up an' back, in a straight line, like.'

'Ah.' But Ahmed didn't look particularly enlightened.

As they rode, they passed scores of Egyptian infantry straggling in small groups back from Mahsama towards the perceived safety of Kassassin. They posed no threat. Most of them had abandoned their rifles and they hardly lifted their heads as the three Bedawi rode between them. It wasn't long before the trio had left them well behind.

Long before the black blob that was Kassassin emerged on the horizon, Simon consulted his compass and turned his camel's head to the north to pass well clear of the end of the entrenchments they had observed earlier. Having gained his ground, he turned back again to the west and, mounting a dune, unslung his field glasses. He stared through them for a moment and then handed them to Jenkins.

'Tell me what you see.'

The Welshman adjusted the focusing mechanism and put

the glasses to his eyes. Then he lowered them, rubbed his eyes with his knuckles, lifted them again and scanned the lines. Eventually he handed them back to Simon. 'As a matter of fact, bach sir, I don't see a bloody thing. It looks to me as if they've all buggered off. Amazin'.'

Simon looked through the glasses again. 'Yes,' he said. 'There's absolutely no one to be seen. Come on, let's take a closer look.'

They goaded their camels into a gentle trot and made their way down the unmanned entrenchments. These had never been as sophisticated as those at Tel el Kebir, and they were largely unfinished, petering out into the desert at the northern tip. But there was no sign of troops, only scraps of paper spiralling up on the occasional eddy of the late afternoon breeze, embers of cooking fires and other detritus to show that the lines had once been occupied. Even the lock was unmanned, although the lock gates had been closed to lower the level downstream. The whole position was like some land-bound *Mary Celeste*.

Simon eased his back. 'There must have been an element of cavalry back in Mahsama who galloped back here to raise the alarm once our heavy boys went in on the charge.'

'Hmmm.' Jenkins pulled at his moustache. 'These Gyppos don't much like fightin', then, do they? Oh,' he turned to Ahmed, 'no offence now, Amen.'

The little Egyptian shrugged his shoulders.

'I am not so sure about that,' mused Simon. 'They could be playing a clever game. They must know that Wolseley's lines of communications are very severely extended by now. They are also sure to know about his difficulties in unloading at Ismailia, so that he has not yet been able to disembark anything like his complete army. They might be luring him on to stretch him so that they can attack from out of the desert and cut his lines, surround and outnumber the forward troops and polish them off. Or even tempt him to keep coming, without a full force, and entice him on to the guns at el Kebir.'

Jenkins nodded his head slowly. 'Ah,' he said. 'I never thought of that, see. Just as well that I'm not paid to be the thinkin' one, isn't it, then?'

'Don't worry about that – but can you operate lock gates?'

A great beam came across Jenkins's face. 'Well now, bach sir, it's funny you should say that, see, because as a matter of fact, I used to do it sometimes on the canal near 'ome, when I was a nipper, like. I reckon I can 'andle those little things.'

'Good. Open 'em up so there's plenty of water downstream. You come with me, Ahmed, and let's see what we can find.'

In fact there was nothing to be learned except that the defenders had left in a hurry and had moved out west, presumably towards the safer lines of Tel el Kebir. Simon made a decision. He scribbled a note to Major General Graham, informing him that the Kassassin lock was undefended and that, in his opinion, the lines could be occupied and held as a forward post for the final advance. He and Jenkins, he explained, would scout on ahead and report back on the extent to which the Tel el Kebir defences had been completed. He gave the note to Ahmed and instructed him to ride back with it, looping out into the desert to avoid the soldiers retreating from Mahsama.

The little man rode off, and Simon returned to where

Jenkins was completing the opening of the lock gates. They both stood for a moment in silence as they watched the released water surge through the open lock. There was something satisfying, in this arid place, about seeing water flow and hearing it gurgle. Then they mounted their camels and set off once more towards Tel el Kebir to camp out in the desert twilight. They headed slightly to the north to avoid overtaking any of the troops retreating from Kassassin.

They reached the el Kebir entrenchments early the next day, and, mindful of their pursuit by Egyptian horsemen on their last visit, kept their distance, slowly plodding northwards up the line of the fortifications and carefully observing them through the field glasses.

It was clear that this line was meant to be very permanent. A huge, continuous ditch had now been dug in front of the trenches, south to north, and the excavations had been thrown up between the two to provide high earthworks. Any attacking force would have to cross flat open ground, span the ditch and then climb the earthworks – all in the face of a heavy artillery barrage from the redoubts and, by the look of it, an unbroken line of musketry fire from the earthworks. It was a defensive position of some sophistication, only lacking the new barbed-wire entanglements that Simon had first seen in Afghanistan. It was also well manned, for the familiar white-clad soldiery could be seen along the top of the earthworks all the way up the line.

'Can it be turned, then, bach sir?' asked Jenkins.

'Difficult. The end of the line at the south rests on the canal, which would be damned awkward to cross under fire, and the northern tip, by the look of it, curls back on itself and is protected by that second line running back from it at an angle.' Simon frowned. 'Despite his inexperience of field warfare, old Aunt Ada seems to know what he's doing in terms of erecting defensive positions. All right, I think we've seen enough. Let's get back to Mahsama.'

Once more they turned back, heading out into the desert a little way to ensure that they met no Egyptian stragglers or cavalry patrols sent out to scout the ground between the two forces. They halted at midday when the overhead sun beat down on them with such intensity that they were reduced almost to automatons, lolling in their saddles and desperately resisting the temptation to drain their water bottles. They hobbled the camels, and using their rifles and blankets to erect a primitive lean-to shelter against a sand dune, crawled under its shade, ate a handful of raisins and fell into an uneasy doze.

The respite lasted for less than an hour, for Simon found little sense of security in the desert. Empty as it seemed, they were still caught between two opposing armies and it was a dangerous place, with the undulating sand dunes offering cover to anyone approaching and the desert sand, of course, muffling the sounds of footfalls, horses' hooves or camel pads. Two sleeping men were vulnerable, and Simon insisted that they go on their way as soon as they had snatched a few minutes' sleep.

They had been riding again for less than a quarter of an hour and Simon, head down, was consulting his compass when Jenkins whispered, 'Two riders, about a quarter of a mile away.' Simon caught only a momentary glimpse, following Jenkins's outstretched arm, before they disappeared out of sight behind a distant undulation.

'Our own cavalry, d'you think?' asked Jenkins.

Simon shook his head. 'Shouldn't think so. Wolseley promised that he'd send a troop out, but they would never ride in pairs. And, from a quick glimpse, they looked like Arabs.'

'Better avoid them, then?'

'Yes. On second thoughts, perhaps not. We can't be all that far from Kassassin now, and if they are Arabs – Egyptians or Bedawis – they might be able to give us information. So I think we should take 'em in for questioning. Pity Ahmed isn't with us to interpret, but it can't be helped.'

'They could be armed.'

'They probably are, but only with *jerzails*, the old muskets, I should think, and we should be able to intimidate them with our Martini-Henrys. So we will show them we've got them as we approach. If they run off, then to hell with it, we'll let them go. I don't fancy another camel race. Come on.'

They withdrew their rifles from their canvas covers and urged their camels into a trot, setting a course to intercept the distant riders. It seemed for a time as though they had not been seen, for the Arabs made no alteration in their course, and as they approached, it could be seen that they were lolling forwards in their saddles, obviously half dozing in the heat. They were riding camels but they did not appear to be Bedawi, for they were shrouded not in black but in the duns and browns of Egyptian desert dwellers, perhaps traders travelling between oases. Then the smaller of the two figures sat upright as he caught sight of Simon and Jenkins and thrust a hand out to his fellow.

'Show our rifles,' shouted Simon.

They both waved their Martini-Henrys and Simon

unslung his binoculars. Before he could raise them to his eyes, however, the smaller of the Arabs produced a revolver and fired. It seemed to be a warning shot, because the aim appeared to be deliberately high and the bullet whined well over the heads of the two men. Jenkins immediately reined in and raised his rifle to his shoulder.

'No,' cried Simon. 'I've never seen an Arab with a revolver before. He can't do us much harm at this range. Let me have a look at them first before we begin firing.'

'Just as you say, bach sir, but I don't like bein' fired on one little bit.'

Simon focused the glasses. The larger of the two figures immediately came into view: a desert Arab all right, bearded, dark, but not with the Nubian blackness of the Bedawi. The smaller was clean-shaven, and as a movement of his camel caused his *esharp* to slip a little, his face came into focus, revealing a skin quite light in colour. Simon moved the focusing wheel with his thumb, and into clearer view came a strangely familiar square jaw and a wisp of fair hair.

'My God,' he cried. 'It's Alice!'

Chapter 15

'What?' said Jenkins. 'Are you sure? What on earth is she doin' out 'ere?'

Simon put down his rifle and waved his arms. 'Alice! Alice!' He pushed back his headdress. 'It's Simon. Don't shoot. We're coming over.' He urged his camel forward, and as the distant figure extended her pistol again, he attached his handkerchief to his rifle and waved it. 'Alice,' he shouted again, 'it's Simon. Simon and Jenkins.' The extended pistol was slowly lowered, and Simon beat his camel's flanks with his stick, so that it broke into its vertebrae-rattling trot.

She came to meet him and they paused a few yards apart. 'Is it really you, Simon?' she asked, her voice quite hoarse. Although through the lenses of the field glasses her face had appeared quite pale, compared with the blackness of her companion, it was now obvious that it was burned by the sun and that her lips were drily puckered and almost white. Her shoulders drooped but she now made an effort to sit straight in her saddle, and her grey eyes gleamed. 'Oh, my dear,' she said. 'I can't tell you how glad I am to see you. You seem like a . . . a . . . mirage. And, oh my goodness, dear 352.' Her voice cracked and a tear appeared on her cheeks.

Simon fumbled for his water bottle. 'Here,' he said. 'You look as though you need a drink.'

She took it but offered it first to her companion. 'Drink, Abdul,' she said. He took it and gulped greedily before handing it back. Then she raised it to her lips and hiccupped as the precious fluid poured down her throat. 'Sorry,' she gasped, handing the bottle back. 'We ran out some time ago and I was trying to find our way back to the canal.' She summoned a regretful smile. 'Somehow, while I was half asleep on this damned camel yesterday, my compass slipped into the sand, and we have been well and truly lost now for twenty-four hours or so.' She sighed. 'Oh, Simon, you really must stop this business of continually rescuing me. It's getting quite embarrassing . . . but thank you, thank you. I don't know how much longer we could have gone on. I tried to steer by the sun, but with it almost directly overhead, it was so difficult to do . . .'

Simon dismounted and put up his arms. 'Come on,' he said. 'Slip down and rest for a while. We will make you a little shade. We have some raisins left and you can have the rest of my water.'

Alice uncoiled her leg from the saddle cantle and half slipped, half fell into his arms. They stayed locked together for a moment before Jenkins strode over and swept her up into his arms and marched with her to the slope of the dune. He laid her down tenderly, and with their blankets and rifles they re-erected their rough shelter over her head to provide some shade, poured a little water on to a handkerchief and laid it on her forehead.

Simon turned to Abdul. 'Can't you find your way in the desert, man?' he demanded. 'You must know that the

Sweetwater Canal is that way.' He pointed south. 'Easy enough to find.'

The Egyptian gave a half-smile and a shrug. 'The miss did not want us to get too near the army, *effendi*. She say we keep going to west. She very determined, and when compass is lost, in the end I do not know which way I am going myself. I am from Ismailia, *effendi*, and not happy here. Sorry, *effendi*.'

Simon sighed. 'I know she is determined, but you should have insisted. She was in your care, dammit, and you should never have run out of water. Here, have another drink.'

Abdul salaamed and drank deeply a second time. 'Miss's water bottle has leak,' he explained. 'So we share mine. Nothing left for some time. Sorry, *effendi*.'

'Never mind now. Take some rest.' Simon walked back to where Alice was lying, with Jenkins at her side, waving away the flies. She watched him approach, her eyes wide.

'Can you sleep a little before we go on, Alice?' he asked.

She shook her head. 'No. I will be fine in a moment. The water was what I really wanted, although this shade is heavenly. Thank you both so much. But what on earth are you doing out here?'

Jenkins let out a guffaw. 'Blimey, miss, that's fine comin' from you, like. It's what we're dying to know about you, see. It's our job to be out 'ere in this blasted sand, look you. We're army scouts, that's what we are. But you ain't, now, miss, are you?'

Alice smiled. 'I don't somehow think so. If I am, I'm making a fine bloody mess of it, if you'll pardon my army language.'

They both smiled down at her and she sat up. 'I suppose

I owe you an explanation, but first, how are you for water? Could I have just another sip, do you think?'

'Of course. Here.'

She drank, more carefully this time, and wiped her lips with the back of her hand. Colour already seemed to be returning to her face under its tan.

'Thank you. Now, my story. There seems to be a whole army of journalists at Ismailia, but of course we are not allowed to do anything – anything, that is, but report on the endless unloading of equipment and supplies and the heat and the flies, always the damned flies. We were even too late for the first landings on the quay, where,' she looked up at them with a shy smile, 'I hear you distinguished yourselves once again.'

'Not really.' Simon went to take her hand and then thought better of it. 'Do go on.'

'Well, I became extremely tired of all this waiting and writing about the same thing every day. We were forbidden to ride out into the desert, but I don't like being hemmed in, so I went down into the market and recruited old Abdul here and talked him into being my guide and taking me towards whatever action there might be.'

'Humph,' growled Simon. 'He wasn't much of a guide. He got you lost and let you run out of water.'

Alice frowned. 'No. It was not his fault. He always told me that he would not be at home in the desert, but he spoke reasonable English, seemed honest and got us two good camels, and, of course, I had my compass. I did not want to follow the railway line because I felt we might blunder into the army and get sent back right away locked in irons, or whatever the army locks you in these days. I set a course to take us just north of Mahsama station, where I thought there might be some action . . .'

'You were right there, miss,' said Jenkins.

'. . . and I could watch it from a distance, so to speak, and then, maybe, get on to Kassassin.'

Simon sighed. 'You took an awful risk, Alice. You can't just go blundering about the desert, you know. Apart from the Egyptian forces, there are the Bedawi . . .'

'No there aren't. I checked and everyone told me that they have more or less retreated to the south to get away from the armies and all the fighting. And I wasn't blundering. I would have been fine if I hadn't lost that damned compass and if my water bottle hadn't split its seam. Anyway, I was armed.'

'What?' Simon grinned. 'That little peashooter?'

'That's no peashooter. I'll have you know that that's an eleven-millimetre French-officer-issue Chamelot-Delvigne revolver. I could have killed you as you rode up, but I deliberately fired over your head as a warning. You should be more careful, Simon.'

'Very well, ma'am. Now, we had better get you back to Mahsama and—'

'Oh no. I shall be arrested and shot, or probably something even worse. First of all, tell me what has happened out here.' She groped underneath her *burnous* and produced a notebook and pencil.

Simon shook his head in mock despair, then related all that had happened over the last couple of days. 'We are now riding back to Mahsama,' he concluded, 'from where, I believe, Major General Graham will march on Kassassin and take possession of it, so that it can be set up as a kind of springboard for what will hopefully be Wolseley's final assault on Tel el Kebir.'

Alice looked up from her scribbling. 'Wonderful,' she said. 'Now, Simon, you must help me. I can't go back to Mahsama, so Abdul and I will camp out in the desert just north of there and follow the army – shadow it, so to speak, out here – as it goes on to Kassassin. But I can't do that without a compass and a couple of extra water bottles. Do you think, my dear, that you could get those things for me? Could you?'

At this point, Jenkins rose and walked away shaking his head. Simon watched him go and turned back to Alice. 'Alice,' he spoke slowly but with emphasis, 'you are being quite, quite irresponsible, you know. If we had not come along, you could have died out here. If you don't have a thought about your life, think of Abdul, whom you have clearly bullied into bringing you here.'

Alice opened her mouth to protest, but Simon held up his hand. 'Now listen. I believe that it is quite a possibility that Arabi wants Wolseley to occupy Kassassin and then will attack him there. He might even fall on Mahsama before the General has a chance of bringing up his main force. The Egyptians will transport much of their infantry by train to just before Kassassin, but their cavalry will almost certainly come out of the desert in the north. They will find you and Abdul sitting out there like observers at a football match and they will ride through you and, likely as not, slit your throats just for being in the way – or because they think you to be British spies.'

Alice pouted. 'No they won't. I shall show them my press accreditation.'

'And how many Egyptian officers will have heard of the *Morning Post* or even care about it? This is war, Alice. These people are fighting for their country. We are an occupying force. They won't observe the niceties of honourable warfare. You would be trampled underfoot. And as for camping just north of Mahsama, you must realise that Wolseley will be sending out cavalry patrols all the time to protect his position. You would be discovered before you could put up your tent.'

A silence fell between them. Eventually Alice sighed. 'I suppose you are right, Simon. Back to Mahsama it is, then. But if old Wolseley tries to ship me back to Ismailia in disgrace, I shall slip away again into the desert, I warn you.'

Simon smiled, and then asked tenderly, 'How is your throat now, Alice?'

She held his gaze for a moment and then slowly reached out and took his hand. 'Much better now, thank you.' She brought his hand to her throat. 'See? No marks, no lumps.'

He let his hand lie on her soft skin, under the cotton *burnous*, while his eyes looked into hers. They stayed that way, he kneeling beside her, until the arrival of Jenkins made him pull his hand away.

'I think we'd better be gettin' on now, bach sir,' the Welshman said quietly.

'Ah yes, right. Are you fit to get back on that camel now, Alice?'

She lowered her gaze. 'Yes, quite well again now, thank you. Thank you both. Back to bloody Mahsama, then.'

Simon set a more southerly course now to take them directly back to Mahsama. For most of the time they rode in silence, but Alice, after considerable thought, pulled alongside Simon and told of seeing George in the bazaar at Port Said. It was salutary for both of them: for Alice because it brought back the terror and pain of standing on tiptoe with the noose around her neck before that final swing into, as she thought, eternity; and for Simon because it reminded him of unfinished business. The recent skirmishes had, for the time being, driven all thoughts of the sadistic little clerk from his mind. He felt guilty and a little ashamed.

'Don't worry, Alice,' he said. 'He can't reach us here, and when this is over, we will find him and there will be a reckoning.'

She smiled back but could find nothing to say, and they rode on in silence.

They quickly reached the tracks made by the Egyptians retreating from Mahsuma and began following the railway line back towards the station. They had been riding in this way for less than half an hour when they saw what was clearly a British cavalry patrol approaching, the sun twinkling from the brasses of its harnesses and equipment.

Simon reached for his field glasses and focused them on the figure leading them. 'Oh no!' he exclaimed.

'What's the matter?' asked Alice.

Simon lowered the glasses and turned to her. 'The patrol is being led by your husband.' His voice was cold. 'I gave him an undertaking in Alex that I would have nothing further to do with you after the George affair. I fear that this will look bad, Alice.'

Alice could not help sucking in her breath, but she spoke firmly enough. 'Nonsense. You have nothing at all to be ashamed of. Without you both, Abdul and I would be dead by now. It is I who will get the scolding, you will see.'

Through the glasses Simon could see that Covington was similarly studying him. It seemed strange that an infantry officer – although now on the staff, of course, with the rank of full colonel – should be leading a cavalry patrol, but Simon reasoned that with Wolseley's lines of communications so thinly stretched, the cavalry and its officers would be much in demand, policing the long line back to Ismailia. And Covington, whatever his faults, was a brave officer who would seize any opportunity to range out to find the enemy.

When only about one hundred yards separated the two parties, Covington held up his hand to halt his troop and rode forward alone to meet Alice and Simon. He made a fine figure on his charger, sitting bolt upright, of course, his reins somehow looped tightly around his hook and his right hand hanging straight at his side, as though on parade. His white pith helmet was set low and straight on his head, so that its peak seemed to dig into his forehead at the top of his nose, between his one good eye and the black patch. As ever, his moustaches seemed to bristle. His eye – cold, china blue – ignored Simon completely and settled upon Alice.

'Good morning, Ralph,' she said, and gave her sweetest smile. 'I am so glad to see you, my dear.'

The Colonel allowed a pause to develop for a moment between them before replying. 'What are you doing out here, Alice, with . . . with . . . this man?' He still bestowed no gaze on Simon but merely indicated him with a jerk of his head.

Alice's smile remained but her voice dropped a fraction in tone. 'Simon – this man, as you call him – has saved my life for the second time in three months. I hired this guide,' she nodded her head towards Abdul, sitting on his camel to the rear, 'to take me out from Ismailia to witness some of the fighting so that I could report on it. Unfortunately, I lost my compass and we were wandering with no water when Simon and Jenkins found us. We are now on our way back to Mahsama.'

'Why did you disobey the General's instructions and leave Ismailia?' Covington's voice remained cold and his words were precise, as though chipped from stone.

'Because I am not in the army, Ralph. I am an employee of the *Morning Post* and I must go where my work takes me. I do not accept directions from anyone in the army, not even you, my dear.'

At this point, Simon pulled the head of his camel around and tapped the beast into a walk with his stick.

'And where the hell d'yer think you are going, Fonthill?' snarled Covington. 'I haven't finished with you yet.'

Simon replied over his shoulder as his camel plodded past the Colonel: 'I have delivered your wife to you, Covington, and now I must get on with my work and make my report to General Graham. Good day to you.'

'Come back here.'

'Go to hell.'

'How dare you talk to me like that. I shall have you arrested.'

Simon turned round in the saddle. 'If you do, then you will have to answer to General Wolseley,' he said. 'I report to him and only to him, unless he delegates his authority, and he has certainly not done that. Pray continue with your family quarrel; I wish to play no part in it. I met your wife in the desert when she was lost and I was bringing her back to you. I would have thought that would have brought thanks, not threats of arrest. But then I had forgotten what a boorish brute you are. Good day to you. Come along, 352.'

Jenkins urged his camel forward and gave Covington one of his face-splitting grins. 'Nice day for it, Colonel bach, eh?' he said as he passed by.

Covington was about to kick his horse into action when Alice pulled on his arm. 'Don't make a fool of yourself in front of the men, Ralph,' she entreated. 'All that we have told you is true. Now, I am going back to Mahsama, but if you do not wish me to go with Simon Fonthill, then give me two of your troopers to escort me and we can meet tonight to talk. Please be sensible.'

For a moment or two Covington glared at her, then he relented, leaned across and kissed her cheek. 'I did not realise what you had done, you silly puss,' he said. 'If I had known you had pushed off into the desert like this, I would have come after you myself. Off you go, then, for I must continue my patrol. I will send two men to escort you. Go back to the camp, Alice, and for God's sake don't get into any more trouble.'

The little party reached Mahsama just before nightfall. Simon, riding ahead with Jenkins, had set a brisk pace without a backward glance, and Alice, some two hundred yards to the rear with her new escort, had been hard put to keep up. Once they were behind the British lines, Simon turned his head to look at her for the first time since they had left Covington. His face held no smile and he gave her only a curt nod as he pulled away to where General Graham's pennant was fluttering by his tent. Seeing Alice with Covington had reminded him finally that she was lost to him. He must have nothing more to do with her, for meeting her just caused him pain.

Graham was sitting on a camp stool, one booted leg thrust out, scribbling. Simon paused by the entrance and coughed, and the General looked up. 'Ah, Fonthill.' He indicated another camp stool. 'Sit down. My word, you've made jolly good time from Kassassin. Must be a bit short of breath, eh? Anyway, I got your message. Good work. I have sent a cavalry force up to occupy Kassassin and will be following up myself at first light tomorrow, with whatever odds and ends I can scrounge to reinforce the place. You must have passed my chaps on the way here?'

'No, sir. We detoured out into the desert to avoid trouble. But we did encounter Colonel Covington about five miles out.'

'Ah, yes.'

Simon liked Graham. A tall, thin man with a lugubrious air compounded by his drooping moustaches, he had acquired a reputation as a fighting soldier and had won the Victoria Cross, Britain's highest decoration for gallantry, as a young man fighting the Russians in the Crimean War. He looked across at Simon now with some paternalism, for he was aware that Simon's own father had also won a VC, in the Indian Mutiny. This valorous club was exclusive and rather self-serving; a kind of Masonic order of bravery. No son of a VC could possibly offer ill-considered advice.

'Well,' he said, 'I've taken your advice to move in on Kassassin. I hope to God it's not some incredibly sophisticated trap that old Arabi has set us. Eh, what?'

Simon shook his head. 'It has to be rated a possibility, sir, but I should doubt it. The Egyptians don't seem to think like that. And even if they do attack, if you have moved in quickly you should be able to defend the position well enough.'

'Well I hope you're right, young man. Sir Garnet certainly seems to trust your judgement. Now – what about Tel el Kebir?'

'That's the place where Arabi will make his stand all right. The lines have been further strengthened since I was last there. A huge ditch has been dug in front of the entrenchments and the guns are well dug in and command the approaches from north and east. It will be difficult to take. It's my belief that Arabi wants to lure us on to those guns. He might have a go at you in Kassassin, but it won't be serious. He wants the British Army to founder on those guns.'

'Hmmm. Right. Well, go and get something to eat, and then turn in. I leave at dawn and I want you and your man to ride with me.'

'Very good, sir.' Simon thought for a moment. Graham would hear soon enough about Alice. He must report it matter-of-factly. 'I think I should report to you that we found Mrs Covington – that is, Alice Griffith of the *Morning Post* – lost out in the desert about two miles north-east of Kassassin.'

Graham's eyebrows rose. 'God! What was she doing out there?'

'I believe that she was rather irked by the restrictions placed on correspondents at Ismailia, so she hired a guide and decided to see for herself how far we had been able to penetrate along the line of the Sweetwater and the railway track. She's . . . ah . . . a very enterprising young woman, sir, and her heart is always in the right place. She earned a fine reputation in reporting from Zululand, Afghanistan and the Transvaal. Anyway, somehow she had lost her compass and we were lucky enough to find her. By coincidence we met Colonel Covington riding in and he provided an escort to bring her back here.'

'Oh lord!' Graham slapped his boot. 'That's all I need – some bright young woman reporter hanging about the camp. What the hell am I going to do with her, Fonthill?'

The air of distress that had suddenly descended on the General was so abject that Simon could not prevent a grin. 'Can't help you there, sir. I suppose you will have to move her on back to Ismailia. No doubt her . . . er . . . husband could help.'

Graham's eyes lit up. 'A capital idea. Yes. Let him handle her. All his fault. He shouldn't have let her come out here in the first place. All this damned heat and sand and flies – no place for a woman. A woman war correspondent! Ridiculous. Whatever next. Women generals, I suppose. Thank you, Fonthill, go and get some rest. I will put Miss Griffith under guard until her husband returns. We march at dawn.'

'Very good, sir. Ah – one thing more, sir. You said you wish Jenkins and me to come with you to Kassassin. I presume that there is no objection to my Egyptian man coming with us? He has grown to be indispensable.'

'What? Oh yes. That little fellow who brought back your message.' A frown descended above the moustaches. 'Afraid he got himself into some sort of scrape and we have had to put him in shackles in the guard tent. Sorry about that, but he won't be able to go with you.'

'A scrape! What sort of a scrape?'

Graham looked embarrassed. 'I understand that he was

rude to one of my majors. Can't have that, you know. Can't have these natives doing that sort of thing. Anyway, we've put him under lock and key. He will be sentenced tomorrow. The Provost Major will have to do it. I have to get on to Kassassin.'

Simon rose to his feet. 'General Graham,' he said slowly, 'this man is the most trustworthy and gentle of colleagues. He has been invaluable to Sergeant Jenkins and me throughout our time in Egypt. Although he is not a soldier, he faced the mobs in the Alexandria riots and he fought with us against the Egyptians – his own people – at Nefisha, outside Ismailia. He is steadfast, true and even-tempered. I don't see how he could offend anyone. What exactly is the charge?'

Graham shuffled his feet, but the frown remained. 'I can't tell you that exactly. It was brought, I believe, by Major Smith-Denbigh, of the Duke of Cornwall's Light Infantry. It will all be dealt with tomorrow, of course. I'm sorry, but I can't help you further, Fonthill. Now, you must excuse me. I have far more important matters to worry about than your little Egyptian, I am afraid. Good evening.'

Simon stood looking down at the General, who held his gaze firmly. 'Very good, sir,' he said finally, and turned on his heel and left the tent.

Outside, Jenkins was still standing, in the twilight, holding the halters of their two camels. 'Blimey,' he said, 'that took long enough. Are we in trouble again, then?'

'No, but we will be shortly. Now take the camels to the lines and then join me at the guard tent, wherever that is. And bring your knife.'

'Bloody 'ell. Very good, bach sir.'

The guard tent was situated on the extreme edge of the British camp, its entrance guarded by a very bored-looking infantryman of the Second Yorks. Simon rendezvoused with Jenkins at the rear of the tent and then approached the guard, who immediately levelled his rifle, bayonet fixed.

'Push off,' he said. 'No natives allowed 'ere, mate.'

Simon pushed back his headdress. 'I am Major Fonthill, head of General Wolseley's intelligence department here in Egypt. This is Sergeant Major Jenkins. Kindly come to attention. NOW!'

The man's jaw dropped momentarily, and then he picked up his left boot and slammed it alongside its mate, while he brought his grounded rifle butt back into line with his right leg. 'Sorry, sir.'

'Good. That's better. At ease. Now – is the prisoner still inside?'

'Yessir.

'We are going to step inside the tent to question him on the charge that has been brought against him. Kindly make sure that we are not disturbed. Admit no one. Do you understand?'

'Yessir.'

'Very good. We should not be long. Please unthread the opening.'

The infantryman did so, and Simon and Jenkins stepped inside. 'Oh, shit!' exclaimed Jenkins. Ahmed was sitting on the desert floor, his legs stretched either side of the central tent pole and shackled at the ankle. His wrists were similarly handcuffed around the pole. As they came in, the little man looked up, and they saw that two weals stood out on his forehead and cheeks, as though he had been whipped across the face. Blood had congealed on the wounds but a little still dripped down from the lower edges of the marks.

'My God, Ahmed,' cried Simon. 'What has happened?'

'Ah, my friends,' said Ahmed, trying to smile. 'I knew you would come, but it has been a little time, you know.'

'Now don't waste breath, my dear chap,' said Simon. 'Just tell us what happened.'

'Very well, Simon. I delivered your message to the General *effendi* and he seemed pleased and thanked me. Good. Then, as I walk away, I stumble on one of the tent things . . . you know, in ground . . .'

'Pegs.'

'Exactly. And I fall into stomach of large, fat English officer walking by. He call me nasty names. I do not like this so I say, it is not my fault because I fall over. He says, don't talk back to me, black bastard, et cetera, et cetera, et cetera, and I say, I do not talk back but only explain, and he shouts and raises his cane and hits me across face and calls the guard and I am here now for four hours. No drink, no food and,' he looked down in embarrassment, 'nowhere to wee-wee.'

A silence fell and Simon and Jenkins exchanged glances. 'Now, Ahmed,' said Simon, 'answer this question carefully. Did you put up your hand to hit this officer, or touch him apart from when you first stumbled into him?'

'No, Simon. I only raise my hands to stop him hitting me. You know he hit me like a tax-collector. I thought that only Turks did that. Not English officers. It is not right, is it?'

'No, my dear fellow, it is not right. Now, 352, can you prise these bloody shackles off with your knife?'

Jenkins grimaced. 'No. Not a chance. But I've got a bit of

wire 'ere, see, that might do the trick. Never go without it, even when I'm wearin' this Arab rubbish.' He fumbled under his *burnous*. ''Ere we are. Now, 'old these things out straight, like.'

The Welshman kneeled, and after five minutes of poking and manoeuvring the wire with the skill of a brain surgeon, he unlocked first the ankle shackles and then the handcuffs. Ahmed rubbed his ankles and wrists with relief and stood shakily.

'Thanks you, very much. It is great relief.'

'Now, Ahmed,' said Simon, '352 will go and get some food and water for you, and I will find a certain Major Smith-Denbigh. You must not move from here until we come back. Understand?'

'Thank you, yes.'

Once outside, Simon turned to the guard, who had sprung to attention at their reappearance. 'We have unshackled the prisoner,' he said, 'but he will not be removed from the guard tent for the moment. Sergeant Major Jenkins here . . .', the guard looked askance at the unshaven, definitively Arabic Jenkins, who grinned back at him, 'will return with some nourishment for the man, but you are to let no one else in to see him. Is that clear?'

'Yessir.'

'Now, what's your name, soldier?'

'Barraclough, sir.'

'Very well, Barraclough. Now, where are the officers' quarters for the Duke of Cornwall's Light Infantry?'

The infantryman, chin tucked into his chest, nodded to the right. 'Go along the lines that way, sir, an' you'll find 'em.'

Jenkins laid a hand on Simon's arm and led him to one side. 'Now, bach sir,' he said, 'I know that you won't mind me givin' you a bit of advice – in me new position as a skilled lawyer, that is . . .'

'Get on with it. I'm in a hurry.'

'Yes, I can see that. I can also see that you're blazin' furious, like – an' I don't blame you. This Major seems the sort of bloke that gives the army a bad name. I've met plenty like 'im. But with respect, like: cool down a bit. You're at your best, see, when you're cool. No offence now, sir.'

'None taken. Get on with it.'

'Very good, bach sir. But I 'ave a feelin' we could be playin' with fire 'ere. Oh dearie me. Now what does a Mosselman like for 'is tea . . .?' Still muttering, he strode away.

Simon found the DCLI lines easily enough and dispatched a soldier to find Major Smith-Denbigh, telling him, in the crisp tones of an English officer, that the matter was most urgent. The Major arrived four minutes later, wiping crumbs from his mouth with a napkin.

'What the hell is all this about?' he demanded. 'And who the hell are you, interrupting my dinner?'

He was about Simon's height, but predictably stout and red-faced. His inevitable moustache was blond, as was his thinning hair, and he appeared to be in his early to mid-thirties. He had not stopped to put on his jacket, and the end of his napkin was still tucked into his shirt front.

'Major Smith-Denbigh?' enquired Simon politely.

'Ah. You're not an Arab, then. Who the hell *are* you?'

'What's your seniority, Major?'

'What the hell's it got to do with you?'

Simon took a pace closer, so that he could smell the garlic on the other man's breath. He paused a moment, looking into the Major's eyes from a distance of a few inches. 'I asked you a civil question,' he said in level tones, 'and if I have to hang around all night here waiting for an answer, then General Sir Garnet Wolseley isn't going to be very pleased. Now. What's your seniority?'

'Er . . . twenty-eighth of February, '69. What's this about?'

Simon smiled inwardly. Good. The man was, of course, older than him, but not so much that the age discrepancy could be detected easily, particularly as Simon had pulled down the edge of his *esharp* to just above his eye line. He could lie happily. 'I am Major Simon Fonthill, head of Sir Garnet's intelligence operation in Egypt. Gazetted thirty-first of January '69, so I'm senior to you, Smith-Denbigh, and I have to tell you that I wouldn't be in your boots tonight.'

'What? What? What are you talking about?'

'Don't bluster, man. Firstly, are you in the habit of walking about the lines without your jacket? Eh? You may be a soldier, but you look like a fucking butler who's fallen out of his pantry.'

'I was told this was urgent. Here – how do I know you are who you say you are?'

'Don't interrupt me. Now, is it your custom to go around whipping natives with your cane?'

'Oh, that. He was only a native. Impertinent little bugger. Anyone would have done the same – and anyway, what the hell has it to do with you?'

Simon inched even closer. 'The man you thrashed happened to be my best undercover agent in this country.

What is more, he is the favourite nephew of the Khedive, specially seconded to the British army because of his knowledge of the country and his eagerness to help us. He has been out in the desert with me at Tel el Kebir and came back to Major General Graham with a message of great importance. He had just delivered it when you chose to slash him across the face and then have him shackled like a coolie. I have just got in and heard about it. You have created a diplomatic incident of the utmost severity, you stupid, *stupid* bastard.'

Simon stayed perfectly still, his eyes glaring deeply into those of Smith-Denbigh, only some eight inches away. He knew he had won when the other dropped his eyes. Bullies, he had gambled, usually step back first.

'I . . . I . . . didn't know who the little bugger . . . er . . . the chap was.' The Major was perspiring, and he dabbed his forehead with his napkin. 'He should have said.'

'He tried to talk to you but you slashed him across the face. Is that the way you behave in this country, you fat oaf?'

'No. It's the heat, don't you know. And the bloody flies. They make a man tetchy. What's to be done, then, eh?'

Simon stepped back. 'I have spoken to Muharram Pasha, who is prepared to let the matter drop, given an apology from you. I am sure that General Graham, who has enough on his mind just now, will also be prepared to overlook the whole bloody episode. But you must come with me now to release Ahmed Muharram and apologise to him, and then explain to the General that you have dropped any charges against the man. Will you do that?'

'Well, of course. It was all a mistake, you know.'

'Very well. Let's do it quickly. I haven't dined yet.'

'I'd better get my jacket.'

'No time for that. I have unshackled Muharram Pasha and he is just about ready to ride back to Ismailia and take ship to Alex to see his uncle. I have persuaded him to wait. Come along.'

Simon turned and walked quickly away, so that Smith-Denbigh was forced to half trot to catch him up. When they arrived at the guard tent, the guard immediately snapped to attention.

'Open the tent flap, Barraclough.'

'Very good, sir.'

The obvious respect with which the infantryman addressed Simon and the fact that the latter knew the guard's name removed the last doubts that might have lingered in Smith-Denbigh's mind. He followed Simon into the tent, dabbing the back of his neck with his napkin. Inside, Ahmed was chewing on a chicken bone, with Jenkins at his side. Immediately on seeing the Major, the little Egyptian attempted to rise to his feet, but Simon stopped him and stepped back, slightly behind the Major, so that Smith-Denbigh could not see him.

'Please don't get up, Your Excellency.' Simon addressed Ahmed, holding a warning finger up to his lips. 'I appreciate that the shackles must have left their mark. Major Smith-Denbigh has something to say to you. Major?'

'What? Er . . . ah, yes. I do beg your pardon for my . . . er . . . behaviour earlier today and for . . . ah . . . putting you in this sad position. It was a misjudgement of mine and I am exceedingly sorry for it. I shall, of course, withdraw the charge.'

'Immediately,' prompted Simon.

'Ah . . . immediately.'

Ahmed's jaw had now dropped on to his neckband and a great grin was beginning to spread across Jenkins's face. Simon frowned at him and the grin disappeared immediately. The Egyptian blinked and began to speak but was halted by Simon.

'If Your Excellency would be prepared to shake hands with the Major and then perhaps we can forget the incident . . .?' It was another prompt, and catching Simon's eye, Ahmed immediately nodded and slowly extended his hand.

'Of course, sir,' he said.

Very self-consciously, the two men shook hands, then before any more, perhaps revealing, words could be exchanged, Simon took Smith-Denbigh's arm and moved him towards the tent opening. 'Perhaps we can catch the General before he retires,' he said, 'and withdraw this charge tonight so that there is no embarrassment with the Provost Major in the morning.' Nodding to Jenkins, he continued: 'Please escort His Excellency to his quarters, Sergeant Major, and see what can be done to treat those wounds. I shall join you shortly.'

'Very good, sir.'

Simon propelled the Major through the tent flap and towards General Graham's tent. 'I say,' protested Smith-Denbigh, 'all this doesn't have to be done tonight, does it? I mean . . .'

'Better to get it over with now. I don't want Muharram Pasha suffering the indignity of being brought up before the Provost Major in the morning, even if it is only to be given an apology. Let's get the slate cleaned tonight.'

They found Graham still working by lanternlight at his desk. The two men paused for a moment at the opening, and once again, Simon coughed discreetly. The General looked up and frowned at their presence.

'Sorry, sir, to intrude once again,' said Simon. 'You will remember the incident when my Egyptian colleague was arrested?'

The General nodded.

'The charge was brought by Major Smith-Denbigh, as you know, sir, who, on being acquainted with the circumstances, wishes to withdraw the charge and has hurried here to ask your permission to do so. Major?'

Smith-Denbigh looked slightly incongruous, standing to attention jacketless, his napkin still in his hand. 'Yes, General,' he said, his eyes fixed on the canvas above Graham's head. 'I fear the charge was a mistake and I acted too hastily. With your permission, sir, I would like to withdraw the charge against Mr . . . er . . .'

Graham waved a hand irritably. 'For goodness' sake withdraw it, then. I've got too much to do to bother with it anyway. You must inform the Provost Major yourself, Smith-Denbigh. No doubt he'll be glad to see the back of it.' He bent his head to the table again. 'Now good night, gentlemen.'

'Good night, sir.'

Outside the General's tent, Simon wasted few words in parting from Smith-Denbigh. 'I will leave it to you to see the Provost Major,' he said. 'My advice to you, my friend, is to curb your temper in future. Good night.' He turned and strode away, leaving the Major looking after him with narrowed eyes.

Simon found Jenkins dabbing at the marks on Ahmed's face with all the care of a midwife, using cotton wool dipped in a pannier full of warm water. He looked up with a grin. 'Just fixin' 'Is Excellency's make-up,' he said.

'Yes, Simon,' frowned Ahmed, wincing at Jenkins's administrations. 'Why did you call me that, and why did bloody man change his mind? Very strange, eh? Very strange.'

Simon grinned back. 'I had a few words with him about the unfairness of slashing away with a swagger stick. I think he saw the point and wanted to apologise. And you have done such a marvellous job riding with us, Ahmed, that I have decided that from now on you are a pasha and shall be called Your Excellency.' He bowed low to the little Egyptian.

'Ah,' added Jenkins, 'the Captain – sorry, *Major*; e's promoted all of us now – can work the odd miracle when he wants to.'

'Speaking of miracles,' said Simon, 'is there anything to eat? I'm famished.'

Jenkins dropped the cotton wool into the bowl with a sigh and rose. 'Well, I can't do *everythin'*, now, can I? One minnit I'm a master locksmith, the next Florence bleedin' Nightingale, an' the next expected to be, what's 'is name, bloomin' Escoffier. I'll go an' see what I can find.' He spoke over his shoulder as he bowed and went through the tent flap, 'P'raps you'll continue lookin' after 'is Royal 'Ighness . . .'

Simon squatted down beside Ahmed and inspected the livid weals across his face. 'Hmmm. No lasting harm done, I think, though you are going to have a couple of black eyes, I'm afraid. I am so sorry about this, Ahmed. It should never have happened.'

Ahmed nodded his head earnestly. 'No. It is not like British I know, like those that come to my hotel, et cetera, et cetera, et cetera.'

'No.' Simon sighed. 'But there are black sheep in every flock, I am afraid. Now, continue the bathing if you wish, but excuse me, because I desperately need to wash this sand out of my hair and off my body before Jenkins comes back with the caviar and champagne.' He directed a level gaze at the Egyptian. 'Do you think you can come out into the desert again tomorrow? Will you be fit enough? We are being asked to go back to Kassassin again, and I can well understand if you do not wish to ride with us, but I would rather not leave you behind.'

'Oh no, Simon. I shall be good to go. I do not need beautiful face to ride bleedin' camel, look you.'

Simon grinned with relief as much as amusement. He did not want the Egyptian staying in the camp alone, vulnerable to any enquiries a newly suspicious Smith-Denbigh might make about his real identity. Risking the mosquitoes and flies, he stripped off his shirt and pantaloons and washed outside, and was towelling himself down as Jenkins returned.

'Bloody chicken again, I'm afraid,' said the Welshman. 'But don't worry, I'll dress it up so that it tastes like old boots an' rat's tails. After all, on this postin', I can do *everythin'*, can't I?'

'Of course you can, old chap. You certainly used to be a good wine waiter, so where's the bloody whisky, then?'

Chapter 16

Once back in Mahsama, Alice resigned herself to the inevitable dressing-down from, first, her husband and then, probably and more seriously, from the C-in-C himself, Sir Garnet Wolseley. Covington arrived back late that evening, dusty and tired from his patrol, but they ate together outside the little bivouac tent she had unloaded from her camel. She did her best with the meal, but it consisted mainly of army tinned rations, with a very little rice, that her man had been able to buy from the stores. She and her husband were both subdued and spoke little during the meal.

Eventually Covington looked at her across the firelight and spoke quietly. 'You know, Alice,' he said, 'you are now becoming that thing that all generals hate the most.'

'And what is that, pray?'

'A bloody nuisance.'

She shrugged. 'Well, Ralph, I can't help that. It is Wolseley's fault for cooping up the journalists in Ismailia with nothing to write about but the weather. He is trying to corral us like sheep. Why, he has even appointed an officer to "see to our needs" – which means keep on eye on us and ensure that we don't stray. We are bound to break out a bit.'

'No. Only *you* have broken out.'

'Well, more shame on the others.'

Covington sighed. 'I fear that he might send you home.'

Alice shot him an anxious glance. 'Oh, Ralph, he must not do that. I was only doing my job.'

'No. You were exceeding your brief.'

'Does he need to know?'

'Yes. Graham will have been informed that you are here, and he will be less than delighted to have you on his hands. He is bound to tell Wolseley, and the General, in fact, arrives here tomorrow, I understand. I shall, of course, intervene and tell him myself, and I will put the best face on it that I can. But I fear the worst.'

'Oh blast!' She looked into the fire for a moment, then gazed beseechingly at him. 'Don't let him send me home, Ralph. It will end my career and . . .' her voice grew stronger, 'there will be a hell of a fuss back in England, you know. He will be accused of muzzling the press and all that sort of thing. Questions will be asked in the House and I will become even more of a bloody nuisance to him back home than out here. You know him well and he respects you. Please talk him out of it, my dear. I know you can.'

Covington shook his head slowly. 'You have the reputation of being something of a stormy petrel, you know. Wolseley knows that General Roberts ordered you home from Afghanistan for evading his censorship. I will do my best, but you do have a record, so to speak.'

They fell silent for while, then Alice moved around the fire and seized Covington's good hand, looking steadily into his eye. 'Ralph,' she asked, 'do *you* want me out of here? Do you want me sent home, back to Norfolk in disgrace?'

Covington sighed. 'Of course I bloody well do, you silly goose,' he murmured. 'You must know that. I want you back home, where it is safe, and where you won't get captured by mad booty collectors and strung by your neck from a rafter, or shot at by Arabi's soldiers. That's your place – my home and your home. That's where you should be. When we married, you promised that you would give up this journalism nonsense, so if this *disgrace*, as you call it, means that you go back to dear old Norfolk and lose your job, then I would give at least two and half cheers.'

She opened her mouth to protest, but he frowned and held up his hand. 'I know you well enough, however, to understand that you cannot be reconciled to that. So I shall do my best – short of threatening to run him through with my sword – to persuade Wolseley to let you stay. You can rely on that. But you must realise that you have made a bloody fool of yourself.'

Alice hung her head. 'Yes, I suppose I have. But thank you for promising to help.'

Alice rose early next morning to compose five hundred words on the facts that Simon had given her about the fighting at Maskhuta and Mahsama station, her account threaded through with background colour on the difficulties of travelling in the desert and the problems facing Wolseley in keeping his lines of communication open and supplied. At mid-morning an orderly slipped a note through her tent flap, inviting her to visit the Commander-in-Chief at two p.m. that day. Sighing, she slipped out of her desert clothes and did her best, with a damp cloth and the palm of her hand, to smooth out the wrinkles from the only change of clothing she had: a simple, if slightly low-cut, blouse, with a skirt and sandals. She remembered how, in South Africa, the General had cast what seemed to be a not altogether disapproving eye on her ankle when first they had met. She was desperate enough to use all the weapons in her armoury.

She presented herself sharply at two and was led into the General's bell tent, where Wolseley rose to greet her and indicated a folding chair across from his collapsible table. Alice decided to take the initiative.

'I am afraid I have become a nuisance to you, Sir Garnet,' she said.

'I fear that is so, Mrs Covington.' His tone was icy and he had obviously chosen to address her by her married name to remind her of her marital duties. 'You know that all journalists were ordered to remain in Ismailia until we could establish ourselves out here in the desert. Yet you chose to disobey that instruction. Why was that?'

'Because, General, it prevented me from doing my job, which is to report back to my newspaper on the war and how it is being conducted. I certainly could not do that from a collection of huts on the edge of the Suez Canal.'

'The . . . ah . . . restriction on your movement was only temporary, but it was necessary because myself and my staff have faced very difficult logistical problems with this campaign, and until they could be resolved, or at least reduced, we could not assume the responsibility of protecting the considerable number of journalists we have here if they were allowed to roam out into the desert – a very dangerous place. You must have understood that. The position was explained to you all, I believe, by your liaison officer.'

Alice could not resist smiling at the memory of that harassed young man attempting to explain to his flock why they could not leave their pen. 'Ah yes,' she responded, 'but I asked for no protection from the army. I did not wish to be a nuisance. I merely made my own arrangements and slipped quietly out into the desert, keeping well clear of your posts along the railway and canal.'

'And where you would surely have died had not young Fonthill most fortuitously come across you.'

'That remained to be seen, General. I feel sure we would have found our way to the canal and replenished our water.'

A vein now began to throb in Wolseley's temple. His position of Adjutant General at the Horse Guards made him effectively the second in command of the British Army. Here, as Commander-in-Chief on campaign in Egypt, he was in supreme command. He was not used to conducting a discussion. He *issued* orders, not *debated* them.

He cleared his throat. 'Has it not occurred to you, Mrs Covington, that your actions could have placed the men under my command at great disadvantage? Did you not think of that?'

Alice frowned. 'In what way, pray?'

Wolseley leaned across the table. 'We are fighting a vicious foe. The Egyptian army is not a civilised body of men as we know them in Europe. Torture is still used in Cairo to extract information from prisoners – oh yes, I have evidence of that. You could well have been captured, put to the lash and forced to divulge whatever details you have of my dispositions and the difficulties we are facing in unloading our men and supplies at Ismailia, thereby encouraging Colonel Arabi to launch a preventive action there.'

Alice thought quickly. 'But General,' she said, 'that applies to any of your troops who might be captured. You run that risk at all times.'

'There are two points in refutation of that.' Wolseley's voice had now risen in tone. 'The first is that my men are not allowed to wander, undefended, around the desert asking to be captured. And second, they are trained to resist the sort of interrogation I have described. They are not women.' The last word was delivered with emphasis, leaving Alice in no doubt about the General's views on the frailties of her gender.

Alice flushed. 'Sir Garnet, I am a brigadier's daughter and a colonel's wife. I have never had the misfortune to be treated as you describe, but my work has led me to campaign with the army in many parts of the empire. I am not the sort of person who would wilt under interrogation, I assure you.'

Wolseley sat back in his seat and for a moment his face relaxed. 'My dear Mrs Covington,' he said, 'may I assure you that I defer to no one – except possibly your husband – in my admiration for your pluck, and even the ... er ... competence and skill you show in your work.' He looked down at his table for a moment before continuing. 'I remember well the fortitude and loyalty you displayed in the face of Ralph's terrible injuries in Sekukuniland. And I should inform you that your husband, this morning, has made a very strong and persuasive case for allowing you to remain on this campaign. But I cannot accede to his request, I am afraid. I wish you to leave immediately for Ismailia and to return home to England as soon as you are able to make arrangements to do so. I shall cable your editor and explain the circumstances to him.'

Despite the heat in the tent, Alice felt herself grow cold. 'Sir Garnet,' she said, 'I beg you to reconsider. Perhaps I was a little headstrong, but, like soldiers, journalists must sometimes display that kind of foolishness if they are to do their job. Please let me stay.'

Wolsley shook his head. 'I am sorry, dear lady, but it is not possible. You see, the British Army has never been accompanied before in any of its overseas campaigns by so large a contingent of journalists. As you know, they are here from all over the world. If I made an exception in your case, then I am convinced that we should have all kinds of people – particularly the . . . er . . . Latin types and the Americans – slipping away and getting into trouble. Once they see that you have done it and, forgive me, got away with it, so to speak, then others will follow. No. I am sorry. You must return home. There is a detail leaving for Ismailia at four. It is expecting you.'

Alice nodded slowly. 'I see. I am to be made an example of. Very well.' She stood. 'Thank you, Sir Garnet, for explaining your reasons so carefully, and I am indeed sorry to cause you trouble in the middle of your other considerable worries. I will pack immediately.'

Wolseley stood and bowed to her. At the tent entrance she paused. 'May I beg one last indulgence of you, General?'

He inclined his head. 'If it does not compromise my position on this matter, then of course.'

'I have written a report of the recent fighting at Maskhuta and I would be most grateful if it could be relayed back in the normal way to my newspaper, without prejudice to your decision.'

Wolseley nodded. 'Of course, if it conforms with our

established rules of censorship, Mrs Covington.' He smiled. 'I think we can allow you a valedictory.'

She returned the smile and, bowing her head, slipped through the tent opening. Outside, she looked down at her skirt and the rather dainty sandals. All wasted, dammit!

In her tent, Alice found a note pinned to her bedroll. It was from Covington and merely said: *I am sorry. Did my best. Back tonight. R.* She shook her head at it. 'Sorry, Ralph,' she said, 'I must be on my way.' She scribbled a brief note of farewell to Covington, and then began packing her few belongings before finding Abdul.

On the uncomfortable and monotonous journey back to Ismailia, Alice hardly exchanged a word with anyone but remained within her own cocoon, thinking hard. She let her mind roam, and although at first she tried to avoid it, it was the thought of Simon Fonthill that most insistently thrust itself into her consciousness. She could not but recall the thrill of Simon's hand on her throat, staying there much longer than was necessary, warm and tender to the touch. She summoned up again his look of first amazement and then delight when they met in the desert and she half fell, half slipped down from her saddle into his arms. With a toss of her head, she acquiesced and, just for a little while, allowed herself to fantasise about what might have been, if that spear had not slashed Ralph's face and the elephant gun's giant slug had not crushed his forearm in the valley at Sekukuni. Then, quite firmly, she ended the indulgence once and for all. She would never, *never* think that way again. It was pointless and debilitating. She could not have Simon and that was that. The question now was: what to do next? As her camel plodded along behind the horses and mules of the detachment returning to Ismailia, grains of sand gritting between her teeth, a plan began to formulate in her mind. There was no question, of course, of her leaving Egypt and returning home. To hell with that – and with General Wolseley! There were stories to be written!

Back in the journalists' compound at Ismailia, Alice carefully composed a cable to her editor. It was important that Wolseley's message to him, telling him of her dismissal, should be refuted before the *Morning Post* rushed out a replacement correspondent. It would be running too great a risk openly to contradict Wolseley's decision in a cable sent from the army's headquarters, but Alice gambled that the kind of keen censorship exercised on press reports would not apply to individual messages of a personal nature. In fact, the censor would most likely be quite unaware of her dismissal. Accordingly, she wrote:

NEWS OF MY RETURN EXAGGERATED STOP WILL CONTINUE REPORTAGE FROM DIFFERENT ANGLE STOP MORE LATER STOP REGARDS GRIFFITH

Alice's reappearance in the compound caused some discussion. Her general air of aloofness discouraged questions, but the bright-eyed, curly-haired *Corriere della Sera*, with all his Milanese brashness, had no such inhibitions. She had grown to like his ineffable charm. 'Where you bin, Miss Griffith?' he asked, falling into step beside her. 'I bin missin you. Scoopin' us all out in the desert, eh?'

She rewarded him with a smile. 'Not really, Enrico. Just

getting some fresh air away from this place. Any announcements while I've been away?'

The Italian shrugged his shoulders. 'They give us a few scraps about a bit of a fight at some place called Mahsama, but it only worth two paras. This isn't a war. Nothin' 'appens.'

She increased her smile and slipped away. Good. Her piece about the engagement at Maskhuta and the cavalry charge at Mahsama might be the only story filed in any depth. So far so good! That evening she sought the friendly armourer who had obtained the pistol for her and begged him to find her two compasses and two more water bottles. That would, he said, be no problem. Then she returned to the market in Ismailia and sought out Abdul. He gave her a cheerful grin, but that disappeared very quickly when she made her request.

'Come now, Abdul,' she wheedled. 'We only got lost the last time because I dropped the damned compass. I am now buying two, one to be held in reserve. And this time I want to sweep much further north into the desert so that we will avoid all the trouble. I shall know exactly where to turn south for Tel el Kebir and we will not be involved in the fighting. I just want to observe the battle from a safe distance.'

'No, missy.' Abdul shook his head. 'Too dangerous.'

'I will double your pay, Abdul. And let us find someone else to come with us as well to afford a little further protection.'

The Egyptian grinned somewhat shamefacedly. 'Sorry, missy. I don't like the desert.'

Alice sighed. 'Very well, Abdul. But here.' She pressed a

handful of piastres into his hand. 'Find me someone – two people – who know the desert and whom you trust. Can you do that for me?'

Abdul closed his fingers over the coins. 'I know one man, at least, missy. I will ask. You come back here same time tomorrow. Yes?'

'Good. Yes. Same time tomorrow, but I must meet him first. Can you bring him along?'

'I try, missy.'

'Yes. Do that.'

The next day Alice picked up her compasses and canteens from the quartermaster and made her way to the market. At first she thought that Abdul had decided she was too dangerous to deal with, for there was no sign of him. Then he reappeared, that embarrassed grin on his face, accompanied by a large, turbaned Egyptian.

'This is Mohammed, missy,' he said. 'He good in desert and know English.' The tall man bowed, running his fingers through his long black beard.

'I was trader for some years with the desert caravans from Cairo, missy,' he said. 'Also took English tourists down Nile. I come with you into desert. Know all the oasis.'

Alice looked at him carefully. Abdul had been recommended to her by an Ismailia-based Frenchman she had befriended, and he had been reliable up to a point and honest, if less than efficient out in the sandy wastes. Could she trust Mohammed? His black eyes held hers steadily, so coolly, indeed, as to prompt the question, was there just a trace of arrogance in his gaze? Ah well, she reasoned, confidence of that sort was needed in the desert.

'Good,' she said. 'Abdul has told you of the terms? From

that sum you must find us good camels, and food and water enough for us to survive in the desert for perhaps four weeks. Is that acceptable to you?'

He bowed again. 'Quite acceptable, missy. I am happy out in desert.'

'Very well, I will take you. Now, can you find one other to accompany us? I want to have no trouble with any Bedawi we might meet, and three is better than two in those circumstances. I shall be armed, of course.' She added the last sentence to offer a hint that she, too, could be strong.

His eyes flickered for a moment. 'I have a friend, missy. He called Ehab. He does not speak English but he knows Tel el Kebir well and has many friend in Egyptian army. He will come, I know. But he needs four or five days before we go. He only man I know for this work. I recommend you wait for him, please.'

Alice frowned. She had hoped to get away from Ismailia as soon as possible before questions were asked about the exact date of her departure. However, it was most unlikely that Wolseley could advance on Tel el Kebir for several weeks at least, and if this man knew the Egyptian army dispositions, he could be more than useful.

'Very well, then,' she said. 'Tell him that he is hired. Let us be prepared to leave in five days' time. Mohammed, you must understand that I want no fuss made about our departure. I just want to slip quietly away. I would prefer to leave after dark. Is that possible?'

'Yes, missy.'

'Good. I am in the journalists' compound near to the main camp. Let me know if you have problems. I will wish to see you the day before we leave to go through our supplies and so on and to see receipts for them. Is that understood?'

'Understood, missy.'

'Very well. Good day to you both.'

Ehab turned out to be a small, rather rotund Egyptian with a light-skinned face, although Alice could see little of it, for the man kept his *esharp* wrapped tightly around it. He wore a neatly trimmed beard and the gaze from his dark eyes seemed myopic. Nevertheless, he handled his camel well, and after checking through the list of supplies and inspecting the camels – an extra one had been added to carry their equipment – Alice accepted everything and they made arrangements to rendezvous at the edge of the town just after dusk the following evening.

Alice's plan was simple, even crude. There was no point in attempting to shadow the corps of correspondents when they were brought up to the front line, nor to keep in loose touch with the army outposts along Wolseley's line of communication. That would open her to the danger of being discovered by army patrols. She had obtained a detailed map from the market, which showed the exact stations along the railway line up to and beyond el Kebir. Her intention was to sweep deeply out into the desert and then turn south to the Egyptian lines and camp to the north of them, as Bedawi, and wait until Wolseley launched his attack. She would observe the battle as best she could, then slip back into the camp under cover of the inevitable confusion, find Enrico, her Italian friend, and persuade him to file her dispatch to the *Morning Post* under an Italianised version of her name. Cornford, her editor, already warned by her cable, would recognise her style and would realise that she had had to resort to subterfuge. She would gamble that in the hectic aftermath of the clash between the two armies, when the censors would have reverted to their role as front-line troops, her story would slip through as long as its contents were not controversial.

She shook her head as she contemplated the plan. Crude indeed! It depended upon far too many fortuitous outcomes. But it was the only tactic she could think of employing. She shrugged her shoulders. Better to try and fail than to submit weakly to transportation back to England!

Alice and her two companions met by the ruin of the barracks at Nefisha. Without incident, they turned their camels and headed a little way along the edge of the rail track before turning north-west out into the desert. After an hour, Alice decided it was safe to camp, and the two men lit a fire and prepared a meal while Alice erected her bivouac tent. They ate in companionable silence and were up before dawn to continue their journey, Alice carefully plotting their course with the aid of her compass.

They continued in this fashion for three days, Alice diverting twice to find small oases marked on her map, where they were able to replenish their water. The two men proved to be amenable to instruction and worked easily with the camels and the cooking. It was, however, a silent party, for Mohammed spoke little and Ehab not at all. The latter kept very much to himself, and after a while, Alice realised that she had no idea what he looked like, for he remained shrouded in his voluminous Arab garments and headdress. But it was of no importance. They both did their job and that was what mattered.

On the morning of the fourth day, Alice decided that the time had come to turn south towards Tel el Kebir. Map in one hand and compass in the other, she gestured to Mohammed, riding behind her. He nodded and turned to Ehab in the rear, passing on the order. The little man also nodded, but then urged his camel forward so that it was level with Alice's and caught her wrist. She whirled round and saw that Ehab had donned spectacles – small, round spectacles. Then he hit her hard across the face.

'No, bitch,' he said. 'We continue to the north-west.' And he swung his hand around and caught her a second blow across the face that sent her falling from the saddle to the ground.

Sprawled there, she looked up, wide-eyed. 'Oh my God,' she cried. 'George!'

Chapter 17

The day following the Smith-Denbigh incident, General Graham and his small force moved up and occupied Kassassin without interference from the enemy. He settled down in defence of this post with a mixed detachment of dragoons, two battalions of infantry supported by mounted infantry, men of the Marine Artillery acting as infantry and two guns of the Royal Horse Artillery. The latter's ammunition was limited to that carried in their limbers: thirty-six rounds per gun. It was a thin line, and Graham used his three scouts continually for three days, patrolling to the west and north, riding ahead of troops of cavalry who themselves were deployed as constant, fluid forward screens to ensure that the outpost was not taken by surprise attack. It was a repetitive and tiring task, out in the scorching sun for most of each day, plagued by fitful dust storms and the ever-pervasive flies, but Simon, at least, preferred it to staying in the lines, away from further attention by Smith-Denbigh and where there was no Alice or Covington, for that matter, to distract him.

It was Ahmed, riding out north of his two fellows in the early morning, who first saw the hesitant advance of the

Egyptian army. The clouds of white-coated figures were gathering on high ground, without, however, displaying any strong antagonistic intentions. Nevertheless, the three scouts rode back to report to General Graham. The latter immediately dispatched them back to Mahsama – their camels were still the fastest and most reliable form of transport between the two camps – to direct Drury Lowe to bring up his cavalry to protect Graham's north flank. The horsemen turned out, but before they could advance, the Egyptians retired, having let off a few salvos of artillery fire. The British cavalry were put on stand-by (there was no fodder available for their mounts at Kassassin, so the decision to move them up there could not be taken lightly), only to advance in earnest in the early afternoon when the enemy was observed making a more determined advance in greater strength, with cavalry and infantry supported by guns. Simon, Jenkins and Ahmed rode up with Drury Lowe, but as he and his cavalry wheeled off to the north into the desert proper to protect the British right flank, Simon and his companions peeled away to the south to rejoin Graham and the main force.

They found that the British line was under sustained artillery attack from, Simon estimated, some forty guns. Graham's men had dug in along the Egyptians' original lines and their disciplined rifle fire was holding back the attempts by the enemy's infantry to launch frontal attacks. The artillery duel, however, was very one-sided, for Graham had only his two RHA guns, and although they were splendidly served by their men and accurately laid, their precious shells had to be conserved.

Graham, his face streaked with perspiration, nodded to

his guns when Simon had reported. 'It's a case of firing one bally round to twenty of theirs,' he complained. 'They've also brought up reinforcements by train from Tel el Kebir, so I estimate they've got about ten thousand against my merry band of odds and sods.' Then he tugged at the end of his hanging moustache and gave a lugubrious smile. 'Mind you, we shall hold out all right. They have kindly provided us with reasonable trenches to shelter from their cannon, and our rifles are stopping their infantry from coming at us across the open ground.' His smile was replaced by the suspicion of a frown. 'As long, that is, as Drury Lowe can protect my open right flank. That mustn't be turned.'

The confrontation continued throughout the long day, with the artillery fire forcing the defenders to keep their heads down, only for them to re-emerge above the trench parapets to direct volleys to deter the desultory attempts by the Egyptian foot soldiers to advance across the open ground. It was a stalemate, and as dusk descended, more and more heads turned to the north to detect any sign of the arrival of Drury Lowe and his Horse Guards.

With no scouting role to play, Simon, Jenkins and Ahmed took their place in the line and suffered along with the rest of the defenders from the heat, the flies and, worst of all, the lack of water. The only source for this was the canal, but this was now discoloured and stank from the numerous animal carcasses that floated in it.

Jenkins wrinkled his nose as he uncorked his canteen. 'The bastards 'ave poisoned the canal deliberately by throwin' corpses in it,' he said. 'Now that ain't fair, eh?'

Ahmed, sitting disconsolately with his back to the trench wall, shook his head. The marks on his face had had little chance to heal and he was forced continually to swat away the flies attracted to them.

'No,' said the Egyptian. 'Koran commands that those killed in action are buried with proper ceremonies, et cetera, et cetera. Egyptians would not throw bodies in water. Too precious to be made deliberately mucky, anyway.'

Simon grimaced. 'I'll drink to that.' He did so, and swallowed with difficulty, despite his thirst. 'Best to use this stuff just to wet the lips and dampen a handkerchief to tie around the neck. Cholera is worse than sunstroke.' He glanced up the line to the north. 'It looks as though the cavalry have got through to the top there, otherwise we would have been attacked from the rear by now. I just hope that they've been able to bring cannon up with them. We could do with them.'

It was long after dark when, at last, news came through from Drury Lowe that his brigade had successfully charged the guns and skirmishers of the Egyptians on the right flank, and that the enemy was in full retreat. Graham, who had himself mounted a rather hesitant advance from his trenches in support of what he had hoped was an attack from his cavalry in the north, was now able to withdraw his men and consolidate his line as more reinforcements dribbled in from the east.

The next two days saw a resumption of the scouting work for Simon and his companions. Once, returning to the camp from another uneventful day riding over the hot sand, he exchanged glances with Smith-Denbigh. Simon nodded to him, but the Major gave no obvious sign of acknowledgement, merely following Simon with narrowed eyes as he plodded through the lines. Covington seemed to have disappeared, and Simon presumed that he had rejoined Wolseley and his staff in the east.

In fact, the General himself rode up on the third day after the Kassassin engagement, and within an hour of his arrival, Simon found himself looking into Wolseley's good eye.

'Now, Fonthill,' said the General (no jocular appellation of 'cousin' this time, noted Simon), 'the time has come for me to have a good look at the el Kebir lines. My Indian division has disembarked at Ismailia from Suez, and I am reinforcing Kassassin rapidly, mainly by boat up the Sweetwater now that the canal has been cleared. It won't be long before I have sufficient forces here to launch what I anticipate will be the knockout blow to Arabi at el Kebir. So I need to see the lines for myself. I will ride out at dawn with a squadron of cavalry, and I shall want you and your scouts to come with me.'

'Of course, sir.' Wolseley's face looked drawn, and Simon wondered if the fever had returned.

'Two more things.'

'Sir?'

'You will remember, of course, that message you intercepted at Ismailia from Mahmoud Fehmy, one of Arabi's leading advisers? He spoke of an informer, you will remember.'

'Of course, sir.'

'Well,' Wolseley's face broke into a bleak smile, 'we've captured a man who has told us something about this informer. It seems that he is, or was, an employee of the Thomas Cook Company.'

Simon felt his heart leap. 'Not . . .?'

'It has to be. Your nasty friend Mr George, the man I

appointed to handle my confidential account at the agency. It seems that George turned on us after the bombardment of Alex . . .'

'. . . and told them of my earlier cables to you.'

'Exactly. It wasn't only the bombardment, I suspect, that turned him, but also your own little contretemps with him, when many of his precious belongings were burned. However, it is of no account now, because he was rather too late with his information – or the Egyptians were slow to act on it – and as you know, we were able to land without interference.'

'Ah, yes, but the man is English and remains a traitor.'

'Well, he has certainly lost his job at Cook's and probably left Cairo, but I doubt if he will be able to leave Egypt while the war continues. I shall make sure that he is found and brought to book as soon as hostilities are over. Like you, I have a personal debt to settle with him. But now, Fonthill, the other matter . . .'

Wolseley's tone had been cold throughout the exchange about George, and Simon realised that he was about to be carpeted.

'Colonel Covington informs me,' continued the General, 'that you have been claiming that your little Egyptian scout is the favourite nephew of the Khedive and that you are a major of some seniority in the British Army. He also tells me that you told a pack of lies to ensure that the man was not brought before the Provost Major on a charge of insolence to a British officer. Is this true?'

'More or less, sir.'

'What the hell do you mean, "more or less"? Is it true or isn't it?'

'Put like that, most of it is true.'

The vein that had throbbed so in Wolseley's confrontation with Alice now slipped into action again, although the General made a great effort to control his voice. 'Then you had better explain yourself.'

'Very well, sir.' Simon also kept his voice level. 'My Egyptian is certainly not related to the Khedive. He is a hotel-keeper – a very good one – who has always been helpful to Jenkins and me. We wanted an interpreter for our work here and he volunteered to join us, without pay, I may add. He has proved to be honourable, brave and a hard worker. Although he does not like fighting his own people, he helped us against the mob in Alexandria and also against the Egyptian garrison at Nefisha. He had just returned to Mahsama with an important message from me to General Graham when he fell foul of an officer of the Duke of Cornwall's Light Infantry.'

'Go on.'

'Ahmed, my scout, stumbled across a tent peg into one Major Smith-Denbigh, who swore at him. Ahmed told the Major that he had tripped over the peg, but he was shouted down. Ahmed is not used to being bullied in this fashion and was continuing to try and explain when the man slashed him twice across the face with his swagger stick and ordered his arrest. I found him that evening, after he had been shackled to the main pole of the guard tent for at least four hours. He had had no food or water nor any opportunity to relieve himself. His wounds were still bleeding when we tended them.'

A silence fell over the tent. 'But he *was* insolent?' asked Wolseley.

'Neither Covington nor I was present when the incident occurred. However, I obtained the facts from the Egyptian and confirmed them with Smith-Denbigh. From what I heard, I certainly would not regard Ahmed's behaviour as insolent, but then I am not Smith-Denbigh.'

'But why did you then tell such a pack of lies? Why not intervene with General Graham and ask for the man's release?'

'I did so. The General said that he was too busy to go into the case himself and that it should be left to the Provost Marshal.'

'So?'

Simon took a deep breath and leaned across the desk. 'I had been ordered to ride with the General when he left for Kassassin the following day. I would not therefore be present to speak for Ahmed when the charge was heard. What chance would the word of an Egyptian have against that of a British Army major? I needed Ahmed to scout with me and Jenkins the next day and – far more importantly – I did not want this good man humiliated and given further punishment. I therefore confronted Smith-Denbigh to get the facts – and he corroborated what Ahmed had told me – and I then invented my rank and seniority and Ahmed's false identity to, er, persuade him to apologise to my man and intervene with General Graham to have the charge withdrawn. He did so and that was that. All done and dusted without further fuss.'

Simon sat back and held the General's gaze. Wolseley looked away for a moment and then returned to the argument, albeit with a voice that was beginning to show doubt. 'But you can't go around telling those sort of lies, Fonthill, you know.'

'With respect, General, what do you expect from a man who is more or less employed to tell lies? I am not a line soldier – in fact I am not a soldier at all. I am a spy-cum-scout. But I do work for you and you have given me the pay of a major and that of a warrant officer for my man Jenkins. I assumed that rank formally and momentarily to browbeat a bully who only understands that sort of language. The rubbish about Ahmed being the Khedive's nephew was part of the same game. General, I had no time and no inclination to play this the army's way. I had to do it *my way*. My word, but Smith-Denbigh changed his tune when he heard that he had hit the Khedive's favourite nephew!'

A slow smile spread across Wolseley's face. 'Yes, I can imagine.' He shook his head ruefully. 'Good lord, Fonthill, your methods are certainly most irregular, but I have to confess that they seem successful. I also have to tell you that, so far, I have been most grateful for all your efforts here in Egypt. However, I will wish to meet your man Ahmed when we ride out tomorrow. I shall examine his injuries and take matters from there.'

Simon stirred uncomfortably. 'I think I should warn you, sir, that if Smith-Denbigh or Covington tries to resurrect the charge against Ahmed, I shall bring a counter-charge against Smith-Denbigh for attacking a member of the civilian population.'

Wolseley stood. 'I don't accept warnings of that sort and you will do nothing of the kind,' he said. 'You will leave the matter with me. Now get out of here, Fonthill, and don't go about telling everyone that you are my mistress and claiming the rank of field marshal. Understood?'

Simon grinned. 'Understood, sir.'

At the tent flap, Wolseley called him back. His voice was now almost plaintive. 'Is there anything you can do to patch up this feud with Covington, for God's sake? It could get out of hand, you know.'

'With respect, sir, I think you should take that up with the Colonel.'

Wolseley waved a dismissive hand. 'Very well,' he sighed. 'Be ready to ride at dawn.'

Sir Garnet liked to travel light and fast when on reconnaissance, and he had only a squadron of Dragoons with him when the small party assembled as the red of the sun began to fringe the horizon to the east. It was warm already, presaging another hellishly hot day. Wolseley called to Simon as soon as he rode up.

'Where's your man?'

Simon called over an apprehensive Ahmed.

'Good morning, Mr Muharram,' beamed the General. 'Do you mind if I take a look at those marks on your face?'

'Ah, they are nothing, *effendi*.' Ahmed was obviously as disconcerted at this attention as if he had been struck again. 'Nothing at all, sir.'

'No. Let me see.' Wolseley turned the Egyptian's face the better to get the benefit of the early morning light. 'Hmmm. Nasty. Are you still in discomfort from them?'

'What? Oh no, *effendi*. No hurt at all, at all.'

'Good. Now, Mr Muharram . . .' (where on earth had he got Ahmed's second name from? wondered Simon), 'I believe you are owed an apology for this, ah, incident. And on behalf of the army, I extend one to you now. I do hope that we can leave the matter there, for I do value the work you are doing with Major Fonthill.'

Ahmed gave as elegant a bow as anyone riding a camel could possibly produce. 'Of course, Sir General,' he said. 'Very happy, sir.'

'Good. Then let's get on, shall we?' He pulled his horse's head round and caught a glimpse of Jenkins. 'What the hell are you grinning at, 352?'

'Who, me, sir? Nothin', General bach. Nothin' at all, see.'

'Go ahead, Fonthill, and take your army of irregulars with you.'

The party proceeded as fast as the horses could manage in the sand, Simon and his companions riding ahead, spread out in arrowhead formation, with Jenkins, inevitably, riding in the middle to ensure that he did not stray. They met no Egyptian outriders and eventually Simon pulled up on an incline of sand and granite and waited for the General.

'I think this is as near as we can go, sir,' he said. 'There's a reasonably good view from here through your glasses.'

'Hmmm.' Wolseley quieted his horse with his hand and then levelled his field glasses at the lines, which could be clearly defined ahead, with the black blemish of the village of Tel el Kebir in the distant background to the left. He stayed that way for all of five minutes, scanning the horizon. Then he lowered his glasses and addressed Simon.

'You've been into the village, I think?'

'Yes, sir.'

'What's that tall tower thing I can make out?'

Simon raised his own binoculars. 'Don't quite know, sir. Some sort of old lookout tower, I think. Certainly not a mosque. You will remember that in an early report I mentioned that it could be dangerous to us in terms of it being used as a spotter tower for their guns.'

'Exactly. Wilson.' A colonel of artillery urged his horse forward. 'Take a look at that tower. Could be used to range their guns, don't you think? And what's the chance of bringing it down with our own ordnance from this far out?'

Wilson studied the distant building for a moment. 'Yes,' he said eventually. 'We know that the enemy are good gunners, and they could well use the thing to range their cannon. With powerful glasses they would see where their shells were landing. They would use a heliograph or even a relay of signal flags to pass on corrections for their gun-layers. That tower ought to be put out of action, but we would never reach it accurately with the guns we have, sir. And if we tried, there would be a danger of killing civilians in the village there.'

'Thought so. Right, let's go further north and take a look from there.'

The little party cantered off and reconnoitred the plain that rose from the southern end of the Egyptian lines, near the railway and canal, and stretched out into the desert. As Simon had noted, it provided no cover at all for attacking infantry, for the guns of el Kebir could send low-elevation shot and shrapnel screaming across the gravel that surfaced the plain, with little in their path except for the odd sand hill and clump of shrub.

Wolseley rode the length of the Egyptian lines, scribbling notes on his pad, before turning back to the east. He beckoned Simon to ride with him.

'Now, my boy,' he said. 'I have a problem – in fact I have quite a few problems, but only one of them concerns you directly.' Simon remained silent, but he felt that he would not welcome what was about to come. 'That damned tower,' the General continued. 'It has to come down or the enemy will know exactly where to place their shells. Now, we can't reach it with our own guns and I can't exactly send a disposal squad of sappers to waltz through the enemy lines, nor a spearhead of Dragoons to carve their way through to the village in the face of what's likely to be point-blank fire.'

Simon gave a soulful grin. 'But three men disguised as Bedawi might slip through and blow it up?'

'Indeed they might. Now, I can't order you to go, and for goodness' sake, there would be no criticism of you if you decided to decline the honour and continue your career behind the lines as an impersonator of senior officers.' He smiled. 'But you would be our best hope.'

'Very well, sir. A bargain with you?'

'What's that?'

'We'll blow up your tower if there is no further risk of Smith-Denbigh bringing up his charge against Ahmed again.'

Wolseley gave a theatrical sigh. 'My word, Fonthill, you drive a hard bargain. Agreed.' They shook hands and exchanged grins. 'When we get back, go and see my Colonel of Sappers – I'll give you a note – and explain to him what has to be done. I should imagine that it will have to be dynamite, but he will be the judge of that. You will have to make your own dispositions for getting into the village, through the lines, and out again. Make your plan and then come and see me, because we may be able to create a diversion to assist you. But I want the job done soon, for I plan to attack as soon as I have brought up sufficient men and guns.'

'Very good, sir.' Simon fell back to join Jenkins and Ahmed, and after a brief pause to gather his thoughts, he explained the task given to them by the General. Neither spoke for a few moments, and in the silence Simon realised how dangerous the project must appear.

Predictably, it was Jenkins who voiced doubts. 'It's a bit barmy, bach sir, isn't it? I mean, even if we do the job, 'ow do we get out and back to our own lines? Flyin' would be nice, but I left me angel wings back in Wales.'

'I agree that it's not going to be easy, but I have the basis of an idea.' He turned to the Egyptian. 'Ahmed, I don't like asking you to join us on this trip because it is going to be damned dangerous, there's no doubt about that. But I think we will need your knowledge of the language. Will you come with us?'

The little man grinned. 'In for a penny again, in for half a crown . . .'

'No, in for a pound.'

'Very well, then, I am in for a pound again. Oh yes. It will be exciting as long as I don't have to shoot pistol.'

The camaraderie re-established, the three plodded on, but Simon's mind was racing. As best he could remember, the tower was set in the heart of the village, and bringing it down by explosion could well mean destroying the huts around it, with consequent loss to the Egyptian people living in them. How to demolish the tower without causing the death of innocent civilians? How to get into the village without detection? How to get out again?

On reaching Kassassin he hurried to find Wolseley's Colonel of Engineers. He proved to be a huge Scotsman, some six feet four inches tall, with a red face and a fair beard speckled with grey. He read Wolseley's note and listened with growing enthusiasm as Simon described the task.

'Hey, laddie,' he said. 'This is a lovely job, but it's nae work for amateurs. I'll hae to come with yer an' do it meself.'

Simon smiled. 'Sorry, Colonel, but the only way to get in is to pose as Arabs, desert Bedawi. And with respect, you look as much like an Arab as I do a Scotsman. I also know that the General would not want to risk his Colonel of Engineers on a mission like this. You see, we are expendable – just scouts pretending to be Arabs – but you must survive to fight another day. Sorry, but we have to go alone.'

The Colonel frowned. 'That's a shame.' Then a twinkle came into his eye. 'Don't tell anyone I said this now, but if there's one thing I like more than buildin' somethin' up, it's blowin' it doon. How tall is yon tower, and what's it made of?'

'Brick and stone, I think, and about a hundred and twenty feet high. Oh, and can we destroy it without harming the huts surrounding it?'

'Phew! Yer not askin' for much now, are yer? Right noo. Concentrate.'

It didn't take Simon long to realise that he was listening to not only an expert but also an enthusiast on the subject of explosives and their uses. The destruction would be done, the Colonel explained, by using dynamite, which he insisted on calling 'Nobel's Blasting Powder', its original name. The substance consisted of three parts nitroglycerin, one part diatomaceous earth ('that's fossilised microscopic algae to you, sonny'), with a small addition of sodium carbonate. The mixture was formed into small sticks roughly eight inches long and one inch in diameter and wrapped in paper.

Although the purpose of the earth was to make the nitroglycerin less shock-sensitive, it was still volatile and had to be handled with great care. About ten sticks should do the job, the Colonel estimated, and they would be detonated by the use of two blasting caps, fired by two long fuses, creating small explosions that would trigger the larger ones.

'Where do I put 'em?' asked Simon.

'Ah, laddie, that's the trick. Yer want the tower to fall into its own imprint, so to speak? To collapse into itself?'

'Something like that, yes.'

'Aye, right. Ideally yer would want to plant the dynamite in bits, at the base and, say, halfway up, an' then fire them sequentially. But that's tricky to fuse and I'm thinkin' yer won't have much time to fart about. So the thing to do is to divide the sticks into two lots of five an' attach them at the base, say about five feet up, on either side. That should do the trick. Now, remember what they say on the fireworks packet, laddie: light the fuse and retire quickly.'

Simon grinned weakly. He didn't like the sound of any of this, but there was no way out. 'Are you sure the dynamite can be carried safely?'

'Noo, I'm not. You hae to be very careful. Don't jolt the stuff and don't get it wet and you should be all right. And for lord's sake, sonny – don't forget the matches.'

'Thank you, sir. I'm beginning to wish you *could* come with us. Can I collect the stuff tomorrow?'

'Aye, yer can.'

That evening Simon discussed the mission with Jenkins and Ahmed. 'Getting into the village should not be all that difficult,' he explained. 'It's about a mile behind the Egyptian lines, so we loop out really wide into the desert in the north and then come in from *behind* the lines, virtually from the west. The trouble is that the village itself is on the south side of the railway and the canal and we shall have to cross both to get to it. But the Egyptian line of trenches doesn't cross the canal – its southern tip rests on it – and the only bridge is well behind the defences, so it should be unguarded. I think we should go in at dusk, because I want to do the job and get away in the dark if we can. If we are challenged, Ahmed will explain again that we are Bedawi from the south, on our way to Cairo to trade in the markets there, and that we have come into Tel el Kebir to refill our water bottles. Does that sound reasonable to you, Ahmed?'

'Oh yes. Very reasonable.'

'Good,' said Jenkins. 'Everythin's tickety-boo, then. I'm so relieved.'

Simon ignored the sarcasm. It was always Jenkins's response to a difficult problem. 'Then, as soon as it is dark, we blow up the tower and get away.'

'An' 'ow in the name of Colonel Covington do we do that, with the whole village aroused an' the Egyptian army dashin' about all over the place, look you?'

'It's simple. I will arrange with the General that, under cover of dusk, he will advance say five cannon of the Royal Horse Artillery out into the desert towards the enemy lines and then, when he sees the explosion, the guns will open fire on a section of the line three hundred yards or so north of the canal.'

'What about us, then?'

'Wait a minute. The Egyptians will then believe that that section of the line is under attack and reinforce the area, hopefully drawing troops away from the canal and certainly making everyone there keep their heads down. Then we will escape – by water, on the canal.'

'Blimey!' Jenkins sniffed. 'But we can't swim all the bloody way – and anyway that water's foul. Ugh!'

'Nonsense. We don't swim. We get out by boat – a collapsible boat that we take in on a fourth camel, loaded in sections. We assemble it and paddle out under cover of the bombardment till we reach the dam, which is at the bottom of the enemy lines about half a mile from the village. No one will look for us on the canal behind the dam; they will all be waiting for a frontal attack. If we are stopped, Ahmed will explain that we are taking supplies down the canal to the trenches. Well before we reach the dam, we will disembark, creep on to the southern bank and slip away into the desert on that side. We may be able to take the boat out, carry it around the dam for, say, two hundred yards or so and then put it back into the water and paddle back to our lines. Otherwise we will just walk. It'll be easy in the dark, under cover of the artillery attack.'

Simon's ridiculous optimism was infectious and the three exchanged wide grins. 'I think we shall be shot,' said Ahmed, his black eyes sparkling, 'but it will be fun. Exciting.'

Jenkins blew out his cheeks. 'But, bach sir, it will mean leavin' your camel be'ind, an' you were gettin' very fond of 'er. As for me, I ain't goin' until I am guaranteed at least five Victoria Crosses an' the promise of Colonel Covington bringin' me tea in bed every mornin' till this postin's finished.'

'Very well,' said Simon. 'That's easily arranged. But the boat might be difficult. I need to enlist Wolseley's help in the morning.'

* * *

The next day, the plan was presented to the General. He listened carefully and then nodded. 'Feasible,' he said. 'Getting out will be the difficult bit, but we can certainly use the guns to create a diversion. When can you go?'

'As soon as the boat is ready, sir.'

'Good. Go back and see your friend Fraser of the Engineers. He can build anything.'

Once again, the Colonel was full of enthusiasm. 'It'll hae to be a wooden framework which yer can assemble quickly,' he mused, 'and then a waterproof canvas cover that yer tak' separately and slip on to the frame. Not easy, because it's got to carry three of yer. But we can do it. Oh aye. Leave it to me.'

Chapter 18

Two days later, Wolseley saw them off from the north of the Kassassin lines. He shook hands with each of them and waved as they trudged off into the desert, the three sitting hunched on their camels and leading two additional pack animals, for the boat could not be loaded on to one beast alone. The extra camels, in fact, added credence to their story of being desert traders, for they had strung a few earthenware pots and other ethnic artefacts to the packs to give verisimilitude to their general appearance. In fact, draped in their black robes, faces and hands burned by the sun, their modern rifles tucked away in their canvas covers, they looked for all the world like Bedawi from the Sudan border, bent on selling what they could in the teeming bazaars of Cairo. But Simon was under no illusions about the difficulties of the task that lay ahead.

Along the straight railway line, the distance between Kassassin and Tel el Kebir was fourteen miles. But Simon and his companions were no crows, and their route out into the desert to get behind the Egyptian lines more than doubled that distance. Their progress was slow, for the pack camels were heavily laden, and the further north they travelled the deeper the surface sand became. Their strange course, however, proved to be worthwhile, for they saw no other living thing, except vultures wheeling high overhead, until, nearing dusk on the third day, they glimpsed bright pinpricks to the south-east that could only be the lights of Tel el Kebir.

'Right,' said Simon, 'we'll loop round and come in from the west.' He looked at his watch. 'Unless we meet trouble, we shall probably be in the village at about midnight. At that time, the General will be sending out his guns and we will need to give them a good two hours. We will make straight for the tower. If I remember rightly, there is a bit of open space near the thing where we can erect our tents, tie up the camels and seemingly settle down for the night. Then, at about two, I will slip away and find the best place to launch the boat, while you two unpack and start to assemble it. Then . . . we play it by ear.' He grinned.

Ahmed blinked in the failing light. 'What do we play with our ear?'

'We, er, see how things develop and act accordingly.'

'Ah yes. By ear. We listen, eh?'

'Well, yes. We *look* as well, though.'

'We play by ear and eye, then?'

'Smellin' is important too, bach,' said Jenkins. 'You can't beat a good sniff, see, for sensin' trouble.'

'Yes. So we play by ear, eye and nose. I remember.'

'I think we should get on,' said Simon. 'Stay alert, Ahmed, because from now on we could be challenged.'

In fact, they were challenged twice before they reached the outskirts of the village: once by a patrol of Egyptian cavalry, led by a bored officer, whose boots gleamed in the half-light; and once, on the edge of the desert, by a group of Arabs walking back into the village. Simon was leading when the Egyptian patrol approached, and he was forced to give a growled '*As salaam alaykum*' before Ahmed could ride up and engage the officer in conversation. They were allowed to ride on after a few moments, but not before the officer had prodded the loads on their camels and sent Simon's heart fluttering. An unlucky thrust could send them all to kingdom come.

'What did he want?' he asked Ahmed.

'He ask where we going and what we carried and why we out so late.'

'What did you tell him?'

'As you say, that you are from south with me as guide and going to Cairo. Late because we had made big loop to avoid British, et cetera, et cetera. I play it by tongue, see.' He grinned.

'Amen,' growled Jenkins, 'you're bloody marvellous, that's what you are.'

The second encounter was less fraught, according to Ahmed, and merely involved an exchange of greetings and a jocular conversation about the size of the overloaded pack camels. But he was able to elicit that it was possible to pitch their tents and feed their camels on a bare patch of earth by the tower.

They passed the railway station, black in the half-light, and crossed the little bridge over the canal, which was, indeed, unguarded. The village was a miserable enough collection of mud huts and unpaved, narrow lanes, now seemingly deserted, and it wasn't difficult to make for the tower looming before them. As Simon had predicted, they reached the spot just after midnight on a night when, thankfully, the moon shone only fitfully between slow-moving clouds. Tel el Kebir seemed to be sound asleep. The tower was, as expected, set in a small clearing of beaten earth and surrounded by poor huts and chicken coops. Up close, it looked much higher than when seen from a distance, and at first sight it appeared to be completely unoccupied and probably in disuse. Its wooden double doors were padlocked, but on examination, the lock was well oiled and the chain showing signs of use. Simon breathed a sigh of relief, for the fact that the door was locked would seem to indicate that it was not occupied tonight. The surrounding huts showed no sign of life or light and, he fervently hoped, were far enough away to be unscathed when the tower collapsed – if they could only place their explosives so that it fell in on itself. Even so, the risk was great and Simon felt uneasy.

They tied their camels to a stunted tree, watered and fed them, and then erected their cramped tent, into which they crawled and lay waiting for the night to deepen as they nibbled hard army biscuits. Only a belch from one of the camels and the barking of a distant dog broke the silence. Jenkins soon fell asleep, but Simon could not relax, and the stirring of Ahmed showed that he too was awake. Eventually, at one thirty, Simon could lie still no longer, and nodding to Ahmed, he crept out of the tent. Ahmed and then Jenkins followed him.

'It seems quiet,' Simon said. 'Three five two, can you open that padlock? As quietly as you can, because it is just possible that there is someone inside. Ahmed, you keep watch and warn Jenkins if anyone approaches. Then start to unpack the boat. Keep the framework covered with the canvas as long as possible. If anyone comes, explain that you are setting up a stall to trade in the morning to make a little money before moving on to Cairo. I am going back to the canal to find the best launching site. Right? Off you go.'

Simon walked back the way they had come and then branched off to the right to avoid the bridge. The canal looked terribly narrow and exposed. It was only some twenty-five feet across, and the water had advanced high up the sloping banks of jumbled rock as a result of the erection of the dam. There was precious little cover. There still remained a drop of some five feet to the water, however, and after scrambling for some way over the rocks, he found a clump of willow that would allow them to hide the boat and launch it from there on to the canal.

Back at the tower, he found that Jenkins had had to force the padlock with his knife by splintering the wood around it. 'No one inside,' he hissed, 'though it is in use. Platform at the top an' used cups an' plates an' a glass heliograph thing there.'

'Good. Help Ahmed with the boat and I'll get the dynamite.' Simon looked at his timepiece. Two fifteen. The RHA's guns should be in position now. Dawn came at about four forty-five at this time of the year. They had just two and a half hours to assemble the boat, carry it to the canal, return to the tower and place the dynamite, explode the charges, return to the boat, paddle to the dam, get round the obstacle and be off either down the waterway or out into the desert before daylight came. Could it be done without them being discovered? The odds against were ridiculously high.

He shrugged his shoulders. What was it Ahmed had said about being in for half a crown . . .?

Simon decided that it would be too dangerous to fix the dynamite before they had planned their escape route – he knew too much about its volatility and the danger of self-combustion – so he carefully placed the sticks inside the tower door and closed it so that it appeared to be locked. He then helped Jenkins to assemble the boat while Ahmed stood guard.

There had only been time to carry out this exercise once in Kassassin, but at least they knew how to approach the task. The wooden framework had been constructed to fit together and then be bound tightly with cord that was well dampened from their canteens to make it shrink and tighten the knots. After some forty minutes the frame was complete, showing the semblance of a coracle – not easy, thought Simon gloomily, to paddle or steer. The real problem lay in stretching the canvas over the frame and slipping the projecting frame ends through the holes provided. After much pulling and grunting, the job was done – but another forty-five minutes had slipped by. Just over an hour to go before the sun came up!

'We have to be quicker,' gasped Simon. 'Ahmed, bring the rifles in case we are attacked, while Jenkins and I carry the boat. Move now.'

Luckily, the craft was light and easy to carry and the night was at its deepest and darkest. Within fifteen minutes they had found the clump of willows and slipped the boat down between the rocks, tying its prow to a branch so that it lay half hidden. Then they sprinted back to the little square. Only forty minutes left! Simon realised that he had underestimated the time it would take to assemble the boat. Was it his imagination, or was the sky to the east already beginning to lighten?

'Ahmed,' he gasped. 'Lead the camels away and tether them out of range of the explosion.'

'I knew you were in love with yours,' grunted Jenkins, kneeling on the steps leading to the tower door beside Simon as the latter carefully began unwrapping the sticks of dynamite.

'Now,' said Simon, wiping the perspiration away from his eyes, 'take these two nails and the hammer and knock them into the mortar between the bricks, one on each side of the wall, facing each other, about five feet up. Try and do it quietly. Close the door behind you.'

Simon then carefully separated the sticks. In fact, Fraser had given them three packages of five each – 'Yer may need a few extra to toss behind yer when yer pursued by the hounds of hell on yer way home, laddie' – and Simon decided to use two packages of six each and save the three remaining sticks for emergencies. He then tied the two packages with string and slipped inside the tower.

Jenkins had inserted the nails with minimum noise, and first testing to ensure they were secure, Simon then tied the bundles to the nails so that they lay snugly against the wall, facing each other across the spiral staircase in the centre. With even more care, he now produced the detonator caps with their long fuses and secured them to the bundles. Each taking one fuse, the two men then began to unroll them, backing away towards the door – which suddenly sprang open with a crash.

Turning, they saw a young Egyptian soldier in the

doorway, his jaw sagging. Immediately, Jenkins picked up the hammer, but the soldier was quicker. He raised his rifle and cocked it. As he did so, his head shook and he suddenly slumped to the ground, revealing Ahmed behind him, a large rock in his hand.

'I could not shoot him,' he said. 'One of my people, you see. Anyway, too noisy, yes?'

'Quite right, Ahmed,' said Simon. 'Good work. Is there anyone else about?'

'No, just him. Perhaps he comes to open place up, yes?'

'Quite likely. Quickly now, we have little time left. Can you carry him outside, 352, and tie him up? We have cord left from the boat. Gag him somehow, too. Then we'll take him away from the tower so that he won't get hurt by the falling stone. Put him in a chicken coop, or something like that.'

Simon invested a precious minute in running up the circular steps to the open platform at the top of the tower to look to the east. As far as he could see, the village remained in complete darkness. He could detect nothing of the Egyptian army's encampment in the distance, although the canal gleamed softly whenever the moon appeared between the clouds. He used its light to check his watch. They had just over half an hour before the sun came up.

He leaped down the rickety stairs and lifted the legs of the still inert soldier – had his skull been shattered? He hoped not – while Jenkins took the shoulders. They carried him as far away from the tower as time allowed, dumping him beneath the protection of a mud wall in an alleyway. Then they doubled back.

Simon quickly surveyed the scene. Only the camel droppings and their tiny tent betrayed their presence. The ends of the fuses lay like twin tape worms running down from the door (which Simon had carefully propped open in case a stray wind slammed it shut and extinguished the fuses) and across the steps. He drew a deep breath and took out his matches.

'Right,' he cried. 'Three five two, take the rifles; Ahmed, have your Colt ready. Both of you go, NOW!' He carefully wrapped the three remaining sticks of dynamite in a handkerchief and placed them in a pocket under his *burnous*. Then he lit the fuses. One fizzed and the flame immediately raced away up the steps. The other spluttered and died. 'Damn!' He lit it again and waited until it took firm hold, and then ran after the others.

They had reached the canal and begun sprinting along its length when the tower erupted with a bang that momentarily deafened them and a blast that threw them to the ground. Turning his head, Simon saw a sheet of flame rise up from within the tower, and then, almost in slow motion, the building begin to sag and crumple, falling in on itself like a drunkard collapsing to the ground and shedding outwards what seemed to be only a few particles of brick and stone. Within seconds, all that remained was a cloud of dust and smoke rising to the sky, which almost immediately resumed its previous darkness.

'Bloody 'ell,' said Jenkins. 'We've done it! What a firework!'

'Don't run now,' said Simon. 'Just walk quickly to the boat. Ahmed, if we are challenged, point behind and say that British soldiers have blown up the tower and are still there.'

Walking along the canal bank, they were aware that the village had come to life. Behind them, they heard shrieks and shouts, then the pounding of feet from the direction of the station. But they saw no one along the towpath and reached the boat among the willows without detection. There, they untied the rope and slipped the little vessel into the water.

'Ahmed and I will paddle,' Simon whispered. 'Three five two, you're the best shot, so you stay in the stern with a rifle. Don't fire unless I tell you to. Ahmed, if we are challenged, don't say we are going up the lines with supplies. That's obviously rubbish, because we've got an empty boat. Say that we have been instructed by Fehmy Pasha to patrol the canal and give warning if the English try and steal up this way. Now push off.'

They paddled hard, and although they were conscious of men rushing along the towpath towards the centre of the village, the darkness protected them. Ahmed and Simon kept their heads down and paddled with long, deep strokes, while Jenkins sat in the stern, his rifle across his lap. But where the hell, thought Simon, was Wolseley's artillery diversion? Surely the explosion would have been seen from across that flat desert?

They had left the confines of the village well behind when the inevitable challenge came. Three soldiers loomed out of the darkness on the left bank and shouted something in Arabic. Simon waved his paddle in greeting and Ahmed followed suit, before answering the challenge fluently and with much gesticulation. It did not seem to satisfy the interrogator, however, for he raised his rifle and gestured for them to paddle to the rocks at the side of the canal.

Jenkins raised his own rifle. 'No, not yet,' hissed Simon.

And then, blessedly, the British bombardment began.

With a crump and a flash that lit the sky to the east, the guns of the Royal Horse Artillery commenced firing. To Simon's surprise, the shells were landing surprisingly close to the canal, and it was clear that Wolseley, or Wilson, his gunner, had deliberately laid down the barrage much further south than Simon had requested. Nevertheless, it proved a blessing to the three men in the coracle, for it immediately sent the guards on the towpath scuttling for cover.

'Paddle like hell,' whispered Simon. 'Pay no heed to the shells.'

They dug in their paddles and made their little craft fairly fly over the water. As they neared the dam, at the southern point of the Egyptian line of fortifications, they realised that the British barrage was gradually ranging to the north – and that the dawn was coming up ahead of them, orange fingers of light throwing the dam into relief.

'Paddle to the right bank,' gasped Simon. 'We will never be able to take the boat round. It's becoming far too light.'

'What do we do with it?' asked Jenkins.

'Sink it. Use your knife to cut holes in it and push it out.'

'How do we get back to our lines?'

'We walk.'

'Oh, strewth!'

'What is strewth?' asked Ahmed, his eyes wide.

'Another time, old chap,' said Simon. 'To the right now, quickly. It's getting light.'

They clambered out of their frail craft, Simon crawling up ahead on the south bank of the canal, taking care not to knock the dynamite sticks on the rocks, and then carefully raising his head above the edge. In the half-light, all he could see was desert. There seemed to be no buildings of any kind and no patrols on this side of the canal. He looked behind him. Jenkins was pushing the coracle away with his foot, and as he watched, he saw it slide beneath the green water. The others joined him on the lip.

'I don't know if the Egyptian line extends on this side of the canal,' he said, 'but they won't leave it open-ended, so there will be troops up ahead. That means we've got to go as far south into the desert as we can to avoid them, before turning east. Are the water bottles full?'

Ahmed nodded. 'I just filled them.' He wrinkled his nose. 'A bit green, I think.'

'Never mind. Come on. We get as far south as we can before the sun comes up.'

The flat, gravel-strewn plain on the north side of the canal was not reproduced on the south, where the sand was deeper and swelled into low dunes as far as the eye could see. As they walked, they could hear the crump of the British guns behind them growing less insistent, and then it finally ceased altogether. The sun soon mounted, and its rays brought the perspiration streaming down their faces, inevitably attracting the attention of the sand flies.

They had been walking for about two hours when Simon consulted his compass and indicated that they should turn left. 'I've no idea whether we have gone far enough to bypass the Egyptian patrols,' he said, 'but it's time we headed for home.'

'Hoo-bloody-ray,' said Jenkins. 'Let's break into a shamblin' trot, shall we?'

'Shamblin' . . .?' began Ahmed.

'Don't ask, bach. Just don't ask. I'll tell you over a beer when we get back.'

'I do not drink alcohol, 352.'

'Then I'll teach you.'

They had plodded on for at least another two hours when the Egyptian patrol found them. Simon had just signalled a break for water and a brief rest when four cavalrymen, mounted on tired ponies, appeared over the hill of a dune some two hundred yards away. They immediately unslung their rifles and urged their mounts forward.

'What I say?' asked Ahmed.

'Too late for talking, I think.' The words had hardly left Simon's lips when the first bullet caught Ahmed in the shoulder, spinning him round. A second thudded into the sand at their feet, and two others whistled over their heads. The horsemen were arrogantly overconfident, however, for they did not pause to reload their single-shot Remingtons, but instead followed their leader forward as he unsheathed a long sabre.

'That's your last mistake, bach,' murmured Jenkins, sighting down the barrel of his Martini-Henry. His round caught one man squarely in the forehead and sent him plunging to the ground. Simon's shot took the second in the chest. The two others immediately pulled their horse's heads round, plunged in their spurs and galloped, as best as the sand would allow, back the way they had come – not, however, before Jenkins's second shot had taken a third Egyptian in the back, bringing him down just on the brow of the dune.

'See if you can capture those horses,' shouted Simon as he knelt over the stricken figure of Ahmed. The little man's face was puckered with pain, and blood was oozing from his shoulder. Simon tore away the fabric surrounding the wound and examined it. The bullet had not gone right through the shoulder and remained inside, too deep, however, for Simon to see it or to try and remove it. He brought his water bottle to Ahmed's lips and then poured a little on the edge of his *esharp* and wiped his brow.

'It's not fatal, Ahmed,' he reassured, 'but I don't think we are going to be able to get that cartridge out until we get back to the British lines. I will try and put some sort of dressing on it.'

'Thank you.'

Simon took off his undershirt – the only part of his apparel that seemed dust-free – and tore it into strips. Then he made a pad and carefully placed it over the wound to staunch the bleeding, and with the rest fashioned a crude bandage to keep it in place and protect the wound from the flies.

'Do you think you can stand, old chap?'

Ahmed nodded, his tongue protruding from dry lips, and somehow stood, his good arm around Simon's shoulder, his legs trembling beneath him. Simon became aware that Jenkins had returned.

'Sorry, bach sir,' panted the Welshman. 'Bloody horses 'ave disappeared from sight completely, see. So too has that last bloke, sod it. The others are all dead, though.'

'Damn,' said Simon. 'That means the fellow will bring others down on us, as likely as not. Well, we will just have to make straight for the canal now and hope to pick up a British patrol on the other side. Do you think you can walk, Ahmed?'

The Egyptian summoned up a wan smile. 'I try,' he said. 'No shimblin' trot, though.'

'Good man. Lean on me.'

'No,' said Jenkins. 'Lean on me, Amen. If it gets difficult, I'll carry you.' Ahmed nodded and transferred his good arm to Jenkins's shoulder. Jenkins grasped his wrist with his own left hand and put his other arm around Ahmed's waist, and together they set off, Simon leading with the compass and carrying the two rifles.

It was a horrific journey. By now it was midday and the temperature, Simon estimated, was well into the nineties. They were forced to stop every thirty minutes to rest Ahmed and to take sips of water. Simon noticed that the exertion had caused the wound to bleed again, but there was nothing for it but to plod on. He did contemplate digging some sort of shelter in the sand and waiting until dark, but there was no wind to cover the footmarks behind them, which would surely lead pursuers directly to them. Their only hope was that they could reach the canal before they were overtaken. How they would cross it he did not know, but the north side would be a better bet for meeting a British patrol, because that comprised the no-man's-land between the two armies. He spelled Jenkins in assisting Ahmed, but it was clear that the Egyptian was getting weaker and was now staggering along half conscious.

'Right,' said Jenkins, 'time to carry the little chap.'

'No, you won't be able to get far in this sun.'

'Piggyback's the answer. Look.' Jenkins disrobed and took off his shirt. As Simon supported Ahmed, he wrapped the body of the shirt around the Egyptian's bottom and then tied the ends of the sleeves around his own waist. 'Now,' he said to Simon, 'lift 'im up. Amen, look you, 'ang on round me neck with your good arm. That's the way.'

There was a shout of pain as Jenkins hoisted his burden. 'Now, bach sir, tighten these bloody shirtsleeves. That's the way. Why, I can carry the little feller back to Rhyl like this! You all right, Amen?' But the Egyptian was now virtually unconscious and could make no reply.

How long it took them to reach the canal, Simon never knew. The strength and stamina displayed by the Welshman – not tall himself but a wide-shouldered giant next to the tiny and slim Ahmed – was prodigious. Perspiration pouring down his face so that he could hardly see, shrouded in flies but with no hand to spare to knock them away, he strode on, snorting through his mouth like a camel. Simon had never admired his comrade more.

Eventually they reached the canal. Jenkins lowered his burden to the sand with care and then collapsed at Ahmed's side. Simon limped down to the water to refill their bottles and to wet their handkerchiefs to bring a little relief to their sweating faces and necks. As he did so, a flutter of movement on the far side of the canal caught his eye.

'A British patrol,' he shouted. 'Mounted infantry. Thank God!' Jenkins gave his face-splitting grin, and even Ahmed summoned up a faint smile. Simon tottered to his feet and waved his arms. 'Hallooo,' he hailed. 'This way. We're British!'

As he watched, he saw the officer leading the patrol hold up his hand and level his field glasses. Then the man turned and issued some sort of command. His men remained stationary, but the officer turned his horse and slowly walked it towards the canal, looking through his binoculars at Simon from time to time.

'Blimey, 'e's takin' 'is time,' muttered Jenkins.

It was at least five minutes before the officer arrived on the far side of the canal and dismounted. 'Good afternoon,' said Major Smith-Denbigh.

Simon gulped. 'Thank God you've come,' he said. 'We're all in. We've blown up the tower in el Kebir and we've got Egyptian cavalry on our heels. We've also got a chap with a shattered shoulder. Can you help us across? A couple of horses will do it'

A smile spread across Smith-Denbigh's face. 'Ah, bless my soul, if it isn't the head of military intelligence for the whole of Egypt – and, goodness me, he's got the Khedive's favourite nephew with him. Well I never!'

Simon frowned. 'Look,' he said. 'We're done in. Goodness knows how long we've walked carrying a wounded man. For God's sake, get us across.'

'Well now.' The Major carefully extracted a handkerchief from his pocket and blew his nose. 'If I remember rightly, Fonthill, you made me eat dirt. Now you must do the same. As far as I am concerned, my dear fellow, I have never seen you and,' he gestured with his handkerchief behind him, 'I will make quite sure that my men have never seen you either. Just three bloody Arabs trying to sell me something or other. So fuck off, Fonthill. I am quite happy for the vultures to have you.'

Leisurely, he put his foot into the stirrup and mounted his horse, then turned it and spurred it into a trot. An awful silence fell on the trio. They watched as Smith-Denbigh rejoined his troop and led it away into the heat haze.

Jenkins disturbed the silence. 'I shall 'ave 'im,' he said quietly. 'You see if I don't.'

'Not if I see him first,' said Simon. 'Right. We have rested

369

long enough. Let's follow the canal along. It can't be too far before we see our lines, or perhaps another patrol.'

'Or an Egyptian one,' muttered Jenkins.

'No. We'll get there. Have faith.'

Laboriously, Ahmed was hoisted back on to his sling and the little cavalcade trudged on, Simon taking up the rear, his rifle at the ready. If the Egyptians caught up now, then they would sell their lives dearly.

They had stopped for another break when the second patrol appeared. There were ten men this time. They stopped well out of rifle range as their officer examined the trio through his field glasses. Then he turned, issued an order and the patrol dismounted and began spreading to right and left.

'The hounds of hell,' murmured Simon. 'We've got the canal to our backs, so they can't surround us. How much ammo do you have, 352?'

'About eight rounds. Just enough for this lot. What about you?'

'About the same. But I do have three other little babies . . .'

'Eh?'

Simon fumbled and produced the dynamite. 'I was told to treat this stuff with care,' he said, 'but I've fallen on it, scraped it across rocks and sat on it. I only hope the bloody stuff goes off now, when I want it to, because if it doesn't, we could be in trouble.'

'Amen to that,' said Jenkins. 'Oh, sorry, Amen.'

Leaving Ahmed lying under cover among rocks on the slope of the canal side, Simon and Jenkins took up their positions on a low sand dune near the bank, lying on their stomachs in a V formation, their rifle butts at their cheeks.

'Do you think they'll rush us?' asked Jenkins.

'Not yet. They will probably work round to both sides of us and try and pick off one or the other of us before charging in. Save your fire until you are reasonably certain of hitting. Let's hope they're as bad shots as the other lot.'

'Hmmm. But they still got old Et cetera, didn't they?'

Jenkins voice was cut off by the crack of two rifle reports. The first round buried itself in the sand by the side of his head; the second landed similarly near to Simon.

'Hell!' cursed Simon. 'They've got round further than I thought. Back to the rocks on the edge of the canal.'

They crawled back as quickly as they could to the jagged line of stones and boulders that marked the line of the waterway and took up new positions either side of Ahmed, who lay still, only half conscious, his brow puckered by the pain of his wound. Jenkins eased himself into a crevice between two rocks and took careful aim. His shot was followed by a howl of pain.

'Bugger.' Jenkins swore softly. 'Only got 'im in the shoulder. Must be gettin' tired or old or somethin'.'

'Keep changing position,' said Simon. 'They won't be able to get a fix on us then.'

But that was easier said than done, for it was difficult to crawl among the jagged jumble of rocks and stones and the Egyptians began to lay down a steady fire, forcing Simon and Jenkins to keep their heads down and giving them little opportunity to return the fire. Even so, Jenkins was able to elicit one more cry of pain from the riflemen out among the sand dunes.

'I think they're crawling nearer,' said Simon. 'It's going to be difficult to toss these sticks among them when I can't get a good view of them. Can you keep them occupied while I try and wade up on the edge of the canal and get behind them?'

'Very good, bach sir. Go to the right and I'll concentrate on the devils on that side and force 'em to keep their 'eads down while you get be'ind 'em, see. Go and 'ave a paddle.'

Simon undid the cord with which the three sticks of dynamite were tied and secured it round his head, slipping the sticks through it so that they stood up like candles, well away from the water. He fixed his matches in the same way and, rifle in hand, slipped and crawled down to the edge of the canal. It was unappetising enough, but would it be sufficiently deep to force him to swim? He hoped not, for he did not want to leave his rifle behind. No, at the edge it only came up to his waist, and holding his rifle aloft, he was able to move slowly through the opaque water.

He waded for perhaps a hundred and fifty yards, then scrambled out, still hearing the sharp crack of rifle fire to his left. Ideally he would have wished to have made more ground, but he could not risk leaving Jenkins any longer on his own. Would he lift his head above the bank and find himself staring into the muzzle of a Remington? Gritting his teeth, he edged upwards. Nothing. Making sure that his highly explosive headdress was dry and still in place, he crawled slowly towards the edge of a long, low dune that swelled before him, and gingerly looked over the top.

Four white-clad Egyptian infantrymen were lying spaced along the top of the next dune, their backs to him, their long rifles poked over the top of the mound, firing leisurely at their distant target. Good, that meant that Jenkins was still keeping them at bay.

Simon slipped back and released the dynamite and matches from the cord. He carefully placed two of the sticks to one side and brushed the sand from the third. He gulped, for its fuse was only about an inch and a half long: no time to 'light and retire quickly'. He would have to ignite the fuse and throw almost in one action. And he was too near the target for safety. But what the hell!

He lit the fuse, knelt for a frightening few seconds to make sure that the thing was burning, and then stood and threw the stick, in an overarm action to ensure accuracy, like bowling a cricket ball. It fell neatly between two of the enemy. Simon flung himself down and backwards, certain for an agonising moment that the fuse must have fizzled out, but then a blast of flame and a loud explosion showed that Mr Nobel's Blasting Powder was still effective.

Simon slung his rifle over his shoulder – he had better weapons now – picked up the other two sticks and his matches and peered over the edge of the dune. The four Egyptians lay in varying postures, mostly on their backs with their rifles blasted clear. Their skin, whatever its original colour, was now completely black and their clothing torn. That little hollow smelt horribly of burnt flesh and cordite.

Breaking into a slow-motion run, his feet slipping in the sand, Simon crested the top of the dune and saw that the remaining six patrolmen were spread out in a crescent. Two of them were holding their shoulders and rocking with pain from where Jenkins's bullets had caught them in, and the other four were staring in bewilderment at the black smoke still rising from behind Simon. Immediately, before they could realign their rifles, Simon put a match to another stick and hurled it at the group. Like flies caught in amber, the men lay immobile for a second as they watched it arc through the air, then, at the last moment, their legs fought for purchase in the sand and they attempted to rise and run.

Simon flung himself to the sand again behind the crest of the ridge and so was unable to see the explosion, but he felt it well enough. A hot wave of air surged across his neck and back as he buried his face in the sand, and the noise of the explosion, so near, deafened him and left his ears singing. He looked up. The carnage was as before, except that this time there were six blackened bodies lying on the sand.

He called to Jenkins. Slowly the Welshman appeared from the rocks, rifle in hand. He stood for a second, his mouth open, and then waved his rifle at Simon.

'Come and help me see if anyone is alive and needs help,' shouted Simon. But it was a hopeless mission. Every member of that patrol, caught out in the open at close range to the explosions, had been killed by the blast. It was a nose-wrinkling sight and Jenkins shook his head in dismay.

'Frightenin' stuff, bach sir,' he said. 'But, bless me, you were just in time. They were movin' in on me from all sides an' I didn't know which way to face, see. They would 'ave 'ad me in another couple of minutes. I thought you'd gone swimmin' back to Tel el Watchemacallit.'

'Sorry, 352. Let's see if we can get their horses.' But the Egyptians' mounts, terrified by the explosions, had pulled up their shallow-rooted tethers and bolted into the desert. Wearily, the two men plodded back to the rocks and helped a now fully conscious Ahmed to his feet.

'It's back into your cradle, I'm afraid,' said Simon. 'We can't have far to go now.' But he knew that he was whistling to keep up their courage. There was probably about another two miles to walk before they reached the British lines, not so very far in terms of distance, but hopelessly far in terms of the terrain to be covered under this hot sun. Even the superbly strong Jenkins could not keep going carrying Ahmed for very much further. And if another Egyptian patrol came along? Well, they had one more stick of dynamite . . .

They had been struggling alongside the canal for perhaps another half an hour before, like a mirage, they saw the launch slowly emerging out of the heat haze from the east, the white ensign of the British navy hanging limply at its stern. A Maxim machine gun was immediately presented to them before Simon waved and shouted, 'Don't shoot. We're British. Long live the bloody navy!'

Chapter 19

It took less than half an hour for the launch to take them to Kassassin, steaming astern all the way, for the canal was too narrow to allow it to turn. The young midshipman in command – looking all of twelve years old in his shorts and a topi that seemed two sizes too large for him – told Simon that they had only ventured this far to the west because he had heard the explosions of the dynamite sticks and felt he should investigate. Back in the camp, Ahmed was taken ashore and medical orderlies carried him to the sick bay, escorted by Simon and Jenkins, anxious to ensure that the little Egyptian received as much care as if he had been an English officer. Leaving Jenkins with the doctor, Simon then sought out Wolseley to make his report.

He was made to wait outside the Commander-in-Chief's tent for more than fifteen minutes – unusual, this, for Wolseley had always granted him audience immediately in the past. Simon was eventually ushered in and found the General looking distracted and low (a touch of fever again?). Sir Garnet shook his hand warmly enough, however, and indicated a chair.

'Good work, Fonthill,' he said. 'By the look of it, you did

a splendid job. Casualties?' Simon related the brush with the Egyptian patrols and the resulting wound to Ahmed's shoulder. 'Bad luck. Is he being looked after?'

'I hope so, sir. As long as Major Denbigh-Smith doesn't get near him.' Simon had already decided to keep quiet about the encounter with the Major on the canal bank. That could wait for resolution – one way or another – later.

Wolseley's faced clouded over again. 'Oh, that. Yes. I have had a word with the officer concerned. It won't happen again, I can assure you of that.'

'Thank you, sir.'

'As I say, you did a splendid job on the tower. It looks as though it has completely disappeared from the skyline.'

'Thank you. There was a heliograph there, so it was as well that we moved in and destroyed it. We did our best, sir, to bring it down without damage to the natives living nearby, but I can't be certain about that.'

'That reflects credit on you. Oh, by the way, I am sorry that our diversionary bombardment came a bit late. Damned difficult to get the RHA's guns out through the sand in time under cover of darkness, but it seems as though they did their job.'

'When are you going to launch your attack, sir?'

Wolseley pulled at the end of his long moustache. 'Just a bit late on that too, I fear. We have still been having trouble in bringing up men, supplies and ammunition from Ismailia, but we are using the canal more now and I am hoping to go in four or five days' time. The build-up is going well, though, despite the heat and these damned flies, and I am feeling much more sanguine about the attack now that that blasted tower cannot be used for artillery spotting.'

Simon nodded but remained silent. He had a feeling that the General, usually so forthright, was holding something back – and that whatever it was, it concerned him.

Wolseley sighed. 'What I am *not* feeling sanguine about, however,' he said, 'is something that has cropped up earlier today.' He levelled a searching look at Simon, as though sizing him up. 'To some extent, Fonthill, it concerns you, and once again, I fear, I need your help. I have to confess that what I will ask of you is beyond the call of duty. Here.' He tossed a sheet of paper across the table to him. 'Prepare for a bit of a shock and read this.'

Frowning, Simon picked up the paper. It was unheaded but addressed to Colonel R. Covington CB, c/o British Army Headquarters, Kassassin. The handwriting, printed in capital letters, seemed vaguely familiar. It read:

COLONEL COVINGTON,
ONCE AGAIN I HAVE THE PLEASURE OF YOUR
WIFE'S COMPANY. TO PROVE THAT I HAVE
HER, I ENCLOSE A LOCK OF HER HAIR AND A
SMEAR OF HER BLOOD – ONLY, SO FAR, FROM
HER FINGER . . .

Simon drew in his breath with a hiss.

. . . BUT IF YOU REFUSE WHAT I DEMAND, MY
NEXT LETTER WILL CONTAIN HER RIGHT
EYE. AT LEAST THAT WOULD MAKE YOU
EQUAL, EH? NOW READ CAREFULLY. IN
RETURN FOR YOUR WIFE, I WANT A LETTER
SIGNED BY GENERAL WOLSELEY GIVING ME

SAFE CONDUCT OUT OF EGYPT VIA PORT SAID TO GREECE, PLUS TWO THOUSAND POUNDS IN GOLD.

BRING THESE TO DAKHLAMI OASIS TWENTY-TWO MILES NORTH-NORTH-WEST OF TEL EL KEBIR. COME ALONE. I HAVE MANY MEN AND IF YOU ARE ACCOMPANIED THEY WILL BE SEEN AND THE BITCH WILL SWING FROM A PALM TREE. IF YOU ARE NOT HERE BY THE 10th I SHALL TAKE HER WITH ME TO THE NORTH AND SELL HER TO THE SUDANESE SLAVEMASTERS. BY THE WAY, DID YOU KNOW THAT SHE WAS FONTHILL'S WHORE?

G. GEORGE.

Simon slowly put down the letter and regarded Wolseley wide-eyed. 'Has Covington seen this?'

'Yes. He set off three hours ago to find this oasis place – I am informed that it is very remote. He took with him a letter from me, as demanded, but there has been no time, of course, to find that sort of money in gold if we are to meet the deadline. Instead, Covington has taken a bank draft from me in the hope that this will satisfy the swine. He has gone alone, of course.'

Simon felt his mouth go dry and his brain immediately recalled a picture of George kicking away the table in that horrible room in Alexandria, so that Alice was sent swinging by the neck ... He swallowed hard. 'General,' he said, 'Covington does not know this man. I do. George will not carry out his end of the bargain. In fact, Alice could well already be dead.'

'I think he appreciates that. But we had no choice. We both felt that we had no option but for him to go and attempt to barter for Mrs Covington's life. But I want him to have back-up, whether *he* wants it or not. Certainly, it would be far too dangerous for me to send a cavalry troop trailing behind him. However . . .'

'Yes.' Simon cut in quickly. 'I will go. Jenkins and I make a pretty good pair of Bedawi now, and we can follow Covington without detection, I am sure. I can't help feeling that the Colonel may attempt something stupid and endanger Alice – if, that is, she is still alive.'

Wolseley smoothed back his receding hair with a weary gesture. 'The chances are that she is. Some while ago I put out an order to the northern ports, which we control of course, giving George's description and ordering him to be detained. My theory is that he has tried to leave Egypt by this route and has found it difficult, and that this taking of Mrs Covington is his last desperate ploy. He would not therefore throw away his only bargaining counter at this juncture.'

Simon nodded. The logic was sound – and welcome.

'As for Covington attempting something heroic,' the General continued, 'I'm afraid that may well be true. He left this morning somewhat distracted, I fear.' He sighed, and Simon realised the strain that Wolseley must be under. He was about to attack a well-defended bastion, from an exposed position at the end of a tenuous line of communication and with the eyes of the world upon him. This latest development would be as welcome as an outbreak of malaria. Yet the man was being rational and constructive.

Wolseley continued: 'That is why I decided to ask you to follow him, despite the fact that you have only just returned from a most dangerous and tiring mission. I am most grateful that you have accepted, Fonthill. I am also sorry that your Egyptian cannot go with you, because his linguistic skills would have been useful, no doubt. But you and your Welshman have done heroic things in the past. I cannot advise you – let alone give you orders – on how to approach this task. You must react to the situation as you perceive it.

'Now.' He scribbled something on a pad. 'Take this and get the best camels you can from my transport officer. Here is a local map giving the location of the oasis. Covington refused to take a camel and rode out on his charger, which means that although he has three hours' advantage on you – more than that by the time you set out – you will make better time in the deeper sand and may catch him at some point. But I do suggest you leave him alone unless you have to intervene.' The General gave Simon a penetrating glance. 'He would not want to work with you, Fonthill, and he has no idea, of course, that you will be behind him. Act with great care.'

'Very good, sir.' Simon took a deep breath. 'That last sentence of George's, in his letter . . .'

Wolseley waved his hand dismissively. 'Nonsense, of course. Neither I nor Covington gave it credence. Just an attempt to cause anger and dismay.'

'Thank you, sir.'

The General stood. 'One last point.' His tone now became harsher. 'I am most concerned about Mrs Covington, of course, and the welfare of one of my best staff officers. Nevertheless, Fonthill, I am about to launch what will be a very difficult attack – perhaps under cover of darkness – and I shall need you for that. I will want you back in less than five days. Is that understood?'

Simon gulped. 'Very good, sir.'

Jenkins was aghast at the news of Alice's capture and he willingly went off to find the camels while Simon secured provisions for their journey and ammunition for their rifles. Within two hours, as the sun was beginning to ease down on to the purple horizon to the west, the pair set out into the desert once again.

Following a compass course, they soon picked up Covington's trail in the virgin desert beyond the well-trodden sand surrounding the camp, and they made good time by bright moonlight. But after the exertions of the last twenty-four hours, they both began to nod in their saddles and Simon called a halt. Without lighting a fire or eating, they tumbled into their bedrolls, too tired to set a guard. Within five hours, however, they were up and riding off again into the star-sprinkled darkness.

They rode on through the next day trusting to the compass alone, for two brief desert storms had long since removed the signs of Covington's progress, although the ashes of a small dung fire and an empty British cigarette packet showed that they were on the right track. Otherwise, they saw and heard nothing in that empty desert.

It was early on the morning of the third day that they heard firing, directly ahead of them. Simon checked his compass and the map. They should indeed be very near the oasis of Dakhlami. Dismounting, they hobbled the camels and, taking their rifles, crawled up to the crest of the sand dune facing them and carefully looked over its edge. Only another, higher dune faced them. They ascended that on their hands and knees and looked down on to the little oasis below them.

Some twenty palm trees stood tall and still, no desert breeze disturbing their hats of green fronds. With relief, Simon also noted that no body swung from their tops. Twenty or so mud huts were scattered around a number of stone-lined wells, linked by narrow irrigation channels that meandered between the roots of the palms, sometimes giving enough moisture to sustain what looked like patches of rice and little clumps of fig trees and so bestowing life on the village in this desolate spot. More importantly, however, Simon could see Covington's charger tethered outside one of the huts. Three Arabs were spread out in front of the hut, sheltering behind palm trunks and firing in sequence with their rifles at a fourth figure, who was taking inadequate shelter behind the low wall of one of the wells and attempting to return their fire with a revolver.

'Is Alice with him?' hissed Simon. The answer came when Covington sprang from behind the wall to shelter behind the slightly more hospitable cover of another hut.

'No,' said Jenkins, easing his rifle to his shoulder. ''E's tryin' to get back to the 'ut where 'is 'orse is. Perhaps she's still in there.'

'The idiot. He's made a mess of it. I knew he would.' Simon put his hand on Jenkins's shoulder. 'No. Don't shoot. I don't want anyone to know we are here yet.' He bit his lip. 'The question is, is Alice still alive and is she still in that hut, or has George taken fright and bolted with her? And where the hell are the villagers?'

That question, at least, was answered when they caught a

glimpse through the palms of a cluster of dark-shrouded figures, men, women and children, crowded together on the crest of a dune on the far side of the village. Then they heard the cries of frightened children.

'The firing has driven them out. Good. Let's see if we can get round that side, creep into the village that way and get behind the hut where Covington's horse is. If George has fled, we should be able to see his tracks and follow them.'

'What about Covington?'

'I'll worry about him later.'

Bending low, to be beneath the skyline, they scrambled round the edge of the village, Simon using the top of the tallest palm as a marker. They were heartened to hear the firing continuing, showing that Covington was still putting up a fight. They crossed Covington's tracks approaching the village and showing where he had been met, presumably by George's men, and forced to dismount. Their route took them up behind the gaggle of villagers, who were all intent on watching the gunfight below them. The arrival of Simon and Jenkins from behind them, carrying their rifles, caused great consternation and Simon gestured to them to keep quiet.

He beckoned to one man, who came forward reluctantly, his eyes wide with fright. Simon pointed to the hut. 'George?' he asked. '*Effendi* George?' The man shook his head, clearly not understanding. Simon desperately tried to recall George's Arabic name – the name he had used to rent the house in Alexandria.

Then it came to him: 'Ahmed Kamul?' he asked. Again, the man looked uncomprehending. Simon repeated it, giving the 'Ah' the rasping sound that Ahmed had taught him.

'Ahmed Kamul?' Now the man nodded his head eagerly, delighted to understand and not be shot. He pointed to the hut.

Simon drew in a slow breath. He had remembered the Arabic for woman, but he dreaded the answer to the next question. '*Mar'a hurma?*' he asked, pointing again to the hut. '*Mar'a hurma inglizi?*' Again the man nodded his head, his eyes wide, and pointed to the hut.

Simon blew out his cheeks in relief and turned to Jenkins. 'They're still there, then – but whether dead or alive I don't know.'

'Right, bach sir. Let's go down and see, shall we?' The Welshman's face was as though set in stone.

'Yes.' Simon looked down on the village and frowned. 'We will approach the hut by the back. If there is a back door, we will get in that way. But there's usually only one way in to these places. If we have to go in by the front, we must remain hidden until the last moment – from Covington as well as George's men, because he will take us for Arabs and could well shoot. Now, wait a second.'

Simon turned to the villagers. Slowly he swung the muzzle of his gun across them and held his finger to his lips. The man he had spoken to and several of the women nodded in eager acquiescence. Then Simon led the way down the sloping dune and began running from hut to hut, Jenkins close behind.

When they reached the central hut, Simon held up his hand. There was no door at the rear. 'You go round the hut to the left and I'll go to the right,' he whispered. 'I will take the man on the right; you take the other two. Shoot to kill. I will go into the hut, and you shout to Covington to cease firing. Don't forget to reload. Right?'

Jenkins nodded.

'Right. Go!'

They ran their different ways, and once he had reached the front of the hut, Simon found that the three Arabs were close and easy targets. Without compunction, he fired into the back of the nearest man and heard Jenkins shoot also. Quickly thumbing a cartridge into the Martini-Henry's magazine, he took a deep breath and crashed the heel of his boot into the door of the hut, sending it swinging open. He ducked inside and presented his rifle to the interior.

At first, the contrast of the darkness after the brightness of the sun outside rendered him sightless. Then, as his eyes grew accustomed to the gloom, they took in a scene that he would remember always.

Alice, in a déjà vu tableau from the house in Alexandria, was standing on a low table near a mud wall, her feet bound together. She appeared to be soaked in blood from throat to feet. Around her neck was a noosed rope with its end looped over a piece of timber spanning the roof of palm leaves – but this time the rope was not taut but hanging loosely. She was gagged and her left wrist was secured by a steel handcuff to a large staple in the wall, but her other hand was free and she was working the end of a bloodstained fork into the handcuff in an attempt to open the mechanism. Across her feet, like some stone hound in effigy at the bottom of a Crusader's tomb, lay the body of George, blood still oozing from a ghastly wound at his throat. She froze as Simon jumped through the doorway, and for a second, the two gazed at each other across the spartan room.

'My God,' cried Simon, and leapt to Alice, taking her in

his arms. He kicked away George's inert form and lifted her down, the rope around her neck sliding down from the beam. Then he sat her on the table and untied the gag.

'Oh, Simon.' Her voice was hoarse and little above a whisper. 'How amazing! Thank God you have come. Don't worry, it's not my blood. Now, this damned handcuff. The key is in his pocket but I couldn't reach him. Unlock me, please. Where is Ralph?'

'He's all right. He's conducting a one-man war with George's bodyguards.' Simon pushed away the body of the clerk with his foot and fumbled in his pockets. He realised that the firing outside had stopped, although he could hear Jenkins's unmistakable voice shouting. 'I think Jenkins has seen to them. Here, now.' He found the key and unlocked the handcuff. Then he bent and undid the bindings around her ankle. A sudden thought struck him.

'How many men did George have?'

'Three.'

'Good. Then we have got rid of them all. Water?'

'Oh yes. Over there, on the big table.' She drank quickly, sending little streams down her chin, before handing the gourd back to him. Then she regarded him in silence for a moment, a tear emerging from her eye, before she began to shake. Immediately, Simon took her in his arms and began rocking her and patting her back, whispering, 'It's all right, my darling. It's all right. You are safe now.'

That was how Covington and Jenkins found them a minute later. Simon looked up, met the Colonel's gaze and self-consciously released Alice from his embrace. He felt ridiculously guilty. 'She was trembling,' he said, and moved away.

Covington paid no heed, but strode forward and took Alice in his own arms. 'My God,' he said. 'What have they done to you?'

Alice pushed him away gently. 'It's all right, Ralph.' She spoke firmly now. She nodded to the body. 'It's his blood. I killed him.'

'What!' The exclamation came together from the three men.

'I'll tell you in a moment,' she said. Then her eyes widened. 'What about the others?'

'Ah, don't you worry your 'ead about them, miss,' said Jenkins. 'I've seen to them . . . well, the Captain got one and I finished off the rest, see.'

'Thank you.' Alice summoned up a wan smile for Jenkins. 'It is *so* good to see you again, 352,' she said. 'You always seem to be there when I want you most.'

'Well, I don't know about that . . .'

Simon, his face now set firmly without expression, interrupted. 'We will be outside if you want us,' he said coldly. 'We will get the villagers to dispose of the . . . er . . . bodies and so on. Come on, 352.' He turned on his heel and strode out into the sunshine. Walking to the three bodies, where flies were already circling above the blood draining into the sand, he gestured to the men and women who were now beginning to straggle hesitantly back down the slope of the dune. The man he had spoken to earlier came running. Simon gestured to the bodies, took out a handful of coins and made a digging motion. The man immediately understood and beckoned to his fellows. In less than a minute, the corpses had been removed.

Simon turned to Jenkins. 'Let's get the camels and water

them,' he said. 'I don't want to waste any time in getting back to Kassassin.'

'Yes, bach sir, but what about Miss Alice?'

'Her husband will look after her. Come on.'

Haltered, the camels had not strayed far, and Simon and Jenkins also gathered Covington's horse and the five camels that, by the look of them, had served as mounts for Alice, George and his three accomplices. 'We'll leave one of these camels for the villagers,' said Simon, 'and use the others. The army will be glad to have them and the extra beasts we can use to spell each of us in turn. Remember, we have to be back before the attack starts.'

'Yes, but—'

Jenkins was interrupted by the emergence from the hut of Alice, leaning on Covington's arm. The Colonel, his face set grimly, ignored them and led Alice to a low wall under a palm tree where there was shade. Without looking at Simon he called, 'Fonthill. Make yourself useful and see if the villagers can get us some food. Smartly now, dammit.'

Simon exchanged glances with Jenkins, but nodded and found again the man who appeared to be the leader. Cursing Ahmed's absence, he made eating gestures with his fingers and mouth and found more coins. But his sign language was immediately understood and the man issued orders. Within minutes, they were sitting in the shade of the palms, drinking blessedly cool well water and eating dates, figs and a little rice. Alice, the blood now caked on her well-worn desert garments, seemed calm but quiet, as though stunned by her experience.

'Now, my darling,' said Covington, who spoke as though Simon and Jenkins were not present, 'you don't have to say a word if you don't want to, but perhaps it might do you good to tell me what happened. Get it off your chest, so to speak. Be a bit cathartic, don't you know. Eh?'

Alice took a deep breath and looked at them all in turn. 'The first thing I want to say,' she said, speaking slowly and so quietly that they all had to bend forward a little to hear her, 'is to express my gratitude to all of you and to apologise for leading you into this terrible place.'

'Noo,' beamed Jenkins. 'Not a bit of it, miss. Glad to be of service, see.' Covington turned to the Welshman as though to rebuke him, but thought better of it. Simon remained silent, looking as though hypnotised by the pale, drawn, bloodstained face opposite him.

Alice sighed and continued her story, explaining how she had been tricked into hiring George and how she had been brought to the oasis, where the other two men were waiting. She looked up apologetically. 'It was all carefully planned. George told me that he would use me as a bargaining counter to enable him to get out of the country. He said that we had ruined his business and that he was wanted by the British in the north and could not find a ship to take him to Greece.' She frowned. 'He seemed to know all about me – about you, Ralph, and you, Simon. He seemed to have spies everywhere and must have been watching me somehow, since he saw me in Port Said. Of course, he wrote that letter to you, Ralph, from here.'

Covington swallowed hard. 'Did they . . . did they . . . er . . . hurt you or interfere with you at all, my darling?' You know what I mean.'

'No,' Alice replied quite coolly. 'Not in that way. George hit me several times, and, of course, he pricked my finger to put the bloodstain on the letter, but otherwise, no. I had the impression that he was reaching the end of his tether and was becoming more and more desperate. That was the worst thing. I thought he might just go over the edge and kill me, out of hand. So I tried to be placatory . . . you know.'

Alice shook her head for a moment, as though in denial, then summoned a rag from her pocket, blew her nose vigorously and sat very upright. She looked at the ground and continued her story in a dull monotone. 'However, I could not keep up that pretence and I flew at George one evening, shortly after we arrived here. He then had me bound and gagged and, as you could see, handcuffed by one hand to that staple thing in the wall. That was very uncomfortable.'

'The bastard,' Covington hissed. 'What a swine,' agreed Jenkins. Simon remained silent.

'The problem was,' continued Alice, 'that I had no weapon because, of course, they took away my revolver. I refused to eat with my fingers and insisted on being given a knife and fork, in the hope that I could hide the knife. But they always took it away after each meal – although I did manage to keep the fork.' She looked at them all quickly. 'I presume that they felt I could do no harm with it.' She gave a mirthless smile and her voice dropped to little more than a whisper. 'But they were wrong.

'Sitting for days in that hut, with one hand shackled, I had plenty of time to think, and I can tell you, I was not very proud of myself. I felt I had been selfish and unthinking.' She looked at them all very quickly once again and gave a brief shrug of the shoulders. 'I tried to devise ways of attempting to escape but I was completely helpless. Then, this morning, there was a great commotion and you, Ralph, were brought into the village.'

Covington frowned and nodded. 'Yes,' he said. 'I was intercepted just outside and did not try to resist – produce my rifle or that kind of thing, and I kept my revolver in its holster. I was, of course, quite prepared to parley.'

'What happened?' asked Simon quietly.

'I demanded to see you.' Covington spoke only to Alice, still ignoring the others, as though it was she who had asked the question. 'This was to see if you were alive, of course. They allowed me a glimpse of you, in that hut, with that disgusting rope around your neck, standing on the table. Then I was told to go outside and I met George for the first time. You can imagine . . .' he paused and smoothed his moustaches, 'that I was very upset to see you like that. But I kept myself under control and tried to deal with the little swine rationally. He seemed in a state of some anxiety and demanded to see Wolseley's letter, of course. That was satisfactory and seemed to quieten him down a bit. But when I had to explain that I was not able to bring him gold coins but only a bank draft, he lost his temper and began to scream and shout that we were trying to cheat him and that you would swing.' He paused and coughed. 'And that, I am afraid, is when I rather lost my temper.'

'Go on,' said Alice.

'Yes, well . . . I hit the little bastard with my hook and tried to get to the hut. Two of the others then piled into me, so to speak, but I was able to throw them off. I confess I was fighting like a madman by now, and this was one of the few times when this damned hook actually was an advant-age. The third chap was standing off with a rifle but couldn't get a line on me, what with the scuffle and all. Then a rifle bullet went by my ear and I sprinted for the nearest tree and drew my revolver. I winged one of them, I think, and I was trying to work my way round to the hut and making some headway, mainly because, luckily, those chaps weren't good shots.' Covington looked appealingly to Alice. 'I couldn't see George anywhere and I was desperate at the thought that he might have run back to the hut to do you harm.'

Alice nodded slowly. 'Indeed he had. When I was trussed up for inspection, so to speak, the end of the rope was tied fairly loosely to a peg in the wall. When George went out to talk to you, I was able to reach it and untie it, but keeping the end near me so that if an attempt was made to hang me . . .' She paused for a moment, and the silence hung heavily between them. Then she regained her composure and went on: 'I would at least have some sort of chance to make a fight of it, even though I only had one hand.'

She gave her wan smile. 'And so it proved. You see, earlier in the desert, when we were still quite near to Kassassin and George had to conceal his identity, he did not wear his glasses and I realised that he was myopic. So when he came rushing into the hut and lunged across me to get the rope to finish me off, I was able to knock his glasses off and then jump on them. He was at a disadvantage immediately – you will remember that his spectacle lenses were very thick – and hysterical with rage. He groped for my throat to strangle me but I struggled and was able to use the fork to . . . to . . . to my advantage.'

The silence returned, with none of the men able or willing to break it. The day was windless and seemed at its hottest. It was as though a dry woollen blanket had wrapped itself around them all.

Alice continued, but now her voice was very low. 'I jabbed the fork into his throat very hard,' she said, 'and twisted it, and I suppose I . . . sort of . . . tore out his windpipe.' Her voice dropped to a whisper. 'You see, I was fighting for my life and was desperate. He made a terrible gurgling noise and his blood gushed everywhere. It was quite . . . quite . . . disgusting.' Slowly she put her head into her hands and then broke into a series of convulsive sobs.

All three men rose to go to her but Covington was the nearest and the others sank down again as he took her in his arms. 'My brave girl,' he murmured, 'my dear brave girl. You could do nothing else. He deserved to die. You had no choice. You were very, very brave.' He continued to hold her, rocking her to and fro, as Simon and Jenkins looked at each other and then slowly rose to their feet and walked away.

They stood for a moment in the centre of the village, outside the hut where George had died. For once, even Jenkins could think of nothing to say. 'I suppose,' said Simon eventually, 'we had better remove the bloody man. We don't want Alice upset even more.'

Jenkins nodded glumly and they turned towards the hut, but found, to their surprise, that the villagers had already removed George's body and, presumably, buried him with his accomplices. Simon summoned the headman again and presented him with one of the camels, which was accepted with eager gratitude. Shortly afterwards, three of the women from the village produced cotton garments of impeccable cleanliness and indicated that Alice should change into them. They led her away to help her do so. It was as though they were trying to make up for the terrible way they knew she had been treated in their little community – or perhaps they feared reprisals.

Simon did his best to avoid Covington, but in Alice's absence, the Colonel sought him out. 'Why did you follow me, Fonthill?' he asked.

Immediately Simon was on the defensive. 'General Wolseley asked me to do so,' he said. 'He felt that you should not go alone and that it would endanger Alice's life to send soldiers with you. We have been passing as Bedawi with some success for a while now, so it was obvious that we had the best chance of helping, should you need it.'

'Well I damn well didn't need it.' Simon found it disconcerting to look into Covington's only eye, of well-remembered china blue. Now, it was watering slightly, whether from emotion or the strain of the harsh sunlight, he would never know. 'I had the matter well under control and would have killed those three Arabs within minutes. There was no need to come blundering after me. I don't need nannies and am well capable of looking after my wife without your so-called help, thank you very much.'

Simon flushed. A succession of conflicting emotions flashed through his brain: anger at Covington's sheer unreasonableness, and jealousy at having once again seen Alice in close and intimate contact with the man who was her husband. Listening to Alice tell her story, reflecting her courage, fear and despair, he had longed to rush across and take her in his arms and comfort her; tell her how much he loved her frailty and admired her pluck. But, of course, it was Covington who assumed that role – and who had the *right* to assume it.

He controlled himself. 'It didn't look to me that you had the situation under control, Covington,' he said. 'But it's of no account now. Alice is safe and that is all that matters. Look, the General is probably going to launch his attack tomorrow night and he has asked me to be back in time to take part. No doubt he will wish you to be involved too. If Al . . . Mrs Covington is up to pressing on, we could arrive at Kassassin in time. We have extra camels to spell the others. But we should move soon.'

'Tomorrow night, you say?' Covington eased his eye patch and continued, as though musing to himself: 'A night attack will be damned difficult to carry out, but Wolseley knows what he is doing. Of course I must be in the attack. Alice will ride with me. She is my wife, and anyway, I am sure she will wish to leave this disgusting place behind pretty quickly.'

And so she did. They were mounted and moving out within the half-hour, with the Egyptians standing mute as though with embarrassment at what had happened within their village, watching them ride away.

Chapter 20

Their journey back was uneventful. Covington was persuaded to lead his charger and mount one of the spare camels, with the result that they were able to make good time. Mostly they rode in silence, with Simon scouting a little way ahead and Jenkins bringing up the rear. They arrived at Kassassin in late afternoon to find that the camp had been considerably extended and was now bustling with the preparations for the great attack on the Egyptian stronghold.

'I think the correspondents have all come up,' Covington called to Alice. 'Can you make your way to their compound? The liaison officer will find you a tent and I will come and see you as soon as I have reported to the General.'

She nodded, and Covington gave her a perfunctory kiss on the cheek, then, still ignoring Simon and Jenkins, rode away. Simon watched him go, and after asking Jenkins to look after the animals, fell in alongside Alice. They rode in uncomfortable silence for a while before she reached out to touch his arm.

'Simon,' she said, her eyes brimming with tears. 'I am so sorry. I . . .' She broke off and turned her head away.

He gave the back of her head a sad smile. 'So am I. Don't worry. It can't be helped. I just want you to know that you are the bravest girl in all the world and that I shall always love you. But I will never speak of it again.' He cleared his throat. 'Will you go back down the line to Ismailia now?'

She looked at him with tearstained cheeks and eyes that were now wide. 'Thank you for saying that, my dearest,' she said. 'I shall always remember it. And,' she reached across and touched his arm, 'you know that I shall always love you, too. Nothing has changed.'

They rode in silence again. Then Alice summoned up a brave smile. 'Go back to Ismailia? Good God, no. I shall cover the battle, whatever bloody Wolseley says. I have not suffered all that for nothing. I still have a job to do. Ralph is going to plead for me with the General. But whatever he says, I shall stay somehow.'

Simon shook his head. 'Alice,' he said, 'you are incorrigible.'

They found the young captain who was the correspondents' liaison officer and whose jaw dropped when he saw Alice. However, he was persuaded to find her a bivouac tent and a bedroll so that she could rest awhile. Simon left her there and made for the General's tent, crossing with Covington on the way.

'General wants to see you,' said the Colonel. 'Probably wants to give you a bloody medal for saving my wife.' Leaving the sneer hanging in the air, he rode on. Simon did not reply.

Wolseley was sitting at his table, dictating orders and surrounded by his senior officers. He waved Simon in. 'Well done, Fonthill,' he said. 'Glad that the miserable business has been cleared up. I haven't got time to hear much about it but you should know that I have decided to let Mrs Covington stay and report the show. She has shown such amazing pluck that I can't find it in my heart to send her back down the lines.'

Simon smiled. 'Thank you, sir. I know she will be delighted.'

'Right, now to business. Now that the 1st Royal Irish Fusiliers have come up, I am ready to have a go at the enemy, and I intend to advance during the night and attack at first light. Now listen carefully.'

Gone was the languor that had characterised much of Wolseley's behaviour during the build-up at the little forward post. His good eye was now aglow and he seemed to be bursting with energy. It was clear that he knew what he wanted to do and how he wanted to do it. He was a man who clearly had found release at the prospect of battle at last.

'Although we are moving forward in a straight line across a plain,' the General continued, 'marching a whole army in the dark as one unit is a devilishly difficult thing to do. My idea is to be in position to attack just before first light, so I can't afford to have sections wandering off into the bloody desert like lost cattle. If we are caught in the open at sun-up, those guns will mow us down. The whole attack is to be silent, with no preliminary bombardment. I want to catch the Egyptians when they're half asleep.'

Simon nodded in comprehension. It was an audacious idea and perhaps the only way to nullify the threat of the guns of el Kebir. But could it be done without alerting the enemy? Sounds carried for hundreds of yards in the still night air of the desert. How could you move thousands of men, with their clunking equipment, forward in line for six miles in darkness without the line being broken and some sound, at least, escaping to betray their presence? It was almost asking the impossible. But Wolseley was continuing.

'Now, navigation is to be by the stars, and one of the navy's best navigators, Lieutenant Rawson, will give direction roughly from the centre. But you, Fonthill, and your Welshman must know this bit of the desert now like the back of your hand, so I want you to go forward and guide from the left ahead of the Highland Division.' Simon suppressed a smile at the thought of Jenkins guiding anyone anywhere. 'You were with the Jocks at Majuba – the Gordons, weren't they?'

'Yes, sir.' He marvelled at Wolseley's memory for detail. The mark of a good general?

'Excellent. Well, you should feel at home, and being Welsh, your man should be able to communicate well with 'em.' The officers surrounding the General's table chortled at the joke. Simon summoned a smile.

'The battle plan is to break in at dawn with my two infantry divisions, but with the artillery, about forty guns, advancing behind the foot divisions ready to support the attack as soon as surprise is lost. We shall go in with the bayonet. No rounds in the rifles. Each division will move with one brigade forward, the other in reserve a thousand yards behind. Now, the frontage of each assaulting brigade is to be a thousand yards, with an interval of about twelve hundred yards between the inner flanks of each division. Your lot, the Highlanders on the left, should leave a gap of about two thousand yards from the railway.'

'Are you leaving that open, sir?'

'Not quite. I haven't got infantry to fill it, but it's rising ground there and I am putting in two squadrons of the 19th Hussars to watch it. The Indian Brigade will push forward south of the canal, with a naval gun coming up on the railway later, but never mind those. Your job is to ensure that the Jocks don't go blundering into the railway and the canal on the left, or into General Graham's brigade on the right. It's a sort of sheepdog role. Appropriate, I should think, for a chap from the Brecon Beacons. Eh. What?'

Once again a low murmur of laughter filled the tent. Looking around briefly, Simon could not help but feel how incongruous the little gathering would appear to an uninformed observer: a middle-aged general, surrounded by his senior officers, most of them of a similar age, carefully briefing a young Arab, covered in the dust of the desert, with the plans for his intended battle.

He smiled again and gulped. 'Most appropriate, sir. I shall try not to bark.'

Wolseley chuckled. 'Jolly good. Now, when the attack starts, I don't want you to lead it. Let the Jocks go through. You have won enough glory on this campaign. Is that understood?'

'Quite so, sir. But I would like to attack with them.'

'Very well. Does you credit. Ah, one more thing. Colonel Covington has patrolled this bit of desert almost as much as you. He will act as guide for the division on your right. But we shall all take our main direction from Lieutenant Rawson. Any questions?'

'What if the stars are obscured?'

'We go by compass bearing, of course. Due west.'

'Very good, sir.'

'Right, Fonthill. Go and get some rest. We march shortly after one a.m. and we shall want you ahead before then, of course. Good luck.'

'Thank you, sir.'

Simon left the General's tent, his head whirling. If it was a clear night, then good, but that meant that the enemy would be able to see them from a distance. If visibility was poor, then they should be able to approach quite near to the enemy trenches and guns – if, that is, the whole army had not strayed all over the desert. He sighed. He hoped to God that there were a few other good sheepdogs with compasses to help him!

Resisting the urge to make one last visit to Alice to ensure that she was comfortably housed, Simon made for the field hospital. He was relieved to find that Ahmed was sitting up in his cot, heavily bandaged but smiling.

'I am flattered by all attention,' he said. 'Three five two has already been but has gone now to do, he says, something important. He tell me about the lady, et cetera. I am glad that she is really safe now.'

Simon smiled back. 'Thank you. I must say, we missed you on that journey, but Ahmed, I am glad that you are not going to be with us for the big battle. That would not be easy for you.'

Ahmed frowned. 'No. But I think it has to be done, this big fight. Otherwise this silly man Arabi will continue to muck up country. Egypt needs stability, quietness, et cetera, et cetera, et cetera, to rebuild country. I just hope not too many killed.'

'Absolutely right, old chap.' They shook hands and Simon slipped away, his thoughts on the coming battle.

Jenkins was not at their tent, and Simon crept inside hoping to steal a few moments' rest, but the bustle of activity in the camp made sleep impossible. Over the preceding week, Kassassin had grown into a tented city about half a mile from north to south and some three miles deep, with streets swarming with a multi-ethnic, colourful collection of fighting men from the Empire: kilted Highlanders, red-coated infantry of the line, pipe-clayed marines, tall guardsmen, blue jackets of the naval brigade, turbaned Indian cavalry and sepoys, dour artillerymen, swaggering cavalrymen and camp followers of every description. Now everyone was preparing to go into battle, and Simon strolled through the lines, fascinated to see an army stripping down to move and fight. Round the commissariat stores parties of men from each regiment were drawing the rations to be carried in the haversacks – a hundred rounds of ammunition per man and two days' basic rations, with water bottles filled with tea. The regimental transports were being loaded to carry two days' full rations and thirty rounds of reserve ammunition for each man. Line by line, the long rows of tents were falling to the ground and were being rolled up and stowed away so that the village was now a vast expanse of stamped-down sand, with soldiers scurrying everywhere, laughing and joking now that the long waiting in the heat and flies was over.

Jenkins returned just after dusk saying that he had been 'for a little stroll, like', but he brought back sufficient provisions for them to eat well. Simon briefed him on the task ahead and, predictably, the Welshman's face fell.

'Oh noo, bach sir,' he said. 'I 'ave trouble findin' me way to the pub even. I'm not leadin' no army through the dark, thank you very much. I'll 'ave to stay by you, see.'

'Of course.'

Then they too had to break down their tent, and change out of their Arab clothing into trousers, shirts and European wide-brimmed hats – there was no worse fate than being brought down by 'friendly fire' – then Jenkins was dispatched once again to find lungers to fit to their Martini-Henrys. Wolseley had given orders that there was to be no firing when the attack was launched. Indeed, no rifles were to be loaded; it was to be bayonets only at first light.

Shortly after six p.m., the troops took up their assault formations on the sand hills outside the camp, falling in by posts rammed into the ground by the Royal Engineers. There were no bugle calls, shouted orders or waving lanterns. Everything was muted. It was as if a ghost army was being assembled for the darkest of journeys. Then came anticlimax, for the men were ordered to pile arms, lie down and rest until the order for the advance was given at one a.m. This vast host – some fourteen thousand men – accordingly lay down on the sand and did its best to go to sleep.

Predictably, the sky was overcast and only the north star and the great bear were to be glimpsed occasionally through the cloud cover. Simon strode along his front but saw no sign of the navigating officer, and was relieved to find that a handful of officers were being ranged out in a loose line behind him to act as communicating links between him and the division behind. Even so, the responsibility being thrust upon him was heavy, for he could see very little in front of him and he was forced to hold up his compass a few inches from his eyes to take in its message. At least the worry helped to divert his mind from the dull glint of steel that tipped the long barrel of his rifle. Bayonet fighting was for gung-ho warriors, not for him. For the first time for years, Simon felt beads of perspiration form on his forehead at the prospect of hand-to-hand fighting. He remembered the searing pain of a Zulu assegai as it penetrated his shoulder (he had been told years before that you felt no such pain in the excitement of battle – not true!), and the noise it made as the warrior twisted it to pull it out. In fact, they called the spear *iklwa* after the sucking sound it made on withdrawal. He shook his head to clear the memory. There would be no fighting at all unless he kept his mind concentrated on his compass and the way ahead. He looked to his right, but of course, Covington was too far away to be seen. He turned left and regarded Jenkins. The little man was quiet. That was significant in itself.

At last the signal came to advance, and ponderously the great army began to move forward. For Simon, way out ahead, it was the beginning of an eerie, never-to-be-forgotten experience. Little sound came from the thousands of boots sliding into the soft sand behind him, but from the deep rear he could just hear the faint jingling of chain harness from the guns and the crunching of wheels on pebbles. An occasional soft cough told him that the officers behind him were on station. The night was cool and the desert seemed to be all-enveloping. Yet at his rear was an army of fourteen thousand men and ahead perhaps twice that number, and, of course, the guns of el Kebir.

Frequently as the night wore on, a call came from behind telling him to halt while the line was adjusted. After just under two hours' marching, a halt was called to rest all across the line. In the Highland Brigade, just behind Simon, the order was passed quietly down the line but it took time to reach the flanks, which marched on so that the brigade halted in a crescent. Similar disruption occurred on the right of the line, and it took some time and many whispered curses before the army straightened and resumed its orderly advance.

Striding out ahead into the velvet darkness, with only Jenkins on his left for company, Simon tried to recall the last time a whole army had advanced so far in the dark, line abreast, to launch a dawn attack. He could dredge up no previous example from British military history. Wolseley, of course, was taking a huge risk. His front stretched, in all, nearly two miles. If the flanks deviated to north or south they could wander off into the desert on the one hand or the canal on the other. If the line bulged then the middle could stumble right into the Egyptian fortifications and give the whole game away. And none of the foot soldiers had cartridges in their rifles! Simon gulped and looked again up at the north star and then down at his compass. The risk wasn't just huge. It was gigantic.

Eventually, Simon sensed rather then saw that the darkness was receding, and he looked at his watch: 4.55. Behind him he could now make out the forms of the communicating officers, and also, a lightening of the sky. Ahead, however, still nothing . . . or, at least, what was that? A smudge of blackness running from left to right as far as the eye could see; a black line that was higher than the ground ahead. Yes, the ramparts in front of the trenches! He lengthened his stride, and, as he did so, there was a flash of light directly ahead and a shot rang out, followed by several more. Instinctively, he flung himself to the ground and then, ashamed, rose to his feet to be suddenly flanked by two large

Highlanders, fixing their bayonets as they trudged on past him.

'Well done, laddie,' said one. 'You've got us there.'

Suddenly a bugler blared from behind Simon and a solitary bagpipe began to wail, then another and another as breath was blown into the bags. As they did so, the parapet ahead began to be pinpricked with rifle flashes, and bullets hissed overhead. But the earth walls were not alight with rifle fire. For the moment, the firing was intermittent. The Egyptians were not manning the parapet in force; the defence was coming from individual sentries and the dreaded guns were silent. Most of the enemy were still asleep. Wolseley's gamble had paid off – or at least his first throw of the dice had. The ditches ahead still had to be crossed and the earth mounds behind them climbed.

Simon took a deep breath and realised that his mouth was completely dry. He licked his lips and looked across at Jenkins in the half-light. The Welshman's white teeth flashed under the black smudge of his moustache, and he ran across to take his place at Simon's side.

'Let's do a bit of fightin', et cetera, et cetera,' he said. 'For old Amen.'

Immediately, Simon felt better – and braver. 'Why not?' he grinned. He slipped a cartridge into his rifle and they broke into a run beside the Gordon Highlanders, who were now thronging forward as the pipes wailed all around them.

The open ground to be crossed was about three hundred yards, and at first the Egyptian firing remained intermittent. As he ran, Simon looked to his right beyond the accompanying Black Watch to where the blue-coated marines should show the start of the first division's lines. But there was nothing. Obviously the division had fallen back somehow during the night and the Highlanders were out on their own. The marching line had, in fact, bulged at its end. As he realised this, the top of the high wall of earth beyond the ditch ahead of him exploded into a line of flame as defenders were thrown into the battle. Simon put his head down and sensed rather than saw that men were falling all around him as the first volley crashed deeply into the Scotsmen.

Jenkins, however, was still at his side as he dropped into the ditch. They exchanged grins briefly and then dug the toes of their boots into the loose sand and gravel and began to claw their way up the mound. Looking up, Simon caught a glimpse of a red fez-like *tarboosh* behind the barrel of a long rifle pointing down at him. Instinctively he ducked, and heard the report of a rifle beside him. 'Got 'im,' gasped Jenkins.

Somehow they reached the top of the rampart and immediately became part of a mêlée of men balanced precariously along the narrow causeway, all thrusting at each other with rifle and bayonet in a series of strangely silent, atavistic encounters. Apart from grunts, shouts and the occasional cry of agony, there was little gunfire, for many of the attackers had had no time to insert a round into their rifles and the defenders themselves equally had had little time to reload before the Highlanders had climbed up to be among them.

Simon linked bayonets with a tall Egyptian whose eyeballs showed whitely in his dark face as they swung their yards of steel in a parabolic circle, each trying to force the other back and down. Simon suddenly reversed his rifle, crashing the butt into the face of his adversary and sending him crashing into the trench below. He turned to his left and found Jenkins desperately engaged with two men, their blue-black faces showing that they were Sudanese. In a brief flash of memory, Simon recalled that they were reputedly the best of the Egyptian fighting men, and he lunged forward, thrusting his bayonet into the side of the nearest one, withdrawing it as the man slowly fell to his knees, clutching at the wound, blood spurting from between his fingers, before he too tumbled into the trench below.

Simon felt immediate revulsion. This was the first time since the chaos of Rorke's Drift that he had plunged a bayonet into living flesh, and the terrible, close, personal nature of the act – he could smell the body odour of his opponent – shocked and, for a brief moment, stunned him. Then a cry from Jenkins revived him. The other Sudanese had twisted his bayonet inside that of Jenkins and pierced the left upper arm of the Welshman, so that blood was pouring down his shirt. For the second time Simon swung his bayonet and felt the point sink through the other's breast. The man fell to the ground with a sigh and Simon twisted his blade and retrieved it, with an insouciance he did not feel.

'Thank you, bach,' panted Jenkins. 'You're one ahead now, look you.'

'Let me bandage that wound.'

'No. No time. It's only a scratch. Ah, look be'ind you now.'

Simon whirled and fired his rifle at point-blank range into the breast of a white-clad figure who was swinging a large curved sword above his head. He then presented his bayonet to another man, who, perhaps seeing the bloodstain on the steel, thought better of his attack and turned and plunged down into the trench below, before taking to his heels across the plain. Simon fumbled for another round and slipped it into the breech.

'Load your rifle,' he ordered Jenkins.

The Welshman, his breast heaving, inserted a cartridge into his own Martini-Henry and grinned. 'By God, bach sir. You're becomin' a bit 'andy like with that lunger. I didn't think officers were taught 'ow to use it, see.'

'I don't like it. It disgusts me.'

'Well, it's best to stay alive and be disgusted, look you.' Jenkins glanced along the top of the mound as he regained his breath. The hand-to-hand fighting had diminished and the ramparts were strewn with bodies, mainly the white-clad forms of Egyptians. 'Whoever said that these blokes couldn't fight – and I think it was me – was wrong. My word, I thought I was done for there, I really did.'

Simon took out a knife and tore a length off his shirt, then bandaged it tightly around Jenkins's arm to stem the bleeding. 'That should serve for now,' he said. 'Go to the rear and see if you can get it treated.'

'What are you goin' to do, then?'

'I shall go on with the advance. There's the second line to take yet.'

'Then I shall stay with you. It would be awful to be attacked by some terrible English doctor without you there to defend me, see.'

They exchanged grins. The sun was now up, and Simon looked to the south and then the north. It seemed that the Gordons had broken through their section of the Egyptian line, although they had left many kilts strewn over the desert to the east. From that direction, British reinforcements were now clearly to be seen advancing in perfect order. But the battle was far from over. There was no sign of the first division, who should have now been trotting across the plain towards the northern section of the line, so far, of course, unbroken. The Black Watch, to the right of the Gordons, were obviously having trouble in attacking a big redoubt, the five guns of which were now beginning to play on the first division. The redoubt itself was defended by a double line of emplacements, strongly held, and the dark-kilted Scots had been forced back, leaving a scattering of bodies on the slopes.

'Those guns will have to be taken or they will tear the first division apart,' said Simon. 'We must go and help the Watch.' He shouted at a small group of Gordons who were climbing to the top of the mound and gestured to the north. 'You men. Come with me to support the Black Watch.' Eyebrows were lifted at first at an order coming from a young man in dishevelled mufti, but his air of command, coupled with the blood still dripping from his bayonet, swayed the Scotsmen.

'My view is that the bloody Watchmen should be big enough to look after themselves, sir,' said a diminutive young corporal, 'but we'll come wi'ye to help out the wee lads. Lead on, then.'

The group, nine in all, ran along the top of the earthworks, jumping over the bodies that littered the narrow way, slipping and sliding where the conflict had torn up the beaten-down sand, until they reached where the mound rose up to form the redoubt housing the five guns. Two lines of semicircular emplacements ringing the redoubt below were lined with Egyptian infantry coolly firing their Remingtons into the men of the Black Watch down on the plain, now being rallied by their officers to make a fresh assault. Doubling forward to help them were men of the Rifles, part of the reinforcements from the second brigade.

'Fire down on to the riflemen,' shouted Simon. 'Select your target.'

The nine, now kneeling, began directing a steady fire on to the Egyptian infantry in the trenches below them. This attack from a new quarter immediately unsettled the enemy riflemen, who could not hear the crack of the rifles behind them above the boom of the cannon and had no idea from which direction this new attack was coming. The consequent slackening of their fire down on to the Black Watch on the plain in turn encouraged the Scotsmen, and they now followed their sword-waving officers in a new attack on the emplacements.

'Good,' shouted Simon, his voice cracking amidst the dust and smoke. 'They'll be through there in a minute. Now up to the guns. We've got to stop them firing on the first division. Follow me.'

The climb up to the redoubt was more difficult, but at least it was not defended, for the gunners were intent on laying and firing their cannon. The boom of the Krupps at close quarters was deafening, and the edge of the redoubt was ringed in smoke as the heavy fourteen-pounders flashed and rebounded on their carriages. Simon tasted again the tang of cordite on his lips. He found that he was looking down from the rear of the redoubt at more than twenty white-shrouded Egyptian artillerymen, working their pieces with discipline and skill.

He turned to the Gordons. 'Fire two rounds,' he shouted, 'and then down among them with the bayonet. Fire now!'

Nine reports sounded as one and seven of the enemy fell across their guns. The volley was repeated and another six crumpled. Then, with a whoop, the little band jumped down from the lip of the ramparts and launched themselves on the remaining gunners. But these Egyptians were made of stern stuff. They seized whatever was at hand to defend themselves – rifles and bayonets, officers' swords, long sponging rods – and for a minute the gun emplacement was a scene of fierce individual duels, with steel clashing on steel and cries of anguish and triumph melding into a devilish cacophony as the smoke from the now quiet cannon drifted away.

It was a one-sided conflict, however, for the gunners were not trained in hand-to-hand fighting and the last two threw down their weapons, leapt over the rear of the redoubt and scuttled away across the plain.

'Well done, lads,' cried Simon, drawing in deep breaths as he leaned on his rifle. 'Are you all right, 352?'

'Right as rain, bach sir. Bit puffed, that's all. An' I'm not much good at fightin' with just one 'and, see.'

'Blast. Yes. You're bleeding again.' He turned to the Gordons. 'Have any of you boys got a field dressing?'

The corporal fished in his knapsack. 'You're lucky, sir. I'm the platoon doctor – which means Ah carry the bandages. Here yer are.' He handed a paper package to Simon, who tore off the cover, threw away the blood-soaked piece of shirting around Jenkins's wound, applied a piece of lint to the gash and then tightly wrapped the dressing in a bandage. He had hardly finished when a subaltern of the Black Watch, sword in hand, his face glistening with perspiration, jumped down into the redoubt and regarded Simon and Jenkins with some wonderment.

'Well done, whoever you are,' he said. 'I doubt if we could have broken through without your help.' He held out his hand. 'Fraser, Black Watch.'

'Fonthill ... er ... Intelligence.' They shook hands. Simon turned to his Gordons. 'Thank you, lads. Better see if you can rejoin your units now.' He nodded to the west, where some three hundred yards away, a line of smoke and gun flashes showed where the Egyptian second reserve line of trenches was under attack. 'They'll be over there.'

'Very good, sir.' Soldiers of the Black Watch were now pouring into the redoubt. The little corporal nodded to them and grinned. 'We wouldn't want to be seen in the company o' these hooligans, anyway. Top o' the mornin' to yer, sir.' With that he led his section away, at the trot.

As he spoke, a battery of the Royal Artillery was to be seen crashing through the line of trenches. It broke a wheel in the process, but it carried on and then unlimbered and opened fire, directing its shrapnel shells over the heads of the British troops on to the defenders of the second Egyptian line.

Simon turned back to Fraser. 'How is the day going?'

The young man brushed the back of his hand across his brow and then his moustache, leaving black cordite smudges. 'Good, I think. It looks as though the whole of our brigade in the south has broken through. But there's the problem.' He pointed with his sword to the north. 'The first division is damned slow coming up, and unless they look sharp, they could get caught in a blast from the guns across this open ground. Our lot won't be able to run up the line to hold it for them. We're under orders to go on to the second line, you see.'

Simon shielded his eyes with his hand and looked to the east. Yes, the first division was at last coming into sight. Even at that range he could see a single figure in the front. Covington?

He held out his hand. 'May I borrow your glasses for a second?' Fraser dipped his head under the strap holding his field glasses and gave them to Simon.

'Thanks.' He focused across the scrub and sand, and eventually the unmistakable figure of Covington came into view, striding out ahead of the massed ranks, revolver in hand. Simon twirled the wheel on the binoculars and brought up the blue-jacketed marines behind Covington. 'Good God!' he cried. 'They're marching in close order. That's stupid. They'll be cut down like corn when the guns open up. Perhaps they think they have already been captured. They've got to open out. Stay here, 352. I'll go. Someone's got to tell 'em.'

He threw the glasses back to a startled Fraser and leapt over the edge of the redoubt, sinking his heels into the soft sand and earth and plunging to the plain below. There, on impulse, he stopped and turned.

'No, no,' he yelled up at Jenkins. 'You stay there. It only needs one of us.'

'Sod that,' gasped Jenkins, floundering down the slope. 'Where you go, I go.'

The two men began running diagonally across the plain to the north to meet the blue lines slowly advancing, with the lone figure ahead of them. Simon realised that the division had, of course, lost its line during the night and opened up a

415

gap to the south. This, however, could be turned to advantage if Covington deployed it to his left, opening up the thick lines and making them less of an obvious target for the Egyptian artillery. He looked over his shoulder, behind and to his left. The guns were strangely silent. Were they holding their fire until the last moment, the better to create havoc; was it that the gunners were late to their posts; or had the Gordons turned back and attacked the line north of them, to help the advancing first division?

Simon was short of breath and losing speed – and he realised that he had left the wounded Jenkins some way behind. But he was near enough now to be within hailing distance of Covington, who was striding out some hundred yards ahead of the marines. To his right, the first division curled away into the distance, a formidable sight.

Waving his arms, Simon shouted: 'Covington! For God's sake, deploy into open order. The guns have not been taken. You'll be cut down.'

'What?' Covington waved his hook. 'Damn you, Fonthill. Get out of my way—'

His words were cut short as the Egyptian guns facing the approaching first division at last opened up, in a great boom that seemed to split the heavens. Simon was conscious of a hissing sound above his head, and he instinctively threw himself flat as the ground ahead erupted in a fiery mass of exploding stone, sand, earth and goodness knows what else as the shells crashed into the lines of advancing troops. He buried his face in the sand and clasped his hands over his head as debris rained down upon him. Then, desperate at what he might see, he turned his head to search for Jenkins and glimpsed the Welshman, equally prostrate, but head up and waving a hand to show that he had survived the first wave of shells. Ahead of him, however, there was nothing but smoke.

Simon stayed there, hands over his head and attempting to burrow into the sand for shelter, dreading the next salvo from the Egyptian lines. It came seconds later. Whether the gunners had adjusted their sights to direct their shells deeper into the advancing mass, or whether some of them had already fled their posts, he would never know, but the second salvo seemed far less concentrated and he was aware that marines, now trotting, were passing him on their way to attack the Egyptian lines.

Crawling to his feet, Simon went back to Jenkins and knelt by his side. 'Have you been hit, old chap?'

The Welshman gave a weary grin. 'No, bach sir. Just takin' a bit of a rest in all this noise, see. Out of bloody breath, look you. Are you all right?'

Simon flung himself down as a third salvo whistled over their heads, but as before it was markedly less accurate, or so it seemed. 'No, I'm unharmed. You stay here. It looks as though the guns are ranging further back now. I'm going to look for Covington.'

'Not on your own you're not.' And Jenkins hauled himself to his feet, the bloodstain on the dressing spreading.

They found Covington lying some hundred yards ahead, marines stepping over him as they advanced. He was alive, but shrapnel had torn a hole in his stomach which he was desperately trying to cover with his one good hand. Blood oozed through his fingers and from another gaping wound in his thigh.

'Covington,' cried Simon, kneeling by his side. 'Don't

move. We'll get a medic to you.' He looked down, winced and lied desperately. 'It's not serious. We'll soon have you right.'

A half-smile crept over Covington's features. 'Wish you'd stop intruding into my life, damn you, Fonthill. And you're a bloody liar. Can't see very well, so I know I'm done for.' His voice started to tail away. 'Shame. I would have liked to have a go at those chaps. Bloody guns.' Then his eye blazed fiercely for a moment as blood began to ooze from the corner of his mouth. 'Tell Alice that . . .'

His head fell to one side and the blood ran down his chin into the sand. He lay quite still.

Simon felt for a pulse but found none, and then Jenkins leaned over and, with his thumb, closed the sightless eye. 'Well,' said the Welshman, 'that's that, then. Brave bloke, despite 'is faults.' He looked across at Simon. 'Better get out of 'ere while we can, bach sir. We can't do nothin' more for 'im. They'll pick 'im up after the battle, like.'

Simon nodded. Then they both ducked as another salvo boomed over their heads. 'Let's go. No. Wait.' Gently he withdrew Covington's sword from its scabbard. 'I'll take this back. Alice might like to have it.'

Almost unaware of the guns, whose firing was now more intermittent, they trudged back to the southern section of the Egyptian lines, where the fighting had now completely ceased. It was continuing, however, at the Egyptian reserve line of trenches, although less intensely now.

'I suppose we had better get on over there,' said Simon. 'There might be something we can do.'

'All right, then, but I'm not rushin'.'

'How's the arm?'

'Just 'urts a bit when I laugh, see. Nothin' much.'

'Come on then. We can probably find you a field doctor over there.'

In fact, by the time they reached the second line, it was clear that this too had been broken, and bagpipes were wailing in triumph. Bodies lay less thickly here, but it was obvious that the Egyptians had suffered badly. British medical orderlies were busying themselves among the wounded, British and Egyptian alike, and stretcher parties were carrying the worst cases to the rear. Along the length of the line, smoke rose as though from a funeral pyre.

Simon sat on the edge of a trench and looked at his watch. It was nearly six o'clock. The boom of guns from the north had fallen silent. He removed his hat and immediately felt the hot sun on his head. He ran his hand over his eyes, sore from the dust and smoke, and blinked. As before after a battle, he felt an overwhelming sense of depression descend upon him, seeming to replace the adrenalin that had surged through him during the fighting and leaving behind an emptiness – no, more a feeling of shame at the waste of it all. He looked again at the crumpled figures around him. So many lives lost, to preserve . . . what? The ownership of a few miles of waterway carved out of sand dunes? The restoration of stability to a country unsettled by foreign domination? Well, at least Ahmed seemed to think it had all been worthwhile.

Simon realised that he had deliberately been avoiding any thought of Covington, as though his death was a momentary aberration – a mistake that would be righted as soon as the smoke cleared. He shook his head. No, the man was gone. Covington, his old oppressor, his rival in love for Alice, the man who had stood between him and happiness, was dead. Yet there was no feeling of elation, of new hope for the future. The tragedy of the man's death, its brutality and suddenness, was too prevalent. How would Alice take it? Simon sighed. Would she welcome him back now – emerging from the debris of the battlefield with her husband's sword, as though he had just slain him in mortal combat?

He shook his head again. Whatever Alice had said about her love for him, he knew that she had always been fond of Covington, had admired his courage and his soldierly qualities. She was bound to be upset at being so rudely thrust into widowhood. Would she even, perhaps, blame him for it? Well, whatever the answers to those questions, one thing was certain: it looked as though the battle of Tel el Kebir was over and that Arabi's insurrection, revolt, uprising – whatever it was – had been broken. Sir Garnet Wolseley's great gamble had paid off and he had won the day.

As though to mark the fact, he heard cheering. A group of officers was riding the length of the line, led by a small man with drooping moustaches on a black charger. He was smiling and saluting to acknowledge the ovation. Wolseley was savouring his victory.

Simon felt Jenkins sink down beside him, and they both watched the approach of Wolseley with tired, lacklustre eyes. They failed to rise as the little cavalcade approached, and then, at the last minute, hauled themselves upright, leaning on their rifles, but neither could raise a cheer.

The General halted and looked down at them, noting their bloodstained bayonets and the dressing on Jenkins's arm. If he also noticed Covington's sword on the ground at Simon's feet, he paid it no attention. Instead, he nodded. 'Ah, my two indefatigable A-rabs. Been in the thick of it by the look of it, Fonthill,' he said. 'Not hurt badly, I trust, 352?'

'No, thank you, General bach, just a scratch, see.'

'Good. You both look all in. Fonthill, no time to talk now, and you need to rest, but come and see me at about six tonight. I shall probably have set up a temporary headquarters at the station. See me there. Good work, both of you.' He put a forefinger to the edge of his topi and rode on. The cheering broke out again as he made his way down the line.

Simon sighed. 'Well, that's obviously that, then. The battle must be over.' He ran his fingers through his hair. 'I wonder if Alice got her story. I hope so. Come on. Let's find someone who can have a look at that arm. Then perhaps we can snatch a couple of hours' sleep before I have to see the General again.'

Chapter 21

In fact, tired as he was, Simon found no sleep throughout the day. Instead, he lay on his bedroll contemplating his future. Would it be with Alice, and more to the point, would she want him? He was old enough now to know that what was unattainable often seemed the more desirable, until, that is, it *became* attainable. And then the bloom went off the rose. With reality came revision, and what? Rejection? Covington had been rich and Alice would inherit. He, Simon, had nothing in comparison. He looked at the snoring figure of Jenkins on the other side of the tent, his arm freshly bandaged, and not for the first time envied the little man's ability to sleep.

He felt, then, tired and dejected when he stirred himself that evening to keep his appointment with the General. He left early for he was anxious to detour on the way to the station to visit the site of the tower. He was gratified to see that the building had, indeed, seemed to have collapsed in on itself. A stump remained, poking through the pile of rubble, but the huts around were undisturbed, and this did a little something to relieve the depression that now consumed him. Unsurprisingly, he was asked to wait at the station, and he perched gloomily on a stool provided for him outside the tiny office, as a succession of young aides and clerks swept by him attending to the General. He sat back, leaning against a wall, his hands thrust deep into his pockets, pondering. Alice, ah, Alice . . .

His reverie was ended by a summons at last, and he found Wolseley sitting behind a makeshift desk scribbling furiously. For a man who had presumably had little sleep for twenty-four hours, he looked surprisingly sharp. 'Bring your stool in,' said the General. 'There's nowhere else to sit. Shan't keep you long. Got far too much to do.'

Once Simon was seated, Wolseley put down his pen and regarded him. 'Good,' he said. 'Sorry to keep you waiting, but I often think that there's more to do after a battle than before it.' He lifted up a tin cup at his side. 'Take a brandy with me, Fonthill. You look terrible.'

'Thank you, sir, I will.' Dutch courage, to face Alice. Why not? Then he remembered the formalities. 'Congratulations, Sir Garnet. It seems to have been a quick and most comprehensive victory.'

The General nodded. 'I have to say that it was.' He yelled through the door to an aide sitting at a campaign desk on the station platform: 'Smithie, bring me another cup, there's a good fellow.' He took a sip from his own mug. 'Yes. Considering the difficulties of logistics and so on, it was a considerable relief to me, I must say, to see how well it went in the end. I hear that Arabi himself is running back to Cairo with what's left of his army. All the fight's gone out of them and I've got the cavalry on their heels to make sure there's no question of them attempting to defend the capital. I shall enter Cairo as soon as I can.'

'What will you do with Arabi?'

'He will be tried by a properly constituted court. I shall make sure that he's not hanged out of hand, or anything of that kind. He will probably be deported. Here.' He lifted up a bottle from the floor by his foot and poured a little amber liquid into the cup handed to Simon. 'Take a gulp.'

Simon drank from the cup and coughed as the harsh aftertaste of the cognac hit his throat. 'You will have heard the sad news about Covington, I presume, sir?'

Wolseley nodded. 'This is the kind of price that always has to be paid for a successful action, but I can never come to terms with it. I know you had your problems with him, but to me he was a fine comrade and soldier. A great loss to me and to the nation.'

Simon could think of nothing to say. He nodded mutely.

'Damned shame,' the General continued. 'The division he was guiding got a bit bent, so to speak, during the night, so it was late arriving, as you know. They caught one or two salvos from the Egyptian guns before the line could be stormed. The cursed thing is that the gunners didn't really cause all that much damage in the end because so many of their shells just buried themselves in the sand. Just bad luck that Covington caught it. But he died as he would have wished, in the heat of battle.' Wolseley looked out of the door with unseeing eyes. 'That's the way I would like to go, when the time comes.'

Simon took another draught of the brandy. 'What about Al . . . what about his wife? Has she been told?'

'Yes. Broke the news myself. Felt I had to. She seemed to take it well, but I know she will be broken. In fact, Fonthill, I would be grateful if you would go to her and give her whatever comfort you can. I know that you were friends more or less from childhood, wasn't it?'

Simon nodded. 'More or less. Our fathers served together in the 24th and remain great friends.' The cognac was now beginning to warm his stomach and bring him to life again. 'Where is she now?'

'She said she must file her story for the *Morning Post*.' He shook his head. 'She's got guts, that girl, you know. To have this terrible news so soon after her dreadful experience out in the desert with that infernal scoundrel George is just too much. My word, she's got pluck. But she's probably back in her tent by now. The correspondents' quarters are just south of the village here.'

'Thank you, sir. I'd better go, then.' Simon stood and made for the door.

'Hold on.' Wolseley gestured to the stool. 'You've got time to finish your brandy, man. And anyway, I have something I wish to say to you.'

Slowly Simon regained his seat.

'Right. Now. Your work for me here in Egypt has been exemplary. If you had rejoined the army I would have cited both you and your Welshman for medals. But I can't give crosses to civilians, even though you clearly fought like tigers on the entrenchments there. So you will both receive an extra six months' pay. It's the least I can do – wish there was more.'

Simon thought quickly. 'Thank you, sir. That's much appreciated. But there is something . . .'

'What's that?'

'Our Egyptian comrade, Ahmed Muharram – you will remember, he sustained a wound when we were coming back from Tel el Kebir, south of the canal.'

'Ah yes. Of course.'

'Would it be possible to reduce the money coming to Jenkins and myself and give him a commensurate one-third share from the total amount? He has worked so bravely for us and supports the British one hundred per cent in what we are trying to do in Egypt. And he could use the money for his hotel. He has not earned while he has been away in Cairo.'

'Of course.' Wolseley made a note. 'I shall increase the overall sum accordingly. I don't want you and Jenkins to suffer. Which reminds me . . .' A scowl came over the General's face that he vainly tried to stop lapsing into a half-smile. 'That officer who hit your Egyptian – Smith-Denbigh, wasn't it?'

'Yes, sir.'

'The most amazing thing seems to have happened to him in Kassassin, before the march. I've just heard about it. It appears that he was lured out into the desert a little way that evening just after dark. Don't know the details, but I gather he was told that I wished to see him by the camel lines. Bloody fool went, it seems, and there he was hit over the head by some Arab. When he regained consciousness a few minutes later, he had been stripped naked and covered in camel dung. Nothing had been taken – in fact, his money was carefully laid out on the sand by his side. But his clothes had gone and he had to stumble stark naked back through the lines.'

Simon carefully composed his face. 'Good lord! I hope he wasn't badly hurt.'

'No, it seems it was only a tap on the head. But it's made the man a laughing stock, of course. You wouldn't know anything about this, would you, Fonthill?'

'Of course not, sir.'

'Well, I don't take this sort of thing lightly, I can tell you. Luckily for the perpetrator, I have too much to do now to conduct an investigation, but if you hear anything, please let me know.'

'I will, sir.'

'Now, as far as I am concerned, my boy, you can consider your service to me in Egypt at an end. This campaign is almost certainly over and I will have no need of you in Cairo. Come to my office there when the dust has settled and I will have steamer tickets to take you back home. What do you intend to do with yourself there?'

Simon felt as though his head was still spinning. Alice free at last! But would she . . . could she . . .? 'I have absolutely no idea, sir,' he said, quite truthfully. 'No idea at all.'

'You won't, of course, consider taking up a commission again? You have excellent qualities for the service, Fonthill, and I can certainly advance you.'

'That is very kind of you, Sir Garnet, but I don't think so. I used the bayonet today for the first time for years, and . . .' he paused and shook his head, 'I have to say that I did not like it one bit. As I told you once before, I believe, I don't think I am cut out to be a regular soldier. However . . .'

'Yes?'

'I don't know how my circumstances will change now, sir, but Jenkins and I have always enjoyed working for you, and if you feel in the future that we can be of service to you,' he coughed, 'in our rather irregular way, then I am sure we would be interested. But not as regular soldiers, I fear.'

Wolseley allowed a grin to spread under his moustaches. 'I seem to remember that we had this conversation once before.' He stood and extended his hand. 'I could well be interested, Fonthill, although I rather see my life now extending before me in a damned office in Whitehall. But we shall see. Goodbye, my boy, and thank you.'

'Goodbye, sir.'

Simon stood outside on the station platform and gazed unseeingly at the young officer working at the desk there. He turned, and then turned back again and walked along the bustling station's little platform, deep in thought and quite unaware of the activity all around. How would Alice have taken the news? She had married the man, after all, and lived with him for two years. Of course she would be grieving for Covington. Perhaps he should leave her with her grief for a while. Yes, that was the sensitive thing to do. But then . . . he kicked away an empty shell case . . . better to get it over with. Ask her to marry him straight away, so that they both knew where they stood. Brutal surgery, so to speak. Too brutal, though? And what about Jenkins? His future would be affected too. He had the right to express an opinion. His mind suddenly made up, Simon turned and strode off in search of his servant and best friend.

Jenkins was cooking when Simon found him. He had purloined a two-man bivouac from somewhere, lit a fire at its entrance and foraged a large pot, the contents of which he was stirring with his bayonet, his bandaged arm tucked inside his shirt. He looked tired but unperturbed, doing his job without fuss. A rock, a solid rock. Simon felt a sudden surge of affection for his old friend.

'How is the arm now?' he asked.

Jenkins gave a glum smile. 'Stiff an' achin' a bit, but I'll live. More'n you can say for the old CO, though, eh?'

'Yes.' Simon lowered himself down and sat cross-legged. 'What did the General want? When do we get our Victoria Crosses?'

'We don't. Civilians can't get army decorations, but we are going to be given six months' extra pay – and so is dear old Ahmed.'

Jenkins's face broke into the familiar beam that seemed to stretch his great moustache to his ears. 'Now,' he said, 'that's more like it. Blimey! We shall be rich.' Then the smile slowly left his face and he looked down into the pot he was continuing to stir. 'So, what ... er ... are you goin' to be doin' now, bach sir?' He continued staring down into the pot. 'With Miss Alice, like?'

'Ah yes.' Simon fixed his gaze on Jenkins's wounded arm. 'Shouldn't that arm be in a sling?'

'They gave me one, but I can't cook with it like that. What are you goin' to do about Miss Alice?'

'Yes.' Simon looked up at the sky and then into the coals of the fire. 'That's what I wanted to talk to you about.'

'Go on, then. I'm not goin' anywhere.'

'Quite. Yes. Well.' Simon looked directly at his old friend at last in desperation. 'Look. Do you think she will have me?'

Slowly Jenkins withdrew his bayonet from the pot, licked the end and nodded in satisfaction. 'Comin' on well,' he said.

'What?'

'The stew. Comin' on well.'

'Oh, yes.'

A deep smile spread across the Welshman's face. 'Of course she'll 'ave you, man. She loves you, an' in my opinion she always 'as. God knows what she was doin' goin' off with the Colonel in the first place, though you tried to explain all that to me. But the way's clear now, isn't it? I suppose you're poppin' off now to propose?'

'Well . . . I don't know. I wanted to talk to you first.'

'Very kind of you, I'm sure.' Jenkins dipped the bayonet back into the cauldron and resumed his stirring. Head down, he asked, 'An' when she's said yes, where will you be livin', then, when you've sort of settled down, like?'

Simon frowned. 'I don't really know. But Alice will inherit what I understand is quite a large estate in Norfolk, so perhaps it will be there, although I would not fancy the thought of living on her late husband's money, so to speak.'

Jenkins snorted. 'Well, it'd be poetical justice, if you ask me, after all he did to bring you down in the army, an' after for that matter.'

'I never thought of it quite like that, but I still don't like the thought. You'd come with us, wherever we are, of course.'

The Welshman looked up sharply. 'What?'

'You would come to live with us. Naturally. I would still want a servant – and a friend. I couldn't do without you, you know that.'

Jenkins shook his head. 'No, bach sir. Very kind, I'm sure, but you wouldn't want me 'angin' about the place, gettin' drunk an' all that.'

'Nonsense, and anyway . . .' His voice tailed off.

'Yes?'

Discomfort sat on Simon's face. 'I hate talking like this when I don't know if Alice will have me, but the fact is, I can't quite see either of us – that's Alice and me – just staying at home, farming all the time, even if we have children. I am jumping to conclusions, but knowing her, I think she will want to go on reporting again, if ever there was a good campaign to follow, although I wouldn't be too happy about that. But I will feel restless if you and I can't do a bit of scouting again for someone like Wolseley. Someone one can respect, you know.'

A slow smile spread across Jenkins's face. 'Really? Ah well, bach sir, that could be quite interestin' now, couldn't it? Quite interestin'.'

Simon rose to his feet and stood, still without certainty. Then his face lit up. 'Ah. I knew there was something I had forgotten to tell you. It seems that someone hit Smith-Denbigh over the head on the eve of the battle and took his clothes so that he had to walk back naked through the lines.'

Jenkins lifted his great eyebrows. 'Good gracious me! What a thing to 'appen.'

'Yes, I don't suppose you know anything about it?'

'Who? Me, sir? No, sir. Not me, sir. But it's all very interestin'.'

'Yes, well, I thought you ought to know.'

'Thank you. Very interestin'.'

Simon took a deep breath. 'Dammit. I'm going to go and see Alice now. This very minute.'

'Are you takin' 'is sword?'

'What? Oh no. Not quite appropriate just now, I think. She can have it later.' He gulped and stood still. 'Right. Right. Yes, well. I'm off.' And he set off at last with a resolute step.

Jenkins looked after him sadly. 'Good luck. Bring 'er back for a bit of stew.' But Simon did not hear.

Author's Note

As with all the Simon Fonthill novels, I have woven fiction around a solid thread of fact. The fact, of course, is the British invasion of Egypt in 1882 to put down the insurrection of Colonel Arabi, and the subsequent campaign of Lieutenant General Sir Garnet Wolseley, culminating in the battle of Tel el Kebir. This war, this 'little war', led to the British occupation of Egypt, which lasted for the next seventy-four years and was ended by what the British called 'the Suez Crisis'. This seminal event of 1956, which comprehensively removed whatever hope Britain still retained of being regarded as a global power, shared, in a deliciously cyclical manner, several of the main features of the Arabi revolt: it was caused by an uprising of a nationalist leader holding the rank of colonel in the Egyptian army; fears of the British losing control of the Suez Canal prompted the invasion; and the French initially played a part, though a less prominent one than the Brits.

The Suez invasion of 1956, however, was a political and economic disaster for the British, while Wolseley's campaign was undoubtedly a masterpiece of logistical and strategic planning. His night march and dawn attack on the Egyptian entrenchments was hailed by Hugh Childers, Gladstone's Minister of War, as 'the most perfect military achievement England has seen for many a long year'. Equally important was Wolseley's handling of his cavalry after his victory. By sending it out in force to pursue the remnants of Arabi's fleeing army to the very gates of Cairo, he was able to prevent any defence of that city and to enable ten thousand Egyptian troops to be peacefully disarmed and returned to their homes. Even the critics in Berlin, Paris and Vienna were forced to concede that the whole exercise had been meticulously planned and executed – so very different from the repetition in 1956, when the American-inspired threat of a run on the pound forced the British government into the humiliating position of having to abandon its occupation of the Canal Zone and withdraw its forces.

In December of 1882, Arabi and seven of his chief lieutenants were tried in Cairo on charges of rebellion against the Khedive, found guilty and sentenced to death. As Wolseley had promised, however, the Khedive commuted the sentences to 'perpetual exile' and Arabi was transported to Ceylon, returning to Egypt in 1901, where nobody remembered him. I have taken Arabi's arguments in his interview with Alice from his defence at the trial, as reported in several of the books contained in the brief bibliography in my Acknowledgements.

My descriptions of the main battle and the skirmishes that preceded it are as accurate as my readings of respected contemporary and later accounts can make them. As far as I know, however, the tower in Tel el Kebir was not blown up before the battle. It was certainly built in the time of Mohammed Tewfik, the Khedive of Egypt from 1879–92, and there is no record of it having been used in the battle. However, when I climbed to its top in 2006, I felt that it would have made an ideal spotting site for the Egyptian guns during the battle, and the fact that it is now known as 'Orabi's Tower' makes me suspect that it played some role in the events of that time.

Wolseley did take a huge risk in advancing his army on foot across the desert in the darkness before attacking at Tel el Kebir. The sky was overcast and the young naval navigator's skill in celestial navigation was therefore negated. Compasses were used in the darkness by the officers who advanced ahead of each British section to lead the way, but as Simon feared, the long British line did bulge at its southern extremity and the first division in the north was accordingly late in attacking, although the Highland Brigade, immediately behind Simon, sustained the highest casualties in the battle. In this context, I must confess to exaggerating slightly the effect of the Egyptian artillery on the belated advance of the first division. I did so in order to give Covington a proper send-off. He has been such a strong character in the first five novels of the Fonthill story that I felt he deserved to go with a rather louder bang than that of, say, a sniper's bullet.

The incident I described briefly of a battery of the Royal Artillery driving its guns over the Egyptian defences in aid of the Jocks did occur, and the unit went down in Gunner history as 'the Broken Wheel Battery'.

Of course, Simon, Jenkins, Alice, Ahmed, George, Smith-Denbigh and Covington are all fictional characters, although a real-life Captain Coveney was wounded during the battle. In addition to Wolseley and Arabi, the other senior officers I have mentioned all existed, and Wolseley did make a feint to invade at Alexandria before slipping away to invade at Ismailia. A fake message *was* sent from that town, under the name of the traffic manager there, and was instrumental in forestalling any attack by the Egyptians during the landing of the British troops and supplies.

A young woman as a war correspondent for a distinguished British daily newspaper? Yes, completely and utterly credible, for, as I have described in previous Simon Fonthill stories, there were precedents for English women as foreign correspondents for British national papers reporting from war zones in both the Franco-Prussian War and the first Anglo-Boer War of 1881. Determination, guts and competence existed in British womanhood long before the Suffragettes!

JW

Last Stand At Majuba Hill

John Wilcox

'There's nowhere to go, 352. We make a last stand here.'

It is 1881, and General George Pomeroy-Colley, commander of the British forces in Natal, is planning to stamp out a rebellion. He is convinced the Transvaal Boers can pose no serious threat, but he needs reliable information. He calls on former army captain Simon Fonthill.

A veteran of the recent Zulu and Sekukuni campaigns, Fonthill knows to never underestimate an enemy. He and his servant, '352' Jenkins, agree to carry out a covert diplomatic assignment. But the greatest test is yet to come. As the two armies converge on the heights of Majuba Hill, Fonthill and Jenkins are first into the fray. If they are to break the enemy, Colley's men must hold the summit at all costs . . .

Acclaim for John Wilcox's Fonthill series:

'Fast-paced, full of action and brave deeds. If you are a fan of Simon Scarrow or Wilbur Smith, then this is for you' *Historical Novels Review*

'A hero to match Sharpe or Hornblower . . . Wilcox shows a genius for bringing to light the heat of battle' *Northern Echo*

'A rollicking account of a turbulent period in Britain's imperial past' *Good Book Guide*

978 0 7553 2719 5

headline

The Diamond Frontier

John Wilcox

It's 1880, and the atmosphere is explosive in the South African province of the Transvaal. The discovery of diamonds has bred greed and violence, while British forces contend with murderous bePedi tribesmen and subversive Boer farmers.

Former army captain Simon Fonthill has had his fill of conflict. But when he hears that an old friend has been kidnapped by diamond smugglers, he and his servant '352' Jenkins embark on a rescue mission. Yet this is only the beginning. For when the acclaimed General Wolseley decides to lead his column against the bePedi stronghold, Fonthill and Jenkins once again find themselves marching to war.

Acclaim for previous Simon Fonthill novels:

'A hero to match Sharpe or Hornblower . . . Rip-roaring stuff' *Northern Echo*

'A swashbuckling tale, slashed through with adventure, bravery, and the utmost danger' *Good Book Guide*

'A thrilling tale of courage and fortitude' *Historical Novels Review*

978 0 7553 0987 0

headline

Now you can buy any of these other bestselling
Headline books from your bookshop
or *direct from the publisher*.

FREE P&P AND UK DELIVERY
(Overseas and Ireland £3.50 per book)

Centurion	Simon Scarrow	£6.99
The Templar, the Queen and Her Lover	Michael Jecks	£7.99
The Paradise Trail	Duncan Campbell	£7.99
In A Far Country	Linda Holeman	£6.99
Private Eyes	Jonathan Kellerman	£7.99
Murder's Immortal Mask	Paul Doherty	£6.99
A Small Part of History	Peggy Elliott	£7.99
The Last Gospel	David Gibbins	£6.99

TO ORDER SIMPLY CALL THIS NUMBER

01235 400 414

or visit our website: www.headline.co.uk

Prices and availability subject to change without notice.